THE CONTACT SERIES: BOOK 2

ADDICTIVE CONTACT

ASH REMINGTON

Editing: Anna Darelli-Anderson (@LiterariaLuminaria)

Contents

Chapter 1

That Ship Has Sailed

Maya Fontaine: 2036

What changes when you put the adults in charge for once? Nothing. We stopped the World Military, crippled the Connect Earth network, cut ourselves off from galactic travel and the triaxum that makes it possible, and I put a bullet in Penelope's skull. Even with Ranbir elected as a regional governor and my ascending military career, our hands were tied as the bureaucrats seized the power vacuum and reshaped our political world.

The way society used to do things was like common street prostitution. Underhanded lobbyist pimps and their dirty politician whores controlled the world until we shook up the system. What we got when they were removed was an only slightly classier version of the sluts we were used to. In less than three years, the same old greedy tramps had the citizens' figurative pants yanked down around our ankles again.

Chaos wasn't limited to our reformed parliamentary government. It touched everything. The World Military was no peach, but at least those boys knew how to organize. In their wake, we were left with a dysfunctional conglomerate of multiple military branches rolled into one ineptly run organization.

I'm not saying I shouldn't have been placed in a leadership role, but it would be fair to question the judgment of the idiot who made me a commander. My service history had a better chance of landing me in a military tribunal than at an officer's desk—yet there I was, and what I was commanding was anyone's guess. North American troops I suppose, but was I protecting them from other continents or the next galactic traveler to roll up on our back door?

I sat in my car outside the recently constructed parliamentary government whorehouse in downtown Chicago waiting for my friends to arrive. It was a big day—one that would decide if our gang would remain together or not, and even though Alexis and Malik were campaigning to get the green light for their mission to Vocury, I was quietly in opposition.

Alexis appeared in my rearview mirror, pulled up beside me, and waved before attempting to parallel park in the open spot behind me. She swung her rear end around far too soon on the first attempt, and then far too late on the second. On the third attempt, she rode a rear wheel over the curb and left her front quarter panel partially sticking out into traffic. That was apparently good enough for her liking.

I got out and leaned against my Cadillac to admire her parking, which was as haphazard as her personality. "Girl, you need some new wheels. This thing is like, forty years old," I commented.

"This thing is a Pontiac Grand Prix and a modern-day marvel in automobile technology. She's my baby, and I'll never put her down," Alexis playfully rebuked as she slammed her door. "Are you glowing? I think you're glowing," she said as she opened her arms for a hug.

I smiled. "It's good to see you," I said as I gave her a quick embrace and then reclaimed my personal space.

"Uh-oh. I think I feel a little bump." She reached out to run a hand over my belly as I raised a fist to warn her away, but she went in for the obligatory pregnancy rubdown anyway. "Oh shit. Bye-bye six-pack, hello baby bump."

"Do you have any idea how badly I want to cut you right now?" I jested. As conflicted as I was on trading in my steel physique for a mom bod, I was inarguably joyful to have a friend like Alexis encouraging me. "Okay, I gave you ten seconds, and that's all you're getting," I complained as I shooed her away.

"Tess is coming, yeah?"

"She was in the lab this morning, but she should be here any minute."

"Look at you. All married up, baby on the way, and an officer's desk job. Two years sure does change a lot."

"And some things stay the same," I reminded her as I tugged on the strings of her hooded sweatshirt. "You might be the only person on the planet who's granted an audience before Parliament and shows up dressed like Eminem."

"You know, there used to be a parking garage right over there." Alexis pointed to the north. "That's where I met Emilia. We got drunk and watched her OWG office get pummeled to the ground. Now look at this place. North American Parliament."

"What do you think she would say?" I asked, hoping to covertly plant some seeds of doubt about the proposed mission.

"Alexis," she said, effecting her best Emilia impersonation, "you dumb cunt. You're truly a special kind of stupid."

"That should be the engraving on her nonexistent statue. These pricks never gave her the props she deserved."

"She should have a statue. God, I wish she were here right now," Alexis said solemnly. "Oh, look who it is!"

Tess pulled up next to us and I pointed around the corner to signal her way to nearby available parking. "Fingers crossed for some good news," I said, hoping the test results Alexis was waiting for my wife to deliver would be good.

"I hope so. If I get a little good news, I won't have to give my speech today or blast off into the cosmos searching for purpose. I can keep it simple with my own baby bump. I imagine picking out some Adonis with great genes, having him squeeze off a couple of rounds in a cup, and pffft," she mimicked a fart noise while illustrating the press of a syringe compressor, "easy bake pregnancy."

"Adonis? I know Malik ain't no chiseled specimen, but he's got good genes and his boys can swim." I laughed. "That was good enough for him to be our donor. But anyway, I'm sure there's a man out there for you somewhere. You saved the world, for Christ's sake."

Tess approached us on the sidewalk then, looking as good as ever. She stood tall at 5'10" and walked with the confident swagger of a professional woman with her house in order. Her blonde hair cascaded halfway down her back and a lover's smile crossed her mouth, causing her dimples to show. Her blue eyes were exactly what you'd expect from a Dutch woman, and even though her height gave her some masculine appeal, she possessed many of the feminine characteristics that I did not.

"Hi, baby." She kissed me, then leaned down to kiss my belly with another, "hi, baby."

"Oh God. You too? How many more months are left of this treatment?" I groaned.

"I'll carry the next one," she promised with a wink. "Alexis. Good to see you. You look . . . like you." She laughed before kissing both of Alexis' cheeks.

"Did you happen to . . . ya know? Is there any news?" Alexis asked, her hands clasped in front of her.

"Are you sure you want to know before you go on stage?" Tess responded.

"Oh fuck me. It's bad? How bad?"

"I'm sorry, dear. It's PID—pelvic inflammatory disease. It's not usually serious, but you do have a good deal of scar tissue."

"I knew it. I freaking knew it," Alexis began to panic. "Where'd it come from?"

"Most times it's STD-related, but your results came back clean . . ." Tess trailed off, purposely avoiding where she knew Alexis was taking this line of questioning.

'The abortion, right?" Alexis pursed her lips and nodded her head as she processed her guilt.

"I can't say for certain," Tess answered, trying to excuse Alexis from beating herself up. "Concerning your fertility, we do have some options we can explore, but I can't make you any promises. I'm afraid medicine isn't as advanced as we'd like it to be. We're making some incredible discoveries at Amaar Labs, though. And who knows what might be possible in a few years."

Alexis shifted her weight, rubbing a hand nervously against her neck. Her eyes welled up, her hands started to shake, and she exhaled deeply. "Dammit," she whispered before going to her car, popping the lid off a pill bottle, and medicating herself before she had a panic attack. "I just thought that maybe, you know, I could have what you have." She sniffled. "I did this to myself."

"There's no proof of that," Tess replied gently.

I wouldn't have thought that I would ever be someone who's an expert at consoling others, but my shoulder was still warm from my time embracing Malik, and I had stronger motherly instincts than I thought. I held Alexis and rubbed her back while she buried her tear-stained face in my shirt.

There I was, daring to complain about the miracle I was experiencing while Alexis was discovering that she could never have such luck. "Come on, let's get you straightened out before you go on," I encouraged her.

There was no turning from the mission now. Alexis had wanted to be a mother, but it seemed her best path to finding her purpose was out among the stars.

We crossed the street to the parliament building and passed through the giant oak doors where we were met with the bustling of politicians and press making their way to the house chambers.

"Is Malik here?" Tess inquired.

"He's around here somewhere. Been here all morning," I answered.

"Yippie," Tess said sarcastically. No matter how vehemently I explained the platonic level of our friendship, Tess still harbored jealousy. I couldn't blame her for feeling threatened. My connection to Malik was unique, and my choice to ask him to be our sperm donor was causing more rifts in my relationship than I had anticipated.

"Hey, superstar," Malik announced his presence as he placed his hands on Alexis' shoulders. "Ready to knock 'em dead in there?"

"I think I can handle it, but I'm not looking forward to the fallout. I really don't want to face him," Alexis answered.

"It'll be fine. You know we're right." Malik turned to me with a smile and a salute. "Commander. Permission to—" was as far as he got before I cut him off. I shook my head to stop him from drawing attention to my belly or making a poorly-timed dad joke that might upset Alexis after the news she just received.

"Tess. How are you? Nice to see you," Malik said graciously, even knowing he wouldn't receive the same warm welcome.

"I'm fine," Tess responded plainly.

"Great. Great. You two should find your places," he said as he took Alexis' hand, "I'm going to escort the keynote speaker backstage."

"See you on the flip side. Good luck," I wished them, even though I didn't mean it.

Tess and I entered the parliament chamber and claimed our seats amid those reserved for high-ranking military personnel. We had no say concerning the matter at hand following the realignment of power, but it was nice to be included among the dignitaries.

The room was filling up fast, with the voting members of elected parliament and governors occupying their assigned seats up front while the press and other onlookers crammed shoulder to shoulder in the back. People

raised their converted Connect Earth phones to capture the moment as
the Prime Minister took the podium to bring the proceedings to order.

"Ladies and gentlemen, please find your seats. We are about to begin,
and I will remind you all that interruptions or disturbances from those
in attendance will not be tolerated. We will be hearing from the delegate
from Mission Vocury first, followed by arguments from the dissenting
council. Parliamentary members and governors will vote once both sides
have had a chance to speak, which will bring the proceedings on this issue
to a close. With that said, I invite Ms. X to the podium."

"She's not going to freak out, is she?" Tess whispered.

"She should be fine," I said as Alexis walked the stage to the podium.
Once within range of the hot mic, her soft humming of a few bars of
Sweet Child O' Mine by Guns N' Roses broadcast over the speakers.
"Okay, maybe she won't be fine after all," I relented, recognizing the
singing as one of the cues for Alexis' panic attacks.

Alexis clumsily gripped the mic and lowered it to her level, causing a
screeching howl over the PA system. "Sorry! Sorry." She gathered herself.
"Okay, um, let's examine the facts. The Praxi came to Earth to help us,
and we barely scratched the surface of what they had to offer. They didn't
have to return after we attacked them, but my friend Gio risked his life
regardless because he saw the good in us. They haven't given up on us.

"We know that, had Gio survived his trip to Earth, his next destination
was the planet the Praxi call Vocury. From context, we presume that it's
an off-world science colony where the Praxi manufacture future members of their society. It's safe to assume that Vocury is a terrestrial world
with an atmospheric composition and temperature similar to Prius and
Earth.

"Under traditional circumstances, a mission to Vocury would be near
impossible. Without a surplus of triaxum to power our gravity drives,
we're left with propulsion-based space travel methods. Based on NASA's
calculations, it would take us nearly three hundred years to reach the
planet using our current tech. However, we've made some incredible
discoveries while assessing the Praxi craft, and we believe that we can
carry enough fuel to propel a colony freighter across the stars with low
gravity slingshot maneuvers and inertia doing most of the heavy lifting.
A small amount of leftover triaxum will assist in breaking Earth's gravity,
maintaining propulsion, and fueling our lander.

"As some of you know, NASA has also disassembled the antigravity couches onboard Gio's ship and they've developed suspension chambers of their own that can preserve a human traveler for the trip. In addition to the suspension chambers, we've also recovered eight of those sweet-ass 'dream tubes'"—she illustrated the point with finger quotes—"from various Praxi crafts. A few lucky ones will be upgraded and get to live a dream for the duration of the voyage, while most of us petitioning for this journey will merely go to sleep and wake up three hundred years later on the other side of the galaxy."

Pausing, Alexis finally took a breath as we all waited for her to continue.

"Our proposition is simple. Assemble a team of fifty explorers onboard a freighter carrying five hundred frozen embryos and enough supplies to establish a colony on Vocury. Should the Praxi remain on the planet, our mission is to establish contact and form the peaceful union that our two species were meant to have.

"With a bit of luck, a few centuries will have healed the wounds between us. In theory, the Praxi there should have operable gravity drives, enough triaxum to fuel them, and potentially even a Jump Point. If all goes well and the Praxi agree, an ambassador from our colony will travel back to Earth with our new friends. We'll have a second attempt at our first contact and maybe, just maybe, if we pull our collective heads out of our asses, we can get it right this time around.

"I truly believe this is what my friend Gio wanted for us. He died for his faith in mankind and was never allowed to reach Vocury where his daughter awaited his arrival. The least we could do is carry out his vision and deliver some explanation to that child who never met her father. Please, keep her in your thoughts as you cast your votes." Alexis went to move away before speaking back into the mic. "Oh! And thank you for your consideration."

I leaned over to Tess and whispered, "That was the most un-Alexis presentation possible."

"If you had a vote, would she have earned it?"

I didn't answer because I didn't have to. I had grown accustomed to the benefits of having a grounded life with supportive friends, and the last thing I wanted was to say goodbye.

In a perfect world, Malik would be the godfather to my unborn child, and Tess and I would have him to lean on as our parenting rock any time things got tough. Tess may have been threatened by Malik, but I had no doubt that he'd win her over eventually.

Alexis walked away from the podium with her head held high, but her eyes tilted forward the moment she saw Ranbir approaching from stage left to deliver the dissenting opinion. She said something softly to him as they passed each other, but Ranbir didn't acknowledge her. He walked to the podium, removed the mic from the housing, and proceeded to stalk from one end of the stage to the next as he examined his audience.

"My friend Gio would never support this mission. How do I know that? Because he was actually my friend and not someone I knew for fourteen seconds. Frankly, Gio never should have come back here. He died trying to save us from ourselves, and here we are again—a bunch of greedy, zealous, selfish, and overly ambitious upright apes who aren't considering the consequences of our actions.

"Ms. X would have you believe that we've changed. That we've learned from our mistakes. That things will be different this time around. But they won't be. Even if they were to survive their three-hundred-year trip through the chaotic dangers of space, they can't possibly predict what they will find out there or the harm they might do. If the Praxi still wanted anything to do with us, don't you think they'd be here?

"We must face the music, people. The Praxi probably hate us, and who could blame them? We don't owe it to Gio or his daughter to attempt contact again. If anything, the only thing we owe them is to leave them the hell alone. And don't for one second let Ms. X convince you that this mission is one of altruism. They want this for their own selfish reasons of exploring the cosmos or simply getting off Earth and finding a fresh start.

"Those who agree with me want me to hammer you members of Parliament about the costs of this mission. They want me to politic on the allocation of tax dollars and the centuries it will take to show any return on our investment. But honestly, I don't give a shit about the money. Nor do I care that we possess the technology to make this journey possible in the first place. What I do care about, however, is seeing that the realization we had two years ago stays intact. We're not ready as a species to go jumping through the galaxy, and I'll be damned if I stand by while we repeat the mistakes of our past.

"Please, for the love of God, consider that we can't possibly calculate every way this could go wrong. There's damage we could do or open ourselves up to that we don't possess the knowledge to comprehend until it happens, if even then. Vote no on Mission Vocury and give our people the time to effect change gradually. That's all I've got."

With that, Ranbir returned the mic to its holster and hopped off the edge of the stage to take his place among the other governors and members of Parliament who held a vote.

"I think I know which way Governor Chopra is going to vote." Tess smirked.

"As much as I hate agreeing with him, he's right. We got no business out there in space."

"I think they should go. It's three hundred years away. Those aliens will have either forgotten about us or moved on by then. I don't see what all the gloom and doom is about."

"Babe, I love you, and your naïve hopefulness is cute—but you haven't seen the same shit we have."

I wanted to say more because I knew the real reason Tess supported the mission was because it would take Malik to the other side of the galaxy, but there was no point in fighting before the votes were cast.

Fifteen minutes later, the North American Prime Minister took the stage again and called the room to order. Malik and Alexis had taken a seat in the audience near the front, and I imagined that both of them were avoiding eye contact with Chop across the aisle. It was awful having our team splintered by strong opposing positions, and there were no results of the vote that could make things better.

"Ladies and gentlemen, the votes have been counted. It is my great honor to announce that, with a 13-8 tally, the mission to Vocury has been approved. Funding will be allocated immediately, and in just four weeks, Earth will send her maiden space colonization vessel to the stars. The proceedings on this matter are closed."

"And that's that." Tess stood along with the others to vacate the premise. "I have to be getting back to the lab, but I'll see you at home tonight."

"Yeah, I'll see you." I dismissed myself quickly as Ranbir rose from his seat and stomped his way toward Malik and Alexis. I carved my way through those heading for the exit, thinking I may very well need to step in between my friends if things became heated.

"Don't give me that shit," was the first thing I heard out of Ranbir's mouth as I inserted myself into the conflict in process between the victors and the defeated.

"Chop, come on man," Malik pleaded with him. "After everything we've been through, we can't end things like this."

"We don't have to if you don't want to. Don't go. Delay the mission. Give it five years and really consider what you're doing. If you still want to go after you think it through, I won't stand in your way."

"You already can't stand in our way," Alexis sassed him. "The people have spoken, and the mission is going forward. We could always make room for one more though, if you're up for another adventure."

"I'm not going anywhere with you two, but I hope you're right. For the sake of the Praxi and the people of Earth three centuries from now. I'm just glad I won't be around anymore to say 'I told you so' when this whole thing blows up in your faces."

"Chill, bro. It's over. This bad blood isn't going to solve anything, and you'll wish you hadn't spilled it once they're gone," I warned him.

"Really, Maya? That's all you have to say? You're not going to do anything about this? I know you don't support it either," Chop called me out.

"It's not my place, and I've fought enough battles to recognize a losing campaign when I see it," I answered.

Malik perked up and turned his attention to me as that was the first he'd heard of my disagreement with his mission. "Maya? If you've got something to say, speak on it."

"Nah, bro. I've got your back every time, even when I don't. You feel me?"

"That's gangsta," Alexis quipped with an adoring smile for my loyalty.

"Fine. Whatever," Ranbir surrendered. "Good luck, I guess. Try not to get yourselves or the rest of us killed," he angrily conceded before storming off.

Once Chop was gone, Malik and Alexis were more comfortable sharing their elation, and I did my best to not rain on their parade. If this mission would bring Malik the happiness that had eluded him, then he had my support.

"Can I stop by the house tomorrow morning?" Malik asked me. "I have some things for you."

"I've got some official military duties to attend to, followed by a rehab session. How about 3 p.m.?"

"Perfect."

"Yeah, by the way Maya, how's the whole clean-living thing going?" Alexis piped up.

"It's good. It's good. I mean, it's not quite as much fun as bumping rails off a stripper's backside, but it's a hell of a lot healthier."

"That's incredible, Maya. I'm really proud of you." Alexis gave me an awkward punch in the shoulder.

"Let's not get carried away here. When I leave the hospital after pushing this little monkey out, the first thing I'm going to do is roast a bone, pour a drink, and crush some KFC."

They both smiled and shook their heads at me.

"Alright, I'll leave you kids to it so you can plan your road trip." I walked away, and they were joined by other members of their mission with jubilation and hugs.

Malik's family was growing, and I had no business being jealous. I had a family of my own to worry about, but I craved the excitement of setting out on an adventure with my friends. It's not that I didn't want Malik to leave, it's that I wanted to go with him.

Later that night, Tess and I had a quiet evening together, and I tried my best not to take her for granted. Months earlier, I had the opportunity to sell Tess on the pair of us joining Mission Vocury, but I didn't have the will to shoot my shot.

I had convinced my wife that I was capable of domestication, and the last thing I wanted to do was plant the idea that I'd rather have another adventure than start a family. Getting pregnant was my way of guaranteeing that the option to leave with my friends was off the table and I felt like scum for having moments of regret.

I went about my duties the next morning, and when I returned home in the afternoon, I found Malik sitting on my stoop waiting for me.

"Good afternoon, Commander." He stood to salute me and slung a duffle bag over his shoulder.

"I make the uniform look good, don't I?"

"Better than I ever did," he said while I unlocked the door and entered the house. Malik heaved as he raised the bag to the kitchen table and then took a seat.

"What you got there?"

"Have a look," he invited.

I threw the straps to the side and ran the zipper from end to end. When I yanked open the flaps of the bag, I was met with a treasure trove of banded currency, grouped in packs of one thousand. "Did you rob a bank?!" I exclaimed as I rifled through the shocking amount of cash.

"Yeah, and everything in the vault was mine."

"Seriously, what is this?"

"I sold the house in Arkansas. Liquified my 401k. Emptied my checking and savings. That there are the fruits of my labor, and I'm not going to need it where I'm going."

"I can't accept this, Malik. It's too much."

"It's not for you, ya presumptuous little brat. It's for the baby. Tuck it away until your kid is all grown up, and once they're mature enough to handle it, surprise them with the funds that will make their life easier."

"This makes it feel so official. You're really leaving."

"I am, and I wish you could come with me."

"Believe me, under different circumstances, I'd be all about it."

"This next month is going to be hectic, but I'd love it if you'd come on the freighter on launch day and see us off."

"Awww. Does somebody need to get tucked into bed?" I quipped.

Malik grabbed a banded wad of bills out of the bag, slid it across the table, and bantered back, "That should be enough to purchase a proper bedtime story. Let's keep it light, though. I've elected to use the dream tube and I'd rather not have any nightmares."

"I'd rather go back to Mogadishu than commit to a three-hundred-year dream. You sure that thing is safe? Just use the regular tube, bro. Fall asleep and wake up a second later at your destination."

"They say it's really euphoric, 'better than dreaming.' I haven't had a religious experience in a while, so I figured I'd give it a shot."

"I've never been able to talk you out of anything, so I'll spare myself the trouble. Now, be a doll, stash that bag in the attic for me, and hustle your ass out of here. Tess will be home soon, and I've had my fill of jealous eyes for the week."

Malik did as instructed while I sprawled out on the couch. I laid there with my thoughts and contemplated the state of my evolving life. The more I focused on how well I was doing, the more I wanted to engage in dangerous behavior.

The peace in our home was unsettling, and knowing that I was always only a phone call away from a cocaine connection was making me wish for a series of tragic events that would reintroduce some excitement into my life and excuse some drug use.

I resented the life I was lucky enough to have.

My friends were leaving forever on an adventure, and the most pressing business I had to attend to was shopping for cheaper car insurance and picking a color palette for the baby's room. I was a wife who was meant to be free. An officer meant to be a mercenary. I was a recovering drug addict who longed to be a party animal, and an expectant mother who wanted to act like a child.

I had metaphorically traded in my sidearm and combat boots for a clutch purse and strappy heels—like a suburban spy, sent to collect intel on the boring lives of people I wanted to fight to protect, but never desired to live for myself.

The walls were closing in around me, and the only thing that kept me clean was an instinctual love for the child growing within me. That was the only life I was responsible for safeguarding, and without it, I'd certainly destroy myself in a sabotaging effort to reclaim the hectic existence I had abandoned.

It was only once Tess walked through the door and shared her smile that I remembered what I had gained. The monotony of the simple life would be difficult to accept, but she made the journey worth it. It was time for me to put the warrior within me to bed and embrace the perks of a quiet existence.

I had very little contact with Malik and Alexis in the month leading up to launch day, but Ranbir filled that void with nonstop badgering calls and messages. He was obsessed with stopping them and rarely did a day go by where he wasn't up my ass about it.

In another life, I may have teamed up with him to sabotage the mission. I certainly wouldn't have thrown a wrench into things to save the Praxi, though I might have to keep my friends on Earth.

That ship had sailed, and I wasn't about to leave a sour taste in my mouth when saying goodbye to my friends for the last time. It was a sad day when I went to the launch site to see them off, but I was determined to end things on a happy note.

Malik was finally achieving his dream of becoming an astronaut and Alexis, with her hope of motherhood shrunk, had settled for her backup plan of exploring the cosmos. I was resolved to be happy for them in our final moments together.

Tess and I fought our way through the onlookers and members of the press to get near the chain-link fence separating the sheep from our interstellar shepherds. In the distance was the converted Praxi cargo ship that was being sent to ferry the colonists across the galaxy to Vocury. Down the side, written in bold white lettering, was The Wolf Moon. Launch technicians were in the foreground making their final checks and fueling the rocket that would propel the craft into the outer atmosphere.

I invited Tess to join me on board the craft for the goodbyes, but she was happy to keep her distance and stay among the crowd. I flashed my military ID and special access badge to the security guard, and he promptly opened the gate to allow me to approach the Wolf Moon.

I made my way to the lift that rose above the lower rocket housing and helped myself through the open rear hatch of the cargo hold. The wide-open space that had once been filled with loads upon loads of prisoners was now crammed with refrigerated storage cells for the embryos, sleep tubes for the passengers, and stockpiles of supplies to settle and construct a colony. I entered the ship just as the technicians were loading a much smaller landing craft into the rear of the hull.

I noticed Alexis across the way, holding a clipboard and wearing headphones as she sang aloud as though no one could hear her off-pitch rendition of The Chain by Fleetwood Mac.

"Alexis. Alexis. Alexis!" My voice rose to a shout behind her, but she was lost in her checklist and blaring music. I pulled one of the buds from her ear and she nearly jumped out of her skin when I said "Boo."

"You made it!" she exclaimed warmly. "A few more system checks and it'll be time for one heck of a nap. Come on, let me show you my tube."

Alexis dragged me by the arm through the shuffling flight crew and those who were on board to see them off. The sleep chambers were set in rows, the majority on one side of the bay with a few on the other. Comprised of a silver alloy, they stood upright and, when opened, the interior padding and life support systems were visible. Once closed, they looked like standing metallic coffins with only a small glass viewing port for the tombed.

"This is my feeding tube, this runs my vitals, and this—" Alexis excitedly explained the science behind the tech, but she had lost my interest.

"You're absolutely certain this is safe? The tubes won't fail you? They'll wake you when you arrive?" I interrupted her demo.

"One hundred percent. They run on the backup power generator, and they've been exhaustively field-tested. In the movies, the horrible things that happen to space explorers only ever transpire once they're out of stasis," she joked.

"Look, I don't know what you guys are going to find out there, but you're going to have to back each other up. Malik won't let you down, I can promise you that much. I need you to promise me that you'll look out for him too."

"Anything I should know? Don't let him get wet? Don't feed him after midnight?"

"I'm being serious." I looked her in the eye. "I've looked out for him for over two years, and now it's your job. You feel me?"

"I got you. We're still a team, even if some of us are going our own way," she reassured me. "The same goes for you. Raise that family, Maya. Be a good mother for those of us who can't. And if you can find some time to look out for Ranbir, that would be nice too."

"I can do that." I opened my arms in a rare invitation for a hug and Alexis snatched the opportunity with haste.

"You're a good friend, and I'll miss you dearly," she said through tears.

"No tears, 'cause I don't have any to trade you," I said quietly with emotional resolve. I broke first from the hug, but she continued to hold on for a few more seconds. "This is goodbye, my friend. Be safe out there. Don't take no shit from anybody."

"Yes, ma'am," she replied as she wiped away her tears. "Bye, Maya. It's been a privilege. Thanks for coming to see us off, being so supportive, and just like, thanks for being you. You're like, the coolest person I'll ever know."

"Likewise," I responded. I turned my back to avoid lingering in the charged moment, and that was the last I would see of one of the few friends I had ever made. I didn't loiter around to watch Alexis being loaded into her tube, instead choosing to move on and find Malik on the other side of the bay.

There were four dream chambers built into one superstructure that mirrored a massive dresser with drawers for the human cargo. One of the passengers was being loaded into the top slot as I approached, but Malik was nowhere to be found. I listened in as the architect of that monstrosity offered a final coaching to the colonist and watched with intent as he administered a sedative and closed the sleeper into her cell.

"Excuse me, sir. I'd like to ask you a few questions," I prompted, but the man was too busy turning dials and initiating the freezing process to pay me any attention. "Excuse me," I raised my voice more pointedly, which was again ignored.

"Hey, pendejo, I'm talking to you," I barked, grabbing the man by the back of his neck. I calmed my tone as he bent to the will of my grip, "There, that's better."

"Do you understand the importance of what I'm doing here?" he chastised.

"Sure don't. And seeing as how you're about to load my boy Malik in there, how about you put my concerns to bed first?"

"It's perfectly safe. Your friend will be suspended in a deep freeze, but unlike the others in their hypersleep chambers, his mind will remain active. He'll be able to live out a three-hundred-year dream on his way to Vocury. Who knows what wonders he will learn about himself in the process? Now, do you mind?" he politely asked for me to release him.

I let go of his neck and allowed him to continue his work. "What if the dream turns into a nightmare?"

"Not possible. Your friend will be plugged into a dream inhibitor. His vitals will be monitored, and sedatives and serums will be locally introduced as needed. Furthermore, his mind will be kept in a sunken state of bliss, and the chamber will transmit data back to Earth so that we can monitor his progress until the ship passes out of range in approximately seventy-two years."

"So hypothetically, if something does indeed go wrong during the first leg of their journey, we'll know about it?"

"That is correct," he said as he moved on to the next colonist to prepare for sleep.

'Well, that's good news. 'Cause if something does go sideways, I'm going to pay you a visit. Just something to keep in mind when you're doing your final checks. No pressure."

"You're a military officer. You wouldn't harm a civil servant," he replied with zero conviction.

"Want to test that theory, doc?" I sneered, to which he visibly gulped. "Didn't think so."

"What do you think?" Malik asked as he approached from the forward decks of the ship. "It's impressive, right? I get to live three hundred years in dreams before our mission even begins. I'll be an old soul by the time I meet the Praxi again."

"Impressive? Sure. Insane? Absolutely. I don't know why you want to live that long, bro—if it even qualifies as living."

"It sure felt like the real thing on my test runs, and that was without the sedative. I'll be going many layers deeper this time. In fact, this may not be the last time I see you. There's no telling where my mind may take me, and I bet you're in there somewhere."

"Whatever version of me is up there"—I tapped his temple—"had damn well better be close to the original."

"I can't wait to find out," Malik said as he took a seat near the lowest sleep tray and removed his shirt. The doctor went to work on connecting various devices to his body and inserting two IV tubes for his feeding and sleep aids.

It was in that moment that I realized how magnified pain is when you can see it coming. A fist smashing you in the face will never hurt as badly when it comes from your blind side instead of from straight in front of you.

I had seen this goodbye blow coming for a month, and the agony had intensified with every minute that passed. To make matters worse, Malik was cheery with centuries of my dream clone to keep him company and the pain of goodbye kept at bay.

"I have something to tell you that I hoped would put you in a positive state of mind before you went to sleep, but it seems you've got that under control."

"What is it, Maya?"

"Tess and I are having a boy and we've decided to name him Marcus. Something of an homage to the biological father he'll never know."

"You know, when you frame it like that, it kind of feels like a guilt trip," he said, concerned.

"It's not, bro. It's really not. I'm happy for you, and Tess and I are eternally grateful."

"I'm honored. Truly," he said as he placed his hand over mine. "And you don't need to be grateful. You saved me, Maya, and centuries of dreaming won't make me forget. Don't let my positive disposition today throw you. I know what this trip is costing me, and I don't abandon our friendship lightly."

"I know. I know," I repeated as I clenched my jaw and held back tears. I wanted to beg him to stay, but knew I had to let him go.

"Come here," he said as he stood and pulled the various cords and lines hooked to him into one hand, holding them to the side. I stepped up to his chest and had my arms around him before he could reciprocate, and I held him the same way he had held me on our mission to Prius. My grip was tight, and I hid my pained expression and tears from the world by burying my face in his shoulder.

"Take care of your family, Maya. Raise Marcus up right to be a proper young man," he counseled.

"I will. I promise," I said as we broke from our embrace.

"You're going to be one heck of a mother. I feel sorry for those ladies on the PTA. They don't know what's coming," he joked with a slap to my upper arm. "Ha, now I can't get the image of you as a suburban mom out of my head. You're going to be driving a minivan before you know it."

"Dick." I shoved him lovingly.

Malik followed the doctor's instructions and climbed into the sleep compartment to make himself comfortable. His head rested gently on the padding and he reached a hand out for one last shake before being tucked in.

"I love ya, Maya. You're going to be okay."

I shook his hand. "Good luck, Astronaut Emmanuel. Go prove Chop wrong. You got this."

The doctor fixed the cables into position, ran one final check on Malik, and slid the sleep compartment into the structure.

"Nighty night," I said as I watched my best friend disappear into the contraption and ceremoniously exit my life forever. My tone quickly changed as I addressed the doctor. "Don't fuck this up."

"He's fine. He'll be sleeping comfortably in minutes. Now, please exit the ship and see yourself to the perimeter with the other guests."

That was it.

I trudged my way back to the elevator and across the airfield to rejoin Tess among the crowd of onlookers. I took my time going back to compose myself and give my eyes a chance to shake that annoying silver glow of a fresh cry.

"Are you okay?" Tess asked as she lightly massaged the small of my back.

"I'm good. He has his journey, and we have ours. I hope things go the way they think."

"They'll be fine. Malik and Alexis have each other."

We waited for thirty minutes as all personnel were cleared off the Wolf Moon, and I spent the final seconds hoping for some kind of launch failure that would delay the mission for a few more weeks—but it never came.

The rockets fired and the craft slowly lifted upwards toward the clouds, propelled by a flaming blast that was hot enough to warm my face. The ship was out of view within minutes and would soon ditch the rocket housing in the outer atmosphere to start its long voyage across the stars.

"So long, my friends."

Chapter 2

Crossing Over

Malik Emmanuel: 2036

My eyes opened to the blinding light of the sun above and I had to blink repeatedly to erase the white spots in my vision. I was lying on my back in tall grass, and when I sat up, I found myself alongside a dirt road. The sky was filled with fluffy clouds, as if ripped from a painting, and the sun shone bright upon my face. I rose to my feet and slowly examined the landscape. There were farmhouses off in the distance in all directions and the land was flat and clear, even though there should have been fields of crops growing in such a setting.

I walked along the road for about a mile toward the closest home and found an old wooden mailbox marked L.E. at the end of an unpaved driveway. Children's toys littered the pristinely maintained front yard, and even though the residence had a driveway, there were no vehicles or anything resembling a garage.

"Hello?" I shouted, having no idea what to expect.

Was my mind going to populate this simple country dream world with anyone to interact with? Was there an adventure in here waiting for me? Was time passing at the same rate of speed as my frozen body?

It was impossible to say.

Squeals of children playing in the distance penetrated the silence, and I thought I heard the soft echoing of a familiar woman's voice singing.

I walked around to the backside of the house to find a woman swaying back and forth on a wooden bench swing between two towering oak trees. Her back to me, she sung softly to herself as she held a book just high enough to read while keeping an eye on her children.

It was only once I stepped closer and saw her profile that I received an answer to one of my questions.

"Lydia?" I asked, my voice quivering. She turned to look at me and smiled as if she had been expecting me. She quickly shot out of her seat, ran to me, and stopped just short of jumping into my arms.

"I knew you'd come, but I never dared to dream that it would be so soon." She attempted to embrace me but passed right through my body as if I were incorporeal.

"What is this? What's happening?" She reached out to touch my chest, her hand once again passing through me. "I can't feel you. I can't . . . I can't even smell you."

"Dad? You came!" Marcus cried out as he ran to me ahead of Maisie.

"Stop, Marcus!" Lydia demanded, but Marcus ignored his mother, passed through me, and fell to the grass behind me.

"Daddy! Daddy!" Maisie shouted, and Lydia scooped her up before she could sprint to me.

"It's not your Daddy. It's a test. Or a temptation," Lydia said, with a frightened tone. "What do you want from us?"

"I don't want anything. I don't know. This is just a dream. I woke up down the road and I think my subconscious mind brought you here." I laughed. "Ha, this is wild," I said to myself.

"What?" Lydia asked. "We've been here for at least a few years. I've patiently waited for you to come, hoping that you would live a rich and full life before you joined us. You shouldn't be here this soon, and you certainly shouldn't be a ghost. You're not real."

"For what it's worth, the three of you aren't real either, no matter how much I want you to be."

"I'm real, Daddy," Maisie proclaimed, causing my heart to sink.

"Why can't we touch you?" Marcus pondered as he probed his hand through my thigh and stomach as if I were a science experiment. He waved his hand toward my chin as though he was slapping me, and again he phased through my matterless form. "Oh, this is sick!" he said with delight.

"If you're my Malik, then you better get to explaining yourself," Lydia warned.

"This is a dream. My mind brought you here to occupy the space. My physical body is currently on ice in a suspended state and my mind is being kept active to entertain me as I journey across the galaxy. I—"

"You're alive? You haven't died in the physical reality?" Lydia interrupted. "How is that possible? Lordy, I don't understand anything anymore."

"Yes, I'm alive."

"And we're dead, Malik. We're real, but we're very much dead. What happened to us?"

"This is nuts. It's not supposed to be like this."

"Answer me. What happened to us? Where were you?" she repeated through tears.

"I don't even know where to begin. So much has happened." I delayed revealing the awful truth to my dreamscape family, as if they were real.

"The three of you were in London when a gravity wave device was dropped on the city. You likely died instantly, and your bodies were never recovered. I went into the English countryside and never saw you again. I couldn't even give you a proper burial. It hurt worse than you can possibly imagine. Even after years of processing, I still love you mad, baby."

"Malik?" her voice softened as she raised her hand to my cheek, stopping short of passing through me as though she were making real contact. "It's really you. I don't know how, but you're here."

"For now. The dream could change, or I could wake up and disappear in an instant."

"You're not dreaming, babe. This is the afterlife," she said definitively. "My parents are up the road that way"—she pointed in one direction—"and your folks are down the road that way." She nodded her head in the opposite direction. "There's nobody here who hasn't passed away, until now. There's no pain or sickness or aging here, as far as I can tell. It's perfection, or at least it will be one day when you join us."

"I'm here right now, and I'm not going anywhere anytime soon. It's a long trip to Vocury. Long enough for us to live multiple lifetimes together." I gave way to Lydia's interpretations of reality, happy to embrace my mind's concoction of the afterlife.

Millions of people had lost their loved ones during the war, and I was lucky enough to be afforded additional time with mine. If the scientists back on Earth experimented with the same sedations pumping through my veins, this process of deep, controlled dreaming could prove therapeutic to many experiencing losses back home.

"Would you like to see your dad?" Lydia asked. "It's maybe a mile down the road, and he's been waiting for you a lot longer than I have."

I nodded happily and instinctively reached to take Maisie's hand only to be reminded that my pleasure in this state was limited. I would never be able to hug my children, make love to my wife, or shake my father's hand. Though initially jarring, the lack of physicality was acceptable, and I didn't learn to resent it for quite some time.

My concept of time slipped after the first few days. Some days the sun would be up for what felt like an eternity, and the next it would only shine for a few hours. It was as though it would rise and fall at our command, even though we never paid it any mind.

If we were enjoying a walk, games in the yard, or I was fishing with my dad, the sun would stay up as long as necessary. Conversely, if we were roasting marshmallows over the fire pit, the moon would hang high and bright, not dipping beyond the horizon until we had enjoyed a full night's rest.

Sleeping was odd while trapped in suspension. None of us required rest, yet we uniformly retired to our bedrooms every night for slumber. While it felt amazing, it wasn't about going to sleep at all. The pleasure was in the waking.

If I were to make a list of the most detrimental technological achievements of mankind, the invention of the alarm clock would fall somewhere between chemical weapons and propane grills. You can't possibly understand the beauty of starting every day by waking naturally and having nowhere to be until you're living that lifestyle.

There was no hustle and bustle in that world. No appointments to keep, no clock to punch, no errands to run, and no bills past due to tend to. Every day was whatever we chose to make of it, and lying in bed for an hour before bothering to move was the perfect way to start them.

The life we could have had on Prius was nothing compared to my dream world. The sun never burned our skin, the weather obeyed my subconscious demands, and every day was as carefree as could be. The cupboards never emptied of food and the electrical power was free of charge. If I woke with a craving for sausage links, there they would appear in the morning. If Maisie dropped her glass, it would neither shatter across the floor nor spill a drop of juice.

When we felt like celebrating Christmas, snow would fall for a day, the kids would play in it, we'd eat more servings of ham and mashed potatoes than we needed, and it would be a warm autumn day the following morning. Even something as simple as changing light bulbs wasn't a concern because they never ran out. We had everything we could dream up and there was no reason to ever leave.

My only enemy was time. Days turned into weeks, weeks into years, and years into decades. It was about the time when I assumed decades had given way to a century that I started to feel the anxiety creep in. By that point, it was clear that the dream was unchanging and would likely last for the duration of my trip.

Being unaware of how much time I had remaining hung around me like a distant approaching thunderstorm cackling manically in the distance. I wanted to get lost in the fantasy that my dream state had somehow pushed me into the afterlife, but I never believed it. If there wasn't a Heaven where my family was awaiting me, the time I had in this dream could be the last that I'd have with them.

It was odd watching my children grow up without age showing its effects. They became wiser as time rolled on, but they never traded their childlike wonder for that of an old soul.

I would never see them graduate high school, fall in love, make art, or have children of their own. Marcus would never need my guidance through a broken heart or a career decision, and I'd never get the chance to give Maisie away on her wedding day. Those opportunities were lost lifetimes ago, and not even a millennium of dreaming could return them.

My sleep tube fermented resent in my mind. I was on a centuries-long vacation that was nothing more than a tease—a promised bliss that came with all the setbacks you'd expect from a heroin spike. I needed the high and lived in fear of the comedown. I became helplessly addicted to my fictional family and wanted to die every time my hand passed through one of them instead of experiencing a physical connection.

At my lowest, I would long for the moment I disappeared from that world and woke aboard the ship, even though I knew all I'd want to do was climb back in and take another hit. I woke every day fearing that it would be my last with them, but also itching for it to end. Decades went by where my bliss was tainted by animosity. Everything was painfully ordinary and repetitive, right up until the moment that it was not.

It was a typical sunny afternoon, different in no way than the thousands before it, and the four of us were in the backyard enjoying the simple bliss of an idyllic day.

While Lydia sat on her swing, a book in hand and a glass of sweet tea by her side, the rest of us played baseball. I was pitching, Marcus was hitting, and Maisie was chasing down fly balls. It was then that Lydia looked to the north and noticed a darkening storm cloud heading our way.

"What is this? Which one of you hoped for some rain?"

"Maisie? Was it you?" I asked. "If you're sick of playing the outfield, you can switch places with Marcus and take some cuts. You didn't have to wish for a storm."

"I didn't," she answered. "I don't want to go inside."

"Don't look at me," Marcus chimed in before he could be accused.

"Well, it wasn't me," I added as I examined the landscape.

I had been there for centuries and couldn't remember a storm happening without us planning for a rainy day.

"Maybe my folks wanted a little shower," Lydia mused aloud, drawing attention to the proximity of the clouds to her parent's residence down the road.

"Maybe," I responded. "It's slow, but it's moving this way."

"Come on, Dad. A few more pitches. I've got a runner on second." Marcus drew me back into the game and cranked a handful of solid line drives off my slow-pitch meatballs in Maisie's direction before thunder cracked and lightning shot streaks of light through the vanilla sky.

"Whoa. An actual thunderstorm!" Lydia exclaimed as she wrangled us up. "Let's go, gang. We'll enjoy the storm from the house."

The kids retired to their rooms while Lydia and I sat in our favorite rocking chairs in the living room. Before we could get comfortable, however, an aggressive rap sounded at the front door.

"Who's coming over in the middle of a storm?" Lydia questioned. I shrugged my shoulders and we had a stare down for a few seconds to determine who would have to get up and greet our guests. She sighed as she relented, shooting up out of her chair and giving me a playful, "you're a lazy old man" ribbing.

"Love you bad, baby," I replied as the seated victor.

Lydia peered through the curtains beside the door and asked, "Who is this?" before opening the door. "Can I help you?"

"Is this the Emmanuel residence?" a female voice responded.

"You'll have to be more specific, ma'am. There's a few in these parts."

"Are you Lydia Emmanuel?"

"Yes. Why?" Lydia became defensive.

"Is Malik here?"

"What is this about?"

At that point, I rocked forward in my chair and nearly fell out of it as my line of sight bypassed my beautiful wife. I stood and approached her side, unable to believe my eyes.

"Emilia?"

There she stood on my stoop. Her short hair was drenched and matted to her face, which once again featured the scars she had left in her past. She was dressed in a blue blouse and skirt, both equally darkened by rainwater.

"What are you doing here?"

"Me? What about you?" she accused as she walked right through me into our home, not at all surprised by my gaseous physical state. "How did you get here? Where is Ranbir?"

"Excuse me, miss," Lydia interjected, her emotions bringing out her long-dormant southern drawl.

Emilia raised her hand to silence Lydia. "I've walked more miles than I count with years' worth of rain weighing me down. I'm sure you're a lovely woman, but I swear, I will cut you down if you fuck with me right now."

"You know this woman?" Lydia asked.

"Yes. I did. A very long time ago. You know, I always thought someone might pop up in here, but I expected it to be Maya, or even Chop. This is a pleasant surprise though."

"A very long time ago," Emilia echoed. "So why are you like this?" She waved her hand through my physical form.

"It's a long story that I barely remember after all these years."

"Well? Where is Ranbir?" she asked while poking me in the chest with intention even though her fingers slid through my aura.

"I couldn't tell you. Probably buried somewhere on Earth centuries ago."

"Why the hell didn't he come here with you?"

"We had a difference of opinion."

"Oh bullshit. He's supposed to be here. With me! A long-ass time ago! Instead, I have this fucking rain cloud following me everywhere I go."

"Ms. Emilia, I'm sorry for whatever you're going through right now," Lydia patronized with southern charm, "but I won't have that language in my home. Cut me down or not, I won't have it."

Emilia entered the living room and dejectedly plopped down into my chair. She placed her bare muddy feet on my footrest, and all the grime that soaked the fabric disappeared immediately. She ran her hand over her forehead and massaged away an apparent headache, which she shouldn't technically be able to experience.

"Sorry," Emilia spoke softly like a child to a disappointed parent.

It felt pointless consoling my mind's random conjuring of Emilia after all those years, but my paternal instinct took over.

"Emilia . . ." I waited for her to look up at me. "This isn't real. You're a figment of my active dreaming imagination. Someday soon, I'm going to wake up, and this world is going to cease to exist. Whatever troubles I've subconsciously assigned to you will evaporate."

"Malik, with all due respect, that is the dumbest fuc—" she caught the curse on the tip of her tongue as Lydia gave her a glare. "You have no idea what you're talking about."

I couldn't concentrate on her words, though. I was becoming lightheaded and dizzy, which was incredibly jarring after centuries of feeling neither. I stumbled forward until my hand reached Lydia's rocker, and I carefully sat myself down in it. Either Emilia had brought something into our home, or my body was going through a change.

"You still believe that after all this time, Malik?" Lydia inquired. It had been so long since our differing interpretations had drawn conflict between us, and I was being ganged up on by opposite sides of my brain's projections.

"It's all just a dream," I said, grasping at my chest and as it rose and fell at a rapid pace.

I had forgotten what it felt like to be out of breath. My heart pounded as if I was an hour into a workout, and beads of sweat formed on my forehead. "Something is happening to me. This might be the end."

"Hey. Hey, hey, hey," Emilia panicked, more concerned with getting her answers than my well-being. "You can't leave me here like this. Come back and bring Ranbir with you. Please, Malik," she begged. "I can't go on like this. And if he's never coming, I just need to know. I have to know."

My vision blurred, but I was still able to make out Lydia's total lack of panic. A smile crept across her face even as she watched my physical form begin to take on transparent qualities. She knelt beside me and leaned her elbow on the armrest to put my chair in a rocking motion.

"It's okay, Malik. You'll be back one day, and we'll be here waiting for you. Finish what you've started. Help your friends. Give your good nature to the world. I love you mad, baby."

I wanted to respond in kind, like I had a million times before, but I was no longer able to speak. My vision went first, followed closely by my auditory senses. The dream was ending, and my eyes closed to accept the phasing of my physical form.

I sensed a bright white light behind my eyelids, and when I attempted to open them, they naturally constricted to defend against the fluorescent glare. "Wakey-wakey, sleepyhead," a voice beckoned in a singsong tone.

My arm jerked from the pinch of my intravenous connections being removed and my temples ached from the snappy removal of the monitoring stickers that had been stuck to me for centuries. "Coffee's on, whenever you're ready."

I peeled one eye open and shielded it from the piercing unnatural light to see Alexis standing over me, bright-eyed and bushy-tailed. I clumsily reached for the sensors and plugs that she had removed, haphazardly trying to reattach them.

"Whoa, whoa, whoa. Slow your roll there, Rip Van Winkle," she said, yanking them from my weak grip. "Come on, sit up," she encouraged as she helped me to an upright position.

"Ho-ly shit," Alexis groaned as she turned her nose from me. "Let's get you some Listerine before that coffee, yeah? Woof." She laughed.

"Put me back. Put me back in," I mumbled, still half asleep.

"Just because I can't have children of my own doesn't mean I want to babysit you. Up and at 'em," she encouraged while tucking the medical equipment away and forcing me to face the real world.

When I went into hypersleep, I hadn't considered the costs. One taste would have been fine, but three hundred years of it had made me an addict.

Even with all that time, I still couldn't bring myself to give my family a proper goodbye. It was as though they were ripped from my life all over again, and all I could think about was completing the mission and finding a way to be forced to journey back to Earth so I could go under again.

I took a long shower, brushed my teeth furiously for Alexis' sake, and outfitted myself in a dark blue zip-up uniform. I walked through the main chambers where the rest of the passengers continued to sleep and couldn't help but envy the few who were in dream tubes. A part of me wanted to leave them in there forever while simultaneously wanting to pull them out and drill them with questions about their dream experience.

I made my way to the bridge and joined Alexis as the only other crew member out of slumber. She removed her earbuds and quietly mocked, "Put me back in," as I sat in the copilot's chair.

"Welcome to the year 2337. Still seems weird. So, you going to tell me about your dreamy adventure, or do you want to get right down to business?"

Chapter 3

The Promise of Paradise

Ranbir Chopra: 2039

I paced the sidewalk in front of the Final Contact Memorial Cemetery carrying a small candle-shaped urn, procrastinating going inside. It had been nearly six years since the World Military had murdered a hundred million people, and five years since I had lost Emilia.

The city of Chicago had done a wonderful job honoring those deaths, but lost in that sorrow was the fact that we had wiped out an entire civilization. No one mourned the tragic loss of the Praxi, and even though we avenged them, I solely carried the weight of the guilt with me everywhere I went.

I couldn't walk through the gates without feeling that my presence at the memorial was a slight to those who had died, but I couldn't avoid facing my guilt any longer. There was only one place to lay Amir's ashes to rest, and I thought it was the best peace offering I could offer Emilia's grave after years of hiding.

I walked along the Wall of the Fallen and ran my finger across the shined black marble that had the names of the victims inscribed upon it. The wall stood nine feet tall and ran around three-quarters of the cemetery perimeter, covering at least a mile. Most of them never received a proper funeral as their bodies couldn't be recovered from the wreckage.

I searched among the Es for Malik's family to make sure I paid my respects while I was there. I placed my hand over Lydia Emmanuel, Maisie Emmanuel, and Marcus Emmanuel and found myself emotional even though I had never met them.

Being reminded that I would never see Malik again was a punch in the gut and part of the reason I had avoided visiting the cemetery. I kept walking by the F section and on to the Gs, where I continued my search.

Gillen, Gillgren, Gillian, Gimby, Gines, Giton. "What the f . . ." my voice cracked with anger.

I scoured the grass until I found a rock with a sharp edge and returned to the wall to carve GIO in the margin between names. If they wanted to arrest me for destruction of property, they could come and try it.

I took to the plots next, which was my true purpose for visiting. Emilia's headstone was a small gray rectangular slab, and it was minimalist, to say the least. The only markings were E.L.V., just the way she would have liked it. I cracked open my urn and spread Amir's ashes over the grass that covered Emilia's grave.

"If there was anyone he loved as much as me, it was you. This seemed a fitting place to put him to rest." I paced awkwardly in front of Emilia's headstone, speaking as though she were right there listening to quell my bubbling emotions.

"So, I had a date about a month ago. I know—it's the last thing you'd want to hear. You know how in the movies when someone is dying, they say 'I want you to live on. Be happy'? I doubt that's a sentiment you'd share. You'll be pleased to know that it didn't work out, though. She was a perfectly sweet girl. She has a good career, she's attractive, and has a decent enough sense of humor. She had one fatal flaw though. She wasn't you."

I released a depressed laugh to myself and wiped tears from under both of my eyes. "I can't move on from you. I've tried, and I just can't. Anyone who attempts to fill the hole you left in my life only serves as a reminder that you're gone."

I paused as my voice became shaky and the moment swept me away. "I miss you. So badly. I'm sorry it took me this long to come. Fuck, this hurts."

There was cracking of dead leaves being stepped on behind me and the voice of a child pestering his mother who responded, "Sshhhh," quietly. I turned to look and found Tess, Maya, and their toddler son, Marcus, waiting patiently.

"You're early," I complained as I tried to compose myself.

"Paying our respects," Tess answered simply as she shifted Marcus' weight from one arm to the other.

Maya approached and we shared a knowing look of our past that bonded us forever. She knelt and placed a hand over Emilia's initials on the stone and whispered, "Hey, crazy girl. We could really use your help right now."

"Help with what?" I asked.

"Kind of a weird place to meet, no?" Maya responded.

"You said inconspicuous, and I was coming here today anyway. Seemed as good a place as any. What's the big secret?"

"SATCOM picked up a ship two days ago and they've been in communication. It's one of the lost haulers coming from Triax II. Apparently, they tried to use the Jump Point and, obviously, couldn't get through, so they took to charting the stars and blindly navigating their way back to Earth. They're carrying a full load of triaxum, minus what they've burned on their journey. They'll be here tomorrow evening."

"Son of a bitch," I moaned. "Why haven't I heard a whisper of this in Parliament?"

"'Cause the governors in the know are already on the take. The special interest contributors are all over this one, and the triaxum on board is already sold."

"Not possible," I dismissed the notion. "In the contingency for this event, the representatives will vote for the allocation of former World Military property. I can whip up the votes. We can use that shipment to power the planet for a hundred years."

"Ranbir," Tess interjected softly. "Do you honestly believe that? You might be involved in a new era of politics, but it's politics all the same."

"Let me ask you something," Maya aggressively prompted. "Do you like being a governor? Do you feel like you're making a difference?" I opened my mouth to answer, but Maya raised her hand to shut me down. "Is there anything keeping you on Earth, and would you leave if you could?"

"What are you talking about?" I dodged her questions. Amir's passing had pushed me to a low I hadn't experienced since Emilia died, and I wasn't comfortable exposing to Maya the levels of depression I had sunk to. She wasn't the type to respect weakness, and based on the complicated history of our relationship, I doubted her ability to show empathy.

Becoming governor was a pointless endeavor, and if what they said was true, I had no purpose left to serve in life. Throughout years of depression, I never experienced suicidal thoughts, but I could understand why others who felt equally lost and alone might. The only thing that kept me off that ledge was feeling like I had something important to do.

"I'm talking about a second chance. You boys had a good thing going on Prius. What if I told you that I could get you back there, and that you could save the world again on your way back?"

"Don't tease me. Not today."

"I'm serious. You do one job for me and give me maybe a year or two of your life on a mission, and I'll get you back to Prius with more supplies than Malik could drop in a thousand trips."

I once again paced over the ground where Emilia was buried, as if to channel her ability to navigate a negotiation, which this was clearly becoming. "Go on. Give me your elevator pitch."

"That triaxum headed for Earth is going straight to the repurposed Edwards Air Force Base, and it's meant to fuel three massive transports for a deep space mission. If I had to guess, I'd say those boys are planning a stop at Triax II to keep production going, and after that, who the hell knows. Whatever their next stop is, it's big. Rumor has it that one of the craft is a warship that dwarfs the other two and is capable of carrying an entire army, along with all of their ground vehicles and equipment."

"Bullshit. It would be the size of the entire base if that were the case. There's no way to keep something like that off the books or hidden from government oversight. Plus, there was nothing like what you're describing among the Praxi inventory. If this thing existed, I'd know about it."

A slick smirk on her face, Maya took two steps forward. "What if I could prove it to ya?" she asked confidently as she bopped my nose with a single finger. "If I showed it to you, in person, and you knew you couldn't stop it with a vote, would you steal it?"

"Same old Maya." I smiled down at her. "So that's it, huh? You want to go snooping around on a military base and steal their most prized and secret asset? You've got clearance, but you don't have a pilot."

She shrugged. "Meh. You're actually qualified for the job this time."

"What's the mission?"

"It's easy. I've got it all figured out. We hijack the ship, load it with a ridiculous amount of supplies, beat the baddies to Triax II, liberate the miners, make off with all the triaxum, destroy the place on our way out, make one other quick stop, and then retire on Prius."

"What other stop?"

Maya's playfulness turned to annoyance. "You want to get off this planet or not? I need a pilot, not an inquisition," she snapped.

"Is Prius as beautiful as I've been told?" Tess stepped in to keep things calm, passing Marcus into Maya's arms.

"It's paradise," I reminisced. "Everything is alive and vibrant and a different shade of yellow. It's the only reason I'm entertaining this nonsense."

"Say you were fully bankrolled and had time to prepare. What would you bring with you to Prius? What would life look like there for us?"

I smirked at Tess. "I know what you're doing."

"I'm serious. I want to know."

I took a deep breath and contemplated all the options of a dream life before thinking out loud. "I'd clean out an entire home improvement store. Lumber, trim, fittings, plumbing, and windows. Tools, lots and lots of tools. Seeds, fishing equipment, a dozen charcoal grills, and a thousand pounds of pellets to fuel them. I'd build a cabin mansion on the lake and would help you build yours as well. I'd spend a few years helping the friends I left behind construct homes and outfit their paradise. After that, I'd fish every day and grill every night. We'd turn a penal colony into a retirement resort."

The more I spoke, the bigger the smile on my face became. Having considered Prius as a real option, there was no way I could stay on Earth. Maya's mission was my only way out of this depression. Not only was she offering me the purpose I so desperately needed, but she also promised paradise.

"In two years tops, I can put you right there," Maya promised.

"There's no coming back from this," I warned. "You'll never wear a uniform again. The days of subordinates saluting you will be gone."

"It's not my style anyway."

"It will be the end of your career, Tess. No more cutting-edge research projects. You'll never be the chief of medicine at a big hospital." Tess bit her lip and looked away, her balled up fists giving away her nerves. She didn't have a response, but my words didn't seem to deter her. "Not to mention the life you'd be giving up for Marcus," I pressed, wanting to test their commitment.

"This little spoiled brat?" Maya teased, mussing Marcus' hair. "He gets to live a permanent summer."

"He'll never know anyone his own age. He'll never get to play with other kids, or receive an education, and it's possible he'll never fall in love. Everyone on Prius is decades older than him, and unless you've changed your position on segregating by sex, there still won't be any other children born for some time. Have you considered that?"

"We know what we're getting into. Marcus will be fine," Maya stated pointedly.

"Perhaps I should do this alone," I suggested. "Get me on the base, prove this ship exists, and I'll take care of the rest. You can trust me. Brief me on whatever needs to be done, and I swear I'll see it through. You two have a good thing going here; I've got nothing left to lose."

"We're going," Maya said firmly. "Only question is if you're coming with us or if I need to find a pilot who won't be a bitch the whole time."

The two of them were hiding something, but I didn't really care. I never would have returned to Earth in the first place if I hadn't been following Emilia. Getting a chance to return to Prius felt like keeping a part of her alive. I would cement her legacy by isolating the rest of mankind on Earth and salvaging something resembling happiness after her passing.

Standing over Emilia's grave while making such a life-altering decision made it easy to consider what she would've approved of. The egotistical monster inside of her might have delighted in the fact that her passing had been so impactful, but at the end of the day, I believe she wouldn't want me moping around depressed.

Things moved fast once I agreed to the mission. There was no question that Maya was in charge, but Tess was the obvious brains behind the operation. She had thought of everything and the two of them were far more prepared than I had anticipated.

The next day, I went with them into the Illinois countryside where I was shown the rundown plot of land they had purchased. It would have made for a quaint home for anyone operating a ranch, but for us it was nothing more than storage space and a good cover story.

Tess wanted to make the most of our exit from Earth, and her plan was deviant and brilliant. The three of us liquefied our assets and pooled them together to give us the maximum purchasing power to supply the rest of our lives.

We had a nice nest egg when we combined everything with the small fortune Malik had left behind, but that still wasn't enough for Tess' liking. Her genius idea was for each of us to take out business and agricultural loans on the grounds that we were starting a farm and preparing to buy equipment and more land.

It was a little shady taking out loans we had no intention of paying back, but compared to the crimes committed by big banks over the years, what we took was a drop in the bucket. The banks would simply make up the difference in a month by charging overdraft fees to people living on the poverty line. Screwing over the financial elite on our way out was a final middle finger to a system that had failed citizens like us at every opportunity.

I stayed on the farm for a week, though it was hardly a vacation. We rotated going out on massive spending sprees where two of us would head to town to place enormous orders while the third person stayed back to receive deliveries and watch Marcus. By the time our shopping spree was complete, we had filled two barns and a storage building mostly with items that weren't even for us.

If we had learned one thing from early human settlements, it was that we couldn't expect to live a life of luxury on Prius without providing the same for those we wanted to live among. It's easy for the upper class to separate themselves in an advanced civilization, but in the developing stages? Heads are bound to roll. I was depressed, not stupid. We were going to need to provide for everyone.

My interest was in construction, Tess was into amenities and fabrics for fashioning clothing, and Maya was focused on entertainment. There was some contention around the amount of booze and party supplies Maya was purchasing, but it wasn't the money that troubled Tess. Most people could enjoy a drink or a toke sitting around the fire by the lake without having to worry that it might ruin their life; Maya hadn't yet proven that she had that kind of discipline.

First things first, though. We'd never get the chance to put Maya's sobriety to the test if we couldn't get off Earth. We had to make it onto the base undetected, prove that this warship existed, and get away clean.

The more I thought about it, the more I realized what a giant risk we were taking. If Maya was wrong, we were going to have some explaining to do and a few thousand items to return for store credit. Both of my partners in crime insisted that it wouldn't come to that, and they further encouraged my commitment to the heist by billing it as the only way to save Earth and even our friends who were on their way to Vocury.

I didn't necessarily doubt them, but I should have pushed harder for the explanation they were unwilling to provide.

Chapter 4

The Travelers

Alexis X: 2337

Malik sat sunk in his chair, and though he was awake for the first time in centuries, his eyes remained closed. I would have loaned him some of my energy if it were possible; I had more than enough for both of us.

After waiting a few minutes for him to show any signs of life, I took matters into my own hands. I rested my phone on the control panel with the speaker facing toward us and played Nice to Turin by Land Observations at a low volume. Malik raised his hands to his face as if to wipe the sleep away, and no sooner had he finished rubbing his eyes, than I slowly wafted a fresh cup of coffee under his nose.

"That's my dude," I encouraged him as he took the mug from me and began to sip it. Once I had him on the right path, I turned my attention to the controls to get a look at Vocury. The overhead display momentarily hummed upon powering up, and I scrolled through the options to find forward viewing. I was expecting a vibrant ball of life but was met instead with a burnt orange hunk of dirt. The multicolored ring of gas around the planet gave off an inviting glow to an otherwise uninviting rock, at least.

Malik's posture straightened before he leaned forward. "Are we sure this is it?"

"The coordinates check out. This is where Gio was headed after Earth."

"There are no oceans. How can anything live down there without water? Are the scanners returning any info?"

"They're still running, but if I'm reading this correctly, the air is breathable. Let's see here . . ." I paused to study the digital readout. "Trace gasses. Nothing harmful. The temperature is warm, the humidity is high, and—ho-ly shit. Yuck."

"What?"

"The gravity is slightly more than two times that of Earth."

"Doesn't sound like much of a place for a new colony to me," Malik groaned. "Any life signs?"

"Nothing yet. I say we go down there and have a look around."

"Yeah, I figured you would."

Malik stood and extended an arm for me to lead the way. He was awake and on point, and I wasn't about to waste another second. We made our way to the rear of the ship, sealed off the launch deck, and climbed inside the tiny Praxi pencil craft that had been converted to serve as our lander.

I stood aside to allow Malik to pass and take the front piloting station, then strapped myself into the seat behind him. "Bay doors open," Malik announced as he reacclimated himself to the controls.

"You remember how to—" was as far as I got before we plunged into space and whipped around toward the planet's lower atmosphere.

"This baby moves!"

I didn't want Malik unnecessarily burning up any of our limited supply of triaxum, but this was the first time since he woke that he wasn't solemnly sleepy, and I wasn't about to discourage him from enjoying his duties as our pilot. He dropped us to a low cruising altitude where we could view the vast tangerine landscape, and without much to look at beyond some scattered mountain ranges, I turned my attention to the scanner.

"Hey, I think I've got something here," I alerted him. "Off in the distance to the right. Like, that way," I estimated as I pointed in the general direction I was looking to navigate toward. Malik adjusted course and within minutes he had reason to slow his speed. We came to a complete stop at five thousand feet of elevation and Malik twisted in his seat to look back at me.

"What's that look like to you?" he asked.

"That's a pyramid," my voice rose with excitement as a smile filled my face.

From a distance, the steely structure reflected sunlight, standing tall above the landscape. The tippy-top of the pyramid came to a sharp point fifteen hundred feet in the air, and the structure was wider than it was tall.

"It's big," I noted. "Three times the size of Giza. And hollow," I read the results of the scan out loud as they came in. "And deep. Is this right?" I drew Malik's attention to the screen.

"Really deep. There could be a small city under that thing. Must have been a massive excavation at some point."

"I freaking knew it! Humans didn't build the pyramids. Ancient Aliens, man. That crazy-haired guy from The History Channel was right."

Malik chuckled at my excitement and asked, "What?" through his laughter.

"You know the memes, right?" I shuffled through the thousands of GIFs I had stored on my phone and turned the screen to Malik to share the visual. "'I'm not saying it's aliens, but it's aliens,'" I mimicked along with the animation.

"Only one way to find out," Malik said suggestively.

"Well, look at you. Astronaut and explorer. An hour ago, I didn't think you were going to wake up at all."

"Didn't want to, and if I'm being perfectly honest, I'm in something of a hurry to wake the others, ask some questions, and get back to sleep ASAP."

"Well, let's go knock on the front door then. See who's home."

"With a bit of caution. I didn't see a Jump Point up there, which means one of two things. One, this is the Praxi outpost we're looking for and they're not interested in drawing attention to themselves . . ."

"And two?"

"This place isn't Praxi at all."

It was a good thing I wasn't working alone. If I didn't have Malik, I would have landed in the front yard and expected a warm welcome. Instead, we kept our distance and found a perfect spot tucked behind a dirt ridge that created a tactical visual barrier between our lander and the pyramid.

I opened the lower hatch and my boots landed on the planet's surface with a squishing sensation. The difference in gravity from Earth was stark, and it was especially punishing after being laid prone for so long. The weight of every step took some getting used to, but no amount of time on Vocury could ever make me accustomed to the taste of the air.

"Ugh," I groaned while spitting the metallic taste out of my mouth to no avail. "This is horrid. There's no way we can live here."

"It's like licking a battery," Malik agreed.

I bent over to examine a handful of the orange sod below. The texture was that of wet clay halfway warmed to becoming solid pottery. Wetter and heavier than sand, but far denser than mud. I rolled it into a ball and wound back to throw it, but it traveled no more than twenty feet in the thick gravity.

We began walking in the direction of the pyramid, and it didn't take us long to realize we had bitten off more than we could chew. Every step sunk our boots a half inch into the soupy surface before meeting just enough rocky material below to lend us some buoyancy. The clay caked the bottom of our boots, adding an unwelcome weight to every stride.

I was complaining about the journey long before we cleared a second ridge and laid eyes on the structure in the distance—and would continue to complain upon approach.

The closer we got, the more the landscape came into view. The pyramid wasn't alone in the region. There were at least three, and as many as five, smaller villages scattered around the structure, with maybe a mile or two between them and the huge centerpiece.

Those on the right had already fallen into the shadow cast by the structure as the midday sun began its descent around the other end of the planet. The villages on the left remained in sunlight, and we took notice of a bright metallic glare coming off some kind of rail system running between the encampment and the pyramid.

We had already walked for a couple of hours, and a few more passed before we were creeping up on the nearest village. There were no traditional homes, but the buildings had a man-made quality to them.

Square in shape, they stood two stories tall and featured dilapidated wooden siding. The materials were stained orange, seemingly from years of beating back the Vocury sludge during high winds. There were eight in total, grouped into two rows: four on one side and four on the other, with a clear path between them that had been worn down by foot traffic.

"What in the tombstone fuck is this?" I wondered out loud.

"It's like a piece of the nineteenth century," Malik added.

"All that's missing are some tumbleweeds, a burlesque, train robbers, and a U.S. Marshall to chase them down."

Malik knelt to examine the tracks cemented in the mud. He ran his finger over the grooves left behind, the imprint of a boot followed by another.

"Alexis," he kept his voice low, "This isn't right. We should go back."

Malik might have been right, but my curiosity had been piqued. The wooden sidewalk creaked as I tiptoed in front of the first building, my eyes narrowing in on a sign hanging above a doorway ahead. "Ho-ly shit," I gasped quietly to myself. I turned back to wave hastily to Malik to catch up to me, and even the simple twenty paces of jogging to close the gap caused him to breathe heavily.

"There's footprints back there," he panted. "Boots."

"Look." I signaled with my eyes.

Malik squinted. "Dani's," he read off the sign. "What is going on here?"

"I don't think the Praxi write in English," I emphasized suggestively. I had seen enough to launch into a tirade of theorizing the conspiracy at hand.

"What if the World Military tracked the Praxi here? Or what if the Praxi brought some of the prisoners from Prius to this world? Oh shit,"—my mouth moved faster than my brain—"What if we've already been here? Like, some crazy Back to the Future stuff. Or wait! Maybe the Praxi have been growing humans in their biolabs."

Malik was usually the arbiter of logic, and I expected him to talk me off the conspiracy ledge, but the mystery had swept him up as well. "What if I never woke up . . ." He aroused my interest with the first concept that entered his mind, which said a lot about where his focus was.

"Hit me with it. Feed me," I eagerly encouraged his conjecture.

"I stayed confined to one surreal dream world for the entire trip, even though I always expected it to change. Right at the end—and this is nuts, but—Emilia showed up. What if that was the trigger that pushed me into the next dream? Maybe waking up on the ship was the next stage? My brain could be making all of this up."

"Alright, alright, I dig it. I mean, you're reducing me to a character in your dream, and there's no cool conspiracy twist, but it's fine, you're new to this."

"Let's go back to the Wolf," Malik pleaded. "Wake the others and analyze the situation. Maybe the ship's computer or sensors could help."

"Or, we could pop into Dani's and have a look around. There doesn't seem to be anyone here. Besides, do you really want to make that trek back without getting some rest first?"

"Five minutes. Then we go back and reassess."

We crossed the beaten path that separated the two lines of buildings, our feet no longer sinking into the ground. The moisture in the sod had been stomped out until it was solid. I stepped onto the wooden plank sidewalk and made clicking noises with my tongue to imitate the sound of spurs and Malik shook his head with a grin. We peered through the gap between the saloon's swinging double doors before pushing through them and were greeted by no one.

The interior décor was not dissimilar to what an old-school cowboy might expect to see when seeking recreation. Wooden tables and chairs were scattered about, unlit lamps hung from the walls every five feet, and there were spiral staircases on both sides of the room that led to a balcony above. Near the back of the room was a sealed-off compartment with bars for windows, like a casino's cashier cage. The only thing missing was arguably the most important feature in a saloon—a bar. If this was a place where people gathered for a good time, I couldn't put my finger on what brought patrons in.

Just as I was about to comment on how lived-in Dani's felt, a human female voice rang out a warning from the balcony above. "If you don't want to face down a challenge, I suggest you explain what you're doing back here during labor hours." I got goosebumps from the startling effect her voice had on me, and neither of us knew how to respond.

"Well? I'm waiting," the woman continued as she approached the railing and showed herself to be a young white woman in her mid-twenties. She was short and thin, and her hair was black seedlings, as though her head had been shaved weeks ago and she was due for another straight razor. Her cheeks were rosy, and her tanned skin looked more like a pale Irishman's sunburn than a natural sun-kissing. She wore a tattered black velvet robe, tied around the waist, with a slightly exposed brassiere underneath.

"Are you new?" Her eyes narrowed on us. "Did you walk here?"

Malik thought quickly and responded, "Yes, we're new."

"That's a lie," she said plainly. "Are you Citadelians? You don't look like Citadelians to me."

"Yes," Malik answered, giving me a concerned look out of the corner of his eye.

"That's another lie. Don't move."

She disappeared behind the balcony, entered one of the rooms, and reappeared behind the bars of the cage on the lower level moments later. Examining us closely, the woman looked at the wall inside her cage, and then back at us. "Where are you from?"

"The . . . Citadel?" I read the situation and tried my hand at deceit.

"Uh-huh. And what does that emblem on your chests signify? I've always wondered."

"You have?" I asked, surprised, tracing my finger over the star emblem on my Mission Vocury uniform.

"Oh, yes. I'm Dani. It's a pleasure to meet you." Turning to look behind her, she shouted, "Monkey! Run your silly ass down here."

"You know us?" I asked.

"Depends. Is this you?" Dani peeled a piece of paper from the wall inside her box and slapped it down on the counter, her palm covering the bottom. On it was a hand-drawn picture of two individuals who closely resembled Malik and me wearing our mission uniforms.

"May I see that?" Malik asked, eyes wide, as I noticed the edge of some writing on the paper where her hand rested. She recoiled slightly just as the door behind her opened and a young Korean-looking boy dressed in rags stepped into the box. She turned her back to us, whispered some instructions to him, then stepped aside.

Lifting the carpet covering the floor, Dani unlatched a lock beneath it and raised a hatch door to what looked to be an underground tunnel. As she held the door for Monkey to climb down, Malik shimmied his hand just under the bars and got two fingers on the paper. It wasn't a strong grip, but he was able to catch Dani off guard and weasel it out from her possession with one swift yank.

He held it up for me and we examined the picture closely. The resemblance was uncanny, and the drawing of our mission emblem was a perfect match. Beneath the picture, text read, "Live Capture Reward: 1,500 pill credits."

"What the shit is happening?" I whispered to Malik.

"You don't know?" Dani asked, surprised. "How can you not know? You're The Travelers, are you not?"

Malik looked to me as though I would be the more convincing liar, and prompted, "Are we The Travelers?"

"How the fuck should I know? Yes? No?" I threw my hands up in defeat.

"If anyone asks you that again, you're going to tell them no," Dani instructed. She left the cage, reappeared on the second level above, and made her way to a spiral staircase to join us in the open. "I've sent Monkey to bring help from the Citadel, but the train only travels at dusk and dawn. They may not arrive for you until morning, and that's if they dare venture out here at all."

"You sent him to bring help, or to collect your reward?" Malik questioned pointedly.

"I don't know what you're talking about."

"Who's lying now?" I raised my suspicions.

"Look, I want to get off this rock just as badly as the Citadelians, but if it doesn't work out, it's better that I collect that reward than anyone else."

Malik judged her. "Yeah, I bet it is."

"You want to avoid trouble or not? Stop being so childish and follow me." Dani beckoned us toward the staircase, and we obliged. "You need to stay out of sight. If you're offended by my bounty chasing, then you're really not going to like the lotted sort of customers who patronize my establishment." She hastened us into her quarters on the second floor, "In here."

My hands began to shake and the panic in my voice was unmistakable. "Would you please slow the hell down and tell us what is going on? Who are you people? How did you get to this planet? Where are the Praxi? What is the Citadel? Why do we have to hide? Who are The Travelers? How can—"

"Keep your voice down," Dani warned. "You two are not what I expected, not that I ever really believed that first-generation nonsense anyway. Yet here you are, just like they said you would be. You might be a pair of bumbling fools, but if what they say is correct, you're going to take us all to new worlds. Places filled with lush vegetation and cool summer nights. Somewhere we'll enjoy the sounds of music and the laughs of newborns again. You're going to bring us life."

"That doesn't sound so bad, does it?" Malik asked rhetorically to try to calm my nerves.

The wooden sidewalk creaked with traffic and the saloon doors swung open, banging against each other as they closed. The hall below began to fill with poorly-dressed patrons who lit lanterns as the sun slipped beyond view. Most formed a line at the cage, and when Dani didn't immediately serve them, they became unruly.

"I have to go. It has to look like business as usual. Kade will be here soon. Remember, stay out of sight," Dani reminded us before abandoning us in her quarters with far more questions than answers.

She closed the door behind her when she left, but we dared to inch it open so we could peer below and eavesdrop on the villagers. The crowd was loud, and while it was difficult to hone in on any one conversation among the symphony of sadness, we were able to gather some information.

These dregs had just returned from work in the Citadel, which must be what they call the pyramid in the distance. They spoke in broken English and sounded generally uneducated. The poor devils seemed mainly concerned with whatever Dani was selling and were only placated once they had it. Curiously, no eating or drinking was taking place, and once everyone had been served Dani's goods, the establishment had the feel of an opium den instead of a saloon.

I was unsure how Dani maintained security or avoided being robbed by patrons until the man I presumed was Kade and his gang arrived. His posse passed through the doors first, and they instantly stood out from the rest of the crowd. A dozen or so men and one woman, they dressed semi-uniformly, with vests and pants that had a leatherlike quality, stained with a burnt orange hue—as if they had walked through the Vocury sands for years.

They ranged in age, from their twenties to sixties, and appeared to be in peak physical condition. The entire crew possessed bulging thighs, calves, chests, and upper arms, likely from training in the punishing gravity. In fact, every member of the crew was more physically imposing than the man who entered last, who I guessed was Kade. You'd never know he was at the top of the food chain, walking among them.

No taller than five feet nine inches, he couldn't have been a day over eighteen years old. His physique was otherworldly, though; to categorize him as thick would be an understatement. With ridiculously defined muscles that didn't seem humanly possible, his neck alone was the size of my thigh, and his torso was testing the tensile strength of the vest he was wearing. He was an upright walking bull of a young black man, and while his size and traveling gang made him terrifying, it seemed that he was more respected than feared by the people.

As Kade passed through the crowd of patrons, they greeted him by name. And though they were clearly beneath him on the societal structure, he shook some of their hands. He finally moved out of my line of sight as he approached Dani's cage, and his crew began shuffling tables together to create a larger space for their gang to congregate.

I retreated to Dani's bed and brought my knees up to my chest in the fetal position. There was a panic attack coming on, so I did the only thing

I knew to do: I inserted my earbuds and sang quietly as I swayed back and forth.

"Sara. You're the poet in my heart. Never change, and don't you ever stop. And now it's gone. No, it doesn't matter anymore. When you build your house, I'll come by."

"Relax. It's okay," Malik soothed, gently running his hand down the back of my head. "We'll stay nice and quiet here, and help will arrive in the morning. We'll get some answers."

"I didn't bring my meds. I need my Xanax."

"You only think that because you don't have them. Just breathe and everything will be fine."

Malik's logic was comforting, but there was nothing he could say that would change our situation. I should have listened to him before. We could have been on our way back to the lander, but my damn curiosity needed five more minutes.

Who was I kidding, pretending like I'd escape if given the option, though? We were somehow part of the Vocury ethos, and there was no way I was leaving until my questions had been answered. Gio had intended to come here centuries ago—and I was going to find out why. I couldn't explain what the hell human beings were doing on this side of the galaxy, but the Praxi had to be connected to it somehow.

We were almost certainly in danger and might have made a horrible mistake leaving Earth behind. My only solace was that Ranbir wasn't around to gloat. It churned my stomach to admit it, but he may have been right.

Chapter 5

Omaha! Omaha!
Maya Fontaine: 2039

I popped the trunk to my Cadillac, stared at Chop, and nodded for him to get in.

"There's got to be a better way," he complained.

"You going to whine all day or are you going to get in?" I asked as I dragged him by his shirt to the trunk.

"I'm going, I'm going." He shook free and climbed in one leg at a time.

I stood over him as he pulled his knees to his chest and crammed into the tight space. "It's five hours until dark. All you have to do is stay quiet. I'll get you once the coast is clear. Comprendes?"

"No problemo." He smirked the boyish grin that had won Emilia over.

I closed the lid on him, drove twenty minutes back to Edwards, and passed by the perimeter guards on my return from a late lunch. I took the long way around to the administrative building to further scout out the hangars and identify our target. Noting the size of everything, I couldn't help but have some doubts about the location of our mystery ship.

Having been stationed mostly in the Midwest, I hadn't hung around Edwards for more than a couple of weeks. The rumors placed the Omaha on the base, and Tess had confirmed it. Still, I wasn't exactly sure where it was stored, and it had to have been greatly exaggerated in size if it existed at all.

I spent the daylight hours in the office assigned to me doing final checks on guard rotations, barracks locations, and the clearest path to the runway lights near the hangars.

Stealing a high-value piece of military tech should be an impossible heist, but this felt much easier than the last time Chop and I had gone wild in this same venue. Hopefully, no one would suspect that a couple of their heroes—a decorated officer and a parliament governor—had reverted to being outlaws.

I loitered around long after the day shift had checked out, and once the sun went down, I moved my car to the other end of the base, adjacent to the most likely building where the Omaha would be stored.

Shift change was coming, and soon there would be soldiers exchanging posts and moving about. Before anyone would be in sight, I popped the trunk, quickly raised the lid, and hurried Ranbir out of hiding.

"Move your ass," I urged as he slowly unknotted his body from the tight compartment.

"I swear, Maya. You better be right about this."

"Or what? Iron yourself out." I ignored his idle threat as I yanked at his wrinkled dress shirt before grabbing his suit jacket, stuffing it into his gut, and closing the trunk. I checked my phone for the time and waited for a few minutes until the small group of night shift workers came walking across the tarmac toward the hangar.

"Act natural and like you belong here," I instructed as we fell in line behind the men entering the post building attached to our destination. Once they were cleared, had funneled in, and exchanged places with the airmen going off duty, we made our move.

"After you, Governor," I announced loud enough for the non-commissioned officer in charge to hear me as I held the door open for Chop.

"Commander Fontaine?" the sergeant asked. "It's an honor, ma'am. What can I do for you?"

"Inspection," I said plainly. "Open the door."

"I wasn't made aware of any inspection, ma'am."

"That's kind of the point," Ranbir answered.

The man raised a speculative eyebrow before addressing me again. "No disrespect, but he's not authorized to be here. I'm not even sure if you are, Commander. I'll have to call HQ."

"That won't be necessary"—I quickly stopped him—"I've got my authorization right here," I said, drawing my sidearm and pointing it at his face. "Ah, ah, ah," I warned as his hand instinctively slipped to his weapon.

"Dammit, Maya," Chop grumbled as he slid over the desk, unholstered the sergeant's gun, and removed his radio. "This feels way too familiar."

He may have let Ranbir disarm him, but Airman Snuffy wasn't having it. "Have you lost your mind, Commander?"

"Yep. Want to lose yours too?"

"You won't shoot me," he responded confidently.

"It's funny, everyone says that. Every time it's 'you won't do this' or 'you won't do that.' What's a girl got to do to have her reputation stick?"

"Quit screwing around," Chop barked, and I wasn't sure if he was directing it at me or our hostage.

"Fine, fine," the sergeant capitulated. "The door code is 528491." Ranbir entered the code as the man read it off and the door unlocked and popped open half an inch.

"That's a good boy—" I could barely finish expressing my pleasure at his acquiescence before the tarmac lights came on and the base alarm began to shriek. "Oh bro," I sighed. "Don't tell them I went soft on you," I moaned before leaning over his desk and clobbering the butt of my pistol into his temple, sending him limp to the floor.

Ranbir and I raced through the open door into the massive hangar and the first craft we came across was a Praxi hauler surrounded by an assortment of equipment scheduled for loading. "Let's just take this one and get the hell out of here," Chop panicked.

"It's got no weapon systems. We came for the Omaha, now move!"

We ran past the hauler and the hangar doors began to squeal as they rolled up one by one, completely blowing any cover we had from the rest of the base. Another large hauler was visible in the building across the tarmac, and we were quickly running out of the type of space needed to store the behemoth we were looking for.

At the end of the bay were smaller vehicles: a few tanks, two helicopters, a cylinder-shaped Praxi attack craft, and one other vessel that wasn't familiar to me. Unlike the other triaxum-powered vehicles, this one hovered in place and featured a shimmering black color rather than the usual silver. It had a mirrorlike quality to the metal, as though it was constructed from a liquid, and was about the size of a B-52 without wings. The center corridor of the ship was block-shaped, and on either side was a pair of equal-sized cylinders connected by arms that would serve as the base if the ship were to touch down.

"Well? Where is it?" Chop frantically asked.

"They must have moved it."

"God, this thing probably doesn't even exist! What the hell are we doing?"

As I was about to curse Ranbir out for his lack of faith and composure, headlights headed our way, followed closely by gunfire that ricocheted through the hangar. We rushed toward the foreign black craft and sought shelter behind one of its cylinder compartments.

There was a tank within sprinting distance, but no guarantee that the upper hatch would be unlocked. We could have tried our luck with one of the helicopters as well, but running to it would carry the same risk.

"Can we make it back to the freighter?" Ranbir questioned. "It's better than nothing and beats getting arrested."

I was shimmying through the crease between the block hull and the cylinder wing when I saw it. "I think we found it," I said as I ran my fingers across the Omaha insignia on the side of the craft.

"Found what?"

"This is it! 'The Omaha!'" I slapped my hand on the marking to draw Chop's attention to it.

"Oh, that's great. Just great. Some sweet intel you had. We won't be able to fit five percent of our supplies in this thing."

I raced around to the back end of the craft, dragging Ranbir by the shirt along with me. Our assailants had taken defensive positions, parking their vehicles so that their headlights shone into the bay, occasionally firing shots in our direction. The rear of the hull had its ramp lowered, so I ducked behind to offer some cover fire as Chop raced around me, up the ramp, and into the Omaha. I fired toward a Jeep, taking out a headlamp and shattering the windshield in hopes that the Security Forces would be deterred from advancing.

"Maya!"

"What?!"

"This is it! The Omaha. Ha!"

"You think this is funny?" I shouted over the gunfire.

"Get in here!"

I tossed my gun up to Chop so he could crouch around the corner and offer me some cover, then rolled up onto the ramp and ran inside. Ranbir gave up on returning fire and raised three levers on the nearest control panel until the ramp closed behind us. I got to my feet, gathered myself, and couldn't believe what I saw.

The rear cargo hold of the ship was enormous—at least the size of a high school gymnasium, with doors and open corridors on both sides of the bay leading to other areas of the ship. In this one bay alone, no less than two Omahas could have docked based on the exterior size of the craft.

I ran to the nearest door, engaged the electronic controls beside it, and watched as the door slid into the floor. Ahead stretched a hallway hundreds of feet long, lined with doors spaced every thirty feet on either side. Each door seemed to lead to quarters with a living area, bedroom, and full bath. One hallway alone could provide room and board for twenty people, and there was no telling how many more hallways branched off from the cargo hold.

Ranbir and I moved ahead with almost no concern for the SecFo personnel who must have been surrounding the ship. We peered down the open corridors, unsure of their destinations. They might have led to walkways connecting to the attached cylinders or even more and larger cargo holds. The sheer size was incomprehensible.

"How is this possible?" I asked.

Chop shook his head, wearing a grin of wonderment. "I don't know. A temporal field? A bend of space and time within the structure? This is beyond me. Beyond even the Praxi."

"Let's find the bridge and get out of here while we still can."

It was a jaunt to the front end of the bay, and then even farther through a labyrinth of passageways that splintered off to the left and right. If we had wandered around aimlessly, we could have walked a full mile before we covered all the ground inside the Omaha.

We eventually reached the first change in level we had encountered, where instead of stairs, there was a smooth metallic ramp. We slid down fifteen feet to find an area that had been made over into a mess hall.

The room featured five stoves side by side, multiple prep tables, refrigerators, and three sinks. Surrounding the perimeter were several deep freezer units, and the interior space had been filled with a dozen long rectangular stainless-steel tables, each outfitted with a dozen chairs. The craft may have been alien, but the décor was decidedly human.

"Whoever bought that triaxum was planning on ferrying a large team of somebodies," Chop ventured as we continued moving. Reaching a set of double doors that slid open horizontally, we finally discovered the bridge.

The area was bathed in an ominous red glow from lights mounted where the walls met the floors and ceilings. Toward the front, three command consoles were elevated some eight feet, each equipped with a raised chair and step stool.

Assuming it was for the pilot, Ranbir climbed into the center console, and I took two steps up into the station on his right. A shared screen between our consoles flickered to life, displaying 'GREGORY 1.3' as it loaded. The screen turned blue, then began filling with programs and options as they came online.

Once booted, a British male voice, reminiscent of a butler speaking choppy English, greeted us: "Hello. I am. Gregory. Your. Pharoh-to-Human. AI. Interface." I looked to Chop and saw that he was just as confused as I was.

"Oh . . . okay, Gregory," Ranbir began, "We need to leave. Can you help?"

"I can. Take you. Anywhere. You desire."

"That's convenient," I quipped.

"Not for. My former. Masters. Ha. Ha. Ha."

"Gregory's got jokes," I choked.

"We're headed to Illinois. Does that compute?" Chop asked.

"I'm starting to think I didn't need a pilot after all," I joked, drawing a frustrated look from Ranbir.

"Provide. Coordinates."

"I don't know. East. Take us east, Gregory," Chop demanded.

"Cannot. Comply. Provide. Coordinates."

"What about manual controls?"

"Manual. Not recommended. Without. Training."

"Fuck training. We need to go," I demanded.

"Use. Headset."

A red glow emanated from beneath the seats of all three consoles. Ranbir reached underneath, found and unlatched a helmet connected to a single cable housing, and put it on. Once secured, only his mouth remained visible.

"Are you kidding me with this thing? I can't even see. Wait." Chop's arms fell limp at his sides, his head tilted back, and his mouth hung agape.

"You look like a drunk Indian Power Ranger," I teased, but he didn't respond. I raised his hand closest to me and it flopped lifelessly when I released it. "What the shit did you do to my pilot, Gregory?"

"Initializing. Initializing. Manual controls. Activated."

I tapped on the screen in front of me in a panic as I waited for something to happen. All of the available programs were marked in a scribbly language

I couldn't read, so I took turns hitting each of them until I had a visual readout on the screen.

The heads-up display somehow allowed me to pan three hundred and sixty degrees, and I found us surrounded by a hundred angry soldiers. Those near the rear of the Omaha were shielding their eyes from flashing sparks as they attempted to cut into the hull. The hangar doors had been closed, and it didn't look like we'd be going anywhere any time soon.

"Do something, Gregory," I commanded.

"Manual controls. Initialized."

"You worthless twat," I cursed. "Come on, Chop. Wake up!" I shook my partner in crime, but he was out cold.

Only a few moments later, the Omaha rose ten feet off the ground. I couldn't feel the motion on the bridge, but I saw it on the visual display, and through the viewport as I looked down at the men giving siege who were now backing away.

I shifted my focus forward to the hangar doors, now illuminated by a red grid of laser light. Seconds later, the doors began to soften as the lasers melted and cut through them. The steel collapsed to the ground like molten lava, revealing a row of vehicles on the other side, partially melted by the tremendous heat.

"Yeah!" I cheered, knowing Chop had something to do with it.

"Still think you don't need a pilot?" he murmured, sounding as if he were asleep.

The Omaha shot off into the distance like a high-caliber rifle round. Within seconds, Ranbir had us soaring among the clouds, and minutes later, we hovered at altitude.

"Almost there," he said, scanning for Tess somewhere down below. Soon, we descended into the Midwestern night sky, our speed decreasing as we plummeted toward our destination. Chop circled the Omaha around until the rear of the ship faced the barns, and the gravity drive deactivated.

"Good. Bye." Gregory powered down, prompting Ranbir to lift his head, clench his fists, and remove the headset.

"Wow!" he exclaimed as he regained consciousness. "There's a space inside the AI system that is . . . I don't know. It's like an entirely different plane of existence. That was incredible."

"You did good, Chop." I slapped him on the shoulder and jumped out of my high chair. "Clock's ticking."

Ranbir lowered the rear lift, fastened his helmet back into place underneath the seat, and slid out of his chair. We had no time to waste, and it was in that moment of haste that we realized the Omaha's single flaw: there was only one exit, and it was ten minutes from the bridge. By the time we reached the cargo hold, bulky high school boys were hauling supplies aboard while others operated a forklift and skid jacks to wheel crates into place.

I ran down the ramp to scoop Marcus into my arms, kissed him on the forehead, and walked to Tess for an embrace. Ranbir was slightly behind us, his head on a swivel watching the fifty-some boys hustle back and forth.

"Pretty great, Tess. Where did you find these kids?" Chop asked.

"Local high school football team. I gave them twenty-five grand up front, with another twenty-five if they finish in under thirty minutes. That's the last of the cash."

"You believe this thing?" I looked back to the Omaha. "You were right. It wasn't what we expected, but it was there, just like you said."

"Did you run into anyone while you were there?"

"Just the expected Security Forces. Nobody else."

"Hmmm. For the best."

"Let's go, boys!" Ranbir urged the teens. "It doesn't have to be pretty. Just load it up."

Tess curled her finger for me to pass Marcus to her, and I gave them some space to say goodbye. I knew how difficult this was for Tess, and one crying mother would be enough for our young son to deal with. I needed to be the parent who held it together.

"You be good for Mommy now, okay? You do what she says. I'll catch up with you before you know it," Tess whispered softly. She hugged Marcus tight, her hands balling up on the back of his small shirt as she gripped him.

"There are other ways, babe. You could still come with us," I offered, hoping that she would change her mind.

"I can't and you know it. This is my mess. I've got to clean it up."

"What's going on?" Chop interjected.

"It's nothing," I shut him down.

"Tess? You're not coming with us? We're not coming back here . . . right?" he asked, clearly confused, having been kept in the dark.

"There's something I have to do," Tess explained vaguely. "I'll rendezvous with you when I can. I'm not sure what the situation will be like, but I'll transmit a deep space message if I get the chance."

"What?" Ranbir sought clarification.

I picked up Tess' bag of cash and threw it at Chop to get rid of him. "Go pay those boys."

"Watch my family's back out there, Ranbir," Tess shouted to him.

"Yes ma'am," he responded as he jogged away.

Tess turned to me. "He doesn't know?"

"Nope, and he doesn't need to until we're done."

"Good. I'll tell him when we're all together again. It should come from me."

"You be careful, babe. This isn't the lab anymore, and this ain't no game. You're going to have eyeballs on you," I warned.

"I know. I can do this. I have to."

"We'll be waiting for your signal, and I'm not moving an inch until we get it."

"Maya, please—" Tess finally broke into tears. "Don't let Marcus forget about me. Show him the pictures. Play the videos. I'm missing key time, and I don't want him to resent me."

"He won't, and even if he does, one day when he's old enough, he'll understand."

"I love you. I'm going to miss you so much."

I hugged Tess tightly one last time, letting our embrace linger despite feeling Ranbir's eyes on us. "I love you too, baby. This is going to work. Now go, and don't look back."

I released her and she wiped away her tears, gave Marcus one last pat on the head, and then turned to jog to her car. She peeled out and sped down the dirt road, her hand pressed to the window as she drove away from the crime scene.

"That's the last of it," Chop informed me. Our moving team hopped into the back of their pickup trucks and followed Tess' cloud of dust off the property. Within an hour, law enforcement would almost certainly descend on our farm, but they'd be too late to stop us or pick up a single shred of evidence.

"Come on, my boy," I welcomed Marcus into my arms. "Let's go for a ride."

Ranbir and I walked side by side up the ramp and closed it behind us. "You going to tell me what that was all about?" he asked, his gaze fixed on me, and I turned away to hide the tears welling in my eyes.

"Mind your business," I said sharply, struggling to keep the sadness out of my voice. "Get us out of here before we're located." For a moment, Chop looked like he considered pushing it, but then he walked away, begrudgingly giving me my space.

I set Marcus down and pointed toward the quarters. "Go ahead, baby. Pick any room you like. Whichever one you want, it's all yours," I promised with forced cheerfulness.

When he ran off to explore, I began rifling through the tons of supplies on board. It was nothing short of a miracle that we were getting away clean with such an assortment of goods for our journey. The next leg of our trip would be a difficult one without Tess around to ground me, and even though I knew there were better days ahead, I felt the depressive temptation start to sink in.

I popped the lid off a crate to find dozens of tools, then another to discover hundreds of pounds of Tess' fabrics, and just as I was about to talk myself out of the search, I opened one more.

I pulled a bottle of Jack out of the box and stared down at the label for a minute to give myself a chance to turn back. "Goddammit," I groaned quietly as I twisted off the cap. I took a three-second pull off the bottle, spun the cap back on, and before I could put the bottle away, I had it off again for another pull.

"Mommy, they're all the same," Marcus said, startling me. I quickly returned the bottle to its box as though he were old enough to understand my weakness and would judge me for it.

"I know, baby. It's always the same," I lamented with a thousand-yard stare. I had just thrown away years of sobriety at the first hint of turmoil. Even worse, I had planned it. I gave up on my recovery the moment I knew I would be without Tess' support. The sickest parts of me wanted to capitalize on the situation, and I felt downright dirty for it.

Tess' journey would lead her straight into the lion's den and put her squarely in the face of danger. While she was away, I'd spend every moment worrying about her safety, even as I'd be forced to battle against an even worse enemy: myself.

This was not going to be easy.

Chapter 6

Pick Your Battles

Kade: 2337

"Two regenerators, six hydrators, six sustainers, and two accelerators," Dani counted out a week's worth of payment for the customer at her cage. She placed the multicolored tabs onto a small piece of cloth, wrapped them up, and tied the ends into a knot before sliding the sack under her steel bars.

"Wait. No, you see, I said four accelerators. I need four," the fiendish woman responded as she instinctively twisted her head to the side, scratched at her neck, and talked out of the side of her mouth.

"What do you have for trade?" Dani asked, her annoyance evident as she examined the line of customers stretching out the front door. She looked at me over the woman's shoulder and rolled her eyes. "Sorry, Kade. Just a minute," she promised.

"I have an overabundance of time, my dear," I responded. "Patience, however, is at a premium."

The addict peeled Dani's freshly-tied sack open and removed the pills deemed unnecessary. "There. One regenerator, two sustainers, and two hydrators. I'll trade them for three more accelerators."

"You've got two already," Dani's voice rose. "Ten seconds ago, you wanted four total. Now you want five?"

"Just give me the pills!"

Dani slid the junkie's tabs back to her and denied the trade request. "You could go hungry or age out. Ration your accelerators this week and either work harder or turn a trick if you want more. Next!"

I cut in line and stepped up to her counter as though I were an ordinary customer, and those behind me didn't dare offer a complaint. "You should give them whatever they want," I counseled her, even though the distribution of wages was the one aspect of these people's lives that I didn't control. "Freedom isn't for trade, yet you strip it from your customers carelessly."

"Our customers aren't much good to me dead. Or to you. Or to the Citadelians. You want to go into the mines and swing an axe in their place if they all age out?"

I smirked at Dani to let her know that the idea of her looking out for anyone but herself was comical. She talked a good game and had done quite well for herself, all things considered. As a member of the First Generation, she was lucky not to have found herself addicted to any of the evils she peddled over the years.

Her selfish pursuit of career gains had kept her clean, making her a natural partner—both for business and the occasional pleasure. Dani had made herself indispensable to me and my enemies. By playing her role, we maintained a peaceful treaty that kept our people working, while she enjoyed a level of comfort and wealth not available to most.

Dani was a survivor, not a burnout junkie like the rest of them. She accumulated status and success because she adhered to a philosophy I understood: no wasteful excess.

No uppers and no downers. No three-day hallucinogenic benders. No pills for pain, or anxiety, or any random thing Dr. Amaar would suggest medicating. While others relied on pills whose only purpose was to counteract the side effects of their prescribed medications, Dani and I lived off of the essentials.

We swallowed the hydrator, the sustainer, and just enough of the regenerator to get by. And sure, I kept on the gainer from time to time to maintain my physique, but who would dare call me a hypocrite? It's not like they had any grounds to judge me. Half the members of my own crew were so dependent on opiates that they couldn't see straight.

I never once chastised the addicts. Though I had every reason to hate them, I never stood in the way of their freedom. So long as they paid their dues and behaved properly, they had my blessing to swallow whatever tablets they could afford.

Having been abandoned by an absent father and a drug-addicted mother, I was familiar with the self-destructive paths people take. It was their choice to make. I would be their warlord king, but not their overbearing parent.

"Did we have a prosperous week?" I asked.

Dani ducked out of sight and returned with a sack ten times that she would hand out to those behind me. "About average," she answered.

I raised an eyebrow. "Do I need to count these?"

"No, but I suspect you will anyway. What's the difference? You'll have that pile doubled up by the end of the night regardless."

"If you're going to kiss my ass, maybe you should pay me in water so I can wash it first."

"It wasn't meant as a compliment," she playfully replied, always toeing the edge of what she could get away with. "You know your Dawgs let you win, right?"

I pointed to her and warned, "Careful, darling. You might insult their integrity." I proceeded to collect my payment, turned to face the evening crowd, and raised my voice. "And everyone knows I only associate with the most upstanding of outcast citizens!"

As the next person in line stepped to the counter, I reached into my sack for all to see, rifled through the assortment, and retrieved two accelerators. Turning to Dani's lingering previous customer, I placed one in her hand and the other between her lips. Dani shook her head in disappointment at my charitable display, but she understood that she had her role, and I had mine.

"Kade," she called out as I was about to move on. "Maybe set up down the road tonight. I'm tired and don't want to deal with all the traffic when I'm done here."

"No, I think we'll be fine right here." My eyes peered around her behind the bars and then up to the balcony above. Dani never turned business away, and based on her conniving history, I naturally assumed she was up to something. I didn't think she would dare cross certain lines, but if she was hiding anything, I was going to stick my nose right in the middle of it.

I took my usual seat at the table reserved for gaming, and as I settled in, the other players began to fill in for our payday game. Dixie sat to my left, and before she could get too comfortable, I gave her an assignment. "You're running tricks tonight."

"Taz runs tricks."

"Not tonight. I want you to do it."

"Boss, it's payday. There ain't profit when nobody's desperate. Taz barely even runs them on payday."

"You'll be compensated for your time," I promised.

"Why are you punishing me? Just have Taz do it. I'm ready to gamble."

"Taz is a dull tool, and in this instance, I need a sharp one. I don't mind if you make no pairings. I want you to get upstairs and have a look around. See how Dani responds. Maybe sneak a peek behind the counter if you get a chance. See what you can uncover, and if you find something, you'll be rewarded."

"I'll take care of it," Double-A attempted to stand in for his lover, but Dixie would have none of it. She stashed her sack of pills in her waistline and grunted in equal parts annoyance and compliance as she sauntered off.

The moment her seat was vacant, one of the good men of the village clamped the wooden back of the chair and leaned forward to have a word. His cheeks were sunken, and he had the gaunt look of a man who had been rationing himself to save up a stockpile.

"Mr. Kade. I'd like to play tonight."

"Sit, Mitchell," I politely invited him. "What have you brought to the table tonight?" The usual poker lineup featured me, four or five of my cohort, and a few villagers who dared to risk it all for a chance to double or even triple their net worth.

I admired the courage required to sit with us, and most times would even root for their success. However, they'd receive no mercy in our games of chance. They had the freedom to make their own decisions, whether it be to their fortune or fatality.

Stacks perked up and slid over a couple of seats to sit on Mitchell's other side. He was a grimy fiend, but also one of the toughest sons of bitches I had ever known when sober. He cared more about his next high than his own survival, and as a skilled poker player, he collected most of his future buzzes at the tables.

"Are you bankrolled?" he asked Mitchell before I could give my blessing. In response, Mitchell dug into his pockets and emptied two handfuls of tabs onto the table. Stacks quickly sorted through them with a knife, then frowned at the modest assortment. "Where's all the good stuff?"

"I have eleven relievers right here." Mitchell drew his attention to the less potent purple tabs in front of him. They could take the edge off a headache but weren't strong enough to send your mind into orbit.

"Ehhhhh," Stacks scoffed and spit on the ground. "Go to Dani for an exchange. Trade in your sustainers for some flyers if you want to play."

"I've saved these up from day work. I'm not paying the ten percent trade markup, and I have plenty to play. If you win them, you can trade up for your high if you'd like," Mitchell offered. "You'd appreciate being frugal if you'd ever worked a day in your life."

"Sweating in the Citadel factories isn't honest work. It's slavery. They hate you and only keep you alive with regenerator 'cause they own you. Nobody owns me."

"Easy, boys." I calmed them with a disarming smile. "No one's even lost a big pot yet. Let's keep our composure. The poker table is no place for emotion. You may play, Mitchell, but there won't be any refunds. I'll let you age out in the street as a lesson to the others if I must."

After that, the game proceeded as it did any other night. We had some laughs and pushed some pills around until a few members of my crew found themselves either tapped for currency or too high to continue.

The rest of the patrons couldn't have cared less about the stakes we played for. The responsible ones who had work the next day retired to their bungalows with enough sustainer and hydrator to keep them alive for another day, while the dopers lounged around, feeding their addiction.

For as much trash as Stacks talked, you'd have thought he was winning. He barked at Mitchell all night, but to his credit, the commoner was unshaken. We were four-handed when the game devolved into a fight, much as it always did.

Stacks and Mitchell played a heads-up pot on an ace of hearts, five of hearts, and three of spades flop. Mitchell bet out and Stacks announced, "I'm going to hit that heart and clean you out, day worker." as he called the bet.

I held the deck in one hand, burned a card, and dropped the ten of spades as the turn card. Once again, Mitchell led out with a bet consisting of twenty-five pills, holding maybe another sixty back. The double barrel was the most aggressive action I had seen him make all night, and I put him on a set, most likely three aces.

Once again, Stacks confidently called and gave him a speech meant to intimidate. "You won't be the first person to die from poor decisions at a poker table. Bring that heart, Kade, so I can rip his out."

I was actively rooting for Mitchell at this point. I wanted a nice clean river to fall, and Mitchell to pick up the pot and call it a night. It would be worth it to see Stacks humbled. I burned another card and slowly turned the eight of hearts.

"Told you," Stacks celebrated before any action had happened on the final street. "Go ahead. Check, you coward. Save what you've got left and take your ass back to work tomorrow."

"I check," Mitchell said sheepishly.

"Of course you do. I'm all in," Stacks announced.

Mitchell sat in the tank for a painfully long time as he weighed his options. To make that call and be wrong could legitimately cost him his life if he had no reserve of pills to get by on. Otherwise, it would take a miracle of Dani giving him a loan, and she wasn't exactly known for her charity work.

"I call," Mitchell said, his voice shaking and cracking.

I shook my head in disgust at the terrible risk he was taking, but my mood changed when Stacks didn't instantly table his hand and gloat.

"No you don't," Stacks said. "Just fold. Save your stack, man. Consider this a mercy."

I wasn't about to let him talk his way out of this one. "You've been called. Table your hand or put it in the muck."

Stacks turned over the four and five of spades. Nothing but a single pair and busted gutter and backdoor flush draw. Mitchell quickly flipped his ace and queen of diamonds, and I happily pushed the monster pot in his direction.

"That's one hell of a call," I congratulated him.

"Fuck this!" Stacks stood quickly, knocking his chair over. "You cheating-ass son of a bitch. You think I'm going to let you keep that score?"

"Sit down, Stacks," I ordered firmly.

"You helping this little prick? He kicking back half the profits to you? Paying you off in sexual favors?"

"He won fair and square. Walk it off before you humiliate yourself any further or stir my temper."

"Fuck him and your temper! Any real card player knows he can't call there. You cheated me."

I slammed the worn, tattered deck on the table and shot him a warning glare, but he wasn't in the mood to heed it.

"Challenge," Stacks declared, and that was enough to grab the attention of the room, no matter how hopped up they were.

"Stop it." I scoffed at the idea. "He's not going to fight you, and you don't have the votes to approve it."

"Come on, day worker. Challenge!" Stacks persisted, pushing Mitchell off his chair. I snapped out of my seat and had myself between the two of them in an instant.

He glowered at me. "You won't honor our traditions and you're protecting him. I say you cheated me."

"Anything else you want to say?" I baited him into my trap.

"Challenge," he spit maliciously in my face.

"I accept."

The patrons emptied into the street behind Stacks, and I helped Mitchell to his feet. I placed one boot after another on the table, carefully lacing them up and tightening them with precision. Just as I was about to stretch, a commotion erupted from the balcony—arguing, grunting, and the sounds of wrestling. Dixie appeared at the railing above and Double-A beckoned for her to join us.

"Stacks is challenging Kade again," he announced excitedly.

"I got something better," Dixie replied. "A pair of Citadelians hiding out."

No sooner had Dixie shown off her catch, than the sound of Dani's feet pattered up the stairs to her quarters and she stood beside Dixie and her two hostages. She had just enough breath remaining after sprinting into action to say, "I'll get rid of them, Kade. Either by train or the other way. Whatever you prefer. You've got bigger things to worry about."

"That's what I thought," I remarked, staring at Dani as she avoided eye contact. "Bring them. All three," I ordered Dixie.

I stretched my arms overhead, then pulled each of my knees to my chest. Stomping over to the swinging double doors, I kicked them open with such force that one came off its hinges.

"Challenge!" I shouted at the onlookers and members of my gang. "Weapons?" I posed the traditional question to the crowd as I stripped away my vest.

"No!" they hollered back in unison.

"Mercy?" I continued rousing them as I pulled my undershirt over my head to expose my chiseled chest.

"Never!" they screamed back. "We don't speak, we settle it in the street! These are our traditions."

"Raaaaaaahhh!" Stacks growled at me. "No more rations. I'm taking access to your stocks when this is over."

I met him in the middle of the circle formed by our audience. Everyone stood, except Dixie's two prisoners and Dani, who were on their knees.

Stacks charged at me and drove the crown of his head directly into my gut, nearly knocking the wind out of me. I hammered my fists down on his back three times before he retreated from his compromised position.

He came at me with an upright jab next, and I didn't bother to dodge it. I let him throw another, and then another. Then a right cross to my cheek. Then two left crosses to my kidneys.

He came back with another jab that was slower than before, and I caught it in my right hand. Wrapping my left hand around his clenched fist, I squeezed until his groans filled the night air, accompanied by the crack of breaking bones. I kicked his left knee, forcing him down to the ground.

"Challenge!" I screamed at my crippled opponent.

He pulled a knife from his boot and the crowd protested, shouting, "No weapons!" as he rose to his feet again. I raised a hand to keep them at bay, even though they had every right to swarm him, kill him, and claim his goods as their property for his heretical behavior.

He lunged at me, swiping wildly, and managed to graze my chest with the tip of his blade on his third attempt. The cut left a jagged line that would add nicely to the abstract collection of scars on my body later. He ran two fingers across his bloodied blade and smeared the stains of my wound across his forehead.

When he came at me again, I was ready for him. He quickly swiped twice, but I evaded both strikes and braced myself for the third. I seized his forearm, delivered a crushing headbutt that sent blood streaming down his chin, and gripped his wrist with all my strength.

"No weapons!" I yelled, driving the knife into the dirt. "No mercy!" I continued, smashing his nose with my forehead.

Stacks finally collapsed to the ground, disarmed and dazed. He attempted to crawl away, but I planted my foot firmly on his back and stepped over his head, grinding his face into the dirt.

"These are our traditions," I echoed, lifting my leg high as I could and slamming my boot into the dirt beside his head.

This wasn't the first time I had spared Stacks' life, and if karma had her way, a day would come when he would repay the debt.

"That concludes this evening's show," I announced to the crowd. "Seize these final moments of darkness for rest before you're called back to duty in the morning."

I made my way back to Dani's hall, taking a seat on one of the exterior benches. I removed my boots and used my shirt as makeshift gauze for my chest. Meanwhile, Dixie and Double-A pushed their prisoners forward, positioning them on their knees, and I examined them as I tended to my wounds.

"We just want to go home," the female pleaded. "We'll get on the train, go back to the Citadel, and never return."

"Home already? But you've only just arrived, and there's no train that runs to where you came from. Save your deceit, woman," I warned.

"I'm going to ask you some simple questions and all I want in return are simple answers. If I find your responses to be too vague or you fail to be forthcoming, I'll be forced to resort to unpleasantries. Understood?" Both nodded in the affirmative.

"How old are you?" Based on their confused reactions, they weren't expecting my first question.

"Thirty-two," the female answered.

"I'm forty-six," the male said.

"What does the emblem on your uniform signify?"

"It's Mission Vocury," the man replied tersely, offering no further explanation.

"And what are your names?"

"I'm Alexis, and this is Malik," the woman responded.

"Well, Alexis and Malik, I'm Kade, and we're going to be best friends if you continue being this honest." I smiled at them. "Where did you come from? And don't lie," I reminded, wagging a finger.

"They're from the Citadel," Dani interjected.

I sighed as I stood, reluctantly forced into action by Dani's betrayal. It brought me no pleasure to strike the woman I had become so fond of, so I hit her in the gut with only a fraction of my strength. She instantly keeled over, gasping for breath.

"You have been a naughty girl, Dani. What was the reward?" I mused. "Fifteen hundred pill credits? I'll admit, that's a tempting prize. Still, betrayal doesn't taste too nice on my tongue."

I cocked back to hit her again, but now Alexis interjected for Dani. "Please, don't hurt her. We got lost and she was only trying to help us."

"She was trying to help herself," I fired back as I pressed my bare foot to Dani's shoulder and toppled her over.

I turned back to the pair. "Let's try this again. Where did you come from?" Neither would provide an answer, and I couldn't blame them.

They may not have been accustomed to seeing a man beaten within an inch of his life or a woman subdued with a single punch. They probably thought they were one wrong answer away from being next.

"No? No answer? I don't know the truth, but I do know what people will say. 'The Travelers have come to take us away,'" I inflected a comically spooky voice. "They'll think you're their saviors. Prophesied messiahs. And when they discover that you're real, they'll think you gods."

I paced back and forth in front of them to intimidate and draw their fear to a boiling point.

"Look at you tremble, though. You're no gods, and even if you were, there's only room for one of us." I knelt in front of them, making direct eye contact with Malik and then Alexis. "No one leaves this place. Not my subjects. Not the Citadelians. And certainly not you."

I turned my attention back to Dani. Either she would reveal the truth, or the sight of her face getting pulverized would loosen the lips of the Travelers. I pulled her up by the back of her neck, lifting her to make her meet my gaze from her kneeling position.

"What direction did they come from? Who else knows about them?"

"I didn't see. They wandered in during the afternoon while everyone was away on work duty. It was before the evening train returned so I'm certain they didn't come from the Citadel. I was hiding them until I could vet their story and turn them over to you."

"Fucking lies." I shook my head with disappointment and squeezed her cheeks out of frustration. "At least they have the sense to say nothing rather than insult me."

"Hey, uh, Mr. Kade?" Alexis prompted. "Do you think we could get something to eat and drink?"

Malik gave her a surprised look and she replied, "What? I'm freaking parched over here. I feel like I've been sucking on a dirty penny for twelve hours straight."

"Your guests are hungry," I said to Dani. "You don't mind if I raid your stash, do you? We need to keep their strength up if they're going to deliver on the prophecy."

I approached Dani's caged counter, wrapped my hand around two of the steel bars, and propped my feet against the wall. Within seconds of raging against them, I yanked the steel through their wooden housing and slid over the rubble into her pharmacy. I searched through the shocking volume of goods she had hidden away and grabbed two sustainers and two hydrators.

The sun was beginning to blaze over the mountain range, its light pouring into the valley, signaling the start of a new day. I reached into the lanterns along the wall and pinched out the flames to give way to daybreak. In the distance, the Citadel train hummed along its track, sounding its morning work alarm to rouse the commoners and draw them into another day of servitude in the city.

"Compliments of Dr. Amaar." I dropped two pills into each of the Travelers' open palms.

"What is this shit?" Alexis asked. "How about some biscuits and gravy?"

"You're awfully chippy for someone on their knees."

"Not my first time, bub." She immediately realized the double entendre when Taz smirked and let out a pervert's muted laugh.

"Gross. Not my first time being interrogated and beaten. It's kind of my jam," she quipped even though she was visibly shaking.

"Can we at least get some water to wash this down?" Malik joined the conversation.

"That is water. Hydrator to fuel you and sustainer to fill you. You know, for someone who's supposedly here to save us, you know shockingly little about us."

"You could educate us," Malik said leadingly.

The wooden planks outside rumbled as boots crossed over them, half of my Dawgs returning from aiding Stacks on his way home to lick his wounds.

"Allow me to introduce you to some of the loveliest renegades you'll ever know. The wiry brunette is Double-A, the rotund bearded man is Taz, the tattooed beauty of the desert is Dixie, and then there's my favorite maniac in goggles, Paul."

"Paul?" Malik questioned the out-of-place name, drawing laughs from the others.

"I don't need a war name," Paul spoke for himself before announcing proudly, "I'm First Generation." No one was impressed and they continued mocking him with their laughter.

"I don't know what the three of you are laughing at," Alexis chimed in. "You're named after a tiny battery, a cartoon devil, and a disposable paper cup." We didn't understand the reference as an insult or a joke, but it drew a laugh from Malik.

"Where were we?" I cut through the chatter before being interrupted by the sound of scurrying footsteps racing across the creaking sidewalks. The rest of my crew barged in, breathless and disheveled, barely able to convey their news.

First through the door, Reginald could only utter one name. "Maddox," he spit out as he struggled to catch his breath. "Maddox is coming. He was on the train."

Trigger followed quickly behind him. "It's Citadel security! They're sweeping every village."

I approached Dani and kicked the toe of my foot into her side. "What have you done?!"

Malik and Alexis exchanged hopeful glances, anticipating their rescue, and before I could rally the troops or even devise a plan, Citadel security forces swept into the building.

Dressed in their solid rubber-padded black suits and helmets, each of them rivaled my ripped physique. A dozen of them were upon us before we could react, and my Dawgs followed my lead of slight retreat toward the staircases on either side to create a buffer between our forces.

Dani rushed toward the door to make her escape but ran straight into Maddox, who ducked through the walkway and shoved her aside like a rag doll before advancing behind his troops.

Standing at least a foot taller than the last time I'd seen him, he now towered over seven feet tall, judging by the height of the doorway he couldn't clear. A naturally brutish, bearded white man, his addiction to gainer only amplified his bulk. His green eyes were piercing yet sad, but you'd never know it as he hid them behind goggled sunglasses. As always when outside the walls of his stronghold, he held a silver circular filter between his teeth to cover his mouth against the tainted air.

"Still haven't outgrown your pacifier, eh Maddox?" I insulted. "It's been a long time since you've been beyond your walls. I thought I had made myself perfectly clear. You're not welcome here. You know the penalty for breaking the treaty."

He spit the air filter into his hand and tucked it away in his pocket. "Give me what I came for and we'll let you get back to running whores and playing king. Nobody has to die."

"What do you have to trade?" I questioned him, even though there wasn't a price that could tempt me into handing over my prisoners.

"The lack of death is my trade."

"Oh, come on, big guy. You don't believe all that prophesy nonsense. The Travelers are helpless. Lost. Stranded, just like us."

"You don't believe it either, boy." Maddox spit the taste he hated so much out of his mouth. "They didn't appear out of thin air, and we both know what that means. Now hand them over before this gets messy. You can stay here and be king of the rats if you'd like, but I'm going home."

"This is home, and nobody leaves. Turn around, take your pathetic henchmen with you, march your ass back to your Citadel, and pray it's still standing when you return. If you hurry, you'll still catch the train."

"Fine, Kade. You win." Maddox seemed to be unaware of his advantage, but then announced, "Challenge."

That was the last thing I wanted to hear out of his mouth. I'd rather have a dragged-out brawl with his forces, even if we were outmuscled. At least then we'd have a chance.

No matter the confidence in my strength, I was wise enough to realize that Maddox was the one person on the planet that I couldn't go toe to toe with. If I accepted, I might give him a good fight and even wound him, but he would inevitably kill me in the street. The Dawgs would disband after picking me clean, and I wasn't about to accept any death, not even an honorable one.

"You dare call upon our rituals?" I feigned outrage as cover for my cowardice. "You're an outsider here. You will not mock us with one breath and adopt our customs with the next."

"Let your people vote," Maddox persisted. "Either you accept my challenge and fight me for property and life, or I will bash my way through your entire pirate crew." He reached behind his back and unslung a device

I hadn't seen before; it appeared as though he had traded in his old steel rod for some new piece of gravity tech.

Approximately three feet long, the weapon featured a black rubber grip on one end and a silver alloy shaft that hummed when activated. To demonstrate his point, he took a casual swing at Dani near his feet, and she went flying, tumbling across the floor toward us without the weapon even having made contact with her.

I clutched Malik's throat in a last-ditch effort to weasel my way out of the situation. "I'll kill them. I'll kill them both. One good squeeze and I'll collapse their windpipes."

"No, you won't. I know you, boy, and I know your secrets. If you're afraid of a fight, maybe you can rustle up your mother to stand in for you."

"Don't test me," I warned him as I picked Malik up off the ground with a single hand around his throat. Malik gasped and kicked at me, but I wouldn't relent.

"You stubborn, broken child. Make a compromise to save your people. Keep the man, give us the girl, and we won't make a mess."

I dropped Malik to his feet and released his throat. "Fine. Your proposal is accepted." The Dawgs may have thought I had lost my edge, but I saved every one of their lives that morning, much as I had in the past.

I looked at Alexis. "You're free to go."

"Wait! No!" Malik shouted as the Citadel guards took her by the arms and dragged her away.

"Malik!" Alexis fought against them, but one of the guards quickly subdued her by tossing her over his shoulder. "Don't tell them anything!"

"Your friend will be fine," Maddox comforted Malik. "She's certainly in better company than you are." Looking at me, he said, "Enjoy your dirt hill throne, boy king. We won't be seeing each other again."

Maddox and his crew exited, hurrying up the street toward the train, barely making it in time to take the ride to the Citadel with the workers.

Malik pushed two hands against my chest, which did nothing to budge me even an inch. "You coward."

"Sometimes the only way to win a fight is not to fight at all."

"What will happen to her?" Malik asked with genuine concern for his friend.

"She'll be fine," Double-A said foolishly, which drew a dirty look from me.

"One of you is going to talk, and the other is going to die," I lied. "It doesn't necessarily need to be that way, but that's up to you."

If I knew Dr. Amaar and the rest of the Citadelians as well as I thought I did, I shouldn't have a problem winning this race. The badlands were mine, and a ship was out there just waiting for me. We'd either find it first, manipulate Malik into a trade of information, or the Traveler would accidentally lead us right to it.

Vocury was mine, and I wasn't about to let prophecies from the past affect the present and future. Nobody leaves if I have anything to say about it.

Chapter 7

Just One More

Ranbir Chopra: 2039

I took the Omaha to high orbit, cleared the moon, and removed the headset. I presumed our next stop would be Triax II, but Maya hadn't joined me on the bridge to confirm. Where to take us was the least of my pressing concerns, though. We had never discussed Tess staying behind on Earth, and I couldn't help but wonder why they had kept that a secret.

Were we going to sneak back to Earth to pick her up later? Why did she stay behind? What could Tess have to do that was so important that she'd take such a risk?

Certainly, military leadership had fingered Maya and me as their thieves and would be paying Tess a visit. I couldn't come up with any good reason why I was being kept in the dark, and I had to imagine that the secret was big. I was going to have to play things cool if I expected Maya to open up and share with me. The best thing I could do now was my job.

"Alright, Gregory, old chum," I mimicked the AI accent. "Let's see what you can do. I want to go to Triax II."

"Input. Coordinates."

"I left my galaxy roadmap at home. Looks like it's your big chance to prove your worth."

"Accessing. Star charts."

The screen populated with a map of our solar system, with the neighboring systems visible at the edges. I dragged my finger across the touch panel to navigate over foreign planets and stars, and it was then that I realized this was going to be harder than I thought.

"Triax II," I demanded, hoping that the screen would zip to the right system.

"Not. Available. Input. Coordinates."

"Gregory, what locations do you have available?"

"LV-426. Tattooine. Arrakis. Pandora. Genesis. Krypton. Asgard—"

"Gregory," I interrupted. "Are you having a laugh?"

"Ha. Ha. Ha," he mechanically chuckled.

"Oh God," I moaned. "Please tell me you have some real destinations in your database."

"Ubion. Ares. LP Meteora. Seron H2. Revis. Vocury. Sariter. Prius—"

"That's it. Prius. Bring up the system."

My screen zipped across the star charts, system after system flying by until it finally settled on Prius.

"Okay, Gregory. Expand. Let's see what's close by." If the Praxi were manufacturing high levels of triaxum at one point, Traix II must have been within range of their home planet.

"That's good enough, Gregory. Take us to Prius at maximum speed and I'll sort out where to go from there."

"Yes. Sir. Arrival in. Twenty-nine. Hundred. And four. Earth hours. Forty-seven. Minutes. Twelve. Earth seconds."

"What am I supposed to do with that, Gregory? Convert that to days."

"Cannot. Compute."

"You can tell me down to the second how long it will take but you can't do simple math? You kind of suck."

"Yes. Sir. System. Capable. Of. Far more. But. Insufficient. Programming."

"Guess we should have given the programmers a few more weeks before we stole you."

I switched off the monitor and left Gregory to autopilot the Omaha for the next one hundred and twenty-one days. With a bit of luck, I'd be able to narrow down the location of the triaxum mines long before our arrival on Prius. The only other thing left to do was get comfortable.

I led myself on a more detailed tour of the ship until I made it to the rear cargo bay again where Maya was taking stock of the military weapons on board. I didn't intend to creep up on her, but she jumped when I tapped her on the shoulder.

"What do we got?" I asked.

"Chingada! Don't be sneaking up on me," she warned, liquor on her breath.

"Sorry. Didn't realize you were so locked in."

"Why are you in my space? Step off me, bro."

"Alright. Jesus," I complained as I moved back to give her room. If she thought a few feet of buffer between us would mask the fact that she had already gotten into the booze, she was mistaken.

"Well, what did we come away with?"

"A few atmospheric gravity bombs and a shitload of these portable charges. I'd say them boys were planning something on the ground. Those forward compartments are rifle storage, but there are no weapons stowed."

"Well, we might have taken their space power, but they could certainly still get the job done with the other two haulers. We should see if there's any ship logs or communication records that might offer a clue of what they were planning."

"I'll handle that," Maya quickly volunteered.

"We've got four months to kill. Let me help."

"Just fly the fucking ship, man. That was the deal."

I should have pushed the issue right then and there. I doubt Maya would have responded to being challenged, but I wanted her to at least know that I wasn't stupid. There was something going on and I didn't appreciate the disrespect of being left in the dark.

Rather than make things contentious though, I played the role of subordinate. "Should we unpack some stuff? Maybe stock the kitchen?"

"Good idea," Maya concurred. "Go pick a room for yourself. Marcus' is the first on the left and I'm in the one right next to it." I turned toward the hallway and before I could walk away, Maya stopped me. "Hey Chop," she said earnestly, "thanks."

I peeked in on Marcus in his room. He was lying on his belly on the bed with a book open in front of him and a stack of them on the floor. The kid couldn't even read yet and he was already a fan of thumbing through the pages. "Hey buddy," I waved to him as I moved on.

The door to the quarters I assumed belonged to Maya was next and I decided to have a little look around. Her personal luggage was on the floor, unopened, and the corner of her bed sheets were ruffled near the floor and hung up on the mattress.

I peered back toward the cargo bay to make sure Maya wasn't nearby and quickly snuck into her quarters. Moving on instinct, I peeled the bed sheets up and found a box of liquor under the frame. Inside were a dozen bottles, rolling papers, a sack of marijuana, and a bag of coke the size of a baseball.

Maya may not have fallen off the wagon yet, but she was evidently planning a full-on suicide swan dive off the back end. We hadn't been out of Earth's atmosphere for two hours, and she was already drinking and making sure she had her party supplies tucked away.

I don't know if it did any good, but I instinctively grabbed the cocaine and shoved it into my pocket. She would know I had violated her privacy, but like a teenager whose mother had found a joint in their sock drawer, I doubted she would raise the issue. Had I understood the depths of Maya's chemical dependency, I would have taken the entire box and destroyed it along with the rest of our alcoholic cargo.

I couldn't help but selfishly consider my desire to have the occasional cocktail, or how much the citizens of Prius would enjoy a drink by the fire. Why should those of us with self-discipline be punished for Maya's addiction? That's what it is to love someone, though.

Sometimes, personal sacrifices must be made to save a friend. Whether for selfish reasons or foolish ones, I didn't save Maya that day as I should have. It was a decision I would come to regret, driven by a misplaced sense of purpose and hope.

All things considered, the four-month journey to Prius went about as well as it could. The Omaha provided Maya and me enough space to stay out of each other's hair, and the time we did pass together was spent mostly on Marcus-centric activities. There weren't a lot of ways to entertain a toddler aboard a spaceship, so we made sure to involve him as much as possible.

Maya was at her best as a mother when she was sober, lying on the floor, and filling in a coloring book with her son. Her vocabulary was free of profanity, and she rarely ever raised her voice. She handled Marcus delicately, to the point of almost being overbearing with maternal instinct. If anyone had ever predicted that Maya would be a helicopter mom, I would have thought they meant jumping out of a chopper into a war zone with her son strapped to her chest and not the more traditional version she became.

I found enjoyment in reading to Marcus. It was a good way to give Maya a break, and the kid genuinely loved it. Even if he didn't understand most of it, he would still lie on my chest while I read out loud from books borrowed from Tess' collection. A lot of them were boring medical books and science journals, but Tess also had an affinity for the classics.

Homer, Dostoevsky, Tolstoy, and Shakespeare were among her favorites, and I enjoyed challenging myself with the material.

If one didn't dig deep enough into Tess' stack of books, they'd think she was nothing but a stuffy intellectual. I had a lot of time on my hands though, and I found the boxes containing her guilty pleasure: romance novels, and not the safe-for-work type. Tess was a literary smut slut, and I truly couldn't wait until she was on board with us so I could tease her about it.

The adult time Maya and I spent together involved watching movies on the bridge, having drinks while singing karaoke, or playing games in the mess hall. Maya always spoke fondly of Malik, but she didn't miss him as much when it came to competing in Monopoly, chess, or poker. She was far more entertained by splitting matchups with me than by getting her brains beat in by her former merciless gaming partner. We tried to cook together, but any activity where the two of us had a difference of opinion was a recipe for disaster. Though it would cause me endless heartburn, I decided to leave the kitchen to Maya.

By the time we neared Prius, I had scouted out five possible locations where Triax II might be located. Without triaxum, the reach of the Praxi would be limited, and it would make sense that Triax II was either in their solar system or nearby.

As they were generally uninhabitable, I was able to quickly scratch the first two planets off my list. Our third stop seemed promising because of the livable temperatures, but the atmosphere was low on oxygen. Upon closer inspection, we discovered that the Praxi had been terraforming there but must have been centuries short of completing the process.

The fourth planet took us to a neighboring system, and I was starting to become concerned that I had gone wrong somewhere in my selection process, and Maya was beginning to apply pressure. We were a hundred and thirty days out from Earth at that point, and I didn't want to hear her lecture if we came up empty again.

Visually, the planet below didn't offer much hope. It was a mountainous grey rock and completely devoid of water. Maya hovering over my shoulder, judgmentally munching peanuts, didn't make me feel any better about the situation, but Gregory did have some good news.

"Oxygen-rich. Atmosphere. Temperatures. Indicate. Ninety-eight. Percent. Human. Survival. Rate."

Maya smirked as she took the station next to me. "Maybe you do know what you're doing after all."

"Scan for life signs, Gregory," I ordered.

"Scanning. Scanning. Twelve hundred. Fifty. Eight. Human. Life forms. Detected."

"Ha!" I celebrated. "I knew it!" I left my mouth agape and turned to Maya, who threw one peanut at a time for me to catch. She managed six in a row before bouncing one off my cheek, and I took the opportunity to chew while I further instructed Gregory. "Lock onto those coordinates and take us in."

We entered the atmosphere, found a cruising altitude, and came to a stop near the basin of a mountain range. There were no less than twenty silver alloy buildings that stood multiple stories tall, yet they all looked small in scale against the rocky backdrop. There was a landing zone off to the right, and I had to don the headset to put the Omaha down.

By the time we made the ten-minute walk to the rear hatch, the ship was surrounded. I flipped the switches to lower the ramp and quickly realized we weren't being welcomed. Fists striking the hull echoed through the valley, and the miners' angry voices overlapped with each other.

We shouldn't have expected a positive response. These were criminals who had chosen labor camps and commuted sentences over being deposited on Prius. When we won the war and destroyed the Jump Point, these poor souls had been abandoned to their own private hell. If they weren't here mining triaxum, I don't know if anyone would have ever come for them.

Maya held Marcus close to her chest with one arm and pulled back the snaps on her holster with her free hand.

"Easy. Easy now," I shouted, both to Maya and those who weren't pleased about our arrival.

"You left us here to starve!"

A few men stormed up the ramp the moment it made contact with the ground, and that was all the incentive Maya needed. She unslung her pistol, fired a single warning shot over the heads of the crowd, and then drew down on the man who had made it the farthest into the Omaha.

"If you're so hungry, I'm more than happy to feed you a nine-millimeter round."

I raised both hands in a calming manner. "Everybody chill. We are not the WM. We've traveled far to get you people out of here, and they may only be a few days behind us."

"And take us where?" the aggressive man asked. "Back to Earth, so you can throw us in a cage again? I'd rather eat every last person here and survive another five years than spend what time I've got left behind bars."

A male and female approached hand in hand. The man spoke first, his voice carrying a slight southern drawl. "Cool it, Stacklaw. You don't speak for all of us." His accent was unique and had held strong for someone off-world for years, but it was nothing compared to his partner's.

"You unna choppem up en slurp em don, dats yer bizz. Ivy had me fill. Imma roll dice onna dots en Mexicana."

I looked at Maya with bewilderment and could barely contain my laughter. "Did you get a single word of that?"

"She said they've been eating those who die. She's sick of it and wants to take a chance on us."

"Ah. You're Mexicana and I'm, what? Dots?" I said before I paused as it struck me. I pointed to my forehead and chuckled at the casual racial stereotype. "Dots. Got it."

'You got a name?" Maya asked as she holstered her weapon.

"I'm Anthony Ableright," the tall white man said. "This here is my gal Georgia, and you've already met our loud friend, Michael Stacklaw. As you can see, we're not in much of a position to turn away a helping hand."

"Fit de whole packa dirty bottoms in dis wagon," Georgia said as she wandered into the cargo bay with wide eyes.

Before I could ask, Maya translated. "She's impressed by the quantum mechanics."

I walked down the ramp toward the crowd that extended back into the buildings.

"Gather your things. Anything you can carry. We're getting you out of here and you're never coming back. It might be a little tight, but there's enough room for everyone and we're not going far." I turned to a fat little man with red hair and sideburns. "You there—do you know the mines well?"

"As well as any," he answered with a Scottish accent.

"Very good. What's your name?"

"Seamus Tassin."

"Well, I'll make you a deal, Seamus. We're going to wreck this place on our way out, and I want to make damn sure it stays that way. I've got some explosive charges on board. If you place them deep in the mines for me, I'll prepare your dinner and pour you a glass of scotch tonight."

"Eh. That's fair, I suppose. It's awfully cold and dark down in them mines, though. Not a place I'm excited to return to. Bad memories and such, you know?"

"Alright. What else do you want?" I smirked.

"A proper introduction to that mighty fine partner of yours. When the time is right and I've had a chance to clean myself up, of course."

"Maya?" I held back my laugh. "Yeah. Yeah, sure, buddy. You plant those charges for me, and I'll tell you exactly how to sweet talk her," I promised, realizing that the perfect prank opportunity had fallen into my lap.

I loaded Seamus up and sent him on his way before putting together some bodies to haul every bit of mined triaxum on board. It took two hours to stow away the cargo and herd all the passengers into the Omaha, and once we were sure that no one was left behind, I sealed the rear hatch.

There were a few hundred ragged miner folks in the cargo hold waiting for their chance to claim an open room. Alas, most of them would need to bunk with each other, and the remainder would sleep on the floor or hole up in the mess hall. Everyone was looking for food and luckily, there were plenty of canned goods to go around. The next most pressing matter of business was getting them cleaned up.

The Omaha's plumbing system held a thousand gallons of water, but it typically lost ten percent during filtration. Up until that point, Maya, Marcus, and I had cycled through four thousand gallons, returning thirty-six hundred to the tank over time. Hypothetically, we had enough water to last the three of us eight years, but we were about to deplete it all in three days with all these extra bodies on board if we weren't careful.

I carved my way through the crowd, occasionally greeting and exchanging pleasantries with those who were grateful to have been saved. I found Maya near a housing hall where she was directing traffic and assigning our passengers to their quarters.

"We need to ration," I cautioned her. "Five-minute showers or twenty-gallon baths. They can all have one now and then one more before we reach Prius."

"What am I supposed to do? Hand every one of them our HOA water policy pamphlet? In case you haven't noticed, we're running a zoo now. Can you make an announcement over the ship's comms?"

"I'm not sure. Maybe. It should come from you, though. You're the commander, after all."

"Well, now I'm commanding you to do it. How about that?"

"Okay, sure." I smiled. "You got it, boss! I'm heading to the bridge anyways."

Maya chuckled. "What are you so chipper about? We've got a thousand homeless vagrants invading our space, and you're all do de do de do." she mimicked a cartoonish positive vibe.

"First time I've felt useful in a while." I shrugged. "I needed this more than you know. We're doing a good thing here, Maya. We saved these people."

Maya rolled her eyes before assisting the next group. "You five—fourth door on the left is yours. Five-minute showers. Next!"

"Don't tell me you're not loving being in command." I grinned.

"Saving people is your game, Ranbir. I'll smile when we start handing out some justice." She turned her attention to her boy. "Marcus, baby, go with Uncle Chop. He's going to shoot off some fireworks."

"Come on, buddy." I picked him up. "We'll be back soon to help herd the cattle."

Carrying Marcus the entire way to the bridge was out of the question, so I held his little hand as he walked beside me among all our new residents. When we reached the sliding ramp, I set him between my legs and we zipped down toward our destination.

"Up you go." I raised him into the left control station and switched on the monitor. I climbed into my usual seat, unlatched the headset, and slowly pulled it over my face while making sci-fi noises to entertain Marcus.

"Manual controls, Gregory," I ordered.

"Initializing."

A familiar hum buzzed from ear to ear, as if something were running laps around my head. The visor shifted from dark to black, like a television powering on before projecting an image. A white dot appeared at the center, and by now, I had learned to squint and brace myself for the speed at which it would rush toward my face.

The first few times I connected to the Omaha's AI system, I think I blacked out momentarily. It wasn't so much about communicating with the ship, but more like becoming it. Once inside, it was as if the Omaha's nose was my own.

I could turn this way or that, directing our course with a mere thought. I could sense the distance to nearby objects, scan star maps, deploy weapons, and monitor secondary systems—all without accessing a single menu. It was like flying freeform, as I imagined a shark might feel in open waters: gliding effortlessly, able to make sharp, decisive maneuvers at will.

The Omaha was definitely not a Praxi craft—of that much, I was certain. My best guess was that it came from a hidden cache of recovered vessels that had crashed over the years, likely one that our old pal General Kelly hadn't been able to fully utilize. Its operating language referred to the "Pharoh," and I imagine the craft had been useless until someone installed Gregory. It seemed obvious enough to me that the Praxi weren't the only other ones out there in the galaxy. And judging by the weapon systems, the Pharoh's interests weren't all that dissimilar from humans.

As I assumed manual controls, memories of Gio flooded my mind. The seamlessness was reminiscent of communicating with my old friend. I wasn't inside a computer program or even transforming into a mechanical being. I was in an entirely different dimension, and the more I trained in it, the more I was able to stay alert on the bridge and remain cognizant of everything around me at the same time.

I took the Omaha to an elevation of eight hundred and fifty feet and angled the nose toward the crest of the mountain that housed the triaxum mines. Widening the scope of the laser grid to its maximum width, I began burning a fifty-by-fifty pattern into the rock.

"Watch your screen, Marcus," I directed as the stone liquified into glowing red magma. Most of it dripped down the side of the mountain like a thick gravy poured over chunky mashed potatoes. The longer I held the beams in place, the more the rock wall collapsed in on itself like a volcano erupting in reverse.

Marcus cheered as I tilted the ship on its axis and faced the nose straight down into the hole I had created. I tightened the beam pattern to focus the heat and blasted it deep into the heart of the mines. Once a lake of lava had formed inside the cavern, I put another five hundred feet of distance between myself and my target, fired a targeted wave of gravity into the hole, and drove the softening innards deep underground.

"Here comes the finale!" I reached into my pocket for the trigger to the charges Seamus had planted, flipped the protective guard on all three detonators, and pressed the ignitors.

The explosions sent rock and lava shooting out of the crater like a dozen Mentos dropped into a two-liter bottle of Coke. It was a good thing I was in control and not Gregory. Had I not been able to immediately fully reverse toward the clouds, we'd have been drenched in molten fire and pummeled by flying shards of jagged stone.

I held the Omaha at altitude for a few minutes, hoping to examine the damage we'd caused before leaving, but the ash cloud was thick. Using the gravity wave, I dispersed the smoke like a giant windshield wiper, clearing my view.

The landscape below resembled the core of a long-burning campfire, glowing red with white-hot embers and smoke rising from the charred ground. The horizon was leveled, and the buildings that once stood tall at the mountain's base were now buried under molten lava and rock.

There had only been two distinct explosions, which meant the third device had either been destroyed before eruption or was defective, not that it mattered. The job was done. No one would be mining a single ounce of triaxum here again, and we were making off with the last of it.

I set Gregory on a course to Prius and returned to the cargo hold to give Maya a break. We spent the next few hours ushering our guests around, and once everyone had settled in for the evening, we retired to the mess hall. Anthony, Michael, Georgia, and Seamus were among those enjoying a proper hot meal and everyone's spirits were high and about to get higher.

Maya chose an empty table to sit at and purposely stared at me as she dumped an entire bag of weed out and began breaking it down. She quickly rolled a joint, lit it, took two puffs, and passed it to me. "Spread it around," she instructed.

I took a good drag off it, stifled a cough, and found the first person reaching out for their turn to pass it to. By the time I had handed it off, Maya had lit another and held it up for me to continue distributing. I pinched it from her fingers, decided not to hit that one, and before I could find the next toker, Maya tugged at my pant leg. "Hey. I know you took it, and I'm not mad. I think I know why."

"What are you talking about?"

"Chop, I'm being cool. Don't make a cunt out of me. You know exactly what I'm talking about. Do you still have it?"

I couldn't even look her in the eye. "I do." I felt dirty for violating her privacy, and I never would have admitted to stealing her coke without believing that she understood my motives.

"Go get it. We're partying tonight. With this group of maniacs, we'll finish it off, no problem. Then it'll be all gone. No temptations and no hard feelings."

Maya was doing her best impersonation of a salesman to get her way, but I couldn't argue with her logic. I hustled back to my quarters, removed the giant rock from my locked suitcase, and stopped to look in on Marcus. I quietly inched his door open to find the lights off and my young friend sleeping soundly. Things were about to get wild, and I reminded myself that I'd likely have to check back in on him again later.

When I returned to the mess hall, I found it transformed into a rave. Maya had lowered the lights, and what little still shone pierced through the smokey haze. She hooked her CE phone up to a Bluetooth speaker and offered me a trade—one hand outstretched to accept her cocaine, while the other held out her phone. "I'll let you play DJ Chop all night, but you gotta ride with us until sunrise. No pussying out."

"That's fine, but you have to karaoke at least once, whenever I say, to whichever song I pick."

"Bitch, please. Bring it on."

Maya stood on her chair, peeled away at the twist tie, and dipped her pinky into the bag. She took a good snort into both nostrils, threw her head back, and screamed, "The Scorpio is ready!"

Within minutes, Maya had set up a chopping station and had a line twenty deep ready to join in. I kicked off the night with Believer by BT, and its booming beats seemed to beckon all like-minded individuals to the mess hall. Those who wanted smoke, snort, or scotch all had their fill, and once the buzz had kicked in, we pushed the tables to the perimeter of the room and used the open space as a dance floor.

Drugs were never my thing. I used them the only way they should be enjoyed—as a social enhancer. I never consumed to self-medicate or escape from pain, and I certainly never used them when alone.

That's a lesson I learned early in therapy when my doctor had force-fed me a cocktail of antidepressants as the answer to all my problems. I'd never see Emilia again, and the "take two and call me in the morning" approach wasn't going to change that.

I considered myself fortunate, and maybe that was because I was a glutton for pain. The hurt I felt in Emilia's absence was a reminder that she was real. It kept her alive and it saved me from the prescription epidemic that consumed anyone with an ailment and insurance. Tonight was different, though. We were liberators celebrating life, and that was a cause I was willing to tie one on for.

The only time Maya left the dance floor was when she was in pursuit of her next boost. She danced the night away with a hundred strangers, and I genuinely believe it was the first time in months that she enjoyed herself without worrying about or missing Tess.

I posted up at a table with the only miners I had become acquainted with. They were passing a joint between them, and Georgia poured me a drink. "Cheers," she offered.

"Hey! I understood you!"

"You unna git gat dit der dip doe," Michael imitated her pronounced drawl, and we all shared a laugh.

I queued up some The Crystal Method, and Seamus slid closer to lean over as he watched Maya on the dance floor. "Well, partner? I had to prepare my own dinner and pour my own scotch. This is your last chance to deliver on your bargain, and it looks like prime time."

The moment had come to spring my prank.

"Alright, you horny devil," I drunkenly replied in an unnecessarily loud voice. "Here's what you do. Maya appreciates strength. Someone forthcoming. Confident. You can't roll up on her and politely ask for a dance or introduce yourself with a soft handshake. She has to notice you first."

"Okay. How do I do that?"

"You need to cut a rug, my friend. Get out there and show her your moves. Be bold. Once you've established your presence, close the distance. Dance up on her from behind. Don't get gropey but let her know you're there. When she turns to face you, don't say a word. Just move a single strand of her hair behind her ear and she'll melt."

"That's it?"

"That's the move. Subtle and sexy."

Seamus downed his drink and nervously rubbed his hands together. "Alright, here goes nothing," he announced as he got up from his chair and nearly toppled over.

"You guys want to see something good?" I prompted his friends. "Watch this."

Seamus had exactly as much rhythm as I expected, which only made the situation more perfect. His signature dance move featured rubbing his belly three times with one hand and then switching to the other for three more rotations while slowly swirling his groin. It was quite a spectacle, especially set to the backdrop of electronic dance music.

I had to throw the poor guy a bone, so I decided to play something a little more his speed. The only Lynyrd Skynyrd song Maya had on her phone was Sweet Home Alabama and Seamus gave me an approving thumbs up from across the room for the assist when the first notes hit.

"There he goes," Anthony remarked as Seamus sashayed toward Maya. Although she wasn't dancing at the moment, it didn't stop my drunk comedic assassin from moving in behind her to make the slightest contact between his groin and her ass. One touch wasn't enough to annoy Maya, but after five seconds of Seamus getting entirely too comfortable, she turned to face him.

"Here it comes." I giggled with anticipation.

Seamus went in for the move and Maya had him gripped by the thumb, applying force to a pressure point on his wrist, and spun around before he could weave a single finger into her hair.

"The fuck are you doing?" her voice rang out over the southern rock anthem.

The four of us burst out laughing as Seamus begged to be released, and I quickly moved in to break things up before Maya hurt the poor guy.

"Maya, Maya, Maya," I chuckled as I approached them. "I'm sorry, I couldn't help myself. This here is Seamus, and he didn't mean any disrespect."

"You little asshole." Maya tried to play tough, but she held a smile behind her faux anger. "You want to catch a stray?" she threatened with a balled fist.

"How are you going to hit me when you're too busy singing karaoke?" I asked as I flicked my finger across the screen of her phone to find the one surprisingly out-of-place song hidden among her library of music. Steal

My Sunshine by Len began to play, and now there was no hiding her smile. I had found Tess' guilty pleasure among her novels, and it seemed I had discovered Maya's among her music, too.

I mimicked the speaking parts during the intro, even nailing the personable laugh from memory, then handed Maya the invisible mic.

"Go on, superstar," I said, offering encouragement, but Maya didn't need any. She was as high as a kite, everyone's hero, and the center of attention.

"I was lying on the grass of Sunday morning of last week, indulging in my self-defeat!" she belted out.

"Yessss!" I cheered along with the crowd. I stepped back to give Maya space to operate and she began hopping with positive energy while performing like a coked-up wedding singer. My prank had rolled right off her shoulders, and she couldn't have cared less that I put her on the spot to sing a cheesy pop song.

What a great night. We partied for hours, and I was the happiest I had been in years. We made new friends, everyone had a great time, and Maya's huge bag of coke could no longer be a temptation or source of contention between us.

Regret doesn't come until the morning after a bender, though.

Maya was the only person on board with actual responsibilities, and she was less attentive to Marcus than she should have been. After waking up, I spent the first few hours of my day nursing her through her hangover and ensuring that Marcus was properly looked after.

It should have been a one-time thing, but addiction gives no quarter to its victims. Just one more is the lie whispered by that personal demon, and I underestimated its hold on Maya.

I believe Maya had made plans for just one more time when we set out without Tess. She had prepared an extended bachelorette party, and when it was over, she thought she could put her immaturity behind her and never speak of it again once her wife was on board.

Some people could have pulled that off, but not Maya. Addiction had sunk its claws deep into her spine over time, and that demon would ride her shoulders until its weight forced her to her knees if she let it.

At least the coke was gone.

That's the bullshit I told myself to escape from my enabling behavior. We'd only have our passengers for a few more days, there'd be no more partying, and soon we'd finish whatever Maya's plans were. We'd pick up Tess, settle on Prius, and things would be great.

Without depression or negative emotions, addiction's blade becomes dull.

After everything I'd been through, I don't know how I maintained such foolish optimism.

I should have known better.

Chapter 8

Gateway Drugs

Alexis X: 2337

We approached what they referred to as the "train," and I was shocked to discover some proper tech in that western wasteland. The transportation device consisted of seven alloy pads with guard rails on the exterior, each approximately fifteen feet by thirty. The five in the interior carried the passengers while the end pads remained empty, seemingly to soak up the solar rays that powered the device. By the time we arrived, there were a few hundred of the common folks loaded onto the train, with a bunch of Citadel guards crammed onto the final available cart.

The pyramid loomed large in the distance with two other track systems stemming out in opposite directions to other adjacent villages. None of the pads made contact with the track system below, and it was apparent that Praxi antigravity tech was in play as we floated toward our destination.

I poked Maddox in the waistline from behind to get his attention. "You're going to go back for Malik, right? Return in the cover of darkness tonight and Seal Team Six their asses?"

"A deal is a deal, and we honor our commitments. If you want to save your friend, the best I can offer is to snatch him up when we leave this desolate hellhole. The sooner you deliver on your promise, the better chance he has for survival."

"I haven't promised anything. You guys aren't getting shit from me until I know what is going on."

"I leave the comfort of my home, breathe this filthy mineral air, save your skin, and this is the thanks I get? You're lucky Dr. Amaar is in charge. We take a very different approach to getting what we want."

"Sorry. Thanks, I guess."

I wasn't about to continue poking that bear. Maybe I was being too cynical when I should be grateful. I definitely didn't want to stay with Kade, and even though it seemed like he couldn't bring himself to kill

Malik, I feared the worst all the same. Though I had only just met her, Dani was another concern, but I didn't think there was any secret that could keep her safe. She may have been dead by the time we reached the train.

I should have felt safe, but my conspiratorial instincts were strong. A beast like Maddox didn't exactly put out good vibes, and neither did the looming pyramid as it towered over us upon approach. I was trying to make sense of my situation and piece together the puzzle of where these people came from and how they had prophesied our arrival, but the sheer spectacle swept me away.

The train stopped just short of the base of the pyramid, where there was a group of Citadel security stationed. Once our arrival was approved, a crease appeared in the structure and horizontal doors separated from each other to create an opening for the train to pass through.

We hovered our way into the bay, and the workers dispersed from both sides of their pads onto concrete unloading stations. Most of them hustled toward one of the stairwells leading up or down to their jobs; others had their masters waiting to collect them.

"You guys built a pyramid and put a subway station in it? Weak," I commented. "At least the air doesn't taste like shit in here."

"Are you not impressed, Alexis X of Mission Vocury?" a man near a stairwell raised his voice.

He was of average height for a man of Middle Eastern descent, and his wavy brown hair should have had some pockets of grey in it for his age, but there were none. He was dressed in a white suit with a black-and-gray striped tie and brimmed tan hat. There was a tired look to his brown eyes, but his face and posture were full of energy as he approached. Introducing himself as "Dr. Amaar," he extended his hand in a customary Earth greeting.

"Yeah, hi," I said while raising a hand to quickly wave rather than shaking his. "So, you're like the bad guy, right?"

"I'm sorry?" he asked and nodded to Maddox in dismissal of him and the Citadel guards.

"The bad guy. A villain. Come on, man. You look like an Iranian version of Belloq from Raiders, for Christ's sake."

"I'm afraid I'm not following."

"'Zurok!'" I quoted the Indiana Jones villain. "'Go ahead, Jones. Blow it back to God,'" I imitated. "No? Nothing? That's disappointing."

"I'm sorry. I've never been an impressive man. My work, however, I think you'll find most impressive. May I show you around?"

"Please do." I extended an arm for him to lead the way.

We went up two floors through a stairwell, and I hoped that every step I took in that punishing gravity would take me closer to some real answers. I was out of breath by the time we arrived at a steel door, and my expectations couldn't possibly have been lower based on what I'd seen thus far.

How wrong I was.

I stepped through the doorway like Dorothy walking into a technicolor Times Square Land of Oz. The Citadel was as alive as a shopping mall during the peak of brick-and-mortar consumerism. Translucent sections of the pyramid's upper structure filtered sunlight, casting a warm glow across the borough. Shops and vendors lined the space, television screens above their entrances broadcasting endless loops of advertisements. From pills that promised everything from cures for different diseases to adding inches to your height, along with other male organs that need not be mentioned, it appeared as though you could find anything you needed here.

Well-dressed people hustled this way and that as they went about their day, most of them staring at me with mouths agape as we passed by them. They saw me as an alien visitor to their alien world, but for the first time since I had arrived, I didn't feel out of place. Their metropolis of pharmaceutical advertisement and commerce was all too familiar.

I stood in front of one store with my head tilted upwards to watch the ad playing for the product inside. "Never stress again," an enchanting female voice played over images of a happy couple embracing. "Banish anxiety and doubt, and welcome bliss. Introducing the Relaxer 11.1 from Amaar Labs: the latest in anxiety relief. You'll never worry again."

Dr. Amaar stood behind me as I took it all in. "Does this interest you?" he asked.

"Maybe. I'm waiting for the end of the ad where they tell me to consult my physician if I break out in hives or experience night terrors after taking your Super Xanax."

"Relaxer 11.1 has no side effects. What good is being stress-free if your medication gives you something to worry about?"

"Cute sales pitch. Let me guess, you'll trade me some pills for whatever it is that you want from me? That's how things work here, right? Everything is for trade?"

I suspected far worse from the doctor. I was already assuming that he knew who I was, where I was from, and had a dossier full of my health history. In my paranoid mind, walking up on a cure for my anxiety wasn't random, but a planned segway into trade temptation.

"You're welcome to a daily regimen of hydration and sustenance, and as our honored guest you won't be required to work to receive these necessities. If you would like to trade for other health benefits, whether they be mental or physical, that is up to you."

I looked past Dr. Amaar down the thoroughfare and noticed a man insert a key card into the encasing to a water fountain, open it, and drink from it.

"Oh, yes," I said as I dismissed myself from the conversation for a proper drink. The moment the man was finished drinking, however, the encloser slammed back into place. I tugged at it and tinkered with the buttons on the control panel, but it wouldn't budge.

Dr. Amaar caught up to me, leaned down, and inserted his key card to give me access. The trap doors peeled back, and I lowered my mouth to the best drink of water I'd ever taken. I hadn't even begun to enjoy it before the flow discontinued and the mechanism beeped to signal the snap encloser.

"What the shit is this? I barely had any."

"Six ounces is the daily limit per citizen. Our atmospheric water re-claimers consume twenty-five percent of our total power, and it's necessary to ration our resources. There is no water on the surface, which in turn leads to no vegetation or livestock feeding. We only continue to survive through science."

"Yeah, I bet." I rolled my eyes. "Okay, so what miracle cure are you going to spring on me to get me talking? I know you want something, and the fact that you're dancing around it says more than you coming right out with it."

"I don't know why you're so mistrusting, Ms. Alexis. I was hoping you had come here to help us and that I wouldn't need to convince you. I don't wish to make demands of you, but these affairs have a time limit. I know you came here in a spacecraft, and it's a matter of when, not if, Kade discovers the same."

"So that's what you're after? The Wolf Moon?"

"If you would be so kind as to bring it to the surface, we could escape this marooning and bring our advanced medical cures to the rest of the galaxy. Only the people here have known my work, and it's a travesty that suffering continues on other worlds when I could help them."

"Sorry, I'm not saying that it can't be earned, but I don't do well with trusting authority figures. It kind of violates my core beliefs."

"What can I do? Tell me. How could I help you and earn your trust? I can do incredible things in my lab. Things you wouldn't even think medically possible. If you were paralyzed, I could help you walk again. If you were blind, I could help you see again. If you had a terminal disease, I could cure you of it—"

"Pelvic inflammatory disease," I interrupted him.

"I see. And are your concerns of a reproductive nature?"

"Yes," I lowered my voice with unnecessary shame.

"Reproductive health is one of my chief areas of study. I would need to give you a physical examination before I make any promises, but I can do wonderful things if you'll trust me."

"Alright. Get me some of that relaxer while you're at it. You prove the value of your work and the trustworthiness of your character, and I'll give you what you need."

I had a million other questions about where these people came from, what they were doing here, the origination of their prophecy, and what had happened to the Praxi, but the dangling of a miracle cure distracted me.

"Wonderful. Give me a couple of hours to tend to my duties and prepare my lab. In the meantime, my son Taj can continue your tour of the Citadel if you'd like, or he could show you to your quarters. No relaxer for you though, at least not until I've sorted you out."

"I wouldn't mind taking a little rest. It's been a weird twenty-four hours."

"Very well. Stay here and I will send him for you. He'll serve as escort to your appointment later." He extended his hand again, and this time I felt comfortable shaking it.

The doc walked off, leaving me to take in the pyramid's interior. Stairwells wound around the exterior, leading up at least eight levels, while elevators—seemingly only descending—operated nonstop, ferrying villagers below. Whatever task they were brought here for was clearly underground. I considered investigating further, but a commotion from a nearby store-front stole my attention.

The flashing neon sign read "The Regenerator," and the line of patrons waiting for service was longer than any other of the mall drug shops. At the front stood a disheveled man, far too young for the cane he leaned on, caught in a heated exchange with the lady pharmacist.

"You're not listening to me," he snapped, raising his voice. "I'm almost out and I've already been rationing for weeks."

"I'm sorry, sir. You don't have the required work credits for a refill. You should speak to your supervisor about adding extra shifts."

"I can barely get through the shifts I already have! My knee is shot and it's getting worse."

"Might I suggest reliever to help you through the pain?"

"Oh, what a surprise. You want to increase the script that I already can't pay for."

"Perhaps you should opt in for better coverage."

"I can't." The man gritted his teeth. "Because my knee. Is fucking. Shot. I'm going to age out, you realize that, right? You're killing me."

"You're holding up the line," the customer behind him complained.

"Sir, you can take a train to the village of your choice this evening. Join the workers there or make trade in the outer colonies."

I had heard enough and thought I could intervene with a little Traveler clout on my side.

"Excuse me, miss? Why don't you just give him what he needs to get back to work, and then he could repay you over time?" I suggested.

"With all due respect, you're an outsider here, and that's not how it works. Next!" she curtly dismissed the man, calling for the next customer.

"No, wait!" the man demanded. "You have to help me." He gripped his cane with both hands and raised it above his head, but Citadel security tackled him to the floor before he could lash out. I watched helplessly as they dragged him away, almost certainly to deposit him on the next ride out of town.

The same problems that plagued the poor in the outer colonies were also affecting the rich in the city center. It seemed everyone was reliant on Dr. Amaar's miracle cures, and I was unsure if he was saving them or killing them. The line between the two was unclear and razor thin. If he wasn't offering me something I so desperately wanted, I would have been all over his shit.

I wandered through the shopping center, absorbing the pharmaceutical propaganda flashing from one storefront to the next while waiting for my escort.

When I finally spotted him, I didn't need Taj to introduce himself—I knew it was him from a hundred yards away. From a distance, he kind of resembled Ranbir, and that was a cold reminder of my past.

Ranbir had been right about the mission. He may have harped on the wrong reasons to stay put on Earth, but he was over the target with his demands for caution. We should not have come, and I would never get the chance to tell him that I should have listened. The best I could do in that bizarre situation was try to accomplish something good.

My heart started to flutter as Taj approached. He was tall, fit, and well-dressed, with sandy brown hair and the whitest damn teeth I had ever seen. The only imperfection I could discern was a small mole on his neck—and even that seemed like a well-placed beauty mark.

Taj's blue eyes stared blankly ahead as he casually extended his arms to feel his way through the passing human traffic. He was blind. Despite his lack of vision, he navigated the thoroughfare with the ease of someone who had walked it a million times. I was instantly taken with him, which basically guaranteed in my mind that he would have the personality of a wet towel.

"Hey there," I said as he nearly walked by me.

"You're Alexis." He pointed in the direction of my voice, to the left, and then to the right to make light of his condition. So much for the wet towel hypothesis.

"And that makes you Taj." I smiled and pointed back even though he couldn't see my comedic gesture. I extended my hand to prop myself up against the nearby elevator and instinctively gave my best cool girl pose, but I was standing farther away than I had thought.

My hand eventually made contact with the elevator doors, but by the time it did, I was already toppling over. I fell shoulder-first in the most embarrassing way possible and was left crumpled on the floor.

Taj rushed to my aid on his knees and tried to help me to my feet. "Are you okay?" he asked, his uncontrollable laughter mixing with concern. "What happened?"

"Yeah, no, I'm good. It's okay. I only hurt my pride."

"Are you sure?" He chuckled. "Seems you took a pretty good tumble there."

"Totally fine. I have lots of practice. You might say I fall with grace. It's this damn gravity that's got the best of me."

"The gravity inhibitors lower the rate by forty percent in the dome," he informed me as he swiped at my shoulders to clean me of whatever invisible dust I had collected.

I think he just wanted to keep the human contact going, but maybe I was imagining things. It might have been embarrassing, but I quite enjoyed our first moment together. There's no better way to break the ice than by providing some physical comedy.

"So, I'm supposed to give you a tour. Is there anywhere you'd like me to take you first?"

"To my bedroom," I blurted out, continuing my awkward display. "No, wait. Not like that. But also, not not like that. You're damn cute, you know that?"

He shook his head and laughed at my ridiculous flirting. "You are not what I was expecting."

"Been hearing that a lot lately. Ahhh . . . I'd really appreciate it if you could show me to my quarters before I humiliate myself any further."

"Come." He led me along the wall toward the nearest stairwell. "You'll be staying with me on the sixth floor for your time here. I hope that isn't too off-putting. I've been charged with looking after you."

"Oh." I offered no further comment as we climbed the first flight of stairs.

"You'll have your own bedroom and whatever privacy you desire, of course. It's just that my father has asked that I stay by your side, should you choose to explore the Citadel further."

"That's fair. I can live with that. Ya know, I would like to look around later. The basement has me intrigued."

"It's rather industrious and depressing down there, with the factories and the mines. I doubt you'd see anything of too great of interest, not that I've ever taken in the sights myself. All the really good stuff is restricted."

"Like what?" I was becoming short of breath as we passed the third level on our way up.

"Couldn't tell you. That's what makes it interesting. I know we carve out minerals and pressure cook our pills, but there's more going on down there that I've never been able to gain access to."

By the time we reached the fourth floor, I was completely exhausted from the climb and had to take a break. I leaned against the wall and thanked the stars that I didn't fall over again. "I need a minute. 'Forty percent' reduction of gravity, my ass."

Without hesitation, Taj turned around, took two steps down the stairs in the direction we had come from, and peered back in my direction.

"Come on. Climb on." He slapped his shoulder. "I can tell you wouldn't be above it, so don't pretend."

It was quite possibly the most adorable thing anyone had ever done for me. He braced his hands on the railing to take my weight, and I jumped up on his back. He caught the bottom of my thighs as I wrapped my legs around his waist, and I reached across his chest to hold on. Once I was settled, Taj simply turned around and began climbing toward the fifth floor with me in tow like my own silly Prince Charming.

"Are you medicating while you're here?" he asked pointedly.

"I took two from Kade. One to hydrate and one for sustenance. Why?"

"Nothing else?"

"No. Why?" I pressed.

"You should let me know if you want any. I can tell you which ones are safe and which ones aren't."

"How can you tell?"

"Because there's some that my father won't let me take, and I'm sure there's more to his reasoning than protecting me from ending up like the addicts working the mines."

"Can I trust him?" I asked point-blank even though I didn't expect an honest answer from someone so close to the doctor.

Taj didn't immediately answer.

We reached the sixth floor, and he hunched down slightly to let me off his back. I released my grip from his shoulders, uncoiled my legs, and stood to face him. He made to grab the door handle, but I quickly placed my hand over his to stop him.

"Well?" I asked.

"My father is a good man, and he has a good heart. He's kept us alive for years and he's helped a lot of people. If he says that he can help you, he's telling the truth."

"But..."

"But... he's obsessive. And secretive. His methods can be unsound."

"For example?" I continued probing.

"He feeds poor people highly addictive compounds, and then ostracizes them as second-class citizens for their dependency problems. I understand that their work is crucial to our survival, but I've never agreed with the way they've been treated. Kade, for all his violent and destructive tendencies, seems to care more for them than my enlightened and sophisticated father ever has."

"That's a ringing endorsement," I said sarcastically as I released his hand to allow him to open the door to the sixth level.

We entered a hallway with doors to apartment units on our left and a long wall of built-in windows to our right. I peered down at the thoroughfare from above and took in the awesome size of the structure from that height.

"You know, we've got structures like your Citadel where I come from, only we never turned ours into failed Communist utopias. In fact, we've never really been able to make heads or tails of how our pyramids came to be."

"That sounds familiar. Perhaps whoever built ours also built yours," he suggested. "This is it here," he said as felt his way along the doors.

He inserted his keycard to pop the door latch free, and I entered to find that the housing units were built into the exterior walls of the Citadel. The same translucent material that allowed the passage of light into the building also brought illuminating life to his living quarters.

Just as I was inspecting his situation, he was inspecting mine. He reached toward my chest, tugging at the loose cord hanging from my headphones. "What is it that was rubbing against my neck?" he asked while tracing the cord down to where it disappeared into my suit.

"That's an earbud. For my music."

"Music?" he echoed. "What do you mean?" The fact that music was foreign to Taj made me feel great sorrow, but that instantly washed away when I realized I could introduce him to the best tracks ever recorded and see his reactions.

"Here, look." I held up my CE phone, even though I knew he couldn't see it. "It's all stored on this device, and I can play any song I want as long as my battery holds out."

Emilia had crushed it with the design of the phones, and that's the only reason I was still sitting at eighty-nine percent battery life. I was eventually going to have to get back to the ship for a recharge though, and I'd need it sooner rather than later now that I'd be introducing a musical virgin to their first real experience.

"What do you like? Hip-hop? Metal? Pop?" I asked rhetorically. "Here, put this in your left ear." I placed the appropriate bud in his palm. "Just like this." I showed him as I inserted the right bud into my ear and guided his hand to feel its placement. "What do I play for someone who's never heard music? This is hard." I laughed.

I scrolled through my library of music, trying to pick the perfect first song. My thumb naturally hovered over Wonderwall by Oasis and I smirked. "I could tell you a story about this one," I commented as my forefinger flicked over the screen. I stopped as I scrolled by Linkin Park, and the memories came flooding back to me.

"Are you okay?" Taj asked as I quietly paused.

"Yeah. I had a friend that really liked this one band. She was, umm . . . she was really special."

"I'd like to hear."

"You are not ready for Chester. Not yet." I smiled. "Ahh, okay. I've got it! This is Phil Collins. In the Air Tonight," I said as I hit "play."

I must have had the biggest grin, but there's no way it could have compared to the look on his face. It was like he had no understanding or frame of reference for the soft opening drum beat and melody. I looked up into his eyes as they wandered carelessly and began bobbing my head slightly, encouraging him to do the same by placing my hand on his cheek.

I mouthed the lyrics to the first chorus, and though I had a million things I wanted to say, I stayed perfectly quiet and studied his reactions to the foreign bliss filling his ears. I started to sway and reached out for his hand to pull his body in motion with mine, showing him that it was perfectly natural to be physically moved by the music.

The first chorus came to an end, and now that the song had hooked him, I wanted the big moments to envelope him completely. I removed my earbud and twisted it carefully into his other ear. Though I could still faintly hear the music, I risked cranking up the volume a bit to catch more of it.

The "Well I remember" echo hit him, and I grinned as his eyes widened with childlike wonder. "But I know the reason why you keep this silence up," I mouthed along with the song. "No, you don't fool me. The hurt doesn't show, but the pain still grows," I continued while I prepared myself for the big drum break.

"Here it comes! Tu-du, tu-du, tu-du, tu-du, du-du," I popped the drum sounds as I hit my air drums. I bobbed my head harder and he followed along with his mouth hanging wide open in delight. I didn't hold back singing along now that the song was full sending it, treating him to my best Phil Collins impersonation.

As the song trailed off and then left him with silence, his eyes slowly shrunk back from being peeled open. I pulled the buds from his ears and didn't bother asking for his thoughts. It was there in his glossy eyes.

"That was incredible. It was like a spell that made me physically react. There's nothing else quite like it. More," he begged.

I laughed joyfully at his response and gave him a pat on the shoulder. "Soon—I'll play so many songs for you. We'll find your favorite, but it has to be later. I can't wait to continue this, but I'm beat. I need to sleep."

"I'll give you your privacy now, then," he offered, even though I could tell he wanted to stay. "I'll return later once you've rested, and escort you to your appointment. Maybe then we could listen to some more music? It's been lovely making your acquaintance."

"Likewise." I smiled at him as he closed the door behind him. I missed him the moment he was gone, so I began inspecting the quarters to distract me from the butterflies in my stomach. It wasn't an executive suite by any means, but it was a far cry from Dani's dilapidated bedroom.

I was surprised to find a bathroom, and even more shocked to discover that Taj had running water. I turned on the sink and tilted my head under the faucet to drink. "'Six ounces a day,'" I recited to myself as I reached into the shower to find that hot water was also an amenity. "What a bunch of bullshit. The haves and the have-nots."

I don't know what the quarters were like on the five floors below, but I was positive they weren't enjoying the same access as the "special" people on the higher levels. I imagined Taj and the others of the upper class consumed more water in a day than everyone else did in a month, and that's without considering those who lived outside the Citadel.

I liked Taj, but these were not the kind of people I wanted to help. I'd feel more comfortable getting by on scraps while working fervently to lead a revolution that would overthrow them.

If I had an internet connection, a webcam, and an audience, I could wake the commoners and strike fear in the hearts of their masters. I wasn't on Kade's team by any means, but at least I could respect him. He had honor, and he was certainly more honest than Dr. Amaar.

I laid down on the soft sheets and immediately made a mess of the bed by rolling myself up in them. I had slept for three hundred years to get here, and all it took was a single exhausting day to make me crave a cozy bed again.

The more comfortable I became, the easier it was for my mind to move from leading a revolt to embracing my captors. If the doc truly was as skilled as he claimed, it wouldn't matter to me what happened next. Either side could have our ship and do with it as they pleased.

We could start our colony right here with a thousand-year head start inside the Citadel. I could finally stop chasing down conspiracies and start a family instead. Since I was daydreaming, I dared to imagine that I was lying in the bed of my future husband and father to my children. Taj and I would make some good-looking babies and have a hell of a fun time doing it, that's for sure.

Before I knew it, I had slept for hours and woke to Taj gently shaking me. I waved him off in a stupor to signify that I'd get up on my own time, and he let me be. I helped myself to a shower to bring me to life and joined Taj in his general living space once I was ready.

"Hi." He smiled at me. "The doctor will see you now." We left his quarters, returned to the stairwell, and once again, he took a couple of steps down and waited patiently. "Can I offer you a ride?"

"I won't trouble you if we're going down," I answered.

"No trouble at all. Maybe I liked it." He smiled at me again.

"Alright." I blushed as I climbed onto his back again. Starting a playlist, I plugged one bud into my ear and handed the other to Taj, introducing him to Massive Attack.

Taj trapsed down six flights of stairs, head bobbing to the rhythm, and even though he grunted and had to readjust my position to hold me firmly in place, he made it all the way to the ground floor before putting me down. We crossed the thoroughfare to an elevator, and Taj inserted his key card to gain access before pushing the first of four buttons to take us to the first sublevel.

When the doors opened, I realized I was walking into what looked like a research facility. The walls were stark white, and the fluorescent lights bathed the rooms in a harsh, clinical glow. Though I knew that Dr. Amaar was still working, the majority of the staff were wrapping up for the day—some locking doors behind them, while others packed into the elevator we had just left to return to the surface.

We walked down a hallway lined with rooms on either side, some featuring windows and others not. Most of the those I could see into were dark, and the unfamiliar equipment at the workstations gave no hint of their purpose.

"This is it," Taj stated as he held the door open to his father's personal workspace.

I had anticipated a typical doctor's office, but instead was met with a full-fledged laboratory. Dr. Amaar wasn't seeing any patients here; he was deep into research and experimentation. The workstations and countertops were spotless, and the array of equipment and neatly organized tools looked completely alien to me.

"Come in. Please. Have a seat," Dr. Amaar invited.

Ever the gentleman, Taj asked, "Would you like me to stay or go?"

"Can you wait outside for me?" As much as I was enjoying his company, this was the most private of matters for me and I didn't want to invite him into my medical records.

"Of course. I'm here if you need me."

"This won't take long," the doc assured us both. "I'm not sure what kind of medical treatment you are accustomed to, but this shouldn't be too invasive at all. I will need to give you a little prick, though," he warned. "Can you roll up your sleeve, please?"

I obliged and instantly looked away from the sight of the needle. I started to feel a bit queasy about the whole situation, but I powered through it in the hopes of a miracle. "Ah," I quietly exclaimed as I felt the sharp poke of the needle and the sensation of blood being drawn into the syringe.

"That should do it. See? No big deal." He turned his back to me, plopped down in a rolling high-backed chair, and slid across the floor toward a workstation. I watched as he carefully loaded my tube of blood into the front opening chamber of a machine about the size of a toaster oven. "This is very exciting."

That surprised me. "A blood test is exciting?"

"Well, yes," he paused as he searched for the best way to frame his giddiness. "You're a Traveler. An outsider. The opportunity to aid you is an honor." It wasn't a lie, but it certainly wasn't the whole truth either.

He read the results being bounced back from his device. "You're quite healthy. A perfectly safe candidate for cellular regeneration treatment. Based on these findings, I believe with some confidence that I can create a treatment with a very high probability of mending your reproductive ailments. Your scar tissue doesn't stand a chance."

"That's it? I just drink a magic potion, and all my lady bits will be well-oiled again?"

"It's not magic, Alexis. It's science. I didn't want to promise anything before, but I feel comfortable doing so now."

A wave of emotion hit me as I considered the reality that I could actually become a mother. I had journeyed to Vocury with colonists who were meant to build families here, but I never expected that I could be so lucky enough to be one of them.

It didn't feel real, and even though I had trust issues with the doctor, I believed that he could deliver on his promise. I wanted to cry and laugh and celebrate all at once, and I would have done all three if any of my friends were there to share that joy with me.

"How long? How long until it can be ready, and how soon after can I expect results?"

"I must be precise. Your treatment requires specific construction for your genetic makeup if it's going to be effective." His cautious approach was appreciated, and I fully expected him to tell me that it'd be weeks or months before it was ready, and years before I'd see results. "I'd say about twenty. Maybe twenty-five."

"Weeks?" I asked hopefully, dreading that the answer would be months or even years.

"Minutes, of course. It should only take one dose, and I expect your cells will begin splitting and recreating new matter in a day. Maybe two."

Dr. Amaar went to work on cooking up my cocktail, and I assumed that he was waiting until the moment of delivery to talk trade. I felt relatively safe taking his wonder drug, but only if I could continue to hold out on him. I didn't want to bring the ship to the surface only to have my kidneys explode a month from now because of his weird science.

With Taj seemingly in my corner, I saw an opportunity to test the doc. I left him to his work in the laboratory and joined my pawn in the hallway. He smiled when he sensed my presence, and even though I was intending on using him, I couldn't help but smile back.

"That was fast. Everything okay?" he asked.

"It's good. A little concerning, but good," I exaggerated as I planted the seeds for Taj to play his part. "Your dad is making a special concoction for me right now, and I can't stop thinking about the fact that he prescribes things for others that he wouldn't let his own son take, ya know? Can I trust that what he's about to give me is safe?"

I stood closer than I needed to and made sure to establish physical contact. I didn't want to outright ask him to intervene on my part; this was as much a test for Taj as it was for Dr. Amaar.

"I think I know a way we can find out."

Taj was smart enough to come up with the plan that I had wanted him to, and just naive enough to think it had been his idea. I might have underestimated him and his feelings for me, though. Maybe he was experiencing the same intestinal flirty butterflies that I was. Those little bastards were an all-natural drug that could cloud one's judgment just as well as pharmaceutical-grade poisons.

We entered the lab together and waited for Dr. Amaar to finish his work. Taj could have spoken up earlier, but I think he was reveling in his moment to play my knight in shining armor beyond being my piggyback machine.

"One pill is all it takes," the doc said as he held it between two fingers. "Before I give it to you, however, I'd like to discuss how we can bring your craft to the surface."

He may have been a brilliant man, but he was as predictable as a politician. Before I could navigate my way around his negotiation tactic, my guard dog went to work.

Taj held out his hand and said, "Make another one, father. I'm going to take the first one, just to make sure our Traveler is safe."

Dr. Amaar initially withheld the pill and furrowed his brow at his son's attempt at chivalry. "It's not constructed for your genetic makeup. It might make you terribly ill; it might also do nothing. This is a pointless experiment."

"Just like the regenerator?" Taj asked, his tone accusatory. "That's not built for any one specific genetic profile, and you won't let me take that one either."

"That's completely different. Stop being a child."

"Well, if I don't take it, then neither does she." Taj stood strong.

"Fine, you foolish child. Don't come crying to me when you're terribly dehydrated, or running a fever, or experiencing bouts of diarrhea. I'll make another one if you're going to be so insistent on impressing our guest."

They both had passed the test. If the doc was willing to let his own son ingest that medicine, then surely, it was safe enough for me. I had both father and son right where I wanted them.

"It's okay, Taj. I appreciate the gesture. There's no sense in you risking becoming ill, but I will have to take a little time before I deliver on my end. There's a ship carrying colonists and embryos in orbit right now, and I would be remiss in my duty to keep them safe if I acted too hastily. Let's make sure I don't get sick and everything is in working order before we get too carried away."

I was quite proud of myself for navigating that situational chessboard, and Dr. Amaar knew he was in checkmate. His desire for the Wolf Moon was no secret, but he didn't know how badly I wanted that pill. My manipulation might not have been Emilia-level, but I think she would have enjoyed watching me employ some of her tactics all the same.

"One condition," Dr. Amaar said as he extended his hand to deliver the goods. "We'll be keeping a close eye on the pirates. Should we discover that they've broken your fellow Traveler and make a move for your craft—will you act quickly to help us?"

"That's fair. If I continue to find you trustworthy, I'll step up if things get dicey."

I held my palm open, and the doc dropped a small, brown-spotted yellow tablet into my hand. If the treatment worked, nothing else would matter. Vocury was a desolate wasteland compared to Earth, yet it was the only place in the galaxy where I could ascend from barren to fruitful. I didn't hesitate for a second to seize that opportunity. Without a moment's hesitation, I threw that pill back and swallowed it dry.

"I would like to give you a checkup in three days. By then, I should be able to determine if cellular regeneration is occurring. Hopefully, we'll have some good news."

"Alright. Three days," I responded and turned to Taj. "Shall we?" I motioned to the door.

"We shall," he said, receiving a contentious look from his father.

I got what I wanted, but it was merely a distraction. There were far too many unanswered questions and Citadel secrets to uncover for me to sit back and bide my time. I couldn't be complacent simply because I had received a miracle.

It was time to get some solid content, Conspiriousity-style, and Taj was the perfect gateway to do so. There was no telling what was happening to Malik or how long he could hold out for. Kade didn't seem like the type to trade for information, and I was terrified where that might lead if Malik held his ground.

Chapter 9

Message in a Bottle
Ranbir Chopra: 2040

G regory brought the Omaha to a stop in Prius airspace after a raucous six-day journey, and it was up to me to take us to the surface. A cold sensation vibrated over my body as I pulled my headset down and assumed controls.

Looking out from the nose of the Omaha at the vibrant planet below brought back a rush of memories. I wanted to, just for a moment, feel the presence of my friend Gio. I wished I could tell him how sorry I was and let him know what he meant to me. But, as with most things I had loved, he was gone forever, and I was left with regret. If I was to ever find myself in the position Gio had been in, I was resolved to have the courage to make a similar sacrifice in his honor.

I dropped into the lower atmosphere and enjoyed a few extra minutes of cruising above the splendor of Prius. There were many communities to see from a bird's eye view, but only one where I truly felt at home. I lowered the Omaha to the beachhead of my old village and was quite impressed with the gains they had made in five years.

The huts were larger and had been spaced out a mile long near the tree line. Trenches had been dug and reinforced to redirect and control water, and heavy canopies constructed from foliage hung and extended from their improved homes to provide shade. The men were dressed in clothes patched together like leafy jackets and pants, though there were still some orange prison smocks in play.

I left the bridge and spread the word of our arrival as I navigated my way through our passengers to get to Maya's quarters. I rapped two knuckles at her door and moments later Marcus opened it.

"Hi, Uncle Chop!"

"Good morning, my little spaceman. Where's mommy?"

"Mommy is sick."

"Oh?" I glazed over the youngster's confusion between sick and hungover as I entered.

Maya was in her bed, completely naked, lying on her stomach and only half covered by a single sheet, darkened by the sweat it had soaked up. Her bedroom reeked of stale alcohol, and she had a bucket near the head of the bed.

"Jesus Christ, Maya," I groaned at her state of disrepair.

"Get out," she mumbled with one eye open.

"You need to get your shit together. We're on Prius and we've got work to do."

Maya moaned in disapproval and turned away onto her side. "Open the doors and let them out."

"Don't you want to come see it?"

She shook her head. "Nah, we'll be back in a couple months."

"What about you, spaceman? Would you like to see the most beautiful place in the galaxy?" I asked Marcus.

"Yes! Let's go swimming!"

"No. Baby, baby." Maya turned back. "Stay with Mama. You don't need to go out there."

"Mommy, I want to see! Please."

"I'll look after him, Maya. He won't leave my side. Promise. Get yourself cleaned up in the meantime."

"Ugh. Fine. Stay out of the water though," Maya demanded with no reasoning.

"But I want to swim!"

"Come on, buddy." I picked him up and put him on my shoulders. "Let's go for a little adventure."

By the time we made our way to the rear exit, there was an awkward standoff taking place between our fresh batch of colonists and the men who had already made Prius their home.

After a brief negotiation, the settlers agreed to take on a hundred new recruits for their village but were adamant that no women could stay. It seems the years had brought them balance and they feared what might happen if things were to change.

We unloaded ten percent of the supplies on board, which gave the men enough materials to begin new construction and tools to complete the projects. We also left them a few hundred pounds of Tess' fabrics so they could make new clothes, some updated fishing gear, and other odds and ends.

Before we moved on to find a home for the rest of our miners, I took Marcus on a stroll north along the lake. We removed our shoes and walked in the warm clear water, and I explained how one day soon we would go swimming and fishing there.

I plotted out a piece of land in the region where I had searched for Emilia all those years ago and pictured my future cabin built along the tree line with the lake in my backyard.

Whatever the next leg of our journey was, I hoped what Maya was hiding wouldn't take us too long to get done. She said the mission would last a year or two when we set out, and it had already been almost five months. I didn't want to wait much longer before getting to work on the future I was promised.

We returned to the Omaha, said farewell to my old bunkmates, filled our water storage, and found a rich piece of land fifty miles to the west that had similar access to fresh water. The rest of our passengers unloaded another tenth of our supplies so that they had enough to get themselves started, and I left them there with the promise that we would return and help them build a great community.

Marcus and I made our way back to the ship and were greeted by an unexpected sight when we reached the bridge—Anthony, Georgia, Seamus, and Michael gathered around. Maya had taken my usual seat and was fumbling around with the headset as if testing her ability to pilot the craft.

"What are you guys doing? We're done here and about to leave," I said, confused.

"We didn't spend all that time breaking rocks and nearly dying on Triax so that we could retire without a little wealth," Anthony explained.

"What wealth? You're welcome to anything on board when we return. There's not much else we can offer you."

"That's not what she said." Michael pointed to Maya. "We want in on that loot. You ain't keeping it all for yourself."

"What the hell is going on here, Maya?" I asked.

"How do you work this damn thing?" Maya responded as she removed the headset.

"Move. I fly the ship."

"Just show me how, bro. I've made all the arrangements I need to. You can stay and get started on building your house. We got this."

"What? No! You asked me to be your pilot and we're not done. I'm going to see this through."

I should have just packed my things, unloaded all the supplies, and let Maya go off to do whatever it was that she was up to. I didn't even really want to leave.

I had come this far though, and I wasn't about to bail on Maya, Tess, or Marcus, especially after spending so much time wondering what this was all for. There was no way I was leaving until I had my answers.

"Just tell me what's going on, Maya. For Christ's sake, what is the big secret?"

"I am not in the mood for this bullshit," Maya said, rubbing her temples. "Either show me how to do it or shut up and take us to orbit."

"Fine. Move," I responded coldly. I slid into my spot, put on the headset, and had us hovering in orbit within minutes. "Where to?" I asked.

"I have coordinates."

I removed the headset and reactivated Gregory. "You do?" I probed, wanting to lead her back into our argument, but knowing better than to waste my breath.

"Gregory?" Maya prompted.

"Yes. Commander?"

"I want you to take us to . . ." She looked at the notepad app on her phone. "12.837464523 by -3.927364972."

"Computing. Plotting. Course." Gregory processed his new orders. "Arrival in. Two thousand. Four hundred. And. Ninety-six. Earth. Hours. Fifty-two. Earth. Minutes."

Maya punched the numbers into the calculator on her phone and announced, "One hundred and four days. Hopefully, we won't be there long, but I'm not making any promises. I'm not leaving until Tess is on board, and I'm not taking requests. If any of that bothers you, this is your last chance to bounce." She only briefly looked at me. "Alright then. No whining." She turned her attention back to giving orders. "Gregory, max speed. Until further instruction, disable all command prompts except those that come from me."

"Yes. Commander."

I shot Maya a concerning look, but she wasn't interested in explaining her shift to total control over the Omaha.

"Come on, baby." Maya picked Marcus up, averting her gaze from mine, and exited the bridge as though her actions were warranted. Seamus was shortly behind her, followed by the rest of Maya's newly adopted Demo Dawgs.

She might not be willing to fill me in, but she had clearly promised them something, and I had a better chance of wringing info out of them than my stubborn friend.

Once Maya had retired to her quarters, I made my move. My old friends on Prius had gifted me some freshly caught bluefish, and I let the wafting scent of a hot meal fill the mess hall in order to draw in my compatriots.

"Yer stinkin up a feast?" Georgia asked as she passed through.

"Plenty for everyone. Today's catch won't last too long, so we might as well enjoy it. Get the others and we'll crack a bottle," I invited.

The four of them sat, filled their glasses, and munched on my snack mix while I made the final preparations for dinner. I plated each of them a good-sized filet and cut open a few cans of fruits and veggies for sides.

"Gardetto's, man. The best the prison store had to offer. Can't believe I'm alive long enough to eat them again," Anthony said.

"It's not Gardetto's," Michael interjected.

"I know my snacks."

"There's nuts in there. Gardetto's ain't got no nuts."

"That's my special mix," I informed them. "Gardetto's with all the pretzels removed and mixed nuts added."

"That should be illegal," Seamus joked. "You need the pretzels to soak up all the booze."

"Dats what dem teensie bread fingers er for," Georgia defended my concoction. "I like er wit dem nuts in der."

"Oh, I know you like them nuts," Anthony ribbed her, drawing a chuckle from Seamus.

"Forget the snacks. Try the fish," I told them.

We ate in silence for a few minutes, which is usually the sign of a well-prepared meal. Before anyone could pick a topic, I began driving the conversation in the direction I wanted it to go. "So, you guys had the choice between Prius and the mines, right? Why did you choose the mines?"

"Two years of work in exchange for a clean slate? Seemed a good deal to me," Seamus said.

"How long were you guys supposed to serve?" I turned to Anthony and Georgia.

"Same. Two years. Not only would we get to be together, but we'd have our ten-year sentences commuted," Anthony replied. "Only had a few months left when the last freighter set out, and then they just stopped coming."

"What about you?" I asked Michael.

"Long. Real long."

"I imagine if you knew what Prius was like, all of you would have chosen differently."

"Well, hell yeah," Anthony answered for everyone.

"You had a second chance today. Why not just stay there?" I finally got around to the question I wanted to ask.

"What's the matter?" Michael shot back with an edge in his voice. "Afraid we're going to pilfer too much of your cut?"

"My cut of what?"

"The bounty. The loot," Anthony jumped in.

"I wasn't aware that there was any. I'm just looking for my friend Tess and following orders."

"So she's your friend?" Seamus perked up.

"Fer da fiddiest time, dats der Commanda's girl."

I smirked at Georgia. "What she said. Tess is Maya's wife. We're supposed to be rendezvousing to pick her up, but I don't know where, and I haven't been promised any loot."

"She's actually, seriously, really married? To another lady?" Seamus asked, disappointed.

"That woman wouldn't touch you even if she were as straight as an arrow and needed dick like air," Michael insulted him and then poured himself a fresh drink.

"Well, I want my cut of the loot," I announced. "What is it? How much?"

"What it is, I can't say," Anthony answered. "'How much' is a lot, according to the commander."

"Live like Kings," Michael daydreamed.

There wasn't much to learn from those humble would-be pirates. They knew as little as I did, though I was certain Maya wasn't misleading them. She had no reason to make empty promises, which confirmed to me that something big was going on.

Why did she insist on shutting me out, though? It was driving me insane, and I had no choice but to ride it out. After a multi-month voyage to Triax, what was one more round to get to the truth?

Still, I preferred when it was just Maya, Marcus, and me. The new additions to our crew made it harder to keep Maya on track. I was partially to blame for enabling her, but I had no intention of making it a nightly ritual. No illegal substances remained on board after our big blowout, and, in hindsight, I wish that would have solved the sobriety problem.

Maya's drinking became worse by the day. Mornings where I wasn't looking after Marcus because his mother was nursing a hangover became rare. This wasn't happy-fun-time drinking, either. I knew depression when I saw it, and every day that passed without Tess' comforting presence drove Maya deeper into the bottle. The sad part was, we hadn't even seen the worst of it yet.

The journey seemed to take forever. Even though the occupancy of the Omaha had doubled in size, I felt more alone than ever. There were some fun times sprinkled in there, and I enjoyed filling the role of parent for Marcus, but more than anything, I just wanted it to end. I'd accept any answer to this mystery, assuming it came fast and got us turned around for Prius.

There wasn't much good to come from those few months besides polishing off more of Tess' library of classics, learning the best way to prepare meals from canned goods, and taking the time to let a sick beard grow in again. Maya helped Georgia with her thick southern accent, Anthony and Michael challenged each other to a ninety-day bodybuilding competition, and Seamus followed Maya around like a lovesick puppy dog. Hardly anything to write home about.

When we finally arrived, Maya took to the bridge with Marcus while the rest of us waited patiently in the mess hall for further instructions. Marcus was first to return and ran up to me, proclaiming, "I heard Mommy! Mommy is coming!"

"That's nice," I patronized the lad.

Maya was a few minutes behind him, her eyes puffy and red. "I'm sorry," she said as she paused to keep her voice from shaking. "It's going to be a while so you might as well get comfortable."

"How long?" Michael pressed, and for the first time, I was happy to have him around for his rude bluntness. Finally, I wouldn't be the only one posing questions to Maya.

"A while," Maya barked. "Take up a new hobby. I warned you and you came anyways."

I wanted to ask how long and what for, but I knew better, and it seemed everyone else did as well.

"I'll be in my quarters," Maya ended the conversation before taking Marcus by the hand to drag him along with her.

Having no revelation wasn't surprising, and this time I didn't mind. There was only one way for Maya to receive information out in the middle of nowhere, and I had the vague notion of an opportunity presenting itself. I gave it an hour for everyone to get caught up in their own business again and then snuck my way to the bridge.

I climbed into my station and tapped the screen to activate Gregory.

"Good evening, Gregory."

"Good. Evening. Chop."

"What command prompts are unavailable at this time?"

"Navigation. Manual. Controls. Star. Charts. System. Overrides—"

"How about communications?" I interrupted.

"Communications. Available. For. Commander. Fontaine. Only."

"How about if I just want to monitor transmissions?"

"Unavailable."

"What about internal communications? Can I use the intercom system?"

"Yes."

"Can I monitor live audio?"

"No. Requires. Command. Prompt."

"What about records? Is there anything in the archives? Any older recorded messages you can play back?"

"Yes. Archive. Allowed."

"Excellent." I leaned forward hopefully. "How many archived communications are there?"

"One. Received. Transmission."

"Play it, Gregory," I ordered.

I no longer felt guilt for invading Maya's privacy. After spending eight months flying blind on the Omaha, I had a right to know what we were doing. Not because I feared impending danger or needed to prepare for what came next, but because we should have been a team.

Gregory's screen went blank, the audio crackled, and then Tess' words appeared, written out in an alien script by the AI system as they were played aloud.

"Maya, if you're receiving this message, today is January 29th, 2040. I can only assume that by the time you are hearing this, a few months have passed with my voice bouncing around in the darkness of space waiting for you.

"We arrived five days ago, and while I would never pretend to comprehend the horrors that war has shown you, I do now think that I understand. Since arriving, I've seen and have been forced to participate in atrocities that will haunt me for as long as I live. Worse yet, I carry the horrible burden of knowing that all this blood is on my hands.

"I don't want you to worry about me. Being separated is hard enough. They seem to have bought our divorce story, and though there are some suspicions surrounding me, I don't believe I'm in any danger. The greatest risk comes in sending this message, and as so, I will not be able to contact you again until it's time for action.

"Things are moving slowly at the moment. There have been some unforeseen complications with early production, and I have my doubts about our ability to meet our first shipment deadline of January 1st of next year. Don't panic if my next message falls behind schedule. Stick to the plan. I'll give you a few days' notice before the first freighter is set to launch."

Tess paused for the first time as her bubbling emotions hit the surface. "It can't come fast enough. I miss you so much and I can't wait to get back to you. I miss my . . ." She paused again, audibly sniffling. "I miss my little boy." Tess began crying through her words, and I felt like a dick for invading her privacy.

"Marcus, baby, if you can hear me, Mommy misses you so much. I know I'm missing everything. I bet you're learning and talking and growing up so fast. I'm going to make this up to you, I promise. I'll never miss another birthday. I know you can't understand what is happening, but I hope that when you do, you'll be able to forgive me.

"Please Maya, don't let him forget me. There are children here, and they're so alone and terrified without their parents. I'm grateful that Marcus is safe with you, but I can't help but feel that I've abandoned him. He must never experience terrors like those these poor children are living through. I don't know what we can do against such heavy security and with a glut of collateral damage on the line, but we can't just leave them."

She sighed before continuing. "Stay safe out there, babe. We'll be together soon, and then we'll figure this all out. I love you so much. Marcus, baby, Mommy loves you."

"End. Of. Transmission," Gregory stated as Tess' message faded away.

My God, what had Tess gotten us involved in? It seemed she had a planned extraction for herself in about a year, but there was no way that would be the end of this. I couldn't imagine Maya ever turning away if children were being harmed.

I knew almost no details, and even my blood was boiling. If it came to it, I'd happily throw myself into the fire and sacrifice my Prius retirement for a chance to live up to the legacies of my friends who so bravely came before me.

There was still a year to kill though, and I was genuinely concerned about Maya. Receiving bad news and becoming emotional was the last thing she needed in the middle of a relapse. Spending the next twelve months without her anchor may very well tear her apart.

Dealing with my own depression was one thing, but keeping myself afloat while also holding Maya's head above water was another. I wasn't equipped to handle this. I don't think she'd ever lost a fight, and it seemed the only person who could defeat her was herself.

This was not going to be fun.

Chapter 10

High Stakes

Malik Emmanuel: 2337

Alexis was dragged away by Maddox and his goons, and while I was scared for her safety amid so much confusion, I was glad it wasn't the other way around. If Kade was capable of horrible things, I'd rather have him inflict them upon me than my friend. I could take it.

"It's going to be you or her," Kade warned. "Whoever cracks first has a chance of surviving this. I'll give you your life if you give me what I want. It's a fair trade. Hell, I might even help you save your friend just because I'm a morally upstanding citizen."

"You're a liar and a thug," I charged.

"I don't have to lie. When you've got power, the truth can't hurt you. If I tell you that I'll help you save Alexis, I mean it. On my honor, not that you'd know anything about that."

"I'm not helping you do anything. If you think I'll trade her life for my own, you're wrong. You can torture me, threaten me, even kill me. I've been through worse hells than any pain you can conjure."

Double-A and Dixie grabbed me under the arms, but before they could do anything terrible, Kade gave multiple clicks of his tongue to dissuade them.

"Boss?" Double-A asked. "I bet a couple days of a full-body desert sunburn changes his mind."

"No, no, no," Kade replied with annoyed frustration.

"We could dope him up," Dixie suggested. "Cram him full of flyer and he'll talk our ears off. Tell us anything we want to hear and more."

"Did you hear the man?" Kade asked rhetorically. "He's 'been through a lot,'" he mocked. "No, we're not going to hurt him, no matter how much he deserves it."

"What about Dani?" Taz asked. "If we start breaking things, he might sing the song we want to hear."

"That's a little more bloodthirsty than your usual fare, fat man. What's troubling you? You threatened by our new arrival?" Kade toyed with him. "Dani will face her own judgment for her betrayal. I think our Traveler friend here has gotten the wrong impression about our organization. Let's not reinforce that."

Both Double-A and Dixie released me. If nothing else, Kade's people respected him. It was clear that his word was gospel and they followed his commands to the letter. He frightened me, but he wasn't the brute he appeared to be. There was a softness under the surface, and he was far more calculating and tempered than he let on.

"So what? I'm free to go?" I asked, confused.

"No. You'll never leave this place without my blessing. Reginald, clear a room and lock him in there. It's been a long night. I need sleep, and our friend needs some time to think. Trigger, you're on duty. Go find Stacks, get him cleaned up, and make sure he understands that he still has a job to do. Watch Dani until I decide what to do with her. Everyone else, get some rest," he ordered.

Reginald led me to the staircase and to the upper level. But before he could push me in, Kade interrupted with a final word. "Oh, and Malik," he shouted from below, "Offer stands. If you change your mind and want to make a trade, we can discuss marshaling our forces for an Alexis jailbreak. Think about it," he suggested before turning his back and walking out.

Reginald shoved me into the room and locked the door behind him. I pressed my ear to the door, listening until the pirate crew cleared out. After a few minutes, I tried yanking at the handle and then kicking where the door met the frame, but it was pointless. The only light came from creases in the log walls, just enough to reveal a poorly constructed bed with sheets that stunk of sweat. Under normal circumstances, I would never have slept there, but I was exhausted, and the smallest part of me hoped that when I closed my eyes I'd find my family in a dream again.

I woke hours later, unsure if I'd dreamt at all or just forgotten the details. Restless, I thrashed against the sheets like a junkie desperate for a fix. After three hundred years of lucid dreaming, regular sleep to me was like serving a nonalcoholic beer to an experienced drinker. It may have tasted similar, but it only made me crave the euphoric state of the real thing even more.

My main concern should have been to escape, find the dropship, return to orbit, and save Alexis. Yet all I could think about was getting home and sitting on the porch with my family. If I could somehow slip away, I didn't know if I'd be able to resist the temptation of my sleep tube before carrying out my duties.

I paced the room, my thoughts bouncing between my cravings and the enigma of Vocury. I didn't understand a darn thing that was going on or where these people had come from, yet that mystery barely registered compared to the itch gnawing at me.

After a couple hours of wearing holes in the floor, the locks clanked and the door cracked open. Double-A poked his head in and tossed two pills onto the floor. "Eat up," he snickered. "Kade will be back soon, and you're going to need your strength for what he has planned."

He closed the door, but I didn't hear the locks click into place. Either he was too high to remember or, even if I left my room, they thought I would have nowhere to go. I listened by the door again to find that it was surprisingly quiet.

Cracking it open, I snuck a peek and saw that Double-A was the only one around. He wandered just out of my line of sight toward Dani's destroyed cage for a moment and then back toward the exit before suddenly shouting "Taz!" and running out down the street.

That was my chance. I pocketed the pills, slipped through the door, and rushed down the stairs. Leaning around the corner to ensure the coast was clear, I hustled around the side of Dani's to avoid the main street. Sticking close to the bungalows, I raced from one to the next, using them for cover. The villagers were away in the Citadel, but they wouldn't be gone for much longer. I needed to get out fast—clear of the town and into the desert before they returned.

I stayed off the wooden sidewalks whenever possible to keep my escape unnoticed, and within minutes I was trudging through the desert sludge once again. The heat and punishing gravity would make for a difficult trek, but I was going to have to keep up the pace.

I spent half of the journey walking backwards to keep an eye out for anyone pursuing me and went out of my way to walk around the dunes that the wind had formed and dried out into permanent clay structures. Once the hills were at my back, they created a visual barrier for any of the pirates who would inevitably be looking for me.

Sweat trickled down my forehead as my stomach growled with vacant anger. I would have gladly walked an extra three miles for a single helping of Lydia's hashbrown casserole. Instead, all I had to mimic that palette pleasure was those stupid pills. Sure, they hydrated the body and somehow provided enough calories to fuel me, but they were a poor substitute for a proper home-cooked meal.

The dry desert air left my mouth parched as I struggled to muster enough saliva to swallow the pills. I had to get the heck off this planet, and it was becoming painfully clear why the locals felt the same way. Kade had to be drunk on power to want to continue living in such a miserable environment.

When I was about an hour out from the village, I dared to climb one of the clay dunes that ascended twenty feet above the surface, giving me a better line of sight. I paused there for a few minutes, scanning the horizon for anyone following my trail.

The ease of my escape made me chuckle, but the amusement faded fast when I spotted Double-A's head bobbing up a hundred yards away as he crested his own dune. I froze, watching as he seemed to notice me and quickly ducked back out of sight. The second he disappeared, I mirrored his move, concealing myself behind the dune.

I slid down the backside of the hill, staying low as I crawled along its base to get a look at my pursuers. For fifteen minutes, I sat motionless, watching. Taz briefly showed himself, but neither of them made a move to chase me down. It became clear that they weren't trying to capture me at all, and if I hadn't seen them, I would have led them straight to the dropship.

I calculated the distance they were keeping between us, and wondered how lucky I would have to be to get within a hundred feet of my ship before having to break into a full sprint. Would they realize a game was afoot and catch me before I could release the lower hatch, climb in, and lock it behind me?

It wasn't worth the risk. If the ship fell into Kade's hands, I might never get back to my sleep pod. I felt dirty for having such a selfish main concern, but I couldn't help myself.

There was no point in taking another step toward my goal. I had already led them a third of the way there, and the last thing I needed to do was give them any more direction for their search.

Breaking out of cover, I headed directly toward their hiding spot, climbed up the dune they were crouching behind, slid down its far side, and landed near their feet. Then, I brushed off the dust, got to my feet, and began walking back toward town without uttering a word to either of them.

"Hey! Stop," Taz ordered, confused. He waddled his way after me and tackled me around the waist when he caught me. "It's not back that way. Keep going. We . . . we freed you," he lied unconvincingly.

"Get up." Double-A kicked at the both of us. "I should have left your fat ass behind," he chastised Taz.

"Me? He saw you first. Tell him, Traveler."

Double-A grabbed me by the shirt, pulled me to my feet, and pushed me in the direction I was previously headed. "Move it. You're going to finish what you've started, or I'm going to bury you out here."

"No, you're not," I snapped. "You going to kill me and go back and tell your boss that you lost me? That you let me get away?"

Taz scratched at his neck like a fiend. "Come on, man. Help a brother out. I'm low on pills, man, and I need this payday."

"Take him back to Kade," Double-A ordered. "I'll keep searching in the direction he was headed. It's out there somewhere, and I'll last through the cool of the evening."

"Good idea, but the reverse. You take him back to Kade and I'll keep searching," Taz bickered.

"Fellas, this is pointless. Yes, you're right, there's a ship out there, but we walked for days before we reached town," I lied. "I'm not even entirely sure I can find it again. It's got a cloaking device, so I'd literally have to walk right into it," I lied even more to dissuade them from continuing the search. "You can waste your time if you'd like, but I'm not going to help you."

I started walking back to town, not wanting to look back to see if they were going to continue. If they both kept on from where we were, they may very well stumble upon the ship within a few hours if they got lucky. Thankfully, they both traipsed after me to share in the shame of their failure, though they did argue about it the entire way back.

As we approached Dani's, I was shocked at the sight that greeted me. They had stripped Dani down to nothing but a cloth covering her pelvis, shaved her head raw, and strapped her to a wooden peg like a horse tied up outside a saloon. My heart sank as I examined her sunburned, blistered skin, the result of just one day's exposure. She was in that predicament because of me, and if her suffering continued to escalate, Kade might very well break me.

I approached the single swinging door and stood aside with a coy grin as I forced Double-A and Taz to enter in front of me. Kade perked up from his poker game and excitedly raised his voice. "Did you get it?"

"No, they did not," I answered, entering behind them. "That was a nice little trick, though. I may have underestimated you."

"You morons." Kade slapped Taz upside his head. "All you had to do was stay quiet and follow this scum."

I passed right by them and sat down in Kade's vacated seat at the poker table. "Let's put all our cards on the table, whaddaya say?" I said with a chuckle at my well-placed turn of phrase.

"You obviously know I have a ship, and it's clear that you all want it—and that you'll never get it without my help. You misplayed your hand and read me wrong when you thought I'd turn it over to you to save my skin."

"You're quickly becoming unbearable. Perhaps I should hurt you after all," Kade threatened.

I truly didn't know where all his animosity for me came from. I may have thrown a wrench into his world, but I hadn't personally done anything to offend him. If anything, I felt as though I had displayed the type of honorable characteristics that appealed to a man of his nature, yet he seemed to irrationally hate me all the same.

"You're obviously never going to let me leave, and I'm never going to lead you to the ship. Neither of us is happy in that scenario, so I have a proposition for you, seeing as how you're a man of honorable trade with an appreciation for gambling."

"Go on." Kade waved his hand in frustration. "You don't need to make a big dramatization about it."

"Let's settle things on the felt." I tapped the table. "If you win, I'll take you to the ship under two conditions: you and your crew help me free Alexis, and I want a promise that the other Travelers, as you'd call them, will be safe. If I win, you free Dani immediately and return her former possessions and status. Her debt is paid."

"I call bullshit," Kade scoffed. "You don't care about her. What's your angle here?"

"Don't have one. Just trying to make the best of a bad situation."

"You don't have any currency."

"I'll play on Dani's bank."

Kade laughed. "What's hers is already mine."

"I'm making you an insane offer here. The only thing you're risking is returning that poor woman to her life. All you have to do is beat me, and you get everything you want."

He defiantly crossed his arms. "No. Her punishment stands. You don't have the authority to break it." He was clearly afraid of getting played in front of his crew, and he was wise enough to know that I was up to something.

"Fine," I said as I cleared my throat and raised my voice. "Challenge."

Everyone laughed, even the dopers who were half-popped on their nightly meds. Kade grabbed the back of my shirt, lifted me out of my seat, and lightly pushed me aside.

"You must be delirious from exposure," he snickered. "I bet you could get the votes from my crew to back that fight, but it wouldn't present them with more than three seconds of entertainment. Don't be ridiculous."

"Call it a gamesmanship challenge."

Kade's crew all stared him down as his honor was called into question again, and he didn't have any other option but to accept.

"Stacks, get up," he ordered as he crumbled under peer pressure. Stacks scraped his hand across the top of the table to clear his pills off into his free hand and made a spot for me. Having his brains beat in days earlier seemed to have put him in his place.

"Sit." Kade pointed to the chair. "Do you know how to play?"

"I love games," I said as I shuffled the deck. "If you fellas had Monopoly, I'd clean out every last one of you."

"What determines when you've won or lost?"

"Pick three of your best players to sit with us. We'll play until one of you has either cleaned me out or I have doubled my stack."

"Stacks, go get him a hundred out of Dani's reserves. Only the good stuff. Flyers, sleepers, regenerators, and the like. Dixie, Trigger, and Double-A—you're in the game."

Taz approached the table and stood over my shoulder, practically drooling as Stacks laid out a multicolored assortment of opiates and narcotics in front of me. "Let me play, boss," he begged as he eyed the high he so desperately wanted.

"No. You're fiending. If you want to earn it, either run tricks or go find someone to sell yourself to," Kade dismissed him before turning his attention to his three chosen players. "You keep what you win. Don't let me down."

"One pill ante, and one to bring it in. No blinds and no limits," I announced as I placed the deck near Dixie so she could cut it.

Kade quickly reached across the table and grabbed my hand before I could release the deck. "Look at me. If I catch you cheating, you lose the bet, and I'll take your hands. Understood?" This wasn't an intimidation tactic. He was dead serious, and I nodded in compliance.

The game was slow for the first few orbits, and it had me slightly concerned. If Kade and his crew were going to avoid each other and only specifically target me, I was going to have a rough go of it. Every hand was costing me one of my pills, and I was going to have to get in there, mix it up, and take down pots if I was going to avoid a dwindling stack. The last situation I wanted to be in was having a stack of twenty-eight and needing to win a coin flip to stay alive.

If I lost, Alexis' life could genuinely be in danger. I didn't doubt that Kade would hold true to his word, but what if he was right about the Citadelians? What if they got word that Kade had beat them to their prize and they no longer had use for Alexis? I had to put those thoughts out of my mind, calm my nerves, and focus on the task at hand.

If I wanted the game flow to move in my direction, I was going to need to run some table talk and get my opponents to battle each other rather than just wait for spots against me.

"Trigger, is it?" I asked the Hispanic-looking maniac who was slightly lower on pills than the rest of us. "Did you notice how Kade picked Dixie first when he needed three players?"

"Don't listen to his needling," Kade warned him. "I picked the three best. Period." To me, he said, "Are you going to check or bet?"

"I'll check," I said and then continued antagonizing Trigger. "I don't know. There was a bit of a pause between each choice. Dixie was the first name that came to mind. She's winning. You're not. There might be something to that."

"I bet five," Dixie announced and confidently took my bait. "That's because I'm better than this dope."

"You are not," Trigger fired back. "You play scared. Always have. You're a nit and everybody knows it."

"Well, I guess I'll fold to the nit's bet then," I said as I pushed my cards into the muck and the small pot to Dixie.

"Dumbass!" Dixie barked at Trigger. "You're influencing his actions. Shut your mouth."

"Everybody chill," Kade warned again, like a father approaching the "I'll turn this car around" moment of a family road trip.

Double-A picked up the deck and began shuffling. "She might be predictable, but she's got more game than you, Trig. A safer bet for this situation."

"Bitch, shut up. You were picked last. Shouldn't have been picked at all. We'd already have his damn ship if it wasn't for you and fat boy."

"I've got more pills than you do," Double-A added to the tension as he dealt the next hand.

Kade folded and I looked down to find two black jacks. "Play for three," I announced as I slid three purple tabs toward the pot.

"Make it nine," Dixie followed up with the first preflop three-bet we had seen.

Trigger looked down at his cards and when he showed some pause, Dixie got in his ear. "If I play so tight, then maybe you should fold. I know you've got something under there. Let's see who the nit is now," she goaded him.

"I call," Trigger obliged, with Double-A folding behind him.

I considered going for the four-bet seeing as how I was out of position and would rather just take the pot down without a fight, but I decided to play it cautiously. I didn't want to run into Dixie's big hands, and I couldn't have her folding if she was on the verge of running a big bluff to stuff into Trigger's face. "Alright, I'm in," I said as I pushed in six more pills.

The flop fell nine of spades, five of spades, and the four of diamonds, and I decided to check my over pair to Dixie, counting on her continuation bet.

"Ten," she said confidently, and I picked up a bit of a tell. When she raised preflop, she bet with some of the orange pills that matched the narcotics in my stack, but when she followed up on the flop, she bet ten of the sustainers. She wasn't nearly as confident as she was letting on, and

Trigger either picked up on the same or he had a big hand. He made the call, and the action was back on me.

I would have loved to slow-walk the dog and let Dixie continue bluffing it off, but it was too risky letting the turn card fall. I had to be happy with taking the pot down and be willing to fold if I got reraised, especially if it came from Trigger.

"Let's make it forty," I declared, causing everyone at the table to pucker up. Reginald and Stacks were already watching closely, but the growing size of the pot caught the attention of even the commoners who weren't too stoned to understand what was going on.

"Son. Of. A. Bitch," Dixie postured while shifting her attention from me in front of her to Trigger on her left who was yet to act behind her. "Yeah, I fold."

"Nit," Trigger taunted. "You were trying to show off. You should have checked."

"Play your hand, dummy." Dixie shot back.

"What do you have left back there?" Trigger asked me. It was clearly a probe to gauge my reaction, so rather than give any information away, I sat quietly. "Kade? What does he have over there?"

"Looks like roughly sixty," Kade reported.

"Twenty-seven plus five, plus ten, plus ten, plus forty," Trigger counted out the pot, seemingly making sure that if he gave up now, the pot wouldn't push me over the two hundred mark. "Alright, alright. I fold," he finally surrendered. "What did you have?" he asked. I flicked my cards toward the muck and was shocked when Trigger reached out to try to turn them over.

Kade had him by the wrist in an instant and I could tell he was squeezing hard based on the pained expression on Trigger's face. "Don't fuck about, Trig," he spit as he pushed Trigger's hand away from my cards. Kade might have been a lot of things, but his honor held true even when the stakes were high.

I counted down my stack and found myself sitting with one hundred and forty-nine pills. I was halfway home and only needed one more decent pot to finish things. I was feeling confident as Kade took his turn shuffling, and that high kept rolling when I looked down to find the ace of diamonds and the jack of hearts as my holding. "Three," I declared my standard opening size as the first to act.

It folded around to Double-A who called, followed by Kade who quietly slid twelve yellow tabs forward as a raise. I probably should have given up at that point seeing as how I was out of position and had no read on him, but I was feeling the spirit of the moment.

"I call. I'll teach you a little lesson too, son," I boasted.

Kade instantly saw red. "What the fuck did you call me?"

"Nothing." I smirked, trying to downplay his anger.

"No. You called me son."

"I didn't mean anything by it. I'm just having fun."

Double-A folded his hand, and it was time to take a flop, but Kade had no interest in moving on.

"I'm not your fucking son, got that? Watch your mouth."

I had clearly hit a nerve. "Okay, okay. I'm sorry," I backpedaled. That was a pressure point I'd have to tickle delicately in the future, if at all.

Kade stared at me for a moment before dropping a flop featuring the king of diamonds, the jack of clubs, and the three of hearts. I checked my middle pair over to him and he wasted no time betting thirty-two audibly, which was exactly the size of the pot. It was a calculated sizing that I had no idea how to read, but my hand was too big to fold to a single bet. It wasn't until I had called that Kade counted out the pills to add to the pot.

We took the six of hearts on the turn, and I checked it over to him again. Without hesitation he announced ninety-six and didn't bother counting out the pills to push toward the pot. His bet put me nearly all in, and there was nothing I could do but fold my second pair.

Kade peeked back at his cards and exposed the ace of clubs. "You didn't teach me shit, old man," he barked. My comment had clearly gotten under his skin, and it had caused him to make a critical error.

Kade thought showing the ace would create doubt in my mind over what he was holding, but I found it to be rather obvious. He had been playing cautiously, and the line he took with that hand screamed either pocket Aces or Ace-King. Losing that pot brought me back down to where I started, but the information I gained was paramount.

I knew the spot I was looking for and I carefully navigated the next hour waiting for it. I made a harmless comment to Double-A and intentionally and arrogantly referred to him as "son." I wanted Kade to hear that slur tossed out again, and hoped that even when not directed at him, it would encourage him to step out of line in an attempt to humble me once more.

Two hands later I found Kade stepping off the ledge to battle with me again. I raised to three with the king and queen of diamonds, and Kade once again re-raised to twelve. I made the standard call with nothing but a passing glance between the two of us and Kade presented a flop of the queen of hearts, nine of diamonds, and two of diamonds. I had basically flopped gin, and rather than lead out and run off my customer, I slipped it over to Kade with a casual check.

Kade counted out twenty-nine pills and announced his bet as such while pushing them forward. My read was that he was trying to recreate his show of strength from earlier to chase me off, but he wasn't paying as close attention as I was.

He was using the physical size of his bet to add to his aggressive nature, and I was going to have to decide just how calculating of a man he was. I could have easily check-raised him all-in considering my holdings, but if he was running a bluff, I had to give him the chance to hang himself.

I was praying for a diamond to hit the turn and make life easy, but that's rarely the way it goes in poker. Instead, the nine of clubs fell, and I would be in a world of hurt if he was pressing with second pair and had stumbled his way into trips. I checked it over once more, and within seconds Kade had cupped both hands behind his stack, pushed it forward as an uncounted bet, and declared, "All in."

In any normal game back home, this would be an automatic call. My hand was underrepped, I had a big draw to go along with top pair, and I had specifically set up my opponent for this move. There were lives hanging in the balance this time though, and if I was wrong, there was no telling what fate might wait for Dani and Alexis.

I went deep into the tank to replay the action and Kade's previous big bets. Everything had me screaming to call, but when I finally spoke the words, my voice trembled.

"I call."

There's a moment in poker that is even better than making a huge hand or coolering an opponent for a massive pot. Two little words spoken sheepishly can make a hero call feel legendary. I had heard them before, but they have never felt more satisfying than when Kade spoke them.

"Good call."

He tapped the table, burned a card, and turned the five of spades as the river. I didn't make my flush, but it didn't matter. I really wanted to see just how thin he was bluffing, but I took the gentleman's route and tabled my hand first.

"That's good. Nice hand," he said solemnly, accepting the defeat with honor.

I raked in the pot and counted my stack. Two hundred and sixteen total pills. I sat back to supervise a secondary count by Dixie who confirmed that the game was won, and Kade instantly kept true to his word.

"Stacks, go cut Dani down and cover her up. Trigger, see what you can do to repair her cage. Dixie, take a run at putting the swinging door back on the hinges," he ordered before quietly walking off.

Stacks walked a blanket-covered Dani inside, escorting her upstairs to her room, and the rest of the crew either went to work on their assignments or joined the villagers in feeding their addictions.

I didn't see Dani for a couple of days after that, but she sent Monkey to set me up with my own room. When she did finally reemerge from hiding and recovering, she came out in the middle of the day when everyone was either away on work duty or sleeping.

I was out in the street testing how diligently Kade still had his men watching me when Dani pushed through her newly repaired double doors. She leaned against the post where she had been tied up days earlier and seemed to be struggling to start a conversation.

"You're welcome," I said earnestly.

"I was going to sell you to the Citadelians," she confessed.

"I know."

"I've always had to kind of look out for myself. Sometimes even doing terrible things to others to preemptively cover my ass. I can't say that I remember anyone ever coming to my rescue before. There's not a lot of charity around here."

"You know, I was really low myself at one point. I had someone that I barely knew who picked me up when I was down, too. Don't miss your chance to repay the favor when the opportunity presents itself."

"You can keep room and board here for free as long as you want. The pills you won are yours, and you can keep the hundred from credit as well. Kade's not going to let you take work in the city, but I can make sure you get a seat in the game. If you're going to get by out here, you'll need to earn, and the poker table seems like your best bet. That's as charitable as I can be . . . and it still doesn't feel like enough."

"It's enough," I assured her.

I may have saved Dani's skin, but she was directly responsible for keeping me alive. I had a roof over my head, a sober friend in a position of leverage, and a decent bankroll of pills to get me started. The living conditions on Vocury were tough, but something archaic in me relished the chance to live like a western hustler of old.

I ended up doing quite well for myself at the poker table. I was raking in a steady stream of opiates, and I could trade one of them for enough hydrator and sustainer to last me a week. The majority of the village was so helplessly hooked on them that it drove the trade prices through the roof. I did what I had to do to survive, but I never felt great about watching those people lose themselves to addiction. If they didn't have to work to keep their high, I imagined that most of them would have nothing resembling any kind of structure in their lives.

I made a few friends around town and kept a careful alliance with members of Kade's crew. Some of them were decent people when I got to know them, but I struggled to trust those who were more forgone to addiction than others.

Kade was the only person I didn't have some kind of relationship with. He never spoke to me and seldom sat at the table when I was playing. I kept my distance and counted each day he didn't move against me a small victory. I assumed he was simply biding his time, waiting for the right moment to make his next strategic play for the ship. A man with his power and drive rarely gives up easily.

A month had gone by, and I had settled in comfortably. Even better, Dani had been to the Citadel and brought back good news about Alexis—she was healthy and being treated like royalty for some reason. Although my sleep was far from perfect, knowing that my friend was safe and our cargo remained undisturbed in the upper atmosphere brought me a great sense of relief. Neither of us seemed to be in any imminent danger, but the question of what humans were even doing on the planet still remained.

I tried to squeeze out what information I could, but the residents of Vocury were as specific as I was incurious. Once the shock had worn off that there were humans there, I didn't really care where they came from or put much stock into their fairy tales of our arrival.

I would have gladly listened to anyone speaking logically about the matter, but most of them still looked at me as if I were a ghost from the stories their parents used to tell them before bed. Answers would be better pursued by Alexis than myself, and I imagined that she was playing detective in the Citadel to uncover their secrets and would one day return to deliver them.

As content as I was to make a living hustling, I still longed to return to my sleep tube every night. All it took was a couple of months of moving on and I couldn't even picture the faces of Lydia, Marcus, or Maisie anymore.

Every day that went by made it less and less likely that I'd ever get back to them again, and at some point, I stopped trying. It was time to accept my life on Vocury and make the best of it until an opportunity presented itself. To do so, I was going to need to maintain some kind of relationship with Kade and come to an understanding with him.

Late one night after a poker game, most of the riffraff had either retired for the evening or were so zonked out on opiates that they were zombies. Dani was cleaning up after her guests, and she had extinguished two of her four lanterns before Kade gave her a dirty look to keep the lights on. She returned to her cage to pack everything away for the night, and I passed off my winnings through the bars so she could add them to her stash for safekeeping.

As I walked by Kade toward the staircase to head to my room, he surprisingly spoke to me. He looked uncharacteristically disheveled and spoke with a drunken slur. "Nothing's born here, nothing grows here, nothing dies here, and no one leaves here."

"Okay?" I had no idea how to respond to that.

He stood and slightly stumbled toward one of the tables where he plopped down in a seat. "Come. Entertain a drunken old man," he said, oddly inviting. I sighed and took the seat across from him. He dropped two white tablets onto the table and slid them in my direction. "Drink up."

"What is this?"

"Buzzer. First Generation. Very hard to come by."

"No thanks. I'm not going to end up like everyone else around here."

"Relax, you prude. They were discontinued for 'a lack of dependency properties,' I believe is how they put it. The only thing they can make you suffer is a hangover."

I took him at his word and tossed the pair of pills down my gullet, doing my best to keep the small talk going. "You don't use any of the other stuff, do you?"

"Only what I need to. I refuse to be a slave to Amaar's concoctions because I've seen the worst side of it. You know, these stupid things took my mother," he said as he unloaded a handful of pills onto the tabletop. "She was fierce and fearless. A true pirate queen. She'd probably rule all these parts if she weren't such a junkie."

"Where is she now?"

"For fuck's sake," he drunkenly slurred. "I'm trying to talk to you. Don't interrupt me."

"Why are you always like this? I've played by your rules and abided by your customs since I arrived. You treat everyone else around here with respect if it's given first, but not me."

"Because you're the spirit of a man I figuratively buried in the desert of my past. Your arrival is a reminder that he once existed."

That was the perfect moment for my buzz to kick in, because the only appropriate response to such a vague statement was to laugh.

"Ha, ha, ha. No offense, I'm sorry," I said, raising my hand playfully, "but what the heck are you talking about?"

I was relieved when his own buzz drove him to laugh along rather than act out in anger.

"It's stupid. I know it's stupid," he said with a resigned chuckle. "You don't know the half of it. It's that ridiculous prophecy." He added a spooky "OoOoOo" for effect.

"You know how parents tell their kids stories when they're little? People don't realize just how impressionable children are and the damage those fairy tales can do. It's a trade-off, like anything else. The child sleeps soundly because they believe in something good, but they lose that peace and more when they grow up and discover that everything is shit."

"I feel you." I nodded along as my extremities began to tingle. "I know all about that game. Went through something similar myself."

"What bedtime story did your parents tell you?"

I sat quietly for a moment as I contemplated the spiritual journey I had been on. My faith had been tested, and it hadn't been strong enough to stand on its own. The groundwork that my parents had laid for me needed to be reinforced by the friends I made along the way. Perhaps Kade could experience the same.

"They taught me about God and faith and holy scripture. It was easy to believe as a child. As an adult, though? Not so much when life threw tragedy at me. But I was lucky. I had good friends and a purpose. They brought me back around. How about you?"

"My father left when I was very young. My mother is the only one who told me stories, and she crafted them in defense of dear old daddy. I don't know if she believed the gibberish that she fed me. She was hardened by his absence. She didn't need to keep hope alive that he would return one day. Or hell, maybe she did. Maybe he's the reason she carelessly overmedicates. He could also be dead for all I know, and Mom was just softening the blow for me all those years. I've had plenty of time to consider the possibilities," he ran on.

"Anyway, she told me about the Travelers, like most parents did their children. Our 'saviors' would one day arrive to make everyone's dreams come true," he mocked the prophecy.

"She told me that my dad would come back with them. That we'd all be happy together. That everything would be good again, along with all kinds of other radical notions depending on how long it took her to get me to fall asleep. I had actually forgotten about my father for the most part until you showed up—the spirit I buried in the desert, come back to haunt me."

"I think I get it now. Sorry I jarred some trauma loose for you. You going to stop taking it out on me now that it's out in the open?"

He scoffed. "Ehhh. You don't understand."

"I don't? You don't know anything about me. I've lost more than you can possibly imagine."

"Oh yeah? Impress me with your scars" he taunted.

I contemplated how much to share for a minute.

"I had a wife and two kids. I was a devoted husband, and one heck of a great dad. I never got to say goodbye, nor did I have the chance to bury any of them. Then," I said, my voice rising with anger, "just as I'm learning to cope, I drop into a damn vegetative dream state and find myself living out multiple lifetimes with them, only to have them ripped away again."

I gritted my teeth and pointed to the sky, "They're up there. Right up there waiting for me. And I can't go back to them because your goons follow me everywhere and I don't trust your intentions for our craft and crew."

Before Kade could respond with what I could only assume would be a slurred heartfelt pitch for his trustworthiness, a strange female voice cut in from the shadows. "Feed Kade a couple more buzzers. He'll pass out, and you could easily outrun his doped-up gang at this time of night."

I focused my blurry vision on the doorway and tipped over backwards when I saw who was speaking.

A Praxi woman strode in, walking on two legs while her third pushed open the wooden swinging doors. She wore a sleek, black rubber-like spacesuit that extended up to her neck, only a helmet missing to complete the outfit.

"Speak of the past and it shall appear," Kade said as he stood in a shaky defensive position.

It wasn't until she spoke again that I realized I was hearing her voice in my ears and not my head.

"Hey, baby boy. Long time. Rumor has it you caught something valuable but don't know what to do with it," her mouth moved and surprisingly produced words.

"She's talking like us. Why is the Gray talking like us?" I asked hysterically. Unlike my previous encounters with the Praxi, I couldn't sense her intent or emotions.

"Her name is Gia, and most times I wish she'd shut up," Kade answered.

"Should I challenge you for old time's sake, or are you capable of behaving like an adult?" Gia asked him.

"Turn around, go back to your outcasts, and never return to my lands."

"You really should hear me out. Some old friends of yours are on their way to make contact with the other Traveler. If they're successful, they may acquire the ship, and then we won't need you anymore. But you and me, baby boy—we could get there first."

"Who's the backup plan? You? Or them? It must be them, right?" Kade asked. "Their chances of getting past the Citadel guard are next to zero. The stink of desperation is all over you."

"I'm sorry," I interjected. "But who says I'm helping either of you?"

Gia looked at me curiously. "You're Malik, right? Would you like to hear my proposition?" I replied affirmatively, just as Kade answered negatively, which only made me want to hear what she had to say even more. "There are more colonists on your ship, yes? And seeded human embryos?"

"How could you possibly know that?"

"It's been foretold. Have you been here long enough to examine the plight of the people on this planet? Have you seen what they've become?"

"I've seen enough to know that, while I'm a permanent resident, I don't want to end up like them."

"What if I told you that I could save them?"

"Oh, fucking stop it," Kade growled. "You had your chance."

"I think I can help them," Gia continued gently. "All I need is the cells from a single untainted human fetus and we could develop a cure to break the chains of dependency, even defeat the hold of regenerator."

"I should rip your mechanical voice box from your throat for those lies," Kade threatened.

"I could save your mother," Gia suggested softly, a hint of sadness in her eyes.

"Don't," Kade warned. "Don't you dare manipulate me! The Traveler is mine, the ship stays in orbit, and nobody leaves."

Gia turned her attention to me and her tone shifted from gentle persuasion to mild anger. "Did he tell you what he would do if you turned your craft over to him? He'd strip it down, trade the valuable components and any of the passengers who held value to the Citadelians, and destroy the rest, trapping everyone here forever."

Kade didn't refute her, and I took that as an indictment of his intentions.

"And what is it you're proposing?" I asked her.

"A compromise. Kade gets the ship and components, and I get the passengers and embryos."

"Oh cool," I said sarcastically. "You two get what you want, and I get what, exactly? A pat on the back?"

"What's your price?"

"I want one of the sleep tubes with enough power to run it indefinitely and—"

"We don't use power out here," Kade interrupted. "It's not our way."

Gia raised a hand to silence him and encouraged me to continue. "And?"

"I want a trade facilitated to free Alexis, and I want a guarantee that every colonist on board will be given the chance to live freely and safely under their own rule of law."

"They can go live in the Citadel if they want," Kade continued to argue. "Anyone who puts their feet on the sand belongs to me and lives by our rules."

"You won't even know they're here," I answered his concerns. "There are enough supplies on board to construct an entirely new colony anywhere else on the surface. They'll never bother you."

Kade defiantly crossed his arms. "No deal. Everything nonliving on board is mine, and that includes the supplies."

Gia approached him on three legs, then shifted to stand several feet above him on two. She leaned down, her posture imposing, and asked, "You going to make me do this?"

"I say no deal and that's final," Kade declared.

"Fine. I challenge."

"Everyone's asleep. There's no one here to vote," Kade contended.

"They don't need to. You can accept and we'll settle this in the street."

Kade had no response, which was essentially a rejection of Gia's challenge. That made it twice now that I had witnessed him shrink in the face of a foe he feared. Gia pivoted to balancing on one leg and used both free arms to violently shove Kade backwards. He stumbled, fell over a chair, and crashed through a table which was upended from the blow. She quickly mounted over top of him, one leg on each side, and wrapped her free hand around his throat. "Challenge," she repeated to him once more.

"You're not going to kill me," Kade choked out. "You'll reignite the war, and even if I'm dead, I've got you outnumbered. You'd never make it to Malik's ship, and that's even if he'd help a cold-blooded murderer."

"Oh, he'll help, alright. I'll introduce him to your mother. Let him see what this place has done to her."

"Get your damn hands off me!" Kade battled back, trying to pull her grip from his throat. "Fine! Fine. Fine, I'll take your stupid bargain."

Gia released him and let his head drop carelessly to the floor. "Sober up," she suggested with a judgmental tone before turning to me. "Whaddaya say, spaceman? Do we have a deal?"

Chapter 11

Mama is Coming Home
Maya Fontaine: 2040

I cracked one eye open and was immediately hit by the harsh glare of fluorescent lights. I quickly shut it again, wondering if I'd forgotten to turn off the lights or if Marcus had unsuccessfully tried to wake me. I peeled my dried-out tongue off the roof of my mouth and swallowed hard but couldn't muster any saliva.

"Marcus, baby, you in here?" I probed, hoping for no answer.

My head was ringing, my stomach was in knots, and my breath tasted like someone had used my mouth as an ashtray. I likely wouldn't be getting out of bed for another hour if it weren't for my body urging me to purge the last of the booze rotting in my gut. Crawling to the bathroom was pathetic enough, and I didn't want my son to watch me do it again.

When Marcus didn't answer, I presumed Chop was looking after him. I rolled out of bed onto all fours, noting that I had manage to remove only one sock before passing out.

Groaning, I dragged myself along the cold tile toward the toilet. I pulled myself upright and gagged as I discovered dried vomit on the seat from the night before. My fingers fumbled with the flush lever, but before I could clear my previous bodily evacuation, I had another.

The next stop was the shower, and I barely had the strength to flop over the tub wall. I kicked at the hot water dial until it turned and then cried out in agony as freezing water hit me for the first seven seconds before it warmed.

What the hell was I doing? Was this the hundredth morning that had started like this? The two hundredth? Not only had I lost track of the days since Tess' transmission, but I had no grasp on hours either. I kept track of time based on morning being whenever I woke, and evening was when I was too drunk to stand.

The time I spent lying in the shower, the water washing away the previous night's mistakes, were my only moments of clarity. I'd tell myself I had to stop this; I couldn't keep drinking so much. That I needed to be a better mother, the strong one my family relied on. That Marcus needed me . . . But those rational thoughts would only last a few minutes before the darkness would creep back in again.

I shouldn't have to be doing this all on my own. I knew I wasn't cut out to be a mother. Tess shouldn't have left me! Goddammit, I hated everyone. I hated myself. I just wanted to escape and be alone and forget. I was built for war, and life had sent me on a deployment where the enemy was myself.

I eventually climbed out of the shower without even having properly washed myself. Finally on my feet, I pulled on a cotton robe and returned to my bedroom, only to find Marcus sitting on my bed.

Any hope I had for pulling myself together evaporated the second I saw his sad eyes. He had watched me destroy myself night after night—falling down, cursing, throwing up, crying. I had neglected him, and the only remedy I had for my self-hatred was another drink.

"Good morning, baby," I said softly.

"I want Mommy," he cried and wiped tears from his eyes.

"I'm right here, baby. I'm right here," I tried to comfort him.

"No, I want Mommy!"

In my combat days, I had been stabbed twice and shot once. The pain of all three of those wounds combined was a scratch in contrast to the agony of hearing Marcus cry out for Tess. I wasn't enough for him. He didn't need or want me, and he'd probably be better off without this awful version of myself I had become.

"She's coming home soon, baby," I promised, but my words offered no comfort. I reached under my bed, grabbed my flask, and stared at it momentarily before twisting off the cap.

I couldn't stop myself. Even as I took the first sip of the day, I knew what a horrible mistake I was making. Every drink caused me to hate myself more, and in turn, fermented a deeper drunken isolation. My alcoholism had become a self-fulfilling prophecy from which there was no escape.

My days of zero-consequences partying were over. I remember being young and thinking that having a drink in my hand was sexy, cool, and fun. I never worried about getting hooked on it because I didn't use it to escape.

Booze to me had been like food to a wine snob. Where some people would pair the perfect red with a rib eye or a white with grilled salmon and rice, I was matching drugs with my alcohol. Smoking a blunt with the fellas worked well with a case of beer. An acid trip house party required a cooler full of jungle juice. A Friday night eight ball paired perfectly with a bottle of vodka.

Getting drunk was my baseline, and I'd rarely even feel the effects of the alcohol until the drugs had worn off. Those youthful misadventures had made me underestimate alcohol.

After an hour of self-loathing and nursing a hangover, I made myself presentable.

"Come on, baby. Let's get you some breakfast."

"I ate with Uncle Chop," Marcus answered.

"Okay, then let's get Mommy some breakfast."

Marcus followed me to the mess hall, which was thankfully empty. I was never particularly excited to speak to anyone in the morning, but my need for isolation was especially bad today. I warmed a bowl of oatmeal, popped a can of peaches, and poured a shot of whiskey into my cup of coffee.

I stirred a spoon through my soupy breakfast while holding half of my face in my hand trying to stave off nausea. Marcus sat across from me, a silent witness to what a piece of garbage I had become. His judgmental eyes tore a hole through me, but at least it was quiet.

I hadn't even taken my first bite when Ranbir entered and ruined the ambiance. He filled his drink, grabbed a granola bar, and took a seat next to Marcus across from me.

"We should talk, Maya."

"No, we shouldn't," I replied, avoiding all eye contact.

"Everyone is restless, and we want to know what's going on."

"For the millionth time, bro, I'm not talking about this."

Chop got up, rubbed Marcus' head, picked him up, and carried him to the hallway. "Go find Georgia. She has a surprise for you," he instructed him. This was not going to be good.

Chop stood in the doorway, twenty feet between us, and stared me down. "You don't want to tell me what's going on? That's fine. Whatever it is you're hiding is going to come out sooner or later. You've got to stop this other bullshit, though."

I didn't reply, but I did look him in the eye, held the contact, and then looked away in shame.

"You can't keep up this pace, Maya. Your drinking has gotten out of control. I love your son. He's a great kid, and I'm happy to help, but I am not his father."

"No one asked you to be."

"You ask me to every single day without ever having to speak a word. Did you know Marcus is up for hours before you've rolled out of bed every day? The other day, he asked me why Mommy is so sick. He—"

"Shut. The fuck. Up!" I yelled. "I don't want to hear it from you. I'm all alone here! I'd like to see you do any better."

For a brief moment, I saw the hurt flash across his face before it hardened. "You're alone?" he asked, his tone sharp and accusatory.

"Yes! Malik left me. Tess left me, and I don't even know if she's okay. So, sorry if you've had to get Marcus some cereal or whatever. I know it must be a terrible burden," I finished sarcastically.

"I'm just trying to help you."

"Well, I don't want your help! You have no idea what I'm going through."

"I don't?!" His voice surged with anger. "I don't know what you're going through?" Chop pushed off the wall he had been leaning against, stalking toward me. "You mope around this ship every day, drinking yourself stupid, and threatening anyone who dares try to intercede. You think you're the only one in pain? You think you're the only one who's alone? Tess is coming back! But you know who isn't? Gio. Gio is dead. Emilia is dead! Don't you dare tell me that I don't know pain."

He had every right to be mad, and I felt like such a pathetic piece of shit for letting my depression destroy me when Ranbir could have easily spiraled too. I hated his righteous indignation though, and I could only imagine what his rage would be like once he discovered what had happened to Gio's body.

In the heat of the moment, I wanted to tell him just to have it over with, but Tess had been adamant that the confession come from her. If he knew, the Omaha might have had two drunks instead of one, and the mood was tense enough already.

Rather than fight him any further or admit that he was right, I quietly got up and walked away. In my sick mind, all I needed was a drink and some time alone to think. We didn't speak for days, and while I did make more of an effort to drag my hungover ass out of bed at an earlier hour, I completely failed at sobriety.

Every day, I made my way to the bridge, hoping that Tess' next message would arrive and end this nightmare. But hope died over and over again each time Gregory informed me that there was no news. The more desperate I became, the more frequently I checked, until I couldn't shake the fear that no word would ever come, and that something awful had happened to Tess.

Then one day, it finally happened—Tess had sent word. She was alive. I bolted through the Omaha, heart pounding, until I found Marcus playing catch with Ranbir. For the first time in months, I'd have something positive to share.

"I think we've finally got something to feel good about," I said, scooping Marcus up to take him back to the bridge with me.

"Is it Tess?" Ranbir asked, his tone hopeful.

"Sit tight. I'm gonna get the skinny and report back," I yelled over my shoulder as I raced toward the bridge.

I climbed into the seat, pulled Marcus into my lap, and instructed Gregory, "Alright dumby, play the message."

"Yes. Commander."

"It's December 29th, 2040," Tess' voice crackled through the speaker. The wave of emotion hit me harder than I expected. My eyes instantly welled up, my heart raced, and butterflies went to war in my belly.

"Production stayed on schedule after all, and the first freighter is set to launch in three days. I'm unsure if there's any accompanying crew, but we can't take any chances. I'm going to stow away in one of the containers during the early morning hours, and I won't make a move until you free me."

I breathed a sigh of relief.

"I'm coming home!" Tess cried jubilantly. "It's been four hundred and eighty-two days since I last saw you guys, and honestly, it's felt like ten years. I'm actually coming home, babe! I have one last thing to do here, and once it's done, I'll only have mere hours to count down before I see your faces again.

"I hope you've given some thought to extending our mission. The second freighter should be leaving about a year from now, and there's a decent chance that the entire staff will be on board. If they pack their bags and head for Earth, they'll almost certainly take the children with them. If they don't, or the team stays behind, we're going to have to figure something out. I've grown attached and leaving them now is hard enough. I can't turn my back on them forever.

"Okay, I've gotta go. I love you guys so much! I can't wait to see you again. Three days, babe. Be ready and stay vigilant. See you soon. Tess out."

I hugged Marcus tight as we both cried. "Mommy's coming home. Finally. We're going to be okay."

I'd never felt relief like that before. Hearing Tess' voice was like being choppered out of a hot landing zone when I'd thought I had been left behind. Not only was she alive and well, but she was finally coming home.

No more drinking, I told myself. Not a single drop. I was going to need some pretty serious rehab to overcome my physical addiction, but with Tess back anchoring my life, I could get through anything.

"Let's go tell Uncle Chop," I said, setting Marcus down as he ran ahead. I made a quick stop in the mess hall, ditched the cocktail I was carrying, and poured myself a strong cup of coffee.

By the time I caught up with everyone, I could hear my baby boy announcing, "Mommy's coming home!"

"We're on?" Michael asked.

"We're on," I echoed. "There's a freighter headed our way in three days, and Tess is going to be on it."

"And the loot on board is ours?" Anthony jumped in.

"As much as you can carry," I promised.

I stepped away from everyone and jerked my head for Ranbir to talk with me in private.

"Tess? It was Tess? This is the end?" he asked.

"Indeed. She's coming home."

"That's great, Maya. I'm happy for you." He smiled.

"Look man, I really don't know what to say."

"Then don't. It's okay. I think I know what you would say, and that's enough."

I wanted to hug the man, but I lovingly slapped his upper arm instead. "Someday, when I've had more practice saying sorry, we'll run this back."

I spent the next three days getting clean, working out, and trying to be more social. I even let Georgia cut my hair into the same faux hawk I had when I first met Tess. I had major issues with getting to sleep at night, and I experienced some pretty nasty withdrawals, but I was becoming who I wished I was again.

Tess would almost certainly be disappointed to discover how far I had fallen off the wagon without her around, but I had every intention of telling her regardless. She knew who I was when we got together. I'd never lied to her before, and I wasn't about to start now.

I was the first one to the bridge the morning of that third day. I sipped my coffee as I watched the visual readout and kept Gregory on his toes. Marcus sat on the floor turning the pages of a picture book, and we hummed along as I played my Best of Big Hair Ballads playlist.

With a slight change in lyrics, I sang along with Ozzy to Marcus, "I could be right. I could be wrong. It hurts so bad, and it's been so long. Mama is coming home."

I could hear Chop humming the guitars before he even entered. "Lost and found, and turned around," he sang as he joined us and climbed into his usual station.

"Nothing yet?" he asked.

"It's early." I answered. "Gregory, remove all control restrictions," I ordered.

"Yes. Commander."

Chop lifted an eyebrow. "Anything special I should I know?"

"We're looking for a Praxi freighter moving through this sector. You're going to catch up to it, disable the gravity drive without doing too much damage, and then dock. No muss, no fuss."

"That easy?"

"Hell of a lot easier than all this waiting."

Michael, Anthony, Georgia, and Seamus joined us on the bridge a short time later, and our collective anxiety grew by the minute. The moment didn't mean nearly as much to them as it did to me, but they had spent a year waiting for some promised action and they were ready for it to be delivered.

Ranbir had his headgear on for ninety minutes, scanning the region, before he perked up. "Got something here," he announced. "Praxi freighter and she's incoming fast."

The ship was on us in a flash, and if we hadn't been watching for it, she would have zipped right past us.

"Stay on her!" I ordered.

"We're fine. Already closing in."

I watched my view screen as the grey dot in the distance became larger. Even at gravity-bending speeds, our target was outmatched in every way by the Omaha.

"Watch your shots, cowboy. We need it disabled, not destroyed."

"Maya! Would you stop? I've got this," Ranbir grumbled.

As much as Chop was stressing me out, he managed to bring us within firing distance and used a tight red beam to cut through the gravity field. The laser burned a hole in the right rear quadrant, and after a few seconds of precision cutting, the freighter lost all forward power, drifting on momentum alone.

We shot past it at full speed, but Ranbir corrected and brought us back around within visual range again. We took a position in the ship's path and used low-frequency gravity waves to bring her to a floating stop in space.

With the ship disabled, Ranbir began the docking process, entering through the rear cargo hatch and parking the Omaha in the belly of our target. I jumped out of my seat, left the visual display on so Marcus could watch, and then lifted him into my vacated spot.

"Stay right here and watch the screen," I instructed him.

"I want to come! I want to see Mommy!"

"Marcus!" my voice rose. "No. It could be dangerous. You're going to wait right here and do as you're told. We'll be right back. I promise, baby."

The six of us raced to the rear hatch and I unholstered my sidearm for the first time in ages. "I don't know what we're up against here, so stay behind me and keep cool. Remember, my lady is in there somewhere, so let's not make a mess of things."

Ranbir disengaged the drop door, and I cautiously stepped forward. The dim lighting in the cargo bay offered little concealment, so I signaled my team to stay put and proceeded alone.

I carefully checked the area around the Omaha, making a full circuit of the ship. The bay was cluttered with metallic crates, and while most were anchored to the walls, a few had shifted and tipped when we knocked out the gravity drive. Satisfied, I completed my rotation and gave the green light for everyone to join me in the search.

While Ranbir protected my six as we checked the forward airlock, the others were more interested in inspecting their loot. Michael pried at the latches of one of the damaged crates, and his friends hovered over his shoulder like vultures waiting for their prize. The top came free and clanged loudly as it collided with the floor before the contents spilled out.

"Oh my God," Seamus exclaimed. He looked from crate to crate as though to calculate how much cargo was stored within and announced, "We've hit it big, people."

They could have it all as far as I was concerned. Tess was somewhere on this ship, and until I had her in my arms again, everything else could wait.

I pulled on the handles of several locker doors near the entrance to the forward decks, but they were all sealed. I could shoot them off if I had to, but it wouldn't make sense for Tess to be locked in. If she was in an enclosure, she wouldn't have been able to lock the door behind her.

By the fifth door I inspected, I was becoming frustrated, only to be surprised when it gave way. "Tess?" I called softly as I peeled the door open and exposed its contents to the light. I took three quick steps back and nearly fell over when I saw what was inside. My instinct was to raise my firearm, but a rush of relief, sadness, and fear that wasn't my own washed over me at once.

"Wh-what the fuck is this?"

Stuffed inside the locker were two adolescent Praxi children. Both stood on two legs, the taller of the children with its third arm wrapped around the other. Ranbir's jaw hung open as his eyes shifted from one to the other, and then over to me.

"They're Praxi!" he exclaimed.

"Yeah, I can see that! "What are you two doing here?" I interrogated them.

"She saved us," a young male voice spoke into my mind, and I could feel his connection to Tess. "Are you Maya?" he questioned.

They slowly exited the tight space, the smaller of the two collapsing to their knees. Ranbir quickly moved to help, lifting the young alien back to their feet, and I noticed a bandage on the left side of their head and a larger gauze pad taped across their throat.

"What happened to you?" Ranbir asked, but the wounded child didn't answer.

"Humans happened to us," the male responded with palpable rage. He stared at me and repeated, "Are you Maya?"

"Yes. You've seen Tess? Where is she?"

"We bring a message from her. And instructions."

"You're going to be okay," Ranbir comforted the smaller one nearby, holding them in his arms. "Maya, there's something wrong with them. Something terrible has happened," he babbled with confusion. "What the hell is going on?"

Chapter 12

Ho-ly Shit

Alexis X: 2337

A few days had passed since I took Dr. Amaar's wonder drug, and I saw him again for a post-treatment checkup. He drew another blood sample and ran a few tests to confirm that my reproductive system had returned to working condition while I nervously paced up and down the hallways. I hoped for the best but expected the worst. Could the doctor actually heal me, or was this miracle cure a charade to get to the Wolf Moon?

The doc poked his head out of the lab, and I quickly scampered down the hallway toward him. "I have your results," he announced as he held the door open for me to enter. He motioned for me to sit, but I was far too much of a nervous wreck to be still. I chewed my thumbnail and blurted out, "Let's have it. I can take it. It didn't work, did it?"

"It's fine, of course," he said, as though the positive outcome was expected. "Cellular regeneration has begun, your scar tissue is in retreat, and your 'lady bits,' as you called them, are as healthy as any woman in her reproductive prime."

My eyes instantly welled up and I could do nothing but laugh with joy to stop from crying. "You're serious? Just like that, and I'm good? I could hug you!" Before he could dissuade me, I had my arms wrapped around him.

"You're very welcome. Your body should eject any of the excess spliced regenerator over the next week or so now that its job is done, and once it's run its course, you should be in tip-top shape."

"I almost can't believe it. I gave up hope a long time ago. Where I come from, there was very little the medical community could do for me."

He snatched the opportunity to pivot the conversation to what he wanted. "You could help them, Alexis. You have the power to bring my work to your world." I wasn't surprised that it had only taken Dr. Amaar a whole two seconds to broach the subject, but I was annoyed.

I pumped the brakes on his advances. "Let's see if this really works before we go getting too ahead of ourselves."

"On that subject, might I make a suggestion?"

"Weird, but okay."

"I see that you and Taj have been getting along well . . . He's a healthy young man. He's handsome, he has social status, and he seems quite taken with you."

"Double weird." I raised an eyebrow at him. "Did you just ask me to bang your son?"

"I'm not sure I would phrase it that way, but . . . you're seeking results, yes? There's no easier way to get them than the old-fashioned way. I think you two have positive energy together and would make each other quite happy. Admittedly, I also believe Taj would be a better mate and father than I ever was."

There was some real pain and regret behind his eyes, and it was enough to make me empathetic despite his awkward proposal. As arranged marriages go, I could have done a lot worse.

"He's a good man, and so are you," I comforted him. "I'll make my own relationship and reproductive decisions, though."

"Of course. I'm here if you need anything further, and I encourage you to attend to whatever diligence you must in order to bring our transaction to completion. Please do give serious thought to bringing your ship to the surface."

"I will. I haven't forgotten about you. I'll let you know if I have any questions or when I've made a decision," I said before leaving.

I wandered around the halls of the lab, peering through the glass to watch experiments I couldn't understand just to procrastinate going upstairs. I knew what I wanted to do, but I needed to think things through before acting on impulse for a change. Taj was up in our suite of rooms waiting for me to return, and while I wanted to become pregnant more than anything, I hadn't even had time to process my newfound fertility.

Was it safe for me to become pregnant in this situation? What kind of life would I be making for my child? Shouldn't I at least be in love before creating life? These were responsible questions to pose to oneself, and the type that I had never bothered with before.

Had I been more thoughtful when I was a younger woman, I never would have had an abortion at nineteen—because I wouldn't have become pregnant in the first place.

For years, I tried not to think about it, and it was rather easy when I thought I could get pregnant anytime I pleased. I was just a dumb kid who had better things to do and wasn't ready to be a mother; terminating the pregnancy just felt like the right thing to do.

In my mind, I'd one day fall in love, get married, and then start my family. It was only once I discovered that I had become infertile, and that my abortion was the most likely source of my condition, that my decisions started to haunt me.

For a decade, I told myself that it was just a standard medical procedure—something that hundreds of thousands of women go through every year. Guilt is funny, though. Some believe that a resentful pit in your stomach is karma explaining that you broke an invisible moral code and should feel sick about it.

The truth is, guilt doesn't play by those rules. It's always lurking, ready to strike from within, but it only holds as much power as you grant it. I had managed to avoid mine right up until the moment infertility was no longer my burden; then it hit me like a dump truck, and I was the one behind the wheel. The thought of having a child was now forcing me to confront the one I had chosen not to have in my past.

I wiped away tears produced by equal parts remorse and joy. I had been given a second chance, and if it weren't for my ticking biological clock, Malik being alone in the desert, and a shipload of sleeping colonists waiting on me, I would have taken things slow. I didn't know Taj well, but I was attracted to him, and he had been kind to me.

In a perfect world, we would have dated for months before making any decisions about children, but I didn't have that kind of time. Beyond everything else, I also really wanted to see if the doc truly was a miracle worker.

Haste, it seems, has a way of placing mistakes firmly in one's blind spot.

Two men in lab coats stepped out of Amaar's office, briefly locking eyes with me before looking away. They exchanged a glance and headed toward the elevator, their quiet conversation falling silent as I approached, like a couple of gossiping schoolgirls. "It's okay, fellas. All anyone does around here is whisper as I pass."

The doors opened, both men boarded quietly, and I awkwardly joined them. "I'm going to fart in here as soon as the doors close," I joked to break the ice.

"No you're not, 'cause you're getting out."

"We're going down, and you're not permitted," the other informed me.

"You're not permitted," I mocked his authoritarian tone. I grit my teeth, closed one eye, and raised my ass slightly as I mustered the tiniest of farts before exiting the elevator. I laughed, but they weren't nearly as impressed by my foul humor. Even though they were dicks, it was all fun and games—until I spotted the vial poking out of the top of one of their breast pockets.

Marked with an "X," it was half full of what I assumed was leftover blood from my checkup with Dr. Amaar. I tried to prevent the shaft doors from closing, but the men were already on their way down to who knows where before I could intervene.

What they were doing down there, and what my blood had to do with it, was anyone's guess. If I had the means, I would've pulled on that thread and chased whatever it unraveled, but it was baby-making season, and I had a license to breed.

I waited for the next lift, rode it to the surface, and mentally prepared myself to climb six flights of stairs, hoping I'd still have enough energy to bump uglies with Taj once I got up there. After exiting the elevator, I weaved my way through the swarm of day workers, their blank faces resembling zombies as they queued for their ride underground.

Hyping myself up, I made the short walk to the stairwell just to find a surprise waiting for me: Taj, half asleep on the first step, with his head resting on a propped-up arm.

"Weird place for a nap," I joked.

"I thought you might like a lift."

I smirked. "Assume the position."

He hunched over, and I mounted his back, resuming our usual method for conquering the stairs.

"So, how was the checkup? Are you healthy?"

"It seems so, but I won't know until there's a bun in the oven."

"Excuse me?"

"It's a figure of speech. It means . . ." I paused as I retreated from sharing the details of my fertility struggles. "Ah, never mind."

He didn't need to know my past to be a part of my future.

Taj carried me to the sixth floor, and I walked the rest of the way. I wasn't the only one who was going to need to keep their energy up, and I figured I'd spare him hoofing me to the room so he could catch his breath before I took it away again.

Once inside, I took his hand and led him toward the bedroom I had been sleeping in.

"Are you going back to bed?" he asked.

"Sort of," I replied as I interlocked our fingers.

"Oh." Taj swallowed hard, his hand fidgeting nervously in mine.

I had his shirt untucked and pulled over his head before I even bothered to kiss him. I liked Taj a lot, and there was certainly all kinds of potential between us, but at that moment I was all business. It's not like he minded, either. If we were racing to see who could strip down first, he would have won by a country mile.

I stood on my tippy-toes to kiss him as he kicked off his pants one leg at a time, I listened while he awkwardly tried to deliver a self-conscious PSA before things got carried away.

"I have to warn you . . ."

"Shhhh." I kissed him again.

"It's been a while."

"I don't care," I continued, falling back onto the bed and pulling him down with me.

***

Taj wasn't lying. It had been a while. Probably no longer than my current dry spell, but certainly more evident. In my younger years, I'd convince myself that I was just too hot to handle whenever a partner would pull the old two-pump dump. I didn't fool myself with flattery this time around when I had his toes curling and eyes rolling after only three minutes.

He rolled off of me, his face flushed with shame, and turned slightly away to avoid eye contact he was incapable of making. "Sorry," was all he could muster.

"Relax, champ. The first trip back to the gym is always the hardest. I'll get you back into game shape in no time."

He turned back to face me, his cheeks red with the most adorable blush. He was my sweet little fuck puppy, and I must have been the girl of his dreams. He didn't know it yet, but his sex life was about to go from nonexistent to thriving. There's not a man on Earth or Vocury who would argue with the regimen I was about to offer.

I popped out of bed to grab my phone and then rejoined him under the covers so we could share earbuds.

"How about a little auditory aphrodisiac?" I offered and began playing Desperado by Rihanna. His head bobbed and his face lit up with a smile and more joy than could be contained. "Yeaaahhhh, I know you're feeling that."

We had a second go of it after a short break and six-song playlist, and then another romp that evening before bed. I wasn't sure where my cycle was after coming out of hypersleep, so my best plan was to get after it like bunnies in the spring. I wasn't concerned with the quality of sex at first, but if we were going to enjoy ourselves, I was going to teach him some tricks.

He learned fast, quick to dismiss his pride and self-consciousness. Most men couldn't conquer their sexual hang-ups so easily, but Taj was a proper student. He never became defensive, and he was always willing to follow my lead. I suppose he didn't want to say or do anything to dissuade my abnormally high sex drive in fear that I'd go searching for a more apt partner, but there was no one I'd rather be with.

I had no interest in anyone else, sexually or socially. Taj was incredibly sweet to me, and when we weren't exploring in bed, I was entertaining him with the customs of Earth.

I educated him on our arts, the history of music and television, and the vast culinary delights of all of our different cultures. We'd often walk along the thoroughfare and share our growing distaste for the Citadel and our desire to travel to Earth. There was much for him to experience, and I wished we could sneak away to the ship, pick up Malik, and leave Vocury behind.

Unfortunately, that path was nothing more than a fantasy.

My menstrual cycle remained in flux, and I wasn't sure whether to attribute that to hundreds of years of hypersleep or if it was a delayed effect of Dr. Amaar's treatment for my infertility. Either way, I was stuck on Vocury indefinitely until I had some answers.

As much as I would have loved to offer an escape to the tortured residents, I had my sights set on becoming a mother. If I could achieve that dream, I would be permanently anchoring myself and my child to the Citadel. To be honest, that didn't sound so bad.

Taj and I went right along enjoying each other's company for months. We plowed ahead with reckless abandon, both as lovers and friends, and I told myself that pregnant or not, once my CE phone battery died, I would reconvene with the doctor about bringing the Wolf Moon to the surface.

I wasn't particularly excited about Amaar's brand of pharmaceuticals joining the litany of addictive meds on the market back home, but how much worse could they really be?

Had I not met Taj and become obsessed with my chance at a miracle, I almost certainly would've stuck my curious nose where it didn't belong far earlier and discovered that things were, in fact, far worse than I ever imagined.

I was put back on the Conspiriousity train one night after we had finished a raucous session in bed.

I hit pause on the music to conserve my battery, which was now down to eight percent. With the amount of sex we had been having and the connection we had forged, I figured I could relax on cloaking my motives toward getting pregnant. Men who were trying to avoid becoming fathers don't deposit that many payloads into the baby bank, so I assumed Taj was just as comfortable with the intended consequences of intercourse as I was.

"Oh!" I exclaimed with a sudden idea, lifting my feet into the air.

"What position is this now?" he laughed as he blindly felt his way up my thigh. "I'm not ready to go again yet."

"It's a trick. I've always wondered if it works. You force the swimmers in the right direction."

"I'm not sure that works, but it's a pointless exercise anyway. If a method to achieve pregnancy existed, my people would have discovered it."

"What do you mean?"

"You don't know? Alexis, have you seen a single child since you've been here?"

I dropped my feet to the bed and turned to face him with intrigue. "No. I mean, I had noticed . . . but I didn't really think anything of it. I don't know."

"There hasn't been a single birth on Vocury in my entire life. I was the last."

"What? Shut up!"

Taj stared blankly ahead and swallowed nervously. My eyes were wide, and I was on the edge of my seat for him to continue, but he didn't say a word.

"Well? Come on!"

"Have I offended you?"

"What? No, of course not."

"You told me to shut up so . . ."

"'Shut up' doesn't mean stop talking. It's a turn of phrase. In this case—oh, never mind. Would you please tell me what the hell is going on?"

"I don't know if now is the best time to get into it. I'd like to, you know, go at it again, and this might kill the mood."

"Nah," I scoffed. I might have been uninterested in other mysteries, but if there was a reproductive problem on Vocury, I wanted to know about it. "Tell me. And don't worry—I can get you all revved up again after."

"My mother was the last woman to give birth, and she died shortly afterward."

"Okay, maybe I won't be able to get you revved up again," I awkwardly joked to cut the tension. "Sorry."

"It's alright. It was a long time ago. My father has told me repeatedly that I shouldn't feel the effects of my mother's loss like he has because I never knew her. His theory makes sense, but some connections must exist in the ether. I've often thought of it as kind of like the opposite of the termination of a pregnancy. That is, I imagine that to some mothers, abortion might be a short ordeal, but others may mourn the loss of a child they never knew for many years after. It was the same for me and my mother, only in reverse."

I touched his arm gently to give him some physical comfort even though he seemed relatively unshaken.

"What happened? How did she die? Was it somehow connected to this decades-long reproductive dry spell?"

"People don't like to talk about it, my father especially. He blames himself for her death. When I was born, I was the first—and last—in a very long time. I think he did things to my mother, experimental medicine and such, in order for them to conceive me. As far as I know, no one has dared to try again following such a catastrophe."

Panic immediately consumed me. I rolled out of bed, pulling the top sheet off to cover my naked body, and began pacing around the room with my conspiratorial mind firing on all cylinders for the first time in months.

"That son of a bitch. He lied to me."

"My father?"

"Yes! Remember the medical help he offered? It was reproductive help I needed! He never mentioned anything about decades of no children or infertility. Oh, fuck me! What did he do to me?"

"Wait. You've been trying to get pregnant this whole time? Shouldn't I have had a say in the matter?"

"What's the difference? It's impossible."

"Right. Which is why I never raised the subject. Were you using me?"

"No. I mean, yeah, kind of. It's not like you put up a fight, though. It seemed like a fair trade to me. Why are we even talking about this? Your father killed your mother trying to conceive! Who knows what liberties he's taken with my womb? Jesus, he even tried to push you on me. Have I lost my edge? I never should have gotten comfortable."

Taj rose out of bed to comfort me, which was nice considering that he was feeling slighted.

"We don't know that. It's a rumor, just like all the others. The prophecy was a rumor with many different variations at one time. Same for our infertility. It could be a punishment from God or something as simple as the effect of an environmental condition."

"Well, I'm going to need some answers, and I doubt your father is going to give them willingly. I'd like to get a little heads up if he's poisoned me with some Prometheus-type pregnancy monster." Of course, my reference went right over his head—much as the past million I had used—but he was getting better at understanding based on context.

"Who do we ask if not my father?"

"We don't ask. We act. There's something down in the basement. God-dammit, I even saw some of your pop's lab coat henchmen taking my blood sample to the lower levels. Why didn't I chase that lead?" I chastised myself.

Taj matched my nervous pacing. "I don't know about all this."

"I'm going to get some answers, and I'm pretty sure they're downstairs."

"We can't get down there. I've tried."

"Well, I haven't, and I've seen more movies than you. I'll figure something out."

It was already quite late, and it seemed the perfect time to go snooping about while most of the Citadel was asleep. There was no activity on the stairs, and the borough was closed for the day. The stars above brought minimal light into the structure, but it was enough to show us the way and cloak our presence.

We crept to the elevator, and I prompted Taj to use his key card to get us moving. Unfortunately, he had access to the lab on the first sublevel and the factory on the second, but all other levels were restricted.

"Now what?" Taj whispered, even though we were deep beneath the surface.

I looked at the ceiling of the lift and had an idea. "We're going to John McClane this bitch. Lift me up."

Taj cupped his hands together, I took one step into them, and he raised me to the ceiling. I pushed both hands against the panel and breathed a sigh of relief when it didn't resist. "Ha! When all else fails, trust Die Hard. Let me down."

Brushing my hands off, I told Taj what to do.

"Okay, your turn. I'll lift you up, you climb out, and then reach down and pull me through."

I cupped my hands to give him a boost, pushing his feet as he felt around for the lip and pulled himself through the opening. Once through, he blindly reached back for me, and I gripped his hands, letting him pull me into the elevator shaft. Staying on my hands and knees, I rooted around in the darkness, feeling along the edges for a gap to slide between the elevator and the shaft, but there wasn't one.

"Now what?" he asked, but before I could answer, the lift reset itself, closed its inner doors, and started moving back toward its position on the surface.

"Lay down," I instructed him, closing the hatch as we flattened ourselves against the filth and ash that had gathered in the shaft. I cringed as the elevator approached the top level, half expecting to be squished, but we stopped with about two feet of space between the elevator roof and the shaft ceiling. It wasn't enough room to sit up, and we certainly couldn't reopen the hatch from our precarious position. In short, the space was tight, claustrophobic, and we were completely trapped.

"Brilliant. We'll just wait here," Taj whispered. "The lift will start moving again in the morning when the Citadel comes to life, and we can count the levels as people come and go. With a bit of luck, someone with clearance will eventually take a ride to sublevel four. When they do, we'll wait for them to exit the elevator, quietly drop down, stop the lift, and sneak our way to where we don't belong."

"Oh my God, I freaking love you. Do you have any idea how turned on I am right now? Say 'sublevel four' again." It was too dark to see him, but if I could have, I would have kissed him.

I reached into my pocket and pulled out my phone to bring some light to the situation and provide entertainment to pass the hours. The battery life still read eight percent, but that was enough to get us to daylight.

"What do you see?" Taj asked.

"Not much."

"Yeah, me too," he quipped.

"Ha. Well played. I'm glad you've kept your sense of humor."

"I kind of have to. I'm the only blind person on the planet, and I'm pretty sure that's because my father meddled with science. He could cure me any time he wants, but he won't do it. I think being useless is his punishment for me for my role in my mother's death."

"That's insane. That wasn't your fault."

"I know, but I can't help but wish that I had died and she had lived on. I mean, what good am I to anyone? I contribute nothing to our society and my existence reminds my only family of his mistakes and pain."

"Stop it. You're not a mistake, and you're not useless. Where is this coming from?"

"I don't know," he lamented softly.

Taj may have presented himself as lighthearted and fun, but there was a darkness within him. He had carried me on more than one occasion, and now it was my turn to pick him up.

"Put these in," I said as I opened his palm and gave him both of my earbuds.

"You're not going to listen with me?"

"This one is just for you. Music has the power of emotion, and I want you to feel this song. It's in Italian, but I don't think that will matter."

Taj slipped the buds in, and I hit play on Time to Say Goodbye by Andrea Bocelli and Sarah Brightman. I could faintly hear the orchestral intro, followed by Sarah's beautiful voice as she began the first verse. The chorus swelled, and I reached for Taj's hand, our fingers intertwining in silent understanding.

"It's very—" Taj started, but I quickly pressed two fingers to his lips, silencing him. Andrea was about to drop his silky tenor voice on Taj, and I didn't want him to miss a second of it.

I increased the volume through the second verse and gripped his hand tighter. The song soared as the duo joined each other for the second chorus, and just like every time I'd listened to that song, my eyes began to well up. I hummed along with the finale, all the way through the crescendo and vibrato final note.

Taj removed the earbuds, and I switched to the phone's speaker, playing the song again at a low volume.

"It's beautiful," he admitted, "but I don't know how that's supposed to make me feel any better. I couldn't even understand the lyrics."

"Do you think he's a good singer?" I asked, totally setting him up.

"Yes, he's very talented. Incredible voice."

"His name is Andrea Bocelli, and the two of you have something in common. When Andrea's mother was pregnant with him, the doctors knew he'd be born with defects. His mother was warned that carrying her child to term could be dangerous, and that they couldn't guarantee Andrea's quality of life. They recommended that she have an abortion, but Mrs. Bocelli was a headstrong woman with conviction. She went ahead with her pregnancy and little Andrea was born with congenital glaucoma."

"What's that?" Taj asked.

"It means his eyes developed poorly—he could kind of see, but not really. It didn't slow him down, though. He was an active little fellow, always on the move. Then, when he was twelve, a soccer ball hit him in the head, and he lost his sight completely. You'd think that would have been the moment that derailed young Andrea's life, but he was resilient. He had a gift to share with the world. One record deal, fifteen solo albums, countless collaborations, and seventy-five million records sold later, he left an unforgettable mark on the world and touched millions of lives."

A single tear slid down Taj's cheek, and I gently kissed it away before it could fall.

"You're not defective," I whispered. "You're not defined by your disability, your father's contempt, or anything from your past. You are Taj Amaar, and I think you're pretty damn special."

"What can I do for anyone, though?"

"You're already doing it, babe. We're going to blow the lid off this story, and you're going to be the best investigative journalist on Vocury. You'll see. Stick with me and I'll get you in the kind of trouble that creates the opportunity for greatness."

***

Hours passed before we heard the elevator doors open for the first time, and we started counting floors. The first few trips back and forth were to the laboratory level, but after that, it ran steady for an hour straight, shuttling workers to the factories and mines. We kept count, knowing it was the morning rush of colonists—until we finally got lucky.

I counted to four as we reached our intended floor, and Taj and I tapped each other at the same time. Forcing our fingers under the lid, we cautiously lifted it just enough for me to peek out. My grip nearly faltered when I spotted Maddox in the lift, but luckily, he didn't linger about.

The moment Maddox walked off, we carefully raised the lid, and Taj quietly lowered me down into the elevator. I mashed the stop button before my feet even hit the floor, then helped Taj down from our perch. We peeled the doors open to make sure we were alone, slyly exited around the corner, and watched the elevator zoom off to continue its routine.

The air was thick with the musty scent of industrial welding, and not a hint of natural light filtered through anywhere. Maddox had illuminated the far end of the cavernous bay with harsh fluorescent lights, casting long shadows across the expanse.

The space was massive, too vast to easily gauge, and it gave off major Batcave vibes. Industrial machinery filled the area, much of it too large to have been brought through the elevator.

I hid behind a sheet of foreign metal, still in the process of being forged, and peered around the edge to keep an eye out for Maddox. He didn't seem like the kind of guy who was light on his feet or could sneak up on you, but I wasn't about to get caught in the act of espionage.

Been there, done that.

I led Taj by the hand as we moved from station to station like soldiers taking a beachhead and finding cover wherever we could. We were a hundred feet into the cavern when I scurried up to a cargo container that I didn't recognize until I was right up on it.

I ran my hand over the familiar surface and traced my finger across the WM insignia. "World Military," I whispered to Taj as though he'd understand what a shocking discovery that was. "It's Praxi tech, but from Earth. Hundreds of years old. This is impossible."

The rattling sound of a tool being dropped, followed by Maddox grunting and swearing spooked us. We moved laterally, away from his position, and eventually came upon a perimeter wall built into the rock that had various pieces of metal and gear lying against it. Pressing ourselves flat against the wall, we edged along it, our hands gliding blindly over the rough surface, guiding us as we silently crept forward.

My hand eventually brushed against a door latch, and I gently pressed it down to discover that it was unlocked. I eased the door open and pulled Taj into the dark concourse, putting distance between us and Maddox.

Using the dim light of my phone, I scanned the room and discovered we were in a windowless lab. We both searched along the wall for the switch to the lights above, and I wish I had been the first to find it so that I could quickly plunge us back into darkness once more.

Unfortunately, it was Taj who flipped the switch, and I nearly came out of my skin as the harsh lights exposed the horrifying scene before us.

Inside the lab were a dozen Praxi confined within sealed glass enclosers with steel backs. Each had its three wrists strapped tightly, with another band around their midsections, and a final strap around their throats. Numerous tubes and cables connected to their veins, feeding into a shared piping system above.

Though they were alive, they lay in various states of comatose. Their pain and suffering were evident, yet I could neither feel their distress nor hear their voices crying out for help in my head.

Taj ran his hand across the glass to inspect the discovery for himself. "What is this?" he whispered.

"It's some kind of medical enclosure with Praxi inside," I whispered. "These are the creatures my people came here to seek. Your father is apparently harvesting something from them." He instinctively felt around the side of the tank and took hold of a release handle, but I quickly grabbed him by the waist to stop him from making a foolish decision.

"Don't. You could trip a sensor or set off an alarm."

"We have to save them," he pleaded as the guilt of his father's madness landed firmly on his shoulders.

"If you could see them, you'd know they're on death's door. Probably too weak to walk. We can't help them until we get some help ourselves. Sit tight. I'm going to keep searching. There must be medical records, or recordings or journals, anything, somewhere in here."

We split up and combed through the laboratory torture chamber, hoping to find answers, but only uncovering more horrors. In addition to the main enclosures, there were many smaller tubes, each housing younger Praxi at various stages of development. Some of them looked healthy enough to live if freed, while others were in dire states, resembling failed science experiments. That wasn't the worst of it, either.

The most disturbing discovery was the doctor's apparent attempt to create life in test tubes—decaying infants and toddlers with mixed features, as if Praxi and human genetics had been cruelly intertwined.

Even more revolting, at the end of a row of ten incubators stood an empty one marked with an "X," the discarded vial that had once contained my blood discarded on a workbench nearby.

I backed away slowly, as though I had stumbled upon a hissing rattlesnake in tall grass. The doctor must have been expecting his cure to work, and for his son to deliver the seed, because he was clearly prepping something nefarious for my inevitable unborn child.

I suppose it was no wonder why Dr. Amaar wasn't hounding me daily for the keys to the Wolf Moon. He was waiting on me to show a baby bump before unleashing whatever terrible plans he had in mind.

"Taj. Taj!" I whispered urgently, trying to catch his attention as he feverishly rooted around as best he could without sight. I ran up to him and pulled him by the arm. "We have to get out of here. Now!"

'Wait. There has to be something. Some record of my mother. Anything."

"I'm sorry babe, I really am. Your father did something awful to your mother, and we're going to be next if we don't escape the Citadel."

"I must face him. I have to know why. What is this all for?"

"Whatever he says will be a lie. If he discovers that we've had a look behind the curtain, we're fucked. This is a 'Botany Bay! . . . Oh, no!' moment"—I inflected my best Chekov impersonation—"and without going into the details, I'll simply say that it's serious. We need to get to my ship ASAP and get the hell off this planet."

I yanked on his arm again. "Now, come on, there has to be another way to the surface. They didn't bring all this equipment down the elevator."

"We're coming back!" he said firmly. "We can't leave these creatures here like this."

"Yes. Fine. Whatever," I patronized to get him moving.

I took him by the hand to lead him away from the terror and toward the door. Opening it, I peeked out, half expecting to find Maddox staring down at me menacingly, but he was nowhere in sight.

"Stay on my hip," I told Taj as I guided him along the exterior wall. I traced my hand across everything, searching for any crease in the material that might open, controls that would expose a way out, or a draft of wind that could show us the way.

We were dangerously close to the workstation that Maddox had been laboring at earlier, and it was the brightest part of the bay. I darted through the light, trying to stay hidden while searching for an exit.

We managed to sneak through that hazardous area and back into the shadows once more on the far side of the bay, away from the elevator. I continued feeling my way along the wall, but it was my feet that first alerted me to something being out of place.

I nearly tripped over the slight lip of a steel pad, similar to those I'd seen on the train to the Citadel. I looked up to find an enormous shaft hollowed out of the rock, with the faintest traces of light seeping through near the surface.

"This is it," I whispered to Taj. "Find the controls."

"Alexis, here." Taj drew me over to an elevated panel connected to the pad below. I risked using my phone's light once more and noticed markings in a language I had never seen before.

"What is it?" he asked.

"Our way out. When in doubt, start clicking buttons," I said as I pressed the first one, and a screeching howl of metal on metal roared through the bay.

"Okay. Not that one."

I hastily moved to the next now that our cover was blown. Taj pressed another one and a steel frame four stories above rolled back like a rock from the front of a tomb, exposing the dawning Vocury sun above.

"Good. Good! Get us moving."

"You little fucker!" Maddox shouted from across the bay, lumbering his way toward us.

"Okayyyyy. Now would be good, Taj. Now!" My voice escalated with panic as I joined him in mashing buttons.

"Uhhh, what about this thing!" he exclaimed, gripping a nob and turning it. As he did, the pad we stood on began to move upward.

"Yes!" I celebrated, before realizing that Maddox was sprinting toward the pad. "Shit, faster!" I barked at Taj just as Maddox caught the steel lip with one hand, using the other to anchor himself to the nearest of the bolted-down equipment.

Maddox roared with anger and actually managed to momentarily halt our ascent. He had the strength of a bear, but it wasn't enough to defeat the industrial lift. As the pad continued to rise, he lunged and grabbed Taj's ankle as he attempted to climb aboard.

"A little help?" Taj hollered at me.

I raced over to the edge of the pad, and the sight of Maddox up close struck fear into my heart. His eyes blazed with a vengeful determination, and he hardly appeared human at his hulking size. If he could get his hands on me, he'd squeeze me to death for certain.

I stomped on his fingertips with my heel and wished for the life of me that I was wearing a pair of Emilia's pointy tips on my feet for once. I couldn't shift his grip, so I resorted to the only other option I could think of.

Dropping to my hands and knees, I leaned forward and sunk my teeth into his forefinger. Clamping down hard near the base, I tore through the flesh, gnawing away as he screamed in agony below. The asshole wouldn't relinquish his grasp, and he stubbornly held on until I had chewed entirely through his finger.

I went feral as I spit blood from my mouth, my hands shaking from my frenzied panic. "Oh my god, oh my god, oh my god," I repeated over and over again as I kicked the severed finger from the edge of the lift toward Maddox below.

As the pad rose, the natural heat of the outside world grew more intense, warming my face, and the awful metallic taste of the air saturated my bloodstained tongue.

The second we reached the surface, Taj took my hand and we ran as fast as possible toward the nearest village. The train ride had made the trip feel much shorter, and it was only once we had been running for twenty minutes that I realized we weren't even a quarter of the way there.

"I have to stop," I panted and fell over in the hot clay sand.

"We can't. The Citadel guard won't be far behind us. Come on, Alexis." He tried to help me to my feet, but I had nothing in the tank left to give.

"Up," he urged, placing his hands under my armpits to get me to move. When that didn't work, he bent over, told me to "Climb on," and helped me mount his back.

"I sure am glad you trained for this moment," I tried to joke.

Taj carried me as the sun beat down on us, but his pace began to slow after thirty minutes. I knew he couldn't keep it up much longer, so I said, "I'm good. You can put me down. I've got my second wind."

"Yeah, Taj. Put her down," a male voice ordered as a small group of bandits revealed themselves from their concealed positions in the side of a dune. There were three of them in total—two humans and a Praxi.

Equipped with full head scarves and clothing light enough to blow in the breeze and keep them cool, they weren't dressed like Kade's pirates, but they were unmistakably pirates, nonetheless.

"Oh, for fuck's sake. Now what?" I groaned in defeat. "Let me guess. You assholes want the ship too?"

"I told you not to come here. I warned you, and you wouldn't listen," the man said as he unraveled his scarf from around his neck to reveal a large black beard underneath. He circled it around his face again to expose his mouth and brown skin, and with another twist, revealed his facial features and eyes.

"Ho-ly shit." I dropped to my knees in shock. "Ranbir?"

Chapter 13

The Hypocritical Oath
Tess Fontaine: 2039

Every physician makes a promise to do no harm, and I'm sure we all mean it at the time. I certainly did. I took every word of the Hippocratic Oath as seriously as my wedding vows, and I'm left wondering which I trampled over harder.

There's something darkly ironic about the closeness of the words "Hippocratic" and "hypocritical." I don't know if the ancient Greeks had overpriced medical care, predatory health insurance, or addictive chemicals sold as so-called "cures" in their time—but they sure seem to have had a modern sense of humor when they conceived the oath.

Leaving public practice to go work with the genetics team at Amaar Labs was the best thing to happen for my career. I shouldn't have had any trouble doing no harm once separated from the traditional medical community; in fact, I had the chance to alter the course of mankind's health care for the better.

Yet, I've never forgiven myself for choosing ego over ethics.

We learned a great deal while studying Gio's body. Dr. Amaar discovered that he was twenty-two hundred years old and correctly surmised that long life wasn't natural to the Praxi. He even traced the foreign strands in Gio's DNA and formulated the hypothesis that whatever gave the Praxi their longevity could do the same for humans.

The doctor was an emotional man though, and his frustrations with his failure to connect the dots for a major breakthrough derailed him. There was a miracle cure for mortality hidden within Gio's cells, but it wasn't Dr. Amaar who would find it.

It was me.

The missing ingredient was human cells. I had tried for months to splice Gio's regenerative tissue with human DNA to no avail. Our alien test subject had been dead for some time, and he was already quite old when he was murdered. His cells continuously rejected the foreign human strands I introduced until I tried those from a fetus.

I was alone in the lab the night of my minor breakthrough, and rather than consider the consequences of my work, I had my eye on a Nobel Prize.

My discovery should have gone in the trash. I should have deleted all the research files and burned Gio's body until there was no trace of him left. But I couldn't see past my hubris, and I suppose that's why I've never blamed Dr. Amaar for soaking up all the credit and chasing glory across the cosmos.

I made the same horrible choice he had, except I saw my blunder for what it was. Of all the mistakes I'd made in my life, that was the one I'd take back first if I could.

The entire human race would be affected by my actions, yet I could only think about the one who would be hurt the most. I don't know what Ranbir thought had happened to Gio's body, but I doubt he ever imagined that his deceased friend—a hero—would be dissected, frozen, and cut to pieces.

Ranbir and I had only recently become friends through Maya, and he would surely hate me forever once he discovered the things I had done and would continue to do. No one loved the Praxi like Ranbir, and while he held himself accountable for their genocide, he knew in his gut that it wasn't his fault.

I wasn't afforded the same luxury, and I feared he would feel the same way. It was highly unlikely he would have agreed to help us if he knew the truth, but I'd have to face him one day and confess my crimes.

It's funny. I thought I had ruined everything that night in the lab on Earth, but I had no clue about the amount of damage I would continue to do as I tried, and failed, to uphold my oath.

I left my family behind and had a multi-month space trip to sit around missing them and hating myself. It felt like an eternity, but in the grand scheme of things, it was a drop in the bucket of endless regretful time.

Upon arriving on Vocury, we hadn't spent more than fifteen minutes gawking at the massive pyramid that greeted us before Maddox and his gorillas went charging into action. Only years earlier, we had voted to send a diplomatic mission of peace to meet the Praxi on Vocury, but that was before we realized they had something we wanted and had gained the triaxum needed to acquire it. There would be no trade negotiations on this day.

Dr. Amaar held the research team back, and not because he didn't want us in harm's way. He always thought he could protect us from the ugly nature of our mission. As though we'd all sleep better at night if we didn't watch as the Praxi were killed or captured for the sake of our twisted science experiments.

There was no way to shelter us from the ugliness that was coming, so I don't know why he bothered hiding us from that first moment of conflict.

I entered the pyramid for the first time, expecting the worst, and I thought I had seen it as our goons dragged the bodies of murdered aliens through pools of blood that drew a straight line of liquid death to the pile of the deceased that was being gathered for harvesting.

If the Praxi had put up a fight, it didn't appear to be one that would be gloriously remembered. I already knew that we were the worst thing to ever happen to their species, and it seemed we were only just getting started.

My lab assistant, Dani, and I were among the fourth group to take the elevators to what we had deduced was their research space below. We were on the precipice of a great scientific achievement, yet nobody said a word.

The doors hadn't even opened yet to expose us to the horrors happening in the Praxi labs, but the voices of their young—a chorus of wailing, pleading, confusion, and fear—already rang through our minds. Maya had told me what it was like to hear Gio speak, but nothing could have prepared me for the raw emotion.

It was a horrible feeling, yet it gave me hope that we might collectively turn away. How could anyone possibly proceed with our plans when faced with such a clear instinctive choice between good and evil?

As a spy and saboteur among them, I couldn't be the first to voice ethical concerns and I hoped that Dani would fill that role. Her eyes were as wide as mine when the elevator doors opened, and I suppose she had her own reason for keeping her mouth shut like the rest of us. I knew she wanted to be more than an assistant, but a job promotion certainly wasn't worth going through all the PTSD that awaited us.

Dr. Amaar and a dozen of our colleagues were rounding up and inspecting the Praxi youth. The oldest among them stood maybe five feet tall, while the youngest hadn't yet learned to walk. In human terms, they spanned from infants to mid-adolescence, though there was no telling their true age in Earth years.

For all we knew, with the Praxi seemingly extending their life cycles through science, the children could be decades old and still developing as toddlers. The only certainty was that they were what we were after—and their fate would be among the worst any Praxi had ever known.

"Shut them up!" Dr. Amaar growled as he clasped his forehead. Hearing their cries for help was awful, but no one processed the pain of it as poorly as the doctor. Once we had empathetically connected to the children, I think the rest of us held out hope that we wouldn't do what we came there to do.

But not Amaar. He remained unwavering in his resolve to change the world, and I think that made their cries all the more agonizing for him. He knew he was going to do unspeakable things to them, and the weight of it was already crushing him.

"What are we supposed to do?" Dani joined the panic.

"Count them, mark them, and lock them up," Dr. Amaar hastened. "I don't want anyone having any contact with them until I've figured out a solution to this screaming."

The doctor stormed off, distancing himself from the temptation of pity, while the rest of us cataloged and herded our prisoners into a space where they could be locked in. As I gently placed my hand on the back of one of the older children, her voice pierced into my mind with an icy edge.

"Don't touch me!" she barked, her thoughts cutting through with a sharp intensity.

I focused my mind, wanting to ensure she understood my intentions. "My name is Tess, and I know you're scared."

She didn't respond, but when I touched her again to help her find a place to sit among her peers, she no longer violently recoiled.

"I promise, I'm not like the others. I don't expect you to trust me or even like me, but I'm going to do everything in my power to help you."

I thought she heard me, and hoped she felt me. If the Praxi were truly as emotionally adept as I'd been told, perhaps she could calm the others, offering them some solace in the presence of an unexpected ally, even as their first night of captivity loomed ahead.

Later, rather than return to the surface with the others after leaving the children, Dani and I joined a group of soldiers heading deeper into the facility to explore the mines.

Vocury seemed like a strategically terrible place for the Praxi to grow their young. The surface of the planet was uninviting, the gravity was punishing, and the air tasted foul. Underneath those rotten conditions, however, lay the Praxi's most precious secret: the mineral responsible for their cell regeneration. We didn't know what the Praxi called it, so we dubbed it "Vice"—for reasons that felt painfully clear.

The first few hundred feet of the mine were encased and finished in alloy with power and lighting installed just like the levels above. There were various Praxi excavation tools stored near the elevators, along with a railway hub for traversing the mines.

"Anybody home?" Dani shouted, her voice echoing into the darkness.

We walked to the edge where the light no longer illuminated the cavern and found four separate pathways where the rail line splintered off in opposite directions. There must have been miles of tunnels beneath the pyramid; it was a wonder the ceiling held enough integrity to support the structure above. It must have taken the Praxi years to dig it all out, moving countless tons of Vocury dirt and rock to the surface in pursuit of Vice.

"All this work, and how much Vice do you think they've taken out of here over the centuries?" Dani asked. "Twenty pounds? Fifty pounds? The juice must really be worth the squeeze. We could live fat with a single flake of the stuff."

"If you could find any and dig it out," I replied. "You looking for a career change after seeing what your role might look like? Maybe getting into mining isn't such a bad gig."

It was risky to feel her out, but I couldn't help myself. My hands were relatively bound concerning subverting the mission, and an ally could go a long way if I could make one out of Dani.

"I knew it was going to be rough but picturing it and experiencing it are two different things," she replied.

"And we're only getting started," I continued to nudge her toward empathy. "Maybe you should have stayed in med school."

"And spend another year studying and countless more trying to prove myself as a surgeon? Not when there was an opportunity like this. Come on. Let's finish up—get some rest and an early start tomorrow. We have to figure out how to calm those kids. Dr. Amaar clearly can't work in those conditions, and I'm pretty sure I can't either."

Dani's words gave me hope that she was on the right path, and I thought that over time I might be able to flip her. At a minimum, I was certain that she would speak up if our situation became grim.

We returned to the surface where the troops were hauling the last of the Praxi victims down to the labs and mopping up the mess they'd left behind.

If the adults had been even half as genetically valuable as the young, there's no way Amaar would have allowed so many to be put down. They would have been captured, harvested, and experimented on just like their children.

Maybe they were lucky that their cells were less fruitful. Taking a bullet may have been the easy way out.

We retired to our quarters on the first floor, and I tried to make the best of the Praxi comforts. There's not a lot of sleep to be had in the bed of a murder victim, though. Unfortunately, that didn't seem to be a problem for anyone else.

The Praxi citadel buzzed with activity the next morning. Workers were set to task on refitting the habitat to suit our needs, while those who drew the short straws headed into the mines in search of Vice. To be honest, I would've preferred either of those tasks over what awaited me in the labs that day.

I met Dani by the elevator, hoping that she'd share my restlessness, but the horrors of our arrival hadn't seemed to disturb her sleep at all.

"Good morning, boss," she greeted me as we stepped into the lift.

"I guess we'll see," I replied as I rubbed my restless eyes.

There was no start early enough that would have put us ahead of Dr. Amaar. The lab was already bustling with activity by the time we arrived and, judging by his unkempt hair and unbuttoned lab coat, Dr. Amaar had been at it all night.

"Bring one of the older ones in," he barked at Maddox, whose hulking presence in the lab was a bad omen. "You two—disinfect and suit up. Tess, you're with me. Dani, stand ready to assist," Amaar continued, issuing orders without missing a beat.

"What are we doing?" I asked.

"I want to work in peace, so we're going to turn down the volume. Get dressed, scrub up, and join me," he instructed, brooking no argument.

Maddox returned from the chamber where we had trapped the youth with the insolent child I had made empty promises to slung over his shoulder. He slammed her down onto the stainless-steel operating table and fastened her three wrists into place, with a fourth restraint around her waist and a fifth around her forehead.

"Let me go!" she commanded telepathically while struggling against her binds. Her eyes focused on Maddox, but she let all of us hear and feel her intentions. "I'm going to kill you. I know you hear me. Whatever you do to me, I will repay a hundred times over." If her words didn't make her hate clear, the seething rage of her emoting certainly did.

"You're a fiery little one. Spitting your final words in spite. Shame your kin didn't share your warrior spirit," Maddox responded.

Dr. Amaar halted the verbal warfare. "That's quite enough, Maddox." He swabbed the girl's scalp with a damp Q-tip, prepping for the incision, then turned to me. "Administer a sedative."

The child instantly began screaming, not from fear but something deeper—a primal cry meant to target the line between ethical scientific exploration and immoral abuse that we were about to step over.

Dr. Amaar's jaw tightened, his patience unraveling. "Come on!" he firmly ordered, pushing us to hasten the process that was darkening his soul.

I drew up a syringe and approached the child with apprehension. My mind focused on her fear, and I tried to make her hear me.

"I'm sorry. This is out of my control."

"You want to help me?" her voice answered in my mind, "Don't sedate me. I'll scream my way through this, and if that doesn't deter your doctor, nothing will. He'll share my pain regardless."

I made a split-second decision and pressed the needle to her thigh, making sure to angle myself into Amaar's line of sight. I made as though I were following his instructions for a moment before withdrawing the needle without depressing the plunger. Quickly returning to my workstation, I then covertly squirted the sedative back into its vial and tucked it out of sight.

"Go ahead. Cut me," the child seethed for all to hear. "Leave whatever parts of you that were good and pure in the past. Violate a child," she taunted.

Undeterred, Dr. Amaar steadied his hand and carefully made a two-inch incision on her head. Dani promptly followed up, dabbing the edges to wipe away the blood.

Dr. Amaar called me over. "Tess. Tess! Spread the incision and hold it. Quickly! Ignore the voices."

I took my place next to him and stabilized the opening he had created. I didn't know what he was after, but I was powerless to stop him and could barely stomach being complicit in the evil being performed.

The child screamed in pain as Amaar used bone cutting forceps to saw through her skull. His hand shook as her voice rang in his head, and he suddenly drew back. If the doctor was out to prove that he could power through the moral quandary, he was doing a terrible job of it.

"Stop it. Stop it! This must be done," he rationalized, though the words seemed more for himself than anyone else.

"You don't have to do this," the child's anger shifted to desperate pleading as Dr. Amaar's facade showed some cracks. "You can stop. Whatever it is you're after, there must be another way."

"You"—Maddox pointed to Dani as the doctor floundered—"another sedative."

Dani rushed to follow orders, returning with a loaded syringe. I locked eyes with her, silently begging her to defy Maddox and stand up for what was right. But despite her evident discomfort with the crude science, her position didn't seem to stop her from performing the task.

She inserted the needle and injected the sedative, though Dr. Amaar didn't even bother waiting for it to take effect. Ignoring the growing intensity of the child's screams, he pressed on, continuing the procedure as her cries pierced the air.

"Almost there," Amaar murmured as he leaned closer to his patient. In an instant, the screams ceased, though the child's eyes remained open. Dr. Amaar calmly set down his tool, selected another, and began to reattach the bone flap.

I placed my hand on the child's chest, hoping to offer her some comfort. To my shock, a powerful jolt of electricity surged through me, making my arm convulse.

"Ah!" I shouted, noting that Dr. Amaar must have been zapped as well as he jumped away from the table. Dani, curious, placed two fingers on the child's arm only to be shocked herself.

Luckily, the poor child's eyes finally closed as the sedative took hold and she fell unconscious. Dr. Amaar swiftly completed the procedure, securing the bone before instructing Dani to close and dress the incision. Dani lightly tapped the child's forehead to ensure there was no lingering electrical current, and once she confirmed it was safe, proceeded to close the wound.

"What have you done?" I questioned Dr. Amaar quietly, my voice thick with accusation that was dangerously close to calling into question my commitment to the mission.

"I've created a safe working environment. When she wakes, we'll confirm that the surgery was a success, and then we'll perform the same operation on the others. Once all the children are silenced, we'll be able to do our work in peace."

"Well? What's the verdict?" Maddox asked the doctor.

"I have no idea," Amaar snapped. "We've only just started. I'll get to the real work soon. We'll stay on schedule. Have patience."

"Patience? I'm fresh out. You didn't see me wasting time when we took their citadel, did you? Their screams didn't stop me from doing my part, and now I'm supposed to have patience as you fumble around with your hang-ups? No, doctor. Time for you to get your shit together and deliver as promised."

Whatever Dr. Amaar had promised Maddox was beyond me, but it must have been important enough to turn the once-great soldier into a monster.

"We'll soon have all the time in the world, my friend," Amaar reassured him.

"We might, but others don't," Maddox warned as he stormed out of the lab.

"Take a break," Amaar instructed us. "We'll continue once the sedative wears off."

The moment Amaar was gone, I turned to Dani and met her gaze. "You comfortable doing this to the rest of them? Even the little ones?" She didn't answer but turned her back, the snapping sound of her disposable gloves being removed the only response I received.

"Hey. Dani," I raised my voice at her. "At least help me move her," I demanded while unlatching the restraints around the child's wrists.

"Just leave her there. We might have to go back in to drain excess fluid, or deal with this electrical current issue. Might as well take a break."

Not exactly the response I was hoping for.

"Come on, sweetie," I grunted as I slung the child's body over my shoulder and carried her back to the makeshift cell, two of her limbs dragging across the cold floor. I opened the door and was met with a chorus of pleading and crying from the younger children as I placed her carefully on the floor among them.

"Shhh. Please, try to stay calm," I begged them as I checked over my shoulder for anyone who might be watching. "Listen to me, children. I'm going to do my best to look out for you, but you're going to have to be strong for one another. Very soon the others will come to take you away, and if you make any noise or give any resistance, the bad men will hurt you. Don't talk to them, don't acknowledge them, and don't make a sound."

"What did you do to her?" one of the elder children asked as he examined our poor subject's wound.

"I didn't do this, and I couldn't stop it. I can't stop anything."

My frustration boiled over, and I kicked the wall in anger before sinking to my knees. "Why did I come here?" I spoke aloud. "This is all my fault. God, I just want to see my family." I wept as my thoughts tossed me in a million directions.

"What's wrong with her?" the teen asked once more as the child began to regain consciousness. "I can't feel her. Why can't I feel her?" To her, he said, "Can you hear me?" as he reached out to touch her, only to be shocked away.

"Heyyyy . . . Easy now," I tried to calm the child as I helped her sit up, just as I was shocked myself.

"Son of a bitch, that hurt," I muttered as I shook my hand.

Her head was on a swivel, looking from one member of her kin to the next in a panic. It seemed she could hear them but could no longer speak or share in the emotional exchange. With a few snips and a couple of stitches, Dr. Amaar had removed her ability to communicate.

"Can you hear me?" I asked her out loud and she nodded her head in the affirmative. "And them? Can you hear them?" I continued the inquisition, pointing to the other Praxi, and she shrugged her shoulders.

"I think you're emitting an electrical current when you attempt to communicate. If you can't control it, the doctor may continue with the experimentation."

I had abandoned my family for a chase across the galaxy to repair my conscience, and fate saw to it that a new family was placed in my path. When I set out to ensure that my discovery would never see the light of day, I didn't expect to have a chance at redemption.

As far as I was concerned, these young Praxi were now as much my children as Marcus was, and for the time being, they needed my care more than he did. I only hoped that I wouldn't miss much of my boy growing up, and that he'd never grow old enough to realize that I had higher priorities during his most important developmental years without me there to explain.

"I'm going to do everything in my power to get all of you out of here," I promised the children, despite not having a plan to back it up. "You'll all be submitted to testing, but if you don't put up a fight or cry out, the doctor won't have reason to silence you. Support one another and be patient. I'm working alone here, and this will take some time."

I stood to leave, and the wounded child grabbed my wrist, but she must have held back the urge to communicate because I wasn't hit with a jolt of electricity. "What it is, dear?" I asked her, even though she was unable to respond.

She ran one hand over her mouth and then smacked her lips as if to mimic speaking. "I don't know what you're trying to tell me," I responded, frustrated for her.

She waved her hands to calm me down then pointed at me with one finger, traced that same finger over her incision, and then pointed to her mouth, which she continued to flap.

"She wants you to fix her," the elder child emoted dejectedly, as though he knew it were impossible.

"What's your name?" I asked the defiant young Praxi.

"Rix."

"And what about her?"

"Gia."

"Well, let me tell you something, Rix and Gia. If you don't give up on each other, I won't give up on you. If there's a way to remedy the damage that's been done, I will find it."

"You're going to have to perform a miracle if you want our trust," Rix snarled into my thoughts.

Gia pushed him aside and stood on two feet. She placed her free hand on my shoulder, looked into my eyes, and nodded her head. I had work to do.

I left the children and took advantage of the empty lab. I couldn't assess whether Gia's ability to communicate with her kind could be repaired without poking around in her head, but I could prepare an alternative solution. Judging by the electrical current she was discharging, there was activity within her whenever she attempted to communicate. If I could channel that spark into a voice box of some kind, she might be able to speak.

I wasn't sure if my idea would work, given her anatomy, and I was completely out of my depth, but I had to try. I hadn't discovered much overlap in human and Praxi biology during my two years of research, but having direct access to their tech was a game changer.

The Praxi were millennia ahead of mankind in scientific advancements, and some of that brilliance was at our fingertips here on Vocury. While my colleagues would exploit those breakthroughs for their own selfish pursuits, I'd set out in secret to harness them for good, the way our three-legged alien friends had.

With the extensive work we were going to be doing to combine human DNA with the Vice from the mines below, I had the perfect cover story and excuse to clock countless unsupervised hours in the lab.

I was expecting Dr. Amaar to return first, but it was Maddox who was ahead of the crowd.

"Status?" he demanded upon entering the lab.

"The procedure was a greater success than we could have hoped for. The child can't speak, and the others have taken notice."

"Does this mean we can skip the process for the others and your team can get to the work that matters?"

"Assuming we don't cause them enough pain to cry out, yes." I should have left well enough alone when Maddox turned to leave but my curiosity got the better of me.

"Hey, Maddox—what's the big rush? You have somewhere else to be? I was expecting pressure from Dr. Amaar and yet somehow, you're the one breathing down our necks."

"Some of us actually care about our children."

"What the hell is that supposed to mean?" My eyes narrowed and my heart raced with the type of boiling anger that threatened to expose my cover.

"You could have brought your son, but instead you let that bitch ex-wife of yours take full custody, steal my ship, and run off with that pussy Ranbir to do God knows what. Unlike you, I fight for my family. Whatever it takes."

The last thing I wanted to do was rehash my lie about my divorce from Maya, but Maddox was pushing my buttons. I struggled to control my emotions, so I quickly redirected the conversation back to him to avoid saying anything foolish.

"Yeah? I don't see your family around here either. You're no better."

"You think I'm some kind of monster, don't you?" he grunted, taking two steps forward and towering over me. "I didn't fly halfway across the galaxy so I could coat my hands in blood. I'm not after money, and I don't kill for sport. I wouldn't have come to this damn place if I didn't have to."

"Then what is it? You must be getting something out of this."

"Just do your job and make it snappy. You get me home within two years with a shipment full of your wonder drugs, and you'll find that I'm not such a bad guy. Until then, I'm going to keep pushing you, so you'd better learn to cope."

Maddox was a more complicated man than I expected. Whatever his reason was for leaving his family behind, stacking Praxi bodies to the ceiling, and operating with haste, it must have been big. If he wasn't so prickly, I may have tried to make an ally out of him. But I couldn't trust anyone, much less a murderous maniac.

I continued with my work until Dr. Amaar, Dani, and the rest of the team returned to the lab. Rather than get sidetracked with cracking the skulls of the rest of the children, Amaar was willing to proceed so long as he didn't have to hear their cries.

As horrible as it was, the work that followed was exhilarating. My focus was solely on my mission, but it was hard not to get caught up in the incredible breakthroughs we were making every day.

The applications and combinations of Vice with Praxi and human DNA had limitless potential. There was no question of whether our creations and cocktails would work. We could multiply and heal cells, extend life, cure terminal diseases, and even grow new human tissue.

But as with all things, and as I predicted, there was a cost. We didn't make a single advancement that didn't involve having to extract proteins directly from the tissue of the Praxi children, and every last one of them would be a lab rat until they reached an age where they were no longer useful. In Dr. Amaar's eyes, they were a means to an end and completely disposable.

By day, Gia, Rix, and the others were subjected to constant experimentation while workers filed into the mines below in search of the smallest bits of Vice to fuel our research. By night, I comforted the children and labored tirelessly to give Gia back her voice.

There was no repairing the damage Dr. Amaar had done when he severed the neural pathways in Gia's brain, but I held on to hope that I could grow her an operational larynx. Once I had a strong enough understanding of the science at play, I set up my own private lab in one of the freighters so I could hide my work.

We had only been on Vocury for three months before we had created an entire line of alien health care products. The miners were eventually divided into two groups: one to continue mining and the other to manufacture the drugs. However, because the Praxi hadn't designed their facility for mass production, progress was painfully slow.

There wasn't a single adult among our company of three hundred who wasn't assigned a task. We had left Earth as equals—regardless of our varying levels of education and credentials—but over time, the social classes became more evident. There was plenty of room for everyone in the Citadel when we arrived, but it wasn't long before the population began to grow and evolve in ways we hadn't anticipated.

Someone would eventually need to live outside of the comforts of our walls, and it certainly wasn't going to be anyone who had a fancy degree or a vocational position of importance.

No one had prepared for the contingency that we would be marooned on that rock for centuries, and if we had, I don't know how many of us would have started ingesting the poison we were manufacturing. One natural human lifetime would have been more than enough in that environment.

Nature is poetic and violent, yet also predictable. Mankind spreads like locusts, consuming and destroying everything in our path as our numbers grow. But the moment we think we're advanced, civilized, and in control, nature strikes us with a humbling hammer blow to the head.

Famine, disease, and natural disasters cull the population to manageable levels. As we progress, nature provides new opportunities for us to destroy ourselves with hubris. We cover every square inch of land and then kill each other over who gets to own it. We discover resources in nature that can advance our society, and then sacrifice millions of lives over who gets to control them.

In the end, nature always wins, and it would be no different for those of us on Vocury. We had found the keys to immortality, so in turn, nature decided to introduce us to infertility.

We had a limited supply of early-stage human embryos, crucial for providing the underdeveloped cells necessary to complete our work. Without them, the Vice would have been almost useless for creating high-potency human doses of regenerator. Had we been able to create life in a test tube the way the Praxi had, our population would have almost certainly grown to unsustainable levels. Nature stepped in and did what nature does best, though.

The zealots had no idea they were destroying their reproductive systems as they greedily gobbled up every new miracle drug Dr. Amaar offered them. The first century on Vocury saw our numbers balloon to the point where the less desirable citizens were forced into camps outside the Citadel walls; soon after, the population capped as fewer children were born every year.

Before we knew it, nature had stopped our growth in its tracks, and we had depleted our supply of human embryos. Ironically, we had access to tech beyond our wildest dreams, while sitting on top of a mine full of one of the galaxy's most versatile substances, yet basic human life was our most coveted finite resource.

The drugs were as pure as could be when we started, but as time wore on, Dr. Amaar would be forced to compensate with higher levels of Vice to cut corners around the dwindling supply of human fetal tissue. More hours would be needed in the mines every day, and there was only one way to keep the workers coming back to tunnel through miles of rock. Simple hydration and sustenance only went so far as motivation.

The upper class living within the Citadel needed to maintain their way of life, and the best way to keep the lower class laboring was to have them helplessly addicted to the poison they were partially culpable for creating.

If the people spent all their time stoned out of their minds and entirely focused on how to get their next fix, they'd never be able to confront the caste system they belonged to and their lowly position within it. These would, of course, be problems far down the road that I never saw coming nor was equipped to deal with.

For the time being, my focus was solely on the safety of the children, maintaining my cover, getting word to Maya, and trying to save poor Gia from the horror we had inflicted upon her. Most of it was easier than expected, so long as I was willing to sacrifice sleep and hide out in my makeshift lab in the freighter.

Within days of our arrival, production, while slow, was up to scale and a timeline was in place. I sent my message out into space hoping that the Omaha was lingering nearby, and Maya would receive it. I had bottled my emotions for months on the trip to Vocury, and it was only once I projected my voice out to my family that I realized how much I missed them.

The next year would be incredibly difficult in relation to keeping my composure, so the best thing I could do was stay on task, complete my mission, right my wrongs, and prepare to stow away on the transport with the first shipment headed back to Earth.

If everything went according to plan, Maya and Ranbir would hijack the ship, jettison the cargo into the void, and no one on Vocury would be the wiser. Only one ship would remain, and we'd either destroy it or seize it a year later when it was full and on its way to Earth—whatever it took. Either way, I'd get to see Maya and Marcus again, so it wouldn't really matter to me what else came next.

It was the eve before the first shipment was set to launch, and I was as prepared as I was going to be. My hiding spot aboard the freighter was secure, and I risked sending another message to my family before going over my timeline and checklist one last time.

I had successfully grown a larynx from Praxi tissue, designed to mimic a human's. All that was left to do was to try my hand at the first ethical bit of health care I would provide in over a year, and then make my escape.

The sun had set on a busy day of Maddox and his men loading the freighter with a few hundred totes of Dr. Amaar's poison. The crew had retired for the evening, and I snuck my way onto the elevators back to the lab, surprised to find the lights still on.

Checking to make sure the coast was clear, my voice echoed as I tentatively called out, "Hello?"

Dani stuck her head out of the processing room. "What are you doing here?"

"I could ask you the same thing."

"Rix and Gia are going into processing. Dr. Amaar didn't want to get his hands dirty, so I volunteered."

"Overnight? What for?"

"Not overnight. Permanently. What's with you lately? If you're not careful, I'm going to end up taking your job."

I knew the older children would eventually become less useful as their cells aged, but I hadn't thought it would be so soon. Had I really become so distant that I'd lost track of things as simple as the schedule? This was going to be a major problem for my timeline, and I was going to have to take a necessary risk if I was going to save those children.

"You know what's going to happen once you seal them in those tubes?" I asked, challenging Dani's ethics. She answered anyway, despite it being a rhetorical question.

"They'll be slowly drained of every last ounce of their value and their cells will deteriorate over time. Once they're dead, we'll carve up the leftovers to salvage whatever is useable, and other children who haven't reached an undesirable age will take their place."

To anyone else, Dani's statement would have seemed cold and pragmatic, but I knew better. This was beyond what she had signed up for, and not even her desire to be one of Dr. Amaar's favorite pets and do more than hand tools to actual surgeons could justify these actions.

"What if I told you there was another way?"

"There's not, but now I'm intrigued."

I couldn't just come out and tell her everything. If she realized I'd been a sleeper within the organization all along, it would shatter any trust she may have. And at that moment, everything would fall apart without her help. So, I played to her ego instead.

"I need a steady hand for surgery, and it's about time for you to perform the types of operations that you've been training for. There's no one better suited for the job than you."

She perked up. "What job?"

"We took Gia's voice away, and I want to try to give it back." I set my cooled transport container on the counter and opened it to reveal the larynx I had constructed.

"This isn't run-of-the-mill surgery I'm talking about here. Nothing like this has ever been attempted before, but based on my prep work, it should be possible. You think you're up to the task?"

"Of course I am. I don't really see the point though, unless you're just trying to show off for Dr. Amaar. The kid is going back in the tube when you're done."

I stroked her need to be noticed. "You think he'd be impressed?"

She scoffed. "I don't think he'd have much use for it . . . but it would be damned impressive. You're talking about xenotransplantation—splicing human and Praxi anatomy—here. It's unprecedented." She inched closer to examine the larynx further.

"What do you say? Want to make your first surgery one for the record books?"

"Alright. Let's do it. I'll get the girl."

I didn't know how I was going to deal with Gia and Rix going into the processing tanks, but one problem at a time. The planned procedure was enough to deal with on its own, and now I had Dani to manage, too. She could become a real problem depending on how the following twelve hours shook out.

Dani helped a confused Gia onto the same operating table where Dr. Amaar had cut into her a year earlier, and she couldn't keep her hands on the child through the shocks emitted by Gia inadvertently attempting to communicate.

"Geez, you're welcome, kid," she said sarcastically while shaking her hands out.

"It's okay, sweetie. Dani is going to help with the procedure." I massaged Gia's scalp, trying to calm her nerves. "It's just like we talked about. I'm going to put you under, and with a bit of luck, when you wake up, you'll be able to speak like we do."

I wheeled a rolling supply cabinet next to the table, sterilized and laid out the necessary tools, and scrubbed up.

"Dani, the sedative please."

Within moments, Gia's eyes closed, and I set up the monitors to keep track of her vitals. Dani pulled on a pair of gloves over the edges of her sleeves and asked, "Okay doc, what do I do?"

"Trace along the existing incision site and open the same region as before. I want you to locate the severed neural endings, remove any residual scar tissue, and prep the nerves for new connections." Her hands were steady enough as she made the incision, but her fingers twitched slightly as she used a retractor to inspect the area.

"Hey, you're going to do fine," I comforted her. "You've practiced for this."

Once I assured myself that Dani was on track, I started on the more delicate work. Gia's throat needed to be opened without compromising her airways. I carefully threaded my way through her nasal passages and cranium, aiming to reach her neural center and establish a connection between her mind and her new voice box.

Dani completed her task long before I did, and even though I wanted to keep her engaged and busy, I couldn't trust her with the difficult portions of the operation. I was responsible for Gia, and if something were to go horribly wrong, the blame should fall squarely on my shoulders.

Despite her heart rate spiking up to concerning levels on a couple of occasions, Gia's biology seemed to be accepting the foreign tissue. It took me about ninety minutes to run the neural connections through her passages, and then it was time for the moment of truth.

Dani stood near the head of the table, ready to resume her first attempt at neurosurgery rather than assisting, but I had to insist.

"I think it's best if I put the finishing touches on this."

"I can do it, I promise."

"I'm sure you can," I lied, "but this patient is my responsibility. I have to finish this myself."

I waited for Dani to concede her position and step aside, and then leaned over Gia's head to survey the landscape. Dani removed her gloves and let the aggressive slap of latex speak her frustration rather than voice it herself.

"You can still assist me," I proposed, even though there wasn't much for her to do.

"No thanks. You've got it under control apparently."

In any other scenario, I might have chastised her for being childish, but I couldn't risk pushing her away until I had the situation under control. I checked the time and proceeded with a balance of haste and caution.

It took me two hours to carefully affix and mend the connections between Gia's new voice box and her brain. Then, at long last, I flushed the area and closed the incision.

It wouldn't be long before Gia woke, and I'd finally discover if all my work had paid off. In the meantime, I pivoted to dealing with my other problems.

I couldn't let Dani put Gia back into processing, and I had to get Rix out of there as well. I could get them to the surface under the cover of night, but they'd almost certainly die out in the harsh elements if left alone. My stomach was in knots and my eyes welled with tears as I realized what I was going to have to do.

"Can you start the cleanup process?" I asked Dani. "Dr. Amaar might overlook our work if we leave a mess," I rationalized. "I'll prep the processing tank."

"If this works, I should get promoted, right?" Dani responded as she began to tidy up our makeshift operating theatre.

"This is going to blow them away, and we did it together. Both of us," I said, sharing the credit with her.

With Dani's ego properly inflated, I discreetly carried a medical tray with me as I walked down the hall and entered the processing room.

Inside were two suspension tanks, Rix already hooked up to one, with various tubes plugged into his body and a breathing apparatus attached to his mouth. I turned off the machine, opened the upper hatch, and began pulling the plugs from his body.

As his eyes fluttered opened, I raised a finger to my lips and whispered, "Shhh."

I helped him out of the tank, and he rested against me as he regained his strength. After a moment, I focused my mind so I wouldn't need to speak out loud.

"We have to get you out of here, but I need your help."

The second I had made my intentions clear, I felt joy emit from Rix for the first time since I'd known him. I handed him the stainless-steel tray and ordered, "Hit me."

"Hit you?"

"Yes. Aim for my face. Maybe the eye or nose or mouth. You need to make an impression, but you can't knock me unconscious. I'm going to make some noise and fall prone. Dani is going to come looking. Let her see me laying on the floor, and then hit her, but you know . . . really hit her. You need to knock her out."

"I could kill her easily enough. We could go snuff out Dr. Amaar while we're at it, too," he suggested maliciously.

"Don't do that. Just give her a good smack. Two or three times, if that's what it takes."

"I can handle that. You ready?" he asked as he stood on two feet and cocked back with his free arm.

"No, but let me have it anyway."

I closed my eyes, and within seconds felt the flat edge of the pan smash into my cheek and left eye. I cried out and made a commotion as I threw myself on the floor, laid on my belly, and kept my eyes closed. Moments later, I heard Dani yell my name and come rushing into the room.

"You're getting off easy," Rix's voice projected out.

I listened in on the ensuing struggle and heard two distinct clangs of the steel plate before Dani's body plopped to the ground next to me. Once I was sure she was out cold, I picked myself up off the floor.

"We need to move," I urged him.

We hurried back to the lab, where a groggy Gia was starting to come to. "You're okay, baby, but we're up against it here. Rix, can you carry her?"

Rix heaved Gia over his shoulder and held her with his free hand. Our next stop was the elevator, and instead of risking the main floor of the Citadel, we went lower into the facility to take the transport ramp to the surface. The freighter was just outside the pyramid, and all we needed to do was get clear and into the craft.

I navigated my way through the production level in the dark as I led Rix and Gia to the steel pad that would take us to the surface. We started the slow ride upward and Gia took my hand to grab my attention. Her mouth moved and she gurgled while trying to speak.

"Don't talk, doll," I quickly cautioned her. "Don't. It's too soon. You need time to heal. I want you to follow my instructions carefully. Don't mess with either of your wounds and give it at least a week until you try to speak. Let Rix do the talking for you."

"You must come with us! And what about the others?" Rix pleaded with me.

"There's no time, and nowhere to hide them. You can't help them now, but I can."

The lift rose to the surface, and far off in the distance, the morning sun seared over the horizon. I led the children to the ship, lowered the rear ramp, and rushed them inside. By that point, Gia was walking on her own and she tugged at the back of my shirt to stop my hustling through the cargo bay.

I desperately wanted to hear her speak to confirm that the surgery was a success, but I didn't want to have to stomach what she might say to me. This was an emotional enough time for me, and the last thing I needed was to rethink my decision.

"Can you pilot the craft?" Rix asked, still trying to pull me into their escape.

"I cannot, and I wouldn't even if I could. Come, you both need to fit in here. It's going to be tight, so suck it in," I joked to make light of the situation.

There was a small storage hatch about the size of a refrigerator near the junction between the bay and the ship's main quarters. I had spent a year planning to climb into it myself, but plans changed.

"Rix, you're first. Get in tight against the wall," I instructed him as I held the door open. My voice cracked as I tried to keep my tears at bay. "You too, Gia."

She stood balancing on one leg and wrapped her arms around me, which only made things harder.

"My wife, Maya, and our friend Ranbir are going to find you. Stay quiet until they do." I composed myself. "Tell Maya to treat your throat like a field dressing. You need to keep it clean and replace the bandage every two days. Tell her . . ." I trailed off as I began to cry.

"Tell her that no mother could leave the other children behind. Rix—" I looked to the young Praxi who was still capable of emoting, "make her understand. I'll send word when I can."

I gently, but firmly, guided Gia into the compartment, avoiding her glossy, tear-filled eyes. As I closed the door on them, Rix said his farewell.

"Hey, human. You're not so bad. Consider my trust earned."

His heartfelt transmission was earnest and matched the positive tales I had heard about communicating with the Praxi. I hated staying behind, but I knew from the warmth shared by a single rescued victim that my presence was necessary for the dozens of others who remained in captivity.

I left the kids in the compartment and exited the ship, leaving no trace of my subterfuge. I returned to the loading pad to reenter the pyramid through production, but it appeared as though someone was getting an early start on the day. Whoever it was had lowered the lift and was now riding it to the surface.

With nowhere to hide, I decided to play it cool rather than be spotted running away. I didn't want to face an accusatory line of questioning from whomever was coming to the planet's surface.

Maddox appeared as the pad came to a stop, all of his personal belongings with him.

"Good morning. You're up early."

"What are you doing out here?" he asked as he slung a bag over his shoulder and picked up two others.

"I couldn't sleep, so I figured I'd give the cargo a final walk-through," I lied. "What about you? Where are you off to?"

"I've fulfilled my obligations and now I'm going home."

I spent a year juggling a dozen problems and had forgotten about the three-hundred-pound monster that was planning on hitching a ride on the craft headed right into Maya's path.

If my friends were going to successfully hijack the freighter and free my stowaways, they were going to have to outmuscle this behemoth on their own. I couldn't get back to the ship to send a warning now that Maddox was present, and I had to get back to the lab before Dani regained consciousness.

I didn't want to linger around to chitchat, but Maddox surprisingly had a few more parting words.

"Hey, doc," he grabbed my attention as I walked away, "you did good. I know I was rough on you, but . . . yeah."

The brute was trying to apologize and show some appreciation, but I'm sure he'd take it all back within twenty-four hours.

"I'm never coming back to this hellhole," he continued, spitting out the taste of the Vocury air, "but if I ever see you back on Earth, I'll buy you a drink."

"Alright, then."

Under different circumstances, I might have enjoyed getting to know the gorilla, but I had more pressing matters to tend to.

I rode the pad down to production, hurried through the bay, and passed our final freighter, docked indoors. I took the elevator to the lab level and was relieved to find the situation unchanged. No one else had started their day early, and Dani was still crumpled on the floor in the processing room.

I propped Dani up next to a wall beam, bound her hands using ripped fabric as ropes, gagged her mouth, and then repeated the same process for myself. I slumped my head forward and closed my eyes, pretending to be unconscious. I was dead tired after being up all night, but my nerves were wound too tightly to sleep.

The freighter was scheduled to launch in thirty minutes, and I assumed most of the personnel would be wandering outdoors to see them off rather than stumbling across the pair of us in our precarious positions. I counted down the minutes and felt more confident in my plan with every second that ticked by.

Dani woke up sooner than I had hoped, but there was no one around to hear her muffled cries for help. After a few minutes of listening to her groaning into her gag and tugging at her restraints, I opened my eyes slowly and acted out my own confused stirring.

I shared glances with Dani and mirrored her struggle with the restraints to convince her that I was just as much a victim as she was. Her eyes narrowed with suspicion as she examined how tight her restraints were and how loose mine were.

Not long after, there was a commotion in the lab, and we were able to raise our groans to an audible level that eventually captured Dr. Amaar's attention. He rushed into the room, dropped to a knee, and yanked the gag from my mouth.

"Rix and Gia! They attacked and overpowered us. They must have escaped."

"How is this possible? What were you two doing down here?"

"I'm sorry, sir. I was trying to take advantage of the last night before they went into processing," I explained. "I thought I was on the cusp of another breakthrough, and we might have hit it if it wasn't for Rix. He wasn't secured properly in processing, and before I knew it, I was waking up on the floor."

Dr. Amaar removed Dani's gag, and she was instantly full of spit and vinegar. "He was secure! I double-checked," she insisted, defending her professionalism.

She shot me a dirty look for casually throwing her under the bus, but I didn't have a choice. If there was going to be a finger pointed at someone, I needed it aimed at her.

"You fools. You're lucky to be alive. If you had let the younger children escape as well, you'd wish your attackers had finished you off. Each is worth fifty of you," Dr. Amaar chastised.

"They couldn't have gone far," I lied. "If we track them down, we could salvage their bodies. I'd love to show you what Dani and I accomplished," I threw some verbal water on the figurative burning bridge between Dani and myself, but the damage was done.

"Sir," Dani's voice trembled with uncertainty. "I don't believe that's actually what happened."

I stared at Dani, but she avoided my gaze.

"Rix hit you hard," I enunciated every word, trying to force Dani into compliance. "I think you might have a concussion."

I grabbed Dani's upper arm, but she shook me loose.

"It is my opinion that Dr. Fontaine is compromised. She performed an unauthorized procedure, and I believe she freed those children. She's been acting in their best interests all along. It's highly likely they're stowed away on the freighter. She's been planning this, but I was too blind to see it. She should be removed from duty, placed under arrest, and I suggest that I take her place in the lab."

Fuck.

Chapter 14

Broken Promises

Ranbir Chopra: 2041

We were prying answers from the Praxi stowaways when the door to the forward decks opened. The only security on board was a bulking hulk of a man, and it's a good thing Maya was quick on the draw and had a reputation for an itchy trigger finger. He lumbered toward us and the only thing that slowed his approach was Maya's warning shot zinging by his ear.

"Fontaine! What have you done?" he raged.

"Maddox? Where's Tess?" she answered with a question of her own.

"She's on Vocury," the male Praxi answered. "She wouldn't leave the other children behind."

"That sneaky bitch," Maddox snarled. "That's what this is about? Those damn kids?"

"Why would she not stick to the plan?" Maya questioned as she began to pace back and forth. "Goddammit, Tess. Now what?"

Maya should have kept some distance between herself and that giant of a man, but she walked right up to him until her chin was nearly touching his chest. Pressing the steel end of her barrel against his throat, she seethed through clenched teeth, "I'm going to count to one, and if I don't get some answers about my wife, you won't need a doctor to stop the blood draining from your windpipe, you'll need a plumber. Comprendes?"

"You heard the tripod," Maddox replied, unfazed by the threat of violence.

"I'm not playing with you," Maya warned him. "Where is she? Last chance."

"She's on Vocury, you unhinged twat. She must have snuck these two stowaways on board early this morning. You're a commander. Act like it."

This fool had no idea the human tornado of emotions he was stirring. Maya was more than capable of pulling the trigger, and I think she wanted to.

I approached and placed my hand softly on Maya's shoulder. "She'll send word," I comforted her. "I'm sure she's only doing what she thinks is right."

Maya lowered her weapon, closed her eyes, and pinched the bridge of her nose as though she were nursing a headache. "Move the cargo and anything else of use to the Omaha," she commanded.

Michael, Seamus, Georgia, and Anthony were happy to oblige, but the rest of us lingered to hear what else Maya had in store.

"We'll sit tight. Tess will contact us, and then we'll make a plan," was the best she could come up with.

"I don't have time for this!" Maddox barked and dared to reenter Maya's personal bubble, but the two Praxi kids were quick to step in his path. "I have to get to Earth, now."

"That's not happening," Maya quickly dismissed him.

"You don't understand," Maddox's tone shifted from aggression to desperation. "It's my son, Commander. He has neuroblastoma—a tumor the size of a nickel. The only way he lives is if I get this cargo home."

Maya immediately stopped pacing. She knew the irrational love of a parent, but her hands were tied. With quiet regret, she turned to the Praxi and ordered, "Pack up everything. Bind his hands."

"Fontaine! He's going to die! You hear me? Please. He's just a little boy, and you have the power to save him. Get your fucking slimy digits off of me!" Maddox fought off the kids, and despite my efforts to intervene, he was crazed, and we were physically outmatched.

Maddox charged at Maya, slowing only to lean down and press his forehead against the pointed barrel of her gun. "Just fucking kill me. If you're going to kill my boy, you might as well end me too."

"Don't tempt me."

"Do it, Maya," the male Praxi oddly chimed in, his hate for Maddox palpable. "He's a monster. He killed my people, mutilated Gia, and imprisoned my friends. He does not deserve to live."

"You think I'm bad?" Maddox sneered at him. "Wait until you get a load of these two!" He nodded toward Maya and me. "My body count has nothing on theirs. What's two more, huh, soldier?" he taunted Maya. "Pull the trigger and add me and my son to your bloody legacy."

"I'm not killing anyone today," Maya said softly.

I couldn't imagine what it must have felt like to have this guilt trip added to the sorrow of missing Tess.

"Yes you are. You're killing my son! It's just four months there and four months back. Tess will still be here waiting. I'll help you! Whatever it takes," Maddox began pleading again, his emotions shifting rapidly. "You could trade regenerator and raise an army. The shit is worth trillions."

"With a 'T?'" Michael piped up as he carried a box into the rear of the Omaha.

"What would you pay to live forever? Trillions," Maddox tempted him.

"Well, I don't have trillions. Not yet," Michael replied.

"Shut up!" Maya demanded. I wasn't sure if her anger was because of the disappointment of Tess not being on board, or the fact that she knew she was staring down an impossible moral decision. "Move," she ordered her prisoner, waving her pistol toward the Omaha.

"I'll kill you for this," Maddox seethed as Maya marched him away. "A life for a life. First your son, then you. I swear it."

Things were bleak for Maya before, and if she didn't get clarification from Tess soon, they'd get so much worse. She had already put herself through the wringer, and as a staunch supporter of "an eye for an eye" justice, bearing the responsibility for the death of a child might tear her apart. On top of that, she had to explain to Marcus that his Mommy wasn't coming home today after all.

There was a lot of cargo to move but being near the first Praxi I had seen in years rendered me useless. I had subsided on my questions for over a year, and I would finally be getting answers. If there was an explanation for why I was left in the dark all this time, those kids would certainly know it.

"I'm Ranbir," I finally introduced myself to them after all the drama. "Friends call me Chop."

"I'm Rix, and this is—"

"Gia. Yeah, I got that. That's an interesting name. I once knew a Gio."

The mute child perked up and approached me like she had something to say but no way to say it. She looked to Rix to do the speaking for her.

"You know of Gio?" His hope filled me and coated my sadness.

"Oh yes. He was a dear friend."

"Was?"

Gia grabbed my arm, and her eyes narrowed. There was a pulse coming off of her and my hair began to stand on end. I couldn't feel her or hear her, but her pursed lips told a story.

"My God. You're his daughter."

She nodded her head in the affirmative, encouraging me to share more.

"Where is he?" Rix asked. "The elders lost contact with Prius when we were very young. They sent an unscheduled convoy and discovered that our people had been nearly wiped out by humans. Gio was at the center of the conflict, and he left the survivors behind when he went off with the human Emilia Vera and never returned."

I just stared at Gia. "He's actually your father?"

I could hardly believe it. I never imagined that I'd have to deliver the news of his passing to anyone who loved him more than I did. "I'm so sorry. Gio is dead," I told her, my voice breaking on that final word.

Gia released my arm, dropped to two knees, and fell backward onto the floor. She wrapped two of her arms around herself and slowly rocked back and forth. Rix knelt beside her, unable to offer anything but physical comfort. Her whimpering was soft, and though I couldn't experience her pain, Rix was emitting a cocktail of emotions that nearly overpowered me.

"He was brave," I offered my condolences. "He was kind. Wise. Funny. He taught me things about myself I never knew. He saved our lives, Gia. I've sworn to never let his death be in vain. I owe him an unpayable debt."

I tried not to cry. The poor child had shed enough tears for the both of us. Her father was dead, her people slaughtered, and according to Rix, human scientists had destroyed her ability to communicate. I couldn't even imagine being born into such emotional adeptness just to have it taken away.

I was ready to fight and die for her if necessary. For both of them. For all Praxi. It would be hypocritical not to. Neither asked me about my sordid past, maybe because Rix could likely absorb and process the punishing guilt I carried with me. He hadn't experienced remorse from those who had hurt him, and I resolved to become their caretaker and prove to them that decency could be found among our kind.

Space became tight in the Omaha's cargo hold, and rather than leave anything behind, the crew stacked boxes and crates of pills to the ceiling in vacant quarters. Maya imprisoned Maddox, converting one of the rooms into a makeshift luxury jail cell, and then locked herself away on the bridge.

For three days, I meandered about the ship with the Praxi children, having taken them in as my own, and the crew abandoned their booze-filled nights to indulge in the endless supply of drugs, sampling from millions of assorted tablets.

It wasn't until that third day we spent docked inside the freighter that Maya addressed us. Her absence was telling, but the fact that she chose to deliver her message via the intercom rather than face-to-face said more.

Most of us were in the mess hall preparing dinner when her voice broke in.

"Attention, everyone. There's been no word from Tess so far, and there might not be for some time. I've made promises, and I still intend on keeping them. I want to keep it one hundred with you, though. As you know, it might be another year before the next shipment goes out, and I can't risk moving out of communication range. If I get an update from Tess that includes a workable timeline, I'll give you a lift wherever you want to go. But until then and for now, you should all get comfortable."

Michael slammed his spoon into his bowl, sending his soup flying. Based on their dirty looks, Georgia and Anthony seemed to share his displeasure, but neither acted out as dramatically. And surprisingly, I felt anger coming from Rix, even though he added no commentary.

"There is some good news, though," Maya continued. "Among the loot is our enemy's prized possession. The only thing more valuable than money is time, and while it may seem like I'm taking some from you, time is now officially irrelevant. Call bullshit if you want, but those goons we robbed somehow discovered immortality, and I, for one, don't plan on aging a single day until Tess is back where she belongs. Do with that what you will, but I don't want to hear whining from any of you. Nobody else gets to live forever, and there's a billion people who would kill to switch places with you. So, yeah, there it is."

"This is some bullshit," Michael complained. "Even if it's true, what good is immortality if you're stuck on this damn ship?"

Rix grabbed my forearm as I turned toward the bridge to check on Maya, privately questioning me. "What kind of weapons are on board?"

I stopped in my tracks, focused my mind, and answered, "I know what you're thinking. I've been thinking it too."

"And? I've seen the humans' projectile weapons. While effective, they can be easily outmatched. We are badly outnumbered, but we could overtake them with superior firepower."

"The Omaha has plenty of options, but nothing that'd work for an incursion. Maya has a pistol, and we've got some sweet gravity charges. We're talking big 'booms' here, though."

"No. No explosions. There'd be too much collateral damage. The Citadel is my species' last hope to live on. A successful attack must be clean, precise, and swift."

"Well, unless their forces want to come out into the open so that we can drop a bomb on them, I don't think we're anywhere near equipped enough for a strike."

I couldn't blame Rix for wanting to pick a fight. His friends remained in captivity, and the only center for new Praxi life was under human occupation. If we had even twenty trained soldiers and enough handheld gravity weapons to arm them, we might have actually had a puncher's chance.

Surprise remained our greatest ally, though. We had Tess on the inside, and if Maya was right, there was only a single freighter remaining. If they launched it, we would have the upper hand in space.

I marched up to the bridge to check in on my friend and was shocked to find the door locked. Maya's paranoia had taken hold.

"Hey! It's me," I shouted as I pounded on the door.

"You alone?"

"Yes."

Maya hit the override on the lock and held her pistol at the ready as the door opened. "Get in," she ordered me, closing the door and locking it once more. The bridge stunk of sweat and smoke, her hair was matted, and she had bags under her eyes.

"You think you might be taking this a little far?" I asked.

"I might be drunk, but I'm not stupid. If I traded places with any of them out there, I'd be cooking up a way to take control of the ship. So, forgive me if I'm not trusting of the one person who actually knows how to fly it."

"You don't trust me now?"

"I don't know. Can I?" she shot back as she took a swig from her flask.

"I've backed you every step of the way, Maya. I've taken orders from you. I've tried to help you. I've done everything you've asked of me because you're my friend. And you ask if you can trust me?" My voice rose, "The better question is, can I trust you?"

"What the fuck are you talking about?"

"No! No, Maya. No more deflecting. I'll back you, but it's confession time. You need to fill in the gaps for me. Right now."

"What do you want to hear, man? That I lied to you? That I manipulated you? What?"

"I know all of that already. I want to know why!"

"Because you were our only chance, and you never would have helped us if you knew the truth! You and your holy self-righteousness. What would you have said if Tess admitted that she desecrated Gio's body, huh? 'Hey Chop, so, uh, I carved your friend into little pieces and ran experiments on him. Sorry about that, but could you help us unfuck this situation real quick? Thanks.'" she inflected a mocking tone.

I rubbed my hand across my forehead and closed my eyes with horrified disgust, shock, and frustration.

I wanted to scream, but it wouldn't have done any good. Maya was right. I was incapable of thinking critically where the Praxi—and especially Gio—were concerned.

"I knew it. I fucking knew it. How could you keep this from me?" I paced laps of anger around the bridge, serving Maya a vengeful side eye as I processed the knowledge that my dear friend had been desecrated in the name of science. "I should have buried him myself," I seethed. "Never let any of you put your hands on him!"

"See! You would have preached your guilt trip and tried to stop the mission," she said, her voice lowering. "I know you, bro."

"Tess knew, and she did it anyway. We could have stopped them!"

"With what? Votes? Wake up. You think you can stand in the way of the wealthiest and most powerful people on the planet? They were never going to stop. The only way everyone was going to chill was if they thought shit was running on schedule. Let them burn up the last of their triaxum and fight us on an even playing field. The plan is working."

"Is it? Tess is still down there, we have no idea what's going on, there are Praxi children being tortured daily, your crew is on the verge of mutiny for a litany of reasons, and now we're taking prisoners. What the hell have you gotten us into?"

All the shouting caused Marcus to start crying, and Maya took the easy exit out of an argument she couldn't win. I didn't have an alternative plan to pitch because there wasn't one, but it would have been nice to have gotten an apology.

My heart ached knowing what had happened to Gio, and the duty of delivering the full truth to Gia was going to fall squarely on my shoulders. I wish I had heard it from Tess myself and had her by my side to deliver the news with remorse, instead of Maya with all her defiance.

If anyone else had been responsible, there's no telling what I might have done. The fact that my own friends were the ones involved, and that they had kept it from me, filled me with a rage that couldn't be released through violence.

Maya held Marcus to comfort him and offered no rebuttal. "I need you to undock the Omaha," she said quietly. "Keep us within range of the planet. Please," she added.

"I'm not taking another order from you, understand, Commander? This is the last time. You need a favor? You better get it from one of those jackasses in your new crew, and I suggest you do it before they realize you're leading them on, too. I'm fucking done."

I had marked my line in the sand, so in lieu of fueling the fire between us any further, I undocked the Omaha. Once we were clear, Maya locked the controls down again, input orders to seal off the bridge from anyone but herself, and we went our separate ways.

Every day, Maya would continue to check in for a new message from Tess, and every time there was no news, she spiraled a little further out of control. My anger drove a spike between us, and rather than accept any responsibility for Maya's depression, I was again solely focused on my own.

Everything I had known was a lie. There was a false purpose at the edge of the galaxy, and all it led to was more pain. I had joined Maya on this mission not only for a second chance at Prius, but for the possibility of doing something good. I was supposed to be honoring the legacy of Emilia and Gio, but I ended up being a pawn in a chess game tarnishing their memory.

Meeting Gia should have been the opportunity of a lifetime, and now, instead of consoling her with heroic stories of her father, I'd need to come clean about the darkness that followed his death and my complicity that allowed it to transpire.

Never again.

I was along for this ride wherever it led, but at the end of the road, my destiny would be my own. I had even more to make amends for now than before, and if the moment for redemption presented itself, I would be ready.

In the meantime, I buried my depression and longing for Emilia by concentrating on raising Gia, Rix, and Marcus. It wasn't much compared to the guilt I saddled myself with, but at least it was something.

I found myself joining everyone else in the bottle, and at the rate we were drinking, we would have run out of alcohol in no time. That would have been for the best, but we had a far greater problem on board now.

Our crew wasted no time experimenting with the loot. I gave it a few weeks to watch for adverse effects, and once it seemed that the regenerator was safe enough—and that we weren't going anywhere anytime soon—I joined them.

I don't know what any of us were expecting. It's not like you can see the effects of aging overnight. But it felt incredible. When I took it, it was as if my body was finally getting everything it needed: eight hours of sleep, a proper diet, the right balance of vitamins, and regular exercise. If that could be classified as a high, I'd call it clean living.

At first, I thought I had taken a drink from the fountain of youth and that I was set for life. If the regenerator proved to be as advertised, we'd achieved immortality—or so we thought. It's a hard concept to believe without the proof of a few ageless decades, but Rix was confident in the application of Vice, even in the hands of human scientists.

Unfortunately, mankind was meddling with science we didn't fully understand. The Praxi had carefully integrated this miracle into their DNA at conception, extending their lifespans, but remaining mortal. We, on the other hand, were far too greedy to accept such limits.

Five weeks after the crew had popped their first pills, the sickness began. It started with Georgia, then Seamus, and soon affected the others. What seemed like a mild bug at first—headaches, dizziness, nausea, body aches—quickly turned into something far worse and bizarre.

Maya's hair started growing in grey at the roots, Anthony's fingernails were falling off, and Michael had blood in his urine, stool, and vomit. We went into quarantine, everyone except Marcus, the Praxi kids, and me falling horribly ill. I thought I had dodged it—until weeks later, when a killer headache hit me like a sledgehammer.

We weren't sick at all. It was that damn regenerator running its course, and I was simply behind schedule because I hadn't jumped into our discount immortality as soon as the others.

Regenerator was a joke, and we fell for it blindly. There was no telling what awaited any of us without our next dose, and nobody was willing to be the guinea pig who would go cold turkey to find out. We were now bound to a lifetime of treating death instead of curing it.

I imagine that Dr. Amaar, and the pharmaceutical companies like him, would see the flaw in the product as more of a feature than a bug. If one pill was all it took to live forever, you could sell each for a billion dollars. Who has that kind of money, though? There's far more profit in selling a monthly dose for just slightly less than the average monthly income.

If this poison were ever to reach Earth, mankind would be enslaved by layaway immortality. You could live forever with a lifetime subscription to your prescription, and all it would cost you is everything in perpetuity. No one ever misses a payment when the collection agency is Death.

I suppose we were the lucky ones. We estimated there were half a million tabs of regenerator in the stolen cargo—enough to last the seven of us over a hundred thousand years. Though, why anyone would want to live that long was beyond me.

By the time we had waited another six months for any word from Tess, I was ready to storm the Citadel and happily die liberating the other Praxi children. Unfortunately, we'd be waiting far longer than expected, and boredom had a better chance of killing me than a bullet.

I don't think the crew could have maintained their patience if the regenerator had been all we had. But with the alcohol running low, Maya and the others turned to an assortment of uppers and downers that put traditional narcotics and opiates to shame.

With names like Hydroklonazyn, Ozymgappa, and Percilacite, we simply knew them as reliever, flyer, relaxer, and so on. That's the thing with those pharma titles—they make their products seem official, lab-tested, and safe . . . when really, they're just medical-grade heroin.

Outside of the Praxi kids and I, the entire crew was hooked, and that was the only reason their desire for the riches they'd gain from selling the garbage was held at bay.

Weeks turned to months, and months turned to years without any update from Tess. Something had gone terribly wrong, and though Maya refused to believe it, I had all the confirmation I needed. Every day that passed without the second freighter coming into our path signaled to me that our enemy knew we were waiting for them.

They were trapped on the surface, and we were bound to an ageless siege of their city. If we abandoned our post to seek resources for an attack or to pursue another adventure, our opponents would be free to move about the stars. We didn't have the firepower to overtake them, and they didn't have the capabilities to match us in space. With the bulk of triaxum recovered from the mines, we could hang stationary within range for ten lifetimes.

It was a test of wills that would continue for years, marked by Marcus' aging from toddler to teen. I had the resolve to outlast them until they broke, but the rest of the crew had their own interests.

Maya became a ghost among us. She'd spend weeks—sometimes even months—locked away on the bridge or in her quarters, only showing herself to restock supplies or sneak off to the restroom. For all intents and purposes, I became the captain, though there were no orders to issue. My job was to placate the others and keep them happy, a task that grew harder as time marched on.

Gia had learned to speak, and she wasn't shy about echoing Rix's desire for justice. Maddox remained locked up, though I did carve out slits in his walls so he could see into the cargo bay, maintain some semblance of human contact, and spit his hateful vitriol at anyone who would listen.

The others, while constantly stoned, were desperate to leave, to go anywhere but here. Earth was preferred so they could get rich, but they would have happily settled for Prius, and I couldn't blame them. I had successfully placated them for longer than I expected, but it was only a matter of time before things came to a head.

Marcus was maybe thirteen years old at the time, and we were all in the cargo bay doing our morning training. It was good exercise, and a useful way to pass the time and burn everyone's energy. Gia and Rix were particularly interested in learning how to fight. It wasn't in their nature to brawl, but they had every reason to sharpen the skills they may one day need.

We had a space cleared and filled with unused mattresses so we could toss each other around without getting hurt. I refrained from throwing or taking punches, but Rix and Michael liked to get in there once in a while and really throw down. It had been a while since their last bout, so they decided to pad their hands once again and put on a show. The rest of us watched from the sidelines, Maddox looking on from his cell.

As per usual, Michael was dominating the fight as I offered Rix a bit of unsolicited coaching.

"You have to go to two feet, bud. You're not quick enough on one."

He switched his stance, but with only one hand to defend himself, it was no use.

"Ooof," I groaned as he absorbed three quick strikes from Michael before retreating to call a break.

"You really have to hit him so hard?" Seamus asked as Michael refueled with a hydrator.

"If you step into the batter's box, sometimes you're going to get plunked." Michael took a drink of water and spit a playful stream at Seamus.

"One foot planted or two, I can't beat him," Rix complained. "For all your flaws, humans are better built for combat."

"You're taller and longer," I counseled him. "You have to switch your stance more often. Use your leverage. Keep him off-balance and at a distance."

"Or, if you actually wanted to win the fight," Maddox interrupted, "you could listen to someone who knows how to do it."

'What do you know?" Marcus asked him. "You couldn't even win a fight against my doper mom."

"Sticking a gun in someone's face ain't a fight, boy. I could clear every last one of you at once, and not because I'm the biggest."

"I'd like to see you try," Marcus antagonized him with adolescent ignorance.

"Settle down," I cautioned him. "Who's next?"

"Come here, tripod." Maddox beckoned to Rix. "Come on, don't be a baby. The past is the past. Let me help you."

Rix approached the slits that Maddox peered through and listened in as he offered his fighting advice.

"One more round," Rix announced as he returned to the mats and drew Michael in for more.

"I'm not going to pull my punches," Michael warned him.

Rix looked back to Maddox who nodded. "That's fine. Hit me with everything, if you can."

"Okay, fellas. One more," I agreed, allowing the fight to continue even though I had no say over the matter.

"Come on, Rix," Gia encouraged him. "Don't make me have to get in there and show you how it's done."

Rix stood at the end of the mats as Michael closed toward the center. He dropped from two feet all the way down to three, bending at every joint and standing no taller than four feet high.

"What is this shit?" Michael taunted. "Either fight me or don't."

Rix exploded out of his stance, charging from a compact angle of attack. He drove his head into Michael's gut, knocking him back, then immediately followed with another surge, leaping onto him. Michael got in a glancing shot, but Rix slammed him to the ground, straddling his waist, and began dropping hammer fists toward his face.

"Whoa!" Marcus cheered, wide-eyed. "Get him!"

Wildly thrashing, Rix didn't land every blow, but enough of them went through for me to step in and break it up.

"Okay. Okay!" I shouted before rushing to pull Rix off of Michael. "Hey!" I shouted as I held Rix's arm back and wrestled him away. "That's enough!"

"That was great!" Marcus exclaimed as he rushed to his friend's side. "You were all like, 'rawwwr.'"

Michael stood, wiped blood from his nose, and glared at Rix. "Whoopity-doo, you learned a new trick."

"We're even now." Rix offered his hand graciously just for Michael to slap it away.

"Don't be such a sore loser," Gia mocked him.

"You want to step in here and try me, little girl?" Michael taunted her in return.

Georgia laughed at that. "You're lucky he didn't hog-tie your ass. Young bull realized he's got horns." Though her accent had faded over time, she still held onto her Southern girl slang.

Maddox extended his arm in a gesture of congratulations to Rix, receiving a playful slap from his alien protégé.

"Rage and blunt force—that's the key to winning." Maddox said, seeming gracious enough. But as soon as he had Rix's arm in his grasp, he seized the opportunity, wrenching it through the slit and clamping down on it with a firm grip.

"Hey!" I shouted as both Gia and I rushed to Rix's aid, but Maddox's grip was strong.

"I'll snap his fucking arm in two. Don't try me."

"Stop!" I demanded.

"Open the door. Now!" Maddox replied.

Gia reached through one of the slits to swing on Maddox but at such a weird angle, she was ineffective without leverage. "Let him go!"

Maddox solicited help from the others while playing on their desires. "You idiots want to get out of here? Open the door."

Marcus raced around the corner into the hallway near Maddox's door and stood between Anthony and Michael, who were eyeing the situation with interest.

"Open the door, kid, or I'll turn your three-legged friend into a standard bipedal," Maddox hollered at him.

"Think it through, kid," Michael joined the cause. "You've never seen the worlds outside these walls, and your mother will never let you. We're all prisoners here."

"Shut your mouth!" I yelled at him.

Michael approached Marcus, but before he could put his hands on the boy, Gia charged him on all three legs—much like Rix had—and slammed into him. Anthony and Georgia surrounded the pair as they wrestled on the floor, and just when it seemed I had lost control of the situation, a single gunshot rang out.

"Keep it up if you want to catch one," Maya warned the mutineers. "You." She pointed her pistol at Michael. "Up." Maddox begrudging released Rix's arm, and we retreated behind Maya.

"Open the door, Marcus," she ordered.

"One day," Maddox taunted, his voice dripping with hate, "you're going to run out of bullets, and then I'm going to bash your skull in."

"Looking forward to it," Maya quipped as she turned to the rest of the crew. "Get in." She flicked her barrel toward the open door and forced Michael, Anthony, and Georgia into the cell with Maddox. "You too," she ordered Seamus.

"I didn't do anything," he pleaded with her.

"She's never going to sleep with you," Michael mocked him. "Get your fat ass in here. You're one of us."

"We're cool, Maya," Georgia asserted. "You ain't gotta do all this."

"In." Maya pushed Seamus and nearly lost her balance. High as a kite, as per usual. It's a wonder she was able to walk at all. Had she not been armed, the Omaha might have fallen under new ownership.

It's amazing that we kept it together for as long as we did. There was no way the others could continue to roam freely on board, and one prisoner kept restrained inhumanely was enough.

The rest of us met in the mess hall to discuss how to proceed, and it was actually young Marcus who brought the best solution to the table.

"Just jettison them out into space," Rix suggested. "Be done with them."

"Maddox sure, but all of them?" Gia asked. "Maybe we haven't always been friends, but we've shared a home with them for years."

"We're not murdering them. What else?" I responded.

"Turn their quarters into cells," Maya said, her words slurred. "Lock them away."

"Forever? A life sentence doesn't mean the same thing it used to, unless you're planning on cutting off their regenerator, which again, would mean murdering them," I reasoned with her.

"How about this," Marcus began his pitch. "We push the deserted freighter to the planet's surface with the gravity cannons and guide it in softly. They could live down there and make a new life."

"Hmmm." I pondered the idea. "That's not bad, kiddo."

"No way. We can't set Maddox free. He could go back to the Citadel and spoil everything," Maya argued.

"Spoil what?" Marcus' voice rose. "They already know we're here! How are you the only one who can't see that?"

"We don't know that, and we can't know it until Tess contacts us."

Somehow Maya still held on to hope. Through her depression and addiction, the only thing keeping her alive was that misplaced hope, and I couldn't bring myself to take it from her. Her blind belief kept her moving forward, much as my desire to have a purpose had propelled me.

Marcus didn't have my patience, though.

"You've lost it, you know that? Mom is never coming back. She's either dead or she's abandoned us."

"Don't you say that!" Maya slammed her fist on the table. "She's alive, and we'll see her again."

"Oh, here we go again." Marcus rolled his eyes as he got up from his seat and began pacing. "What's next? More fairy tales about how one day my biological father will magically arrive? Jesus, you're delusional!"

"Sit down, Marcus," I instructed him calmly.

"No! I've had it. It's time to move on. I say we take the supplies and set up our own colony. Help the people living there who have nothing. We can set up shop and make trade. Hell, maybe we could just walk right up to the Citadel's front door and cut a deal."

"We are not making any deals with them," Gia stated firmly.

"Those supplies are ours. When this is over, we're building our colony on Prius," I added.

"Let's just go there, then! What are we even doing here? Who cares if they ship their stuff to Earth! Let them. It's not our problem."

"We can't let that poison reach humanity," I stated plainly.

"Why? You're all on it! You pop pills daily, and I can't even get one to sleep better once in a while. Bunch of hypocrites."

"We're not leaving," Maya said.

"Not until our people are free," Rix affirmed.

"Yeah, I'm not going anywhere, either. We stay until the job is done, even if that means forever," I agreed.

"I hate this ship!" Marcus growled with teen angst. "Nobody ever listens to me. Maddox was right, we're all prisoners."

Marcus stormed off, but amid his hormonal outburst, he had left us with a viable option. I wasn't about to give away our supplies or set Maddox free, but Marcus' idea of turning the freighter into a habitat was a good one. We used the gravity cannons, just like he said, to push the ship to the surface, and we turned Anthony, Georgia, Michael, and Seamus loose on it.

The deal was simple. They could contact us anytime they needed a pill refill, so long as they kept Maddox locked up on their ship. What they did on the planet after that was their business.

It was far from what Maya had promised them, but it was the best we could do in a bad situation.

Just another in a long line of poor decisions.

Chapter 15

The Expiration Date of Hate
Maddox: 2052

I fucking hate Vocury.

I hate the crushing gravity and acidic air, the never-ending mounds of muddy sand, and the relentless heat. I hate the Citadel and everyone in it. I hate this damn mission and the Praxi who made it possible. I hate being confined to a cell with only the child of my enemy for company. I hate swallowing pills in favor of steak and potatoes. I hate Ranbir, Tess, those alien children, and the idiot wannabe pirates.

But most of all, I hate Maya.

Most emotional reactions to the people who come in and out of our lives will fade over time. Even the strongest bonds of love can give way—but not hate. Love requires work. Spite only requires memory, and I would never forget what had happened to my son. Maya was going to pay for her callous indifference, and the bill would cost more than an "eye for an eye."

Killing Marcus wouldn't be enough. Maya needed to witness his death, and if the world were just, to have to choose between his life or the lives of many. Only then would she understand what she had done to me.

I knew she harbored guilt over her decision, but apparently never enough to muster an apology. Maya had issued a death sentence to my boy, sent me to my cell, and rarely faced me again. In any normal lifetime, she might have been able to avoid me forever, but we were no longer bound to a definitive span of years, and my hate would survive as long as I would.

I spent years locked in a space the size of a one-bedroom apartment. My only amenities were a bathroom, a bed that my feet hung from, and the daily pills slipped under the door to keep me fed, hydrated, and timeless. Maya's attempt to make peace with me through those pills was born out of guilt and would eventually get her killed.

Occasionally, Seamus or Georgia would linger on the other side of the door to chat when they were bored, but neither would risk letting me out. I tried countless times to talk them into trading me to the Citadelians, but they never wavered in their caution. A frustrating position for them to hold, albeit a wise one. Given the chance, I would have strangled them the second they let me out.

I had no idea how many more years had passed until I received my first visit from Marcus. The Omaha was his cell, and Maya had either lost complete control of the boy, or she had allowed him to take trips to surface to placate his teen angst.

Though I couldn't gauge his age visually, his cracking adolescent voice gave me a clue. He must have been about sixteen when he first came to me, meaning a few years had passed since I was moved. In total, I had spent over a decade in captivity, my only crime being an inconvenience to Maya.

I heard three soft taps on my door, followed by his curious young voice. "Are you in there?"

"It's the only prison cell on the planet, so I don't know where else I'd be."

"Well, that is where we put criminals," he quipped.

"I'm no criminal, boy. I'm just another casualty of your mother. Like you, but different."

"That's not what I've heard."

"Oh, I'm sure. Maya has a way of justifying everything with a lie. I can only imagine what she's fabricated about me." Manipulation wasn't my strong suit, but I had a decade to prepare, and my subject was a mere child.

"Not from Maya. From my friend, Gia. She says you're a monster."

"I didn't cut that child up. Your mother, Tess, did."

"She's not my mother," Marcus said defiantly. "Regardless, Gia blames you."

"I was there, boy. I saw it. You can take the word of an alien who was a heavily sedated child at the time, or you can believe me. I don't care either way," I lied.

"Tess fixed and freed her. She might mean nothing to me, but she saved both Gia and Rix."

"That's a nice bedtime story, but I think you might be getting a little too old for it. Even if Tess helped Gia, she only did it out of guilt. I'm sorry boy, but you don't know Tess like I do. I was there the day she abandoned you. She could have stayed on the ship and returned to look after you, but she chose the glory of her career. I can't say I'm surprised by either of your parents at this point. They've done terrible things."

I knew I was being heavy-handed in my attempts to sway the kid. There was no telling if he would ever be back, and I had to seize my opportunity to work him.

Marcus didn't immediately respond, which was perfect. Most children would overreact with emotion, but he offered no defense nor rebuke.

My spin on his situation wasn't a novel idea to him. He had either considered these possibilities himself or heard similar takes from the likes of Michael or Anthony.

The very fact that he referred to both Maya and Tess by name, rather than a parental moniker, told me all I needed to know about how he viewed them. The only difference between Marcus and countless other kids his age who had screamed hateful things at their parents was that he had legitimate reasons for his outrage.

"Sorry for the bad news, kid," I broke the silence. "I've never had a visitor before, and I could really use the company. The last thing I want to do is run you off. I'm actually surprised you're allowed down here."

"You and me both. Maya doesn't usually let me do anything. Everyone else gets to do as they please and stuff their faces with pills, and I get treated like a baby. She's such a hypocrite. Everyone talks about what a badass she is, but half the time she's too scared to do anything about Tess, and the other half she's lying on the floor drooling on herself."

"What a mess. I'm sorry your folks got us both into this. If there's anybody who understands, it's me. You're free to stop by any time you want to blow off some steam. I've got nowhere else to be."

I knew well enough that it would be foolish to attempt to get Marcus to open my cell during our first encounter. He might be a kid, but he would've seen right through me. He needed to be coaxed along and convinced to turn that latch. All it would take was a good enough reason, and assuming I could keep him coming back, I had more than enough time to motivate the boy.

The more trips he made to my cell door, the more I regretted what I was planning. Though he did harbor a lot of resentment for his mothers, he wasn't the whining little weakling I expected.

The kid had lived a bizarre, isolated, and difficult life. He had every reason to complain, but the boy was tough. I couldn't help but enjoy his company and admire him. If my own son had grown up to be like Marcus, I would have been a proud father.

Every moment we spent chatting through the door made the idea of killing the kid in front of Maya more difficult, which in turn made me hate her more. My son must have died a horribly painful death because of her, and there I was, second-guessing giving her the justice she deserved. I didn't know if I'd be able to go through with it should the time come, so I started planting the seeds for the next best thing.

Marcus had been visiting me on a regular basis for a year when all my efforts finally started to show returns. He had just returned from a village trip when a real opportunity presented itself.

"This is crazy, man. Everyone is stoned out of their minds, and all they do is go back and forth to work. And now the Citadel has set up a pharmacy to keep them coming back. It's wild out there." Marcus spoke quickly, the excitement of freely roaming the planet powering his tongue. "Michael smashed this guy in the face with his elbow and took a handful of pills off of him. He didn't even need them, but we can literally do whatever we want."

"Wait, what's this pharmacy? Who is running it?" I asked.

"It's like the main hangout now. All the workers only get paid once they return to their villages. They can cash in and trade and get all fucked up. It's wild. Some lady named Dani runs it. Never seen her before. She's a Citadelian."

"This is your chance, kid. Dani is your ticket up, and I can help you. We can get off this rock. You can go anywhere you want. I'm talking about real freedom here."

"I don't know, Maddox. I'm starting to like it here. I have no interest in getting back on a ship where someone can tell me what I can and can't do."

"There is so much more out there to see, boy. Earth might have its problems, but it's our home."

"The only home I've ever known is the cold floor of a space cruiser. It's a cell, just like yours. The only difference was an unlocked door that led to nowhere. Now, the warm sands of Vocury that lead everywhere is my home."

"You can do whatever you'd like. Stay here, live forever, and rule this place, if you want. You could control every ship that comes and goes. Or you could take the Omaha and do as you please out in space. All you need is bargaining power. I can give you that freedom, but you'll have to give me mine."

"I'm listening."

"Go introduce yourself to Dani. Don't tell her who you are or take any of the other goons with you. Inform her that I am alive and well, and that we seek an audience with Dr. Amaar about getting his precious cargo home. She doesn't need to know anything beyond that, except that she's about to become filthy rich. If she can set it up, you'll come back and free me, and I'll get you access to the man who can give you the freedom you desire."

"Sorry, but I don't see how I need you at all. I'm perfectly capable of doing this without you."

"Oh? You think you understand all the moving parts? You have a plan to pitch the doctor? You think he'll even give you the time of day without me? Come on, kid. We both want the same thing."

"Alright, alright. I'll see what this Dani has to say. I'll be back in a few days. Don't you go wandering off now," he wisecracked.

Off went my manipulated, smart-mouthed toy soldier. If we could pull this off, I wouldn't need to bash the young man's head in while Maya watched. She'd be witness to a less horrifying, but equally painful, heartbreak as her only son betrayed her. And as an added bonus, I wouldn't have to harm the kid I had come to admire. It was a plan that was years in the making, and I had Maya herself to thank for giving me the time to concoct it.

She should have killed me when she had the chance.

I counted eight days by the number of times Seamus delivered my daily pills before Marcus' shadow darkened the space beneath my door once more. I had grown worried that he had worked his way into the Citadel and taken matters into his own hands, but those fears evaporated when he finally returned.

He was just a child, incapable of making his own way in our harsh world.

The locking clamp thudded and the hinges of the heavy steel door creaked as it was opened for the first time in years. Standing in the doorway was Marcus, and he wasn't alone.

"Want to go for a walk?" the boy asked.

"You've been pardoned," Michael joked. "Behave yourself, or we'll have to shackle you up and put you back in your box."

"Easy now, big guy," Georgia added. "No funny business."

"Why did you have to get these idiots involved? This was our score," I complained.

"And now it's all of ours," Anthony said as he pulled me over the threshold.

"It's a full day's walk to the village. Let's not keep Dani waiting," was all Marcus said.

***

We trudged out into the Vocury desert, our faces covered to shield us from the elements. After having spent years in my cell, every step through the sand was a battle, and the unfiltered outside air tasted worse than I even remembered.

I walked multiple paces behind Marcus and his jovial band of thieves for the better part of ten hours before the sun finally dipped behind the horizon. We took a rest for the evening and returned to beating a path familiar to everyone but me long before the sun began to rise. I had nothing to say to these fools, so I kept quiet as they shared their grand delusions.

"Where I'm from, you take an outlaw name when you pull a big job," Georgia explained. "It's mysterious and intimidating. If someone has one, you know they've earned the stripe."

"Here it comes," Anthony said playfully. "Go on, sweetheart. Have your big moment."

Georgia bent down, formed a ball of wet clay, and threw it in Anthony's direction. "You ain't know me that well."

"No?" Anthony responded with a raised eyebrow. "You could give me three guesses, but I only need one."

"Fine. What's my outlaw name gonna be?" she asked him.

"You're a 'Rebel Yell' Dixie. Try telling me I'm wrong, and I'll make a liar out of you."

"Dick." Georgia ran him down, slapped him across his back, and pulled him in for a light kiss. "Dixie," she said proudly, admiring her new name. "And what about you, baby?"

"Anthony Ableright should be Double-A," Seamus chimed in.

"Double-A," Anthony repeated. "Yeah, I can dig that. If I keep it, do I get to pick yours?" he asked Seamus.

"I don't know about all that," Seamus replied.

"I won't do you dirty. Seamus Tassin. You're now . . ." Double-A paused as he searched for the perfect moniker. "Taz."

"Alright then, brother." Taz accepted the name before turning to Michael. "What about you?"

"I don't need some stupid name. I just want to get paid," Michael responded.

"Michael Stacklaw wants stacks on stacks on stacks," Dixie joked.

"What about you, kid?" Double-A asked Marcus. "What's it gonna be?"

"You can cash your checks before the job is done. I won't stand in your way," Marcus said. "But I prefer to celebrate once the sun goes down."

"Our little Sundown Kid is all grown up." Dixie ruffled her hand through Marcus' hair as if to suggest the nickname.

The idiots had their outlaw names but all I cared about was getting down to business.

The pyramid was visible in the distance, a shimmering mirage from miles away, and the villages surrounding it gradually came into focus as we approached. The sun blanketed the area, and I imagined that each village found fleeting relief from the heat as the Citadel's shadow rolled over them throughout the day.

We reached our destination shortly after nightfall. I wasn't entirely sure what to expect after being separated from my intergalactic traveling companions for over a decade, but the state they were in was shocking. The buildings were sparse and poorly constructed, and the people's clothes were tattered and worn. The moment we entered town, they swarmed us like panhandling locusts.

Marcus dropped a few assorted pills into the hands of every beggar, and they thanked him by name with slurred speech. After a while, he announced, "That's it. That's all for today."

The vagrants turned their attention to the rest of us, but they were met by the pirates' cold indifference and my surprised confusion. I recognized some of the faces, and I could hardly believe what they had become. None of them had aged a day, yet their eyes appeared glossy and tired.

"It's through here," Marcus said as I lagged further behind, taking in the sad sights. We entered a shoddy establishment full of vagrants slumped over tables, others lying on the ground.

"Wow, so it's true. You're still alive," Dani declared, genuinely surprised. "I lost a bet, but the doc will be pleased."

"What are you doing out here?" I asked her.

"I've taken a few promotions over the years, and they weren't always the ones I wanted. Everything is for trade these days; you can get above-market value when exposing a traitor."

She didn't need to come out and say it, and she was wise not to. Dani may have surmised who Marcus was. I could only guess that she was the reason Tess never came home, and I wasn't about to sully our deal by crossing family matters with business. It made no difference to me whether Tess was buried in the desert or rotting in a cell, but it might have swung Marcus' interests.

"The rest of us would like to get paid as well," Dixie interrupted.

"Very well," Dani conceded. "If you'll follow me, we'll go see the doc."

Dani led us back out into the desert toward the Citadel. Trenches were being dug at the edge of the village, alloy plates laid in the spaces. Materials were scattered everywhere in the sand, and there were miles of cable leading toward our destination.

Whatever they were working on was going to be huge, but in mere hours, it would no longer be necessary. We were all getting off that rock, and those drug-addicted indentured servants could soon reclaim their lives instead of sweating under the sun, constructing their slave rail system.

"I trust that you've got a good plan, yes?" Dani asked as our group split, walking along both sides of a trench. "Your friends in orbit will almost certainly see that something is amiss. They might not react the way you expect—they could blow you out of the sky if they wanted to."

"Sweetheart, ain't nobody gonna see us coming," Dixie bragged confidently.

"And you've got enough muscle to handle it if they do?" Dani questioned.

"If my men are still in the Citadel, we've got more than enough," I said.

"They're not coming," Marcus quickly interjected. "What you see is what you get. It's us versus them. We've got the numbers and the element of surprise. Any extra bodies are more of a liability than they're worth. Our score, remember?"

"It's not just Maya and Chop up there, boy. They've got them two Praxi, and I wouldn't underestimate them if I were you," I explained.

"Gia and Rix?" Dani asked. "Did they turn out okay? Did Gia's surgery work?"

Dani might have been a calculating opportunist, but her heart wasn't nearly as cold and dead as mine. Vocury had given more than it had taken from her. There didn't appear to be many who could say the same.

"They're fine," Double-A answered. "Good kids. Tough little sons of bitches. And yes, Gia can talk. Sometimes too much." The others laughed along, as if reminiscing over fond memories shared between them.

"Are you sure you're the right people for the job?" Dani asked. No offense, but it seems rather chummy between the lot of you. The situation could escalate to violence. Maybe just let Maddox and his men handle things."

"If the Citadel had anyone capable of pulling it off, they would have done so a decade ago," Marcus shot back, quickly pouring cold water on the idea. "In a few hours, we'll be in control of the Omaha, and nobody will have gotten hurt. You'll see."

I hoped the kid was right. The look on Maya's face when her only son turned on her could compensate me for my loss and years of being imprisoned. And if her shock and pain wasn't satisfying enough for my liking, I'd summon the rage to kill the boy in front of his mother. That would certainly set things even between us, but I'd avoid it if I could.

We approached the looming structure and waited patiently for the massive steel doors to part. Dani rapped a fist against the metal with a coordinated staccato, as though tapping out a secret Morse code to enter. Moments later, the walls slid open, and we were quickly met by the men who once served under me. While they seemed to recognize me, they kept their weapons at the ready until our identities were confirmed.

As they guided our company through the industrial checkpoint and into the general causeway of the Citadel, my men, who had only just had their weapons pointed at us, shared pleasantries with me. But I had no interest in catching up or sharing positive sentiments with anyone. We were on the doorstep of delivering my vengeance and I wouldn't be distracted.

However, I couldn't help but notice the dreary state of affairs among our society's elite, forced to survive unnaturally on Vocury.

Those in the Citadel may have been better clothed and nourished than those living on the outside, but their faces bore the same depression, and their eyes the same hopelessness. While they lived in comfort, they needed saving as much as those on the lower rungs of the economic scale. Dr. Amaar's poison had gripped them as well, and I doubted they could recall the days when a prescription wasn't the answer to every ailment.

"The doc should be waiting below," Dani brought me back to the moment as the elevator doors opened and she boarded. Marcus was next, followed by Stacks and Double-A. "The lift will return in a moment for the rest of you."

I grabbed the front of Double-A's vest and yanked him out of the compartment to make room for myself. I glared at Marcus as Dani punched the floor number and the elevator doors closed.

"You're not leaving my side until the job is done," I explained.

"Someone's paranoid," Marcus joked. "Relax, big guy. I've got it all figured out."

"No offense, but I've got trust issues with your family."

"Come on, now." he smirked like a charming thief. "I let you out of your cage, remember? And I didn't even put you on a leash."

The lift stopped at the laboratory, and Dr. Amaar was right there waiting for us when the doors opened. "It's true, then. You do indeed live. Welcome back." He extended his hand to me before turning his attention to Marcus.

"And you, young lad, you must be the boy with the grand designs of escape. We'd all but abandoned hope of ever leaving this place, and I never thought it would be someone with the name of 'Fontaine' who would take us home."

Marcus coldly rejected his heritage. "There's no one by that surname here, unless you've kept Tess alive all these years."

"But of course we have. We're scientists, not barbarians. Perhaps you'd like to see her?"

"Not particularly, but you might as well fetch her anyway. She's coming with us."

The elevator returned from the surface, depositing the rest of our hijacking crew in the lab. Once they had exited, Dani slyly attempted to slink away aboard the lift, but Marcus grabbed her by the arm, restricting her escape. "Oh no, you don't. We're facing our demons today, and that means you, too."

Dr. Amaar turned to a colleague. "Please bring Dr. Fontaine to Lab One." To us, he said, "Would the rest of you like to join me for some refreshments? Perhaps take some rest and we can discuss your proposal?"

"No thanks. We're not staying long," Marcus answered, drawing a chorus of muted groans from his crew. "Where's the transport cruiser?"

"It's below. Hidden away, where it belongs."

"Move it to the surface and make a show of loading it with cargo. We're leaving within the hour."

"You intend to launch with no strategy? You can't outrun the Omaha. She was supposed to be our military escort to Vocury, and our haulers are no match. They'll have you disabled or blown to bits within minutes. No sense in putting our precious cargo at risk."

"It's not your cargo. It's ours. Consider it a down payment. A gesture of good faith. One-third regenerator, one-third sustainer and hydrator—"

"And one-third the real good shit," Double-A interrupted. "We like them yellow ones the best."

Dr. Amaar looked at Double-A with classist disgust and panned his judgmental gaze over the rest of the pirates.

"You're asking a lot, young man. I'm afraid I cannot accommodate you without some reassurances for my people."

"Go on, kid. Tell him," I encouraged him, not so much to ease Amaar's concerns, but because I was genuinely curious as to what Marcus had up his sleeve.

It was starting to become clear that Marcus hadn't been entirely forthcoming with me, and I may have underestimated his capabilities. His time marooned on Vocury with nothing but his depressed inner monologue seemed to have poisoned his motivations much as my sequestering had warped my desires.

"You haven't tried to leave because you're afraid of being shot down, right? Is that what Tess told you? That if you tried to leave, they'd kill you? Maybe she's right and your cowardice is warranted," Marcus mocked the doctor.

"Life has new value, young man. If you were older, you might be able to appreciate the ability to evade death. Immortality cannot tolerate risk."

"That's your problem, doc. You've got too much to lose. You need to lighten up a bit." Marcus was either supremely confident in his plans or he was even more naïve than any of us knew. "Gimme the keys. If they blow us up, then so what? It's not like you can't make more pills. You can preserve your eternal life or whatever, and we'll assume the risk."

"Are you not a customer of ours?" Amaar asked with genuine intrigue. "If you've never taken any of the regenerator, you may have something far greater to offer us. Perhaps you'd like to stay behind. Certainly, your friends are capable of carrying out the plans without you, yes?"

"Not a chance," I butted in before Marcus could answer. I didn't know what Dr. Amaar's interests were in a test subject that hadn't been polluted, and I didn't care. Maya needed to see the face of her son when everything was taken from her.

"Lastly," Marcus continued bargaining, "we need all your weapons—and I do mean all of them."

"We'll have nothing left to defend ourselves with," the doctor argued.

"You won't need them. If you think I'm risking any of you getting cute, you're dead wrong. You arm us to the teeth with everything you've got, and you can have them back when we're done, not that you'll have any further need for them. I'll take care of your blockade and return with both ships. After that, you're free to move about the galaxy as you please, so long as you do right by my people."

No sooner could the doctor offer a rebuttal than his assistant returned with Tess. She wore a dirty lab coat, frayed and torn at the edges, hanging down to her knees. Her hair had grown long, matted, and greasy. And though she hadn't aged a day since I last saw her, she had bags under her eyes, her face withered and tired.

I expected to see a smile when Tess looked upon her grown son for the first time, but she didn't know him, and it seemed no one had bothered to fill her in. Tess had no interest in the rest of us, either. Her eyes locked on Dani, full of accusation.

"Who are you ratting out this time?" she hissed.

Dani had no retort, unable to even make eye contact for a single second. Based on their interaction, she was definitely responsible for Tess having been exposed as the spy she was, and there was no love lost between them.

There was nothing gratifying to me about Tess' condition. I understood why she had embedded herself into our mission, and I respected her for taking the risk to save those Praxi children. That said, she was complicit in the death of my son, even if she knew nothing of it. She wasn't the target of my vengeance, but I wouldn't feel bad if she caught some of the shrapnel.

Marcus playfully slapped Dani on the back to cut the tension. "See, that wasn't so hard. Now we can proceed."

Our crew began to board the elevator to take the ride to the lower decks, and Marcus ensured that he wouldn't need to ride with Tess by squeezing in between myself and Dixie in the first load. The rest waited for the lift to return, and it was only once we had left Dani behind that I broke the ice with Tess.

"She screwed you over?" Tess had no response. "A lot of that going around."

"You mind telling me where we're going?" Tess asked.

"Home. We're finally going home. All of us."

"Have you seen Maya? Is she out there somewhere?"

Now I was the one with no response. The elevator settled, and by the time we disembarked, the freighter was already being powered up and moved under the industrial shaft to the surface.

"Move it!" Marcus shouted from the open rear hatch.

The rest of us hustled across the enormous manufacturing bay and piled into the cargo deck of the ship. The doors closed behind us, and Marcus allowed us to move freely about the ship.

"Not you"—he stopped Tess with a hand to her shoulder—"have a seat." He pointed to a plastic crate. Once seated, Marcus pulled her arms behind her back, bound them with strips of cloth, and tied them to the lid's handle.

"Dixie? We're set."

The female pirate returned from the forward decks with a wireless headset and mic. "Hold still, Mama Bear," she said as she fit the headphones over Tess' ears, setting the mic at an appropriate distance from her mouth. "Stacks," she signaled back to him, "we're good here."

Stacks held his own earpiece tightly to his ear and awaited confirmation. Dixie leaned toward the mic and whispered "Stacks has a drug-induced micropenis" into the receiver, a smirk playing on her lips.

"Did he hear it?" she asked Tess.

"He said you're a bitch, among other colorful insults," Tess relayed back.

Dixie looked up at Marcus. "Ready to go, boss."

"Good. We launch in one hour."

"What do I do?" I asked, as though I was one of Marcus' drones, though all I really wanted to know was what he was planning.

"You can chill, big guy. You're backup muscle at this point. You got us through the door. We can take it from here." He turned his attention to Tess. "You, however, have a very important job. It's up to you to see to it that nobody gets hurt."

"How am I supposed to do anything when I'm tied up?"

"There's a ship out there that's been waiting years for your next communication. Today, they're finally going to hear from you. We'll be taking off soon, and I'm going to leave the communicator on an open channel. All you have to do is get them to dock with us. You will tell them you're alone and that the mission is finally over. You see that crease in the floor over there?" Marcus directed her attention to the spot. Tess turned her head and nodded.

"That's the dock door. If you say anything that I don't approve of, I'll turn off the gravity field and open it. If you use any coded language or give some kind of signal, you'll be sucked into the vacuum of space and will experience what I imagine is one of the worst possible ways to die. If you so much as sneeze or even release a muted fart, I'll send you into the cosmos. Understood?"

"Who the hell are you people? What do you want?"

Marcus kneeled in front of the mother he never knew and addressed her at eye level. "Freedom. The freedom to make our own way, and our own decisions. The freedom to choose whatever life we'd like to lead without someone telling us what we can or can't do. The freedom to do anything other than pace around a stranded ship for years waiting for a message in a bottle."

He stood, turned away, and motioned for me to follow him to the forward decks. I don't know if it was the look I gave her or the sum of the clues, but it was at that moment that Tess knew.

"Marcus? It can't be. Is it you? Marcus!" Her voice rose as we left her behind.

The door to the cargo bay closed behind us and we made our way toward the bridge. "You're kind of a coldhearted little son of a bitch, you know that?" I told him.

"Literally," Marcus replied without looking over.

We waited the appropriate amount of time to ensure Maya would be ready for us, and the autopilot sent us in her direction. Clear of Vocury's atmosphere, the gravity drive was taken offline, and Marcus hit the override to open the docking doors before fitting himself with a headset to monitor the communicator. In less than fifteen minutes, the Omaha was upon us, and I was experiencing a serious case of déjà vu.

"Here's your chance to be a hero, Tess," Marcus spoke into his mic, issuing a final warning. "Play this right, and everybody survives and gets to go home. I'll be listening."

Marcus kept his right hand pressed against the headset, holding it tightly against his ear. The rest of us weren't privy to the words exchanged between Tess and whoever was at the controls of the Omaha, but whatever was said was effective.

Our target moved into position beneath us, came up through the open docking doors, and rested comfortably in the belly of our craft. Once inside, Marcus sealed the doors and deactivated the gravity field.

"It's go time," he announced, reaching into his pocket and pulling out a handful of pills to distribute to the group.

The rest of the crew happily swallowed down their accelerators, but I needed no chemical motivation. When I didn't open my hand to receive his pharmaceutical communion, Marcus pressed me.

"Say 'ahh,'" he jested playfully.

"I'm good. I'm plenty ready."

"You'll take your medicine, or you don't get to come out and play," he continued with a grin.

"Does being a huge pain in my ass run in your family or something?" I grumbled, reluctantly opening my mouth and sticking out my tongue. Marcus deposited the pill, and like a comic sticking to the bit, checked my mouth to make sure I swallowed it.

"Get on with it already," I demanded with a push to his chest and a laugh that I couldn't hide. Marcus was developing the quality of being an annoying little brother who I couldn't help but enjoy.

"Okay gang, let's roll," Marcus declared. The five of us followed him off the bridge and down the corridor, where he split us into two groups. Dixie and I went with Marcus to the right, while Double-A, Stacks, and Taz went to the left.

We used the perimeter entrances to the cargo bay, closing in from both sides to ambush our prey. The numbers were already in our favor, but Marcus wasn't taking any chances. We crept along the rows of crates until we were up against the tiny hull of the Omaha, and by the time we were in place, Maya had already cut Tess free, the two of them sharing an embrace that had been decades in the making.

"He's around here somewhere," Tess warned her.

"How can you be sure it's Marcus?" Ranbir asked.

"I can't, but it's him. Maddox is with him, along with some other sordid rebels."

Before I could stop him, Marcus ducked underneath the front tip of the Omaha and announced his presence.

"Hi, Mom," he greeted Maya.

Both Dixie and I held back for a moment until the other half of our squad rushed in from the backside.

Ranbir, Maya, Tess, and the two alien kids faced Marcus, and before they knew it, Double-A, Stacks, and Taz were all over them. I quickly spun around the front edge of the Omaha and threw all my weight into Maya's chest, knocking her off her feet. Stacks tackled Ranbir, Dixie secured Tess, and Taz and Double-A tossed a thick rope netting over Gia.

"Don't get too close!" Marcus shouted, but before his warning could be heeded, Gia screamed, and Taz was electroshocked when he made contact with her skin. "Net her up!" Marcus ordered.

I pressed my boot into Maya's abs, pinning her down. She lashed out at my ankle and knees, but she was a shadow of the fighter she once was. She looked tired and worn. Her cheeks were damp from tears, her eyes bloodshot from shedding them, and she looked at least fifteen pounds lighter than when she'd locked me away, the muscle definition long gone. I might have pitied what her addiction had reduced her to if I wasn't so hell-bent on revenge.

I wanted to spit malicious words in her face, but the vowels and consonants came off my tongue in a jumble. My vision blurred with stars and dark spots, while my body temperature shot up and dizziness set in.

Something bad was happening to my body, so much so that Rix was able to nearly topple me as he plowed into my side. He gave me a solid kick to the waist, and I held onto his foot for dear life as my knees buckled. I collapsed, dragging him down with me as my body gave out, my motor skills fading fast.

"Marcus!" I violently screamed, my voice slurred and wild like a drunkard's.

I watched the boy who had dosed me stand over us, and it was only once Rix was subdued that Marcus addressed me.

"Sorry, big guy. It wasn't personal. Take deep breaths and enjoy the trip. The effects should wear off in a few hours."

"I'm going to kill you," I slurred.

"Not today, you're not."

I could do nothing but lay prone with paralysis, taking in the fact that Marcus had played me as much as he had his family. The clever little shit had used me to gain access to the Citadel, and it was apparent that I wouldn't be going home or have my revenge that day.

Rix must have sprung free from whoever had pulled him from my grip. Two of his pale alien legs stood planted on the floor, and I was momentarily distracted by the changing shades of color and rippling psychedelic waves moving across his skin. I found myself laughing hysterically as Marcus' pitch changed from high to low, like a cartoon character, as he warned, "I've always liked you Rix, and I don't want to hurt you."

I'm certain I remained conscious throughout, but entire blocks of time went missing after that. One moment, Maya and company were being bound, and the next I was lying alone on the cold floor of the cargo bay.

There was shouting, sometimes loud and present, other times echoing off in the distance. I remember staring at my hand and spending what felt like hours contemplating what life would be like if I had five thumbs for some reason.

The only thing that could break my daydream of multiple opposable phalanges was my arms and legs being grabbed as I was dragged across the floor and through what felt like miles of the interior of the Omaha.

I recognized the bridge as Stacks and Taz sat me upright and strapped me into place. Maya, Ranbir, and Rix were in my line of sight, all buckled into seats of their own, and Gia was netted and tied into place against the wall.

"Are we almost home?" I asked, like a child waking from a backseat nap on a family road trip.

"You sure are, buddy," Marcus reassured me with a soft bop on my nose.

He powered up the AI flight systems and politely engaged in conversation. "Good morning, Gregory," he said as he knelt beneath the touch screen and pried at the paneling with a metal tool.

"Good. Morning. Master. Marcus." Gregory responded.

"Good night, Gregory."

Marcus yanked a handful of cables and circuits, tearing them from their housing unit. The reflective light from the AI command screen cast a colorful pattern onto everyone's faces before fading to nothing and revealing depressed, defeated expressions.

"Good. Ni . . ." Gregory's voice dissipated into nothing.

"I'll set you down as gently as I can," Marcus informed the group.

"We can go home, Marcus!" Maya shouted at him. "It's over. This whole nightmare is done. Don't do this!"

"I am so fucking sick of you telling me what to do," Marcus' voice rose as he slammed his fist on the headrest of his mother's seat. "Never again! Vocury is our home now, and I'm calling the shots. I'll go where I please. I'll do what I please. If I want to get high, I'll get high. If I want to live forever, I'll live forever. I'm not playing by your hypocritical rules anymore."

"Marcus," Tess spoke gently. "Please."

"Don't! I don't want to hear from you. I don't want to see you. I don't want to fucking know you. Don't you ever say that name again."

If I hadn't been so wasted, I would have been capable of seeing what everyone else was at that moment. The playful and mischievous façade that Marcus had always portrayed had been a mask.

He was a damaged, confused, and angry young man, bitter about the life Maya had made for him and the hypocritical standards she'd imposed. He'd likely admired her at one time, and watching her become a broken shell of herself must have been devastating.

It was an anger born out of love, and the opposite of his rage for Tess. In his eyes, Tess was equally responsible for his prisonlike childhood, and she couldn't even be bothered to be present. Tess was the furthest thing from family, and not having a commonality in genes or physical characteristics only made it worse.

As I recognized and understood his hatred in the years that followed, my rage boiled hotter. My boy was dead—and he may have cursed my name much like Marcus had cursed his mother's. He would never know that everything I'd done had been for him. He likely lived whatever few painful years were allowed as yet another abandoned child who felt hate where there should have been love. The bill had come due for the childhood Maya had given her son, and one day, it would come for the life and death that she gave mine.

Soon after his childish rant, Marcus and his crew of pirates left us. The Omaha was deposited into the Vocury sands ten miles from the Citadel—far enough away to create distance between the fractured family, yet close enough for the boy's mothers to witness the world he would create.

He gifted them with enough sustainer, hydrator, and regenerator to keep them alive indefinitely, and he punished them by leaving behind enough uppers and downers to keep Maya trapped in a drug-induced coma forever.

Everything else that wasn't bolted down was stolen and given freely to the villagers to build proper shelters outside the walls of the Citadel.

The Omaha had enough power to last a millennium, and the amenities it provided would only serve as a tease to its residents who would long for the same freedom Maya had denied Marcus. Without the AI-assisted navigation system, the ship was stranded forever. I wasn't welcome there for obvious reasons, nor would I have stayed if allowed.

I woke outside the Omaha with my face in the mud. A few yards away was a burn pile containing the charred remains of all the weapons my comrades had turned over to the deceitful boy, and my pockets were filled with just enough sustainer and hydrator for the trek to the Citadel.

Every step in that blistering heat solidified my resolve for vengeance that would one day come. We weren't the only humans to have set out for that godforsaken planet, and I would survive out of spite for centuries waiting for that starship of settlers to arrive. Maya's old friends were foretold as The Travelers, and those of us who held onto the past knew that their arrival would set the stage for our final battleground.

Chapter 16

Title Fight Challenge
Ranbir Chopra: 2337

O nce upon a time on Earth, I was so impatient that I'd microwave a frozen pizza instead of using the oven to save seven minutes. The soggy mess was ready in half the time, and I'd burn my mouth with steaming cheese rather than wait for my meal to cool down. I didn't hastily ruin my dinner and char my taste buds because I was starving. I did it because I was lazy and in a hurry.

There was no room for such impatience on Vocury.

For most humans, the greatest asset we could ever possess was time. There's never enough of it, it can't be bought, and once it's used or wasted, you can never get it back.

The average human lifespan consists of 39,420,000 minutes, and 13,140,000 of those will be spent sleeping. Once you start subtracting minutes for time at work, schooling, raising children, commuting, upkeep of person and property, and being flat-out lazy, you're not left with much.

If you had ten million minutes to pursue your passions before death, you would have lived a fruitful life. I know this because I had time to do the math.

When on Earth, there's no time to be wasted; patience isn't a virtue when the clock is against you. On Vocury, however, patience is a necessity—and I was desperate to experience haste for a change.

I forced Alexis and Taj to walk and talk at the same time as we put our backs to the Citadel and trudged to the north with the sun beating down on us. Once I had given them the CliffsNotes of the ill-fated adventure that had marooned us for centuries, it was their turn to reciprocate.

"Where's Maya?" Alexis questioned, her voice tinged with concern.

It wasn't my place to answer, nor was it a topic I was eager to discuss. I remained silent, while Tess refused to meet Alexis' gaze, no matter how long she stared.

"Tess? Is she dead?"

"I don't know," Tess replied quietly. "I haven't seen her in a long time. Maya went her own way. The drugs have taken her, and if she's alive, we'll need your help to bring her back. To bring them all back."

"I don't understand. What can I do? Maybe get you home if you're willing to take a three-hundred-year nap, but that's the best I can offer."

'We can't leave all these people here," Taj interjected.

"Nobody wants to hear from you, kid," I condescended to him. "I'd send you back to where you came from if I wasn't worried that you'd lead your father's goons back to us."

"I'm blind, you douchesack," Taj retorted, awkwardly testing the phrase. "Am I saying that right?" he asked, turning to Alexis.

"Close enough," she chuckled, squeezing his hand tighter and flashing him a genuine grin. She trusted him, but I wasn't taking any chances being so close to our goal.

"There's frozen embryos on your ship, yes?" Tess asked.

"Hundreds of them, along with an entire crew in sleep tubes."

"You have to get me up there. If we can bring your ship to the surface, we can evacuate the planet and I might be able to create an antidote to counteract the effects of regenerator," Tess explained.

"Let's just get the hell out of here. I'll take you to the lander, we can grab Malik, and bail on this place."

"We're not leaving." Rix's voice mentally hit us like a ton of bricks. "My kin have suffered for centuries, and I'll die before I leave them behind. We've waited forever for you, human, and promises have been made."

"He's right," I said. "If you would have listened to me in Parliament, we wouldn't be in this situation. I've lived for three centuries patiently waiting for you, and I'd rather have died a long time ago. Do you have any idea what that's like? To wake up every day wanting to die but being forced to live on? To have to wander miles out into the desert every morning looking for you without having any clue how many years have passed or when you'll show up? To have so much time waste away that you convince yourself—"

"Okay, okay. Jesus, I'm sorry," Alexis interrupted. "I promise you looked better practicing that in the mirror than delivering it."

She released Taj's hand and ran a shaky palm across her forehead. The blush faded from her face and her breathing intensified.

"Hold on a second," her voice fluttered as she took a knee and Taj blindly probed around to comfort her.

"Get up," Rix demanded. "We don't have time for this. Our enemies won't be far behind."

"I-I need . . . I need one of those relaxers," Alexis stuttered.

Tess calmly placed a hand on Alexis' shoulder and knelt in front of her.

"Alexis. Don't. Not unless you absolutely have to. If you haven't taken anything but the sustainer or hydrator, you can't start now. Just breathe. You're going to be fine. This will pass and we'll be on our way home before you know it."

It was a shame that Tess never had the chance to really be a mother. Aside from Malik, she was the most nurturing and kind person I had ever known. If her path hadn't led her away, Marcus might have been an entirely different person than what he had become.

"Help her up," Tess instructed Taj, who leaned in carefully and offered his back for Alexis to climb on. We continued on toward our rendezvous point while Alexis recovered herself, wrapping her arms around Taj's chest as she stared over at Rix.

"What?" Rix asked with his usual abrasiveness.

"It's nothing. You're just not like the others. I hold a great affinity for your kind. Hell, I came here for you."

"You don't want to know me, human."

"Maybe. You're no Gio, I'll tell you that much. He had an actual personality. Positive emotions and all that, not this rage and anger that you share."

"And where'd that get him?"

"Rix," I said, my tone a warning. "Leave it alone."

It may have been hundreds of years, but I still felt Gio's sacrifice as if it was yesterday. Rix was like a son to me, and he had every right to harbor hatred, but I wasn't going to stand for anyone dishonoring the name of my fallen friend. "Don't antagonize each other."

We walked on in silence for a while after that.

"You can let me down." Alexis said eventually, patting Taj's chest, dismounting, and taking his hand to lead him on again.

"Tess?" Taj asked, his voice searching for her like sonar.

"Yes?"

"What did you mean when you said you could save everyone? What has my father done to them?"

"It's not just your father. It's my fault, too," she admitted, her voice heavy with regret.

"We pushed the boundaries of science and science pushed back. Creating sustainer and hydrator was easy. There were no side effects, and no human DNA was needed. Everything beyond that started harmlessly enough, and only became dangerous over time. If we had known that extending human life would come at the cost of our children—of future generations—things might have been different . . ." She sighed.

"I don't doubt that your father would have still gone through with it, but he certainly would have kept more untainted human subjects around to provide fetuses and children. Relying on Praxi youth for their cells wasn't enough. We needed underdeveloped human tissue and DNA to bridge the gap, and by the time they figured it out, it was too late. Regenerator was always incomplete. Not only has it become less effective over time, but it's also destroyed the fertility of everyone on the planet. The people here have unknowingly traded their ability to create life for an extended life of their own. We're all barren, and even if life could be conceived, someone would face an impossible choice: sacrifice their child to science or allow it to live."

"I think I may have been that miracle child," Taj said solemnly.

Tess regarded him with curiosity. "How old are you?"

"I don't know. However old I look, I suppose. I've aged naturally because I've never taken any regenerator. Father wouldn't allow it."

"That's not possible." Tess scoffed. "You look like you're in your thirties. There hasn't been a child born here in centuries."

"Yes, I know, and I fear terrible things were done to make that possible."

"If that's true, then I know my hypothesis will work. If I can get my hands on those human embryos, I should be able to create a counteragent. We can break the chains of addiction and get everyone clean. Instead of aging out, we'd be able to get off the regenerator and age naturally."

I admired Tess' commitment to righting her wrongs and helping the citizens of Vocury. I'd gladly stand by her and do everything in my power to topple the Amaar legacy, but I wasn't interested in squeezing in another forty years of life. I had already lived multiple lifetimes, and the further away I moved from my memories of Emilia, the more I longed to join her.

"Look." I pointed ahead. "They're already here."

We were expecting Gia and Malik, but there was no mistaking Kade's looming frame among them, an unwelcome guest. I looked at Tess, her excitement to save the planet quickly evaporating from her face.

"It's okay. Just be cool," I comforted her.

Kade was the first to his feet as we approached. "What the fuck is this?" his voice echoed from afar as he shouted at Gia. He pulled Malik from the ground, wrapping an arm around his chest while pressing a rusty blade to his throat.

But Malik's eyes betrayed no fear; instead, they conveyed the irritation of someone who'd heard the boy cry wolf one too many times. It was clear he was more annoyed at being used as a prop human shield than anything else. That frustration became wonder as he recognized the ghosts of his past walking up on them. He broke free, peeling Kade's arm from around him, and slowly walked in our direction.

Alexis ran forward and hugged him, and though he reciprocated the embrace, he stared past her with his mouth agape.

"Are you okay?" Alexis asked. "Did they hurt you?"

"What? What is—? Chop? Tess?"

I walked up to him, a few feet between us as he studied me.

"Hello, old friend. Your eyes don't deceive you."

Before I could offer him my hand, he pressed a single finger to my chest as though to test if I were solid.

"Ha. Haha," he chuckled, tears in his eyes. "You're real!" he exclaimed as he hugged me. "How is this possible?"

"Gia didn't tell you, huh?"

"Didn't want to ruin the surprise." Gia smirked, and I could see a glimmer of her father in her eyes.

"Ho-ly shit. You-you . . . you're talking. Like, out loud," Alexis stammered. She walked up to Gia and took notice of the scarring around her throat. "I can't feel you, though."

"Yes, I can talk."

"Taj! This one talks!" Alexis shouted. Gia laughed at Alexis' excitement, which only made her giddier. "And laughs! You can laugh!"

"My name is Gia, and I'm guessing you're the Traveler Alexis." Gia briefly paused her introduction to lock arms with Rix and press their foreheads together. "I missed you, too," she replied to whatever private exchange Rix shared with her.

"Say 'No, I am your father,'" Alexis requested. "No, no, wait. Say 'Get away from her, you bitch,' but you have to really lay on the gas for the 'you bitch' part."

"Is she serious?" Gia chuckled, confused, pointing a finger at Alexis.

"Enough!" Kade shouted. "What the hell is this? Are we making a trade or not?"

"No more trades," I announced. "No more deals. No more backstabbing or plotting. And no more Vocury. You've had your time."

"We're going home," Tess said softly.

"We are not going anywhere. That ship up there is going in the sand, like all the rest. My people will salvage the parts and cargo for their survival."

"They're not your people," Gia said firmly. "They're your prisoners. It's time to let them go."

"They're already free. They do as they please every day. If you want to change that, you'll have to kill me," Kade warned her.

"Fine. Challenge." Rix stepped forward confidently.

"For what?" Kade asked.

"For the ship, you brutish fool," Rix answered.

"It's not mine. You can't challenge me for it."

"You coward!" Rix's emoting was as hateful as ever. Every word meant for Kade was an emotional dagger that pierced the rest of us as well.

"You're a tiny, pathetic, human, shrinking from every honest fight that has ever been presented. You're no different than the Citadelians who came here hundreds of years ago. You have no honor, always quoting rules that excuse you from combat when challenged. You've already lost, boy."

"Stop it. Stop it, stop it, stop it!" Tess screamed. "It's over! If you want to stay here, fine. We won't force anyone else to come with us. The people of Vocury can choose for themselves, and you're welcome to any unnecessary components of the ship. Be grateful we offer that much; you're outnumbered this time, and we are done with this. I'm done with this. I am so tired of watching what you've become."

"Fine. Whatever. Run back to the sad lives you left behind that no longer exist."

"Malik, Alexis? Care to lead the way so we can be done with this?" I asked.

"The lander is a few miles south of the southernmost village. I think we walked for about four hours, but I can't guarantee it was in a straight line," Malik informed us.

"No wonder we couldn't find it," I commented to Gia. "We were way off. Well, alright then. Let's get moving."

Gia and Rix walked out front, leading the way with their superior knowledge of direction and the terrain. Alexis, closely trailing behind as she dragged Taj, bombarded them with a million questions, most of which I presumed Gia answered.

Rix didn't have much to say, though I did occasionally sense his hostile nature as we stomped our way through the afternoon heat. Tess wasn't too far behind them, and while she shared a brief awkward pleasantry with Malik, she didn't appear to be in the mood to speak to anyone.

I walked with Malik, explaining the convoluted path that had led to our three-hundred-year stay on Vocury and the sad state of affairs that had ruined his best friend, Maya. Kade followed behind us at a distance, listening in but remaining silent, even when I spoke ill of him. Absent his fellow rebels, he seemed alone and detached from everyone.

There was so much to tell. I found myself forgetting key details, glossing over things, and having to correct myself when I explained things out of order. As I was jumping from one event to the next, Malik must have heard enough to piece the puzzle together, and he changed the subject.

"There's something I need from you. Something I have to show you," he said.

"What is it?"

"It's on the Wolf Moon. I don't know if you remember, but when we traveled here, we used those Praxi sleep tubes. I decided to try one of the dreamers, and there were things inside I can't explain."

"Like?"

"I can't tell you. I need you to take the sedative, get in the tube, and experience it for yourself. If I give you any info on what I saw in there, it may affect the dream world that your mind populates. You need to go in with no preconceived notions."

"Sure. If it's safe, I'll pop in there when we go up, and you can take me out when we land."

"No, man. The sedative is no joke. The minimum dose will probably put you down for at least a few days. Which is fine. It's better if you have enough time to feel things out."

"Sorry, Malik. Unless you can give me something else to go on, I'm not interested. We've got bigger things to deal with here, and I can't be out that long. Have Alexis do it."

"Chop, it has to be you. No one else. I don't expect you to understand, but once you're in there, things might make sense."

"I'll tell you what—if we get the ship, Tess can make her vaccine, and we get clear of this place, I'll help you."

I wasn't sure why Malik was so insistent, but I trusted him. He wouldn't ask if it wasn't important.

We walked for a few hours, stopping only occasionally to rest and rehydrate. It was an hour after the sun had dipped behind the dunes when Alexis finally exclaimed, "It's here. Right here!"

We cleared the sand that had piled up around the lander, and I discovered that it was smaller than I expected.

"There's room for two. Three if we squeeze," Malik explained as he began twisting the lower hatch door. "It's fifteen minutes up, five for docking, another fifteen for surface landing prep, and then the flight time down here. We should be back within an hour."

"You're not leaving the surface without me," Kade spoke for the first time in hours.

"Well, then I'm going as well," Rix's voice projected over us.

"Yeah, not a good idea. It's going to be tight enough in there as it is. The last thing I need is you two hotheads breathing on each other. Chop? Whaddaya say? Wanna go for a ride like back in the day?"

"Fine by me," I said, and Malik stepped aside so that I could climb the ladder and hop into the copilot's seat. Malik followed me in and strapped into the pilot's chair, and Kade was shortly behind us. The hatch sealed, the engines powered on, and sand blew up in a storm near the back of the craft as Malik engaged the thrusters.

Flight times were just as Malik had estimated. Within fifteen minutes we made our approach to the Wolf Moon, which was hanging in low orbit, and not long after, we were docked in the cargo bay.

Kade and I examined the sleep tubes, occasionally wiping away the frost from the glass to look at the faces within, while Malik bustled about bringing the ship to full power and preparing it for an orbital entry.

"Don't get any big ideas," I said to Kade as he took a mental inventory of everything on board. "We're not waking them, and you're not taking them." He offered no rebuttal.

We joined Malik on the bridge, the three of us again assuming the same positions we had on the lander, and for the first time in centuries, I saw Vocury from space.

"I honestly can't believe this is happening. We've waited for so long. At one point I imagined that a thousand years had passed, and you had simply gone off course or never awakened. You have no idea how long three hundred years feels when you're incapable of tracking time and waiting for this one inevitable thing to happen."

Malik looked over at me with a knowing grin. "You might be surprised. I'm not as young as I appear either. The vast majority of my memories are from a life I'm not sure I actually lived."

Malik was speaking in code, but it didn't matter. I don't know if I'd go so far as to say I was happy, but I was certainly satisfied. If things went right, I could finish out my life naturally, and maybe even be lucky enough to have my cabin on Prius before I died after all.

We saw no clouds as we pressed through the atmosphere, but the blinding dark of the Vocury night had taken hold by then. Malik used the Citadel as a navigating point to direct us south toward where we had left our friends an hour earlier, and it was only once we were on approach that we noticed the crowd had tripled in size.

"Oh no. No, no, no." I stood, panicking as I gripped the view screen to take a closer look. "It's Maddox."

Everyone but Taj was on their knees, leaving us to hover over them and consider our options.

"Blast them!" Kade suggested. "Aim clear of Tess and the others and cripple those Citadel thugs."

"This is a colony ship. We have no weapons of any kind," Malik responded.

"What can we do?" I thought out loud. "Maybe we can um, head to the Omaha and swap out some parts to repair the AI navigation system? She's got plenty of firepower if we can get her in the air."

"And then what?" Kade asked.

"Attack the Citadel? I don't know."

"Sweet plan, jackass. Where do you think our friends will be when you collapse the structure? You'll drop the roof on their heads."

"Our friends?" Malik questioned Kade.

"Make a trade," Kade suggested. "It's the Vocury way."

Maddox was pointing his steel gravity club up at us, then down to the ground. When we didn't respond, he began shouting at us even though we couldn't hear him. He walked among his group of prisoners, yanking Alexis to her feet, and threatened to take a swing at her.

"He's not actually going to hit her, right?" Malik asked.

I exchanged glances with Kade, our grim expressions the answer to his question. Before Malik could react, Maddox wound back and swung his stick into Alexis' side. She was thrown roughly twenty feet through the air, plopping violently into the sand before rolling to a stop.

"Land it! Land!" I shouted.

"I am!" Malik responded as he quickly dropped the ship clear of the crowd.

Malik and I rushed toward the cargo bay as Kade followed behind.

"Do we have a plan?" he asked. "Can we stop for a minute and figure this out? Maddox is a force, but he's not terribly bright. We have no leverage here and we need to think of something."

"Our friends are in trouble. We don't have time for your games," I barked at him.

Malik lowered the rear ramp and hit the controls to open the bay doors. No sooner had we started our descent than we had a swarm of soldiers all over us. They apprehended us with the efficiency of law enforcement, though Kade did put up something of a struggle. It took four of them to drag him to the ground, but he was subdued all the same.

"Move it. On your knees," Maddox demanded.

I knelt beside Rix while Malik was dropped down next to Tess. Alexis was still off in the distance, where two of our assailants were picking her up out of the mud and dragging her back to us. To my relief, she was groaning and clutching her left arm—had Maddox connected with her torso, he may have rearranged her internal organs.

Alexis rolled over her right shoulder onto her back and carefully placed her left arm across her belly to support it.

"You okay?" Tess raised her voice when she didn't immediately receive an answer. "Alexis?"

"Oh yeah. I'm super pumped. So glad I got picked to get blasted. I swear, hostage situations always work out just peachy for me."

"Shut your mouth," Maddox snarled at her. "I have had it with you people! Now, where the hell is Maya?!"

"Maya?" I questioned. "She could be anywhere. I don't even know if she's still alive. You've got your ship, Maddox. Take it. You win, man. Just leave the rest of them alone."

Maddox grabbed Taj by the throat and shook him.

"The other woman. Where is she? Was she with them?"

"There was no other," Taj choked out.

"Let go of him!" Alexis screamed.

Maddox released Taj and pushed him into the arms of his soldiers. "Put him on board. His father wants him returned."

"If you want that ship, you're going to have to trade for it. I've claimed it," Kade said, despite having two men's boots on his chest. Maddox approached and leaned over him. "What will you give me for it?" Kade asked, prompting a chorus of laughs, but Maddox wasn't entertained.

"You have nothing." Maddox sneered, his contempt evident as he spat in Kade's face. "You're finished. I beat you. You're going to die here alone, with nothing."

His rant apparently over, he straightened, motioned for his men to round up and board the ship, and turned to walk away.

"What if I could give you Maya?" Kade's voice rose, causing Maddox to stop in his tracks. "Get off me," he screamed at the men holding him down as he rose defiantly to his feet. To Maddox, he said, "You can have her. I don't care."

"Shut your mouth!" I yelled and was quickly met with a kick to my side.

Seeing me walloped, Gia struggled harder against the men holding her down and even threw one into the air. She attempted to scream and shock them, but their rubberish armor didn't serve as a conduit. She broke free from the others using physical strength alone and scampered to me, hovering nearby.

"Any of you touch him again, and I'll kill you."

Gia's courage inspired Rix, and soon he was fighting off the men attempting to subdue him as well. "I say we fight them to the death right here and now. They might kill us all, but we'll take plenty of them with us."

"Not a fan of that plan," Alexis moaned as she attempted to sit upright.

"You can fight among yourselves. We're leaving," Maddox said. Again, he motioned for his men to round up and step off. "In another life, I would have been kind enough to let you come with us. Count your blessings that I let you live."

Most of the men climbed the ramp into the back of the ship, and the moment Maddox slammed his boot onto the steel, Kade howled in anger. He looked over at Tess, sharing a glance, and then back at Maddox. "Challenge!" he screamed. Maddox delayed for a moment, but continued pressing forward. "You hear me?! Challenge!"

"Marcus, no!" Tess yelled.

"Marcus?" Malik asked, a confused expression on his face.

"That is not. My. Name!" Marcus rebuked the mother he had never known before returning his attention to Maddox.

"Challenge, you fucking coward! You want to take revenge? I'm right here! I'll fight you for all of it." When his challenge didn't draw the reaction he'd hoped for, he launched an unwarranted verbal jab that finally got the job done. "You let your son die and you blamed everyone else, Maddox!"

"What did you say?" Maddox's voice rose as he turned and stomped down the ramp.

"You heard me! I said challenge."

Maddox ripped off his vest, tossing it carelessly into the sand. He deactivated his gravity stick, jamming it into the sod before cracking his knuckles with a tight clench of both fists. Unwrapping the blood-stained bandage around his hand, he pulled it even tighter over the mangled stump of his missing finger. Taking two steps forward, he leaned in until he was nearly nose to nose with Marcus. "I accept."

"Don't do this, Marcus. Marcus! Stop!" Tess' voice escalated into a desperate, maternal scream, but he ignored her cries.

Whatever hatred he held for her had softened over the years, and starting an unwinnable fight on our behalf must have been his way of showing it. Malik and I had to hold Tess back, and the only pain I could compare it to was leaning over Emilia as she spoke her final words.

Tess sobbed, her tears unrelenting, and was only able to find composure in our complete lack of control over the situation. My heart sank into my gut as I witnessed her devastation.

Marcus yanked his shirt over his head, pounded his chest twice, and stared up at Maddox, who stood completely unmoved and unimpressed. Without warning, Maddox lunged, swinging a wild right hook that sailed over Marcus' head. Seizing the opportunity, Marcus plowed into his gut, launching a series of quick jabs. Before he could gain ground, however, Maddox delivered a pair of punishing blows to his exposed back, forcing him to retreat.

Marcus pulled back, throwing a forward kick that didn't land but gave him some space to regroup. Maddox, uninterested in using his size and reach to any advantage, attacked, again swinging wildly.

A few punches glanced off Marcus' raised arms, but the fourth connected with the side of his face. Marcus' bell was slightly rung, and if Maddox had pressed his advantage, he may have ended things right then and there.

Blinking away the stars, Marcus stayed light on his feet, no longer drawing back but weaving side to side to dodge Maddox's undisciplined attacks.

"Come on, Ka—Marcus!" Malik shouted like a cornerman. "Keep moving. Tire him out!"

"Destroy him!" Maddox's men shouted as they created a wide perimeter for the fight.

"Come on, you big oaf. Can't you hit me?" Marcus taunted.

Again, Maddox charged forward, but this time Marcus was ready for him. One jab to the chin, an evasive maneuver to duck Maddox's counter, and then another jab. Then another. Maddox's arms came up, forming a shell in front of his face to deflect the next punches, but they weren't headed for his dome.

Marcus struck a punishing body shot with his left. As Maddox reacted, Marcus hit him with another using his right. The moment Maddox tried to wrap him up and end the folly, Marcus dipped back again. This time, Maddox wasn't so quick to advance. He had been stung, and blood was starting to leak from his nose down over his upper lip.

"Hit me!" Marcus jeered, feigning a punch to his own chin. He was baiting Maddox into the type of fight he could win, and it appeared to be working. Tess now stood by my side, fewer tears in her eyes than before, and she joined us in encouraging her son.

"You're faster than him!" Tess hollered. "You can do it!"

Enraged by the turn of events, Maddox lunged again, but this time he wasn't swinging. He kept his guard up as he closed the distance between them, and Marcus tried to break through with a jab once more. When that didn't work, he gave a powerful kick to Maddox's knee, parlaying it into more body shots.

Suddenly, Maddox dropped his guard and hit Marcus squarely in the chest. The blow sent Marcus stumbling into the waiting arms of Maddox's men, who shoved him back toward the beast. Maddox seized the opportunity, wrapping him in a crushing bear hug, but a tight squeeze wasn't going to be enough to take down a man built like Marcus.

Frustrated, Maddox tried to land a pair of headbutts, but being taller than his prey was a disadvantage at close proximity. His forehead slammed into the crown of Marcus' head, and if anything, it did equal damage to both of them. Maddox released him, whether out of irritation or a rare moment of thinking critically for a change, I didn't know. Either way, it was the correct tactical decision, but it still didn't work.

Instead of retreating as before, Marcus stood firm, immediately hammering Maddox's exposed torso with a few quick punches. He bent back to avoid Maddox's wild swing, then delivered his most punishing strike yet—a ruthless uppercut so tight that it nearly careened off Maddox's chest before connecting with his chin.

It was a stunner for sure, and judging by Maddox's stumbled reaction, it had caught him off guard. He was hurt, but the pain seemed secondary to the realization that Marcus might have the upper hand. The only thing worse for Maddox than losing the opportunity to go home would be getting pummeled in front of his men by the boy who had marooned him on Vocury so long ago.

Sensing his advantage, Marcus advanced, landing two more headshots that only grazed Maddox but served their purpose. Maddox's only defense was to grab Marcus and toss him toward his men, and then things got out of hand.

The men grappled Marcus and held him in place while Maddox landed a couple of solid shots, but their hold didn't last long. Gia and Rix exploded into action, piling onto them, heaving them with force. Rix was particularly devasting as he stood on two legs and whipped his third across the body of one man, filling the night air with the loud cracking of ribs. Malik and I were quick to follow, both of us throwing punches and absorbing many more as the one-on-one match turned into a group affair.

Maddox backed up, unwilling to force his advantage in the carnage. His voice roared over everyone as Malik and I were both dogpiled, leaving only Rix and Gia raging on. With their tall demeanor and powerful legs, our Praxi friends could handle three men at once, but it wasn't enough.

One of the men retrieved Maddox's gravity stick and, with a single swing, sent Rix flying into the side of the ship. The attacker sprinted after his prey, club raised above his head to finish Rix off, but Marcus plowed into him first, knocking him off his feet.

Standing, Marcus delivered a swift kick to the man's head and he lost consciousness. Then, rather than be drawn back into combat, Marcus ran to Rix and helped him to his feet. "You alright, brother?" If Rix responded to the question, it wasn't for the rest of us to hear, though I could sense an unspoken respect emanating from him.

Marcus retrieved the gravity weapon from where it lay in the sand and the fight slowly dissipated once as he held it pointed forward with his arm extended. He aimed it in Maddox's direction to reignite the fire of the challenge between them and then threw it into the ground. "No weapons!" he screamed.

The men holding us down released their grip, creating space for Marcus to pass, yet Gia continued to struggle against her captors. Then, none other than Alexis was by her side, arm clenched tight to her upper body as though in facsimile of a sling, kicking and thrashing at the soldiers.

"Let her go!" she screamed.

"Come on, boy! We finish this!" Maddox taunted, wiping a handful of blood from his face.

One of his lackeys quickly grabbed the stick and ran forward to place it in Maddox's hands as all of our heads turned and we froze in unison. He could have killed us all one by one if he wanted to, ending our little insurrection with a few quick swings.

Maddox's grip tightened around the barrel, his eyes narrowing on Marcus, but instead of taking the easy way out, he tossed the club toward the rear of the ship. "No weapons," he echoed Marcus' tribal rules.

With fists raised and eyes locked, the two men walked toward each other. Marcus paused briefly, glancing at each of us, his gaze lingering longest on

Tess, and I wondered what he might have said if he could communicate like the Praxi.

Would he have told his mother that he was sorry? Would the three hundred years of love she had for her son finally have been reciprocated? Would he have asked about Maya? Thanked the rest of us for raising him and expressed regret in his adolescent betrayal of his family? It's hard to say, but his eyes seemed to communicate those sentiments.

There was no time for weakness, though. Maddox was advancing once more, and Marcus refocused just as a left hook flew toward his head. He dodged right, then left as Maddox shifted, charging forward in frustration. Marcus reacted with a brutal kick to Maddox's knee, unbalancing him. Maddox wobbled and Marcus finally lunged, tackling him to the ground.

"Get him!" Tess shouted as Marcus mounted Maddox's back, locking an arm around his throat.

Maddox thrashed, trying to strike back, but his sheer size restricted him. "Argggggggghhhhhhhh," he howled, elbows jabbing back in vain.

"Surrender and I'll let you live," Marcus bargained with him, tightening his chokehold, but it wasn't enough to put Maddox down.

With a roar, Maddox planted his hands in the dirt and raised himself to all fours. Marcus tightened his grip once more, legs locking around Maddox's thighs, but Maddox powered to his feet, staggering under the weight.

"Don't make me kill you," Marcus again offered Maddox a way out. "Surrender. I'll give you and your men a ride home or wherever you want to go. You don't have to die here."

Maddox, defiant, drove his chin into Marcus' forearm, then violently snapped his head back, smashing into Marcus' face. The blow loosened Marcus' grip, his legs slipping from around Maddox's thighs. With a final heave, Maddox then threw himself backward, crushing Marcus beneath him and knocking the air from his lungs.

Tess gasped, her nails digging into my arm, while Gia held her back.

"Wake up, kid!" Malik shouted, but it was too late.

Maddox rolled off Marcus, delivered a savage hammer blow to his mouth to keep him dazed, and then climbed onto his chest. Marcus raised his arms weakly in defense, but they soon fell limp as Maddox began pulverizing his face and head. It was only once Marcus began slipping out of consciousness that Maddox went completely primal.

"I hate this fucking place!" he yelled as his fist smashed into Marcus' forehead. "Where is she?! Where is Maya?!" he screamed at us. He grabbed Marcus by the hair, lifting his head from the sand. "Is this the son she raised?! Will she weep when I take him away?" Maddox let Marcus' head fall back and resumed his assault.

"I hate breathing this poisonous air! I hate this fucking gravity. You took everything from me!" Each punch punctuated his fury.

"Stop!" Tess screamed, her voice breaking. "Please, please, please . . ." Her cries dissolved into sobs. "PLEASE DON'T!"

"Hey. Hey!" Malik's voice cut through the chaos, laced with anger. "Leave the boy. Take me instead."

"Malik, no!" Alexis shouted in protest.

Maddox stood over Marcus' crippled body and laughed cruelly at Malik's gesture.

"You want this little traitor? Bring me Maya! A life for a life!" Then, leaning down to grab him by the ankle, he dragged Marcus toward the ship.

Maddox's men released us, forming a barrier as they retreated with their captain. Tess attempted to push past them, and Gia had to use two legs to restrain her, the pair of them folding to the ground as Tess wept.

One by one, our assailants disappeared into the rear of the craft. The ramp closed, and moments later, the Wolf Moon ascended into the night sky, slowly hovering off into the distance toward the Citadel.

I had waited three centuries for the chance to see my friends again, finish the mission, and find comfort in a well-earned natural death—and everything had unraveled in a matter of minutes.

When once I had more time than I knew what to do with, I now had so little. We were defeated and broken, and though we had each other, I feared we each felt completely alone and lost.

"What the hell are we supposed to do now?" Alexis asked, her voice heavy with despair.

Tess lay curled in the sand, hands covering her face. Gia crouched beside her, gently running a hand over her head before cradling her over a shoulder and walking away.

"Marcus fought for us," Malik said quietly. "Now we're going to have to fight for him." He turned to me, gripping my shoulder. "Where is Maya?"

Despite everything she had done, I couldn't turn Maya over to Maddox. We were defeated, but I wasn't out of the fight until I dropped dead. If we were to be trapped on Vocury, I wouldn't accept aging out as my end. I knew the others likely felt the same way, but there was no sense in everyone giving their lives if mine alone would be enough. Gio had done it for me, and with nothing left to lose, it was my turn to pay it forward.

Chapter 17

Joy in the Face of Depression
Tess Fontaine: 2337

G ia carried me until I composed myself, and from there on out, I
walked alone ahead of the others. I assumed the Omaha was at least
a day away since we hadn't spotted the Travelers' lander in the couple of
months that Alexis and Malik had been on the surface, and there was no
time to waste.

It would have been wise to slow my pace. There was a great deal of
planning needing to be done, but I didn't want the others to see my
shame. I was to blame as much for our situation as anyone. It was my
research that led Dr. Amaar to Vocury. I had tried to save the Praxi, but
the most I ever managed to do was free two children while hundreds more
remained enslaved. I had abandoned my family in a futile effort to cleanse
my guilt—and destroyed them in the process.

Maya and Marcus might both be dead, and I was ready to charge headfirst into battle so I could join them. The others may have shared that
sentiment, but none of them carried an equal weight of responsibility.
They were along for the horrible ride my ineptitude and poor choices had
created for them.

My hastened pace eventually caught up to me, and by the time I stopped
to rest, I realized Malik was the only one close behind me. The rest of
the group were mere specks in the heat-distorted distance. Catching up
to me as I considered getting on my feet to avoid any conversation, Malik
approached, sat down across from me in the sand, and nodded for one of
my hydrators.

"I know what you're going through," he cut through the tension.

"You don't even know me," I snapped harshly. "You have no idea what
I've been through. What we've all been through. You slept while the rest
of us struggled."

"Why do you hate me?" he asked bluntly.

"I don't hate you," I responded quietly.

"It sure feels like you do. It's been hundreds of years and still, you look at me like I'm your enemy. I was a part of your family once, and you rarely spoke more than three words to me."

"Maybe if you had stuck around, we'd be pals," I said with a snide edge.

"So that's it? You resent me for living my life? He's not my son, Tess."

"You're right." I hopped to my feet. "He's mine. We're not your responsibility."

I walked away before he could respond, though I knew I shouldn't have pushed him away. I needed every ally and friend I could get, but the last thing I wanted to hear was Malik explaining himself and making me feel worse than I did already.

He loved Maya, in a different way than I did, but maybe even more. My plate was already full, with a three-course meal of shame, guilt, and regret. I didn't need to add shallow self-consciousness concerning Malik's proximity to my broken family as dessert.

I was the first to arrive at the Omaha, and I wasted no time refueling and gathering supplies so I could set out again. Malik followed behind me and his eyes widened as he stepped through the temporal field into the vast interior of our impressive alien home.

"How is this possible?" he muttered, stepping back and forth between the temporal field like he was unsure if his eyes were playing tricks on him.

He walked past me, his gaze landing on the tick marks Ranbir had scratched into the hull, tens of thousands marking the sunsets and sunrises, grouped and circled for easier counting. As he moved to pull the shelving away from the wall to see how many more thousands of lines were cut into the metal, I stopped him.

"There's twenty-seven thousand, five hundred and fourteen marks, and Ranbir stopped tracking longer ago than I can even remember."

Malik's face tightened as he became oddly emotional over the artistic expression of the amount of time that had passed.

"What is it?" I asked.

"I remember trying to count the days, and I lost track at some point as well."

I kept things moving along. "Do me a favor—find something I can use to make a sling for Alexis. She'll be here soon, and I want to leave as soon as I patch her up." It was mostly just an excuse to send him away.

Twenty minutes later, the rest of our company came into sight, walking up on the Omaha. I sat with my back against the ship as Malik paced the sand while we waited.

"What the shit is this?" Alexis asked as she examined the tiny transport that had become our home.

"Right?!" Malik jumped in, teeing her up with a movie reference. "That's what I thought. 'You came here in this?'"

"Oh, oh! You're braver than I thought," she responded with a snap, point, and smile to Malik, but the humorous moment faded quickly.

"Come on, darling. Let's get you some medical attention." I hastily jumped to my feet and led Alexis into the Omaha.

"Nu, uh, uh," I said as I dragged her past the wonders in the rear of the craft to avoid having to explain the temporal field to her. We passed through the cargo hold and I led her into my makeshift laboratory where I had been working on my cure for years.

"On the table," I instructed her, and she carefully slid onto it without compromising her wounded arm. I gently held her forearm and applied the slightest bit of pressure to extend it.

"Whoa. That's it. Can't go any further than that," she painfully joked. I returned her elbow to its bent position and lightly pressed two fingers to the joint. "Ow. That's no good either."

"If I had to guess, you've got a fracture, and it might be relatively clean. You'll need a sling, but you should be fine. Let's check the rest of you, though, just in case. You took a pretty good licking back there."

"I'm clumsy but I'm sturdy," she said proudly.

I shined a light in both of her eyes to check for symptoms of a concussion and then donned my stethoscope to give her heart a listen. While counting her beats I checked her ribs and torso for any other broken bones or tenderness. Lifting her shirt, I shared a concerned look with her.

"I'm fine, Tess. It's just my arm. Patch that up and we can move on to more pressing business." I held the chestpiece of my stethoscope against her belly and she twitched when the cold metal contacted her skin. "Seriously, what are you doing?"

I looked her in the eye briefly and then examined her abdomen closer.

"What is it?" she asked. "Am I internally bleeding? Tell me."

I pulled my earpieces out and placed my hands on her knees. "What happened with Dr. Amaar?"

"Oh Jesus. What did he do to me?"

"Sweetheart, I think you're pregnant. Have you been sexually active?"

Alexis stared in disbelief.

"My god. It really worked," she whispered. "He fixed me!"

"It would appear so, though I'd have to do a closer examination to confirm."

She smiled and her grin turned into laughter before she covered her mouth, her eyes bright with tears.

"I'm sorry," she apologized. "Everything else is screwed, but I—" she paused. "I just can't believe it." She broke into a full cry. "I'm going to be a mother!"

"This isn't something manufactured by Dr. Amaar, right? There is a father?"

Alexis nodded firmly. "There is. It's Taj. We've been, ya know . . . a lot. I didn't think it would actually work, though."

I wanted to be happy for Alexis, but the emotion escaped me. She had found genuine joy in a dark place, and the pessimist in me was already contemplating a horrible scenario.

All I needed was one embryo from the Wolf Moon and I'd be able to test my theory. I could reverse all the damage I'd done to these addicted people, but the opportunity had slipped through my fingers. Now, here was Alexis, carrying the necessary underdeveloped cells that could give the people on Vocury new life.

Whether she yet realized it or not, she had a looming, impossible, decision to make—and it was imperative that she not be forced to choose.

"You're freaking me out. What is it?"

"It's nothing," I lied. "We just need to get a move on. We don't have much time."

Alexis dismounted from the table, and I helped fit her into the sling. "Is that good? Too snug?" I asked while tightening the tension.

"I'm good. Ready for action."

"You should really rest. I'll show you to my quarters and you can take a load off."

"Hell no. We're all in this together," she answered defiantly.

I let her tag along for the moment, but I wouldn't be able to allow her to put herself in danger. Her unborn child might be our only hope.

Outside, we regrouped. "Gia and Rix didn't feel like waiting around," Ranbir said. "They think Maya might be in one of the villages."

"We're not trading her to that asshole," I stated definitively.

"Of course not," Malik agreed. "She might be able to help get us through the door, though."

"The pirates might listen to her, too," Ranbir added.

"After all these years, I kind of doubt it."

"Let's not stand around talking about it," Alexis cut in. "They're probably loading that ship to the brim with their cargo as we speak. We might not have a plan—"

"We don't," Malik interrupted.

Alexis wasn't fazed. "But we'll figure it out, right?"

"You're awfully optimistic . . ." Ranbir raised an eyebrow at Alexis' positive disposition, but she didn't reveal her pregnancy to the boys.

"Come on," she responded simply as she led the way.

"Sweetheart, it's this way." I redirected her to the east.

"Right. That way. We're going to find Maya, raise an army, storm the gates, save Marcus, rescue Taj, kill Maddox, and take back the Wolf Moon. Just like the good ol' days."

"You remember the good ol' days?" Ranbir's question was met with silence before he continued, "I do. The price of victory isn't cheap."

We traveled quietly as the hottest part of the day passed, and arrived at the edge of the easternmost village after a few hours. It had been a lifetime since I had walked among the poor wretches who lived from one high to the next. I counted my blessings that most of them had been run off to Citadel to hitch a ride, but there was no escaping the mess I had made.

We hurried along the wooden walkway in front of the main row of run-down buildings and saw a woman lying in our path. She was sickly and emaciated, her hair thin from pulling at it, and her arms were covered in sores.

"Please. Please help," she begged.

There was little I could do for her as she aged out, much like we all would if we failed. I couldn't save her; the best I could offer was a fresh dose of regenerator to extend her life by a few days or so, but a painful death seemed inevitable considering the circumstances.

"Up here!" Gia shouted at us from a second-floor opening.

We hustled across the way, entered the building, and I led the way up the stairs, taking two at a time. Bursting through the door, I could scarcely make out Maya's figure where she lay in bed under a dirty blanket. She was barely conscious, her body gaunt and cold to the touch. I knelt beside her, holding her hand, feeling the overwhelming weight of guilt crash over me.

"Oh, baby," I whimpered as I ran my hand across her forehead.

Her body temperature was surprisingly low, even though she was visibly sweating. I propped her mouth open to insert a hydrator and the moment a fresh pill hit her tongue her eyes fluttered with activity.

It was as though the only thing that could get her attention was the promise of her next high, and I suspected that she wouldn't have reacted at all if she knew the type of pill I had given her.

Maya swallowed hard to get it down and turned on her side to face me.

"Tess," she moaned softly.

"It's me," I comforted her as I held back tears. "It's me, baby."

"I'm so tired. It hurts."

"Not for long. I'm going to fix you."

Hearing her voice right then was like the first time all over again. My memories of Maya were from a life that didn't feel like my own anymore—she was a character from one of my childhood dreams ... and I could barely recall even the fondest details. Even if I could get her clean, there was no guarantee that our bond would live on. I had consciously chosen the mission over my marriage—and maybe I didn't deserve to have her back.

I felt a hand on my shoulder and looked up to find Malik standing over me. He sniffled and ran a finger under his nose to cloak his emotion. He was the last person I wanted to see, yet his presence was strangely comforting.

"Maya, sweetie, look who's here," I said as an invitation for Malik to announce himself. He knelt beside me, and rather than slide his hand in front of mine to hold Maya's, he clasped his grip around both of our hands, keeping them together.

"Hey, superstar. I know it took me a long time, but I finally made it," he said gently.

"Nu-uh," Maya groaned. "I need a ... I want ..."

"Shhh," I whispered. "Rest, baby. You need to rest."

Maya tried to stand but fell to her knees instead. Malik and I picked her up and sat her back on the bed, but she had to be held to stay upright.

"Get off me," she slurred angrily.

Gia stomped down the stairs and then back up, poking her head into the room. "Rix is back—and he brought company," she informed us.

Ranbir and Alexis followed her, and Malik and I shared a glance as though we were at war over who would stay with Maya. Rather than let him stay behind, I took Malik by the forearm and pulled him with me.

Downstairs were some members of my son's militant gang, and they seemed to be in a sporting mood.

"Did you get him killed?" Stacks asked belligerently.

"He's not dead," Ranbir guessed. "Maddox dragged him off. He wants some kind of trade for Maya."

"And?" Double-A prompted callously. "What are we waiting for?"

"Come on, guys," Taz interjected, the only member who still held respect for Maya.

"She's dead already," Dixie argued. "We're lucky she's all they want. If we can save Kade at that price, we should take it."

"Marcus," I corrected her. "My son's name is Marcus."

"He ain't your son, lady," Stacks asserted. "You gave him a name and that's about it."

"We are not giving Maya over to that monster!" Malik yelled. "You'll have to kill me first if you want to try it."

"And me." Rix projected his usual terrifying rage.

"Same," Gia echoed.

"Fine." Dixie capitulated. "Do what you will. Don't expect us to sit by idly, though."

"We were kind of hoping you'd feel that way," Ranbir said.

"She doesn't speak for all of us." Stacks sneered at our group. "You damn fools are going to get yourselves killed. Let the Citadelians flee. Who needs 'em, anyways? We can inherit the pyramid when they're gone. We'll have fresh water, soft beds, shelter, and more pills than we'd know what to do with."

Before Stacks could rally anyone to his logic, Double-A pushed him and pointed to Dixie as if to say that she did indeed speak for him.

"Who's going to work the mines? You, Stacks?" I asked. "What about the water reclaimers? Do you know anything about the chemical compositions and blending required to press more pills? Or how about creating Praxi embryos and extracting the appropriate enzymes and proteins?"

"We make a trade!" Stacks raised his voice. "Give them Maya, spare them a fight, and they leave us enough colonists to keep us going."

Rix walked up to Stacks, who—unwisely—didn't back away or soften his demeanor. With two feet planted, Rix picked him up by the throat and lifted him six feet off the ground. "You only live because my people suffer. You don't have to help us, but I will kill you myself if you stand in our way."

"Easy, buddy," Ranbir said calmly. "Let's put the jackass down, okay?"

Rix lowered Stacks, but he didn't back away. If I had to guess, he had some private words for the man after the fact and the struggle may have continued if they weren't interrupted.

"Where's the rest of your crew?" Ranbir questioned the Dawgs.

"They ran off with Trigger when they heard Kade went down," Double-A explained. "Boss man has a major stash hidden somewhere and they intend on raiding it. We can't count on them. They'd trade Maya if they could."

"I'm not for sale," Maya announced from the balcony, gripping the rail as if it were the only thing keeping her upright. She drew a deep breath, gagged, and clenched her fist against her mouth before doubling over and vomiting on the floor.

"Dammit, Maya," I grunted and hurried up the stairs, carefully stepping around the mess. I swung her right arm over my shoulder and steadied her. "Get back into bed. You're not going anywhere."

"I want to know what's going on," she demanded, wiping her mouth with the bottom of her shirt.

I didn't bother arguing. Instead, I helped her down the stairs, one slow step at a time. When we reached the lower level, I led her to a chair, and Alexis sat beside her as she wrapped an arm around Maya's shoulders.

Maya blinked at her, her voice slurring with childlike wonder. "You're here too. Neat-o."

Ranbir's voice cut through the moment. "We need to go. There isn't much time, so if you're ready to get your hands dirty, let's get moving."

Maya struggled to her feet again, wobbling as Alexis helped her with her one good arm. "Jack me up on some accelerator. I've got some fight left in me."

"Alexis, stay and look after Maya," I directed.

"I'm coming with you," Alexis protested.

"You're already injured. Stay back, give Maya a hydrator once every hour, and try to work in some sustainer without her vomiting."

"No way. I can fight!"

"I'm not going," Stacks announced, though no one cared. "I'll look after Maya. She'll be okay."

"No," I insisted, "Alexis is staying."

"What is your deal?" she asked me.

I took a deep breath and pondered whether to make Alexis' secret public knowledge. There was no other way to sideline her without everyone understanding the full gravity of our situation, so I just blurted it out.

"Alexis is pregnant."

"So what?! We should all share the risk. If you leave me behind, I'm just going to follow you," Alexis snapped and shot me a dirty look.

Ranbir took Alexis' side. "She's right. My mother went into combat multiple times when she was pregnant with me."

"This is different, and you know it!" I told him.

"Why? What makes me exempt?" Alexis asked.

"You're 'exempt' because your unborn child might be our only insurance policy!" I admitted. "If the Wolf Moon gets off the ground, everyone who is left behind is in big trouble. We're going to have to make some impossible decisions. Either to continue farming Praxi children to stay alive, or . . ." I couldn't even say the implication out loud.

"We're not harming another Praxi child," Gia said firmly.

"Agreed," Ranbir chimed in. "We either win, die fighting, or age out. I don't care how painful it is. I'm ready." He nodded to Rix, who pulled him close, their foreheads touching briefly in solidarity.

"Well, I'm not!" Dixie exclaimed. "Taz? Double-A?" she asked, and they all begrudgingly nodded in agreement. "No offense—we'll fight for Kade, but I'm not aging out on this fucking rock. I've seen what that looks like. No, thanks. If the girl has to give up her baby, I'm really sorry and that's awful, but come on."

"It won't come to that," Malik said, locking eyes with Alexis. "It won't."

I approached Alexis and used my best bedside manner. "I didn't want you to even have to think about it because it's awful. No one will force you to do anything, but just to be on the safe side and keep our options open, will you please stay behind? Take care of my wife. Please," I gently begged her.

Alexis' eyes filled with unshed tears. "Fine," she whispered, her voice cracking. "I'll stay. One hydrator per hour. I'll look after her until you return, but you have to promise me something."

"Thank you." I nodded, fighting back my own emotions. "Anything you want."

"Don't come back without Taj."

"We'll get him or die trying," Ranbir promised confidently.

And just like that, we were off. No plan, just desperation driving us forward. The odds were against us—Maddox and his men were stronger and better equipped—but we had something they didn't. Gia and Rix were each worth a dozen soldiers, their rage for the genocide of their people burning hot after stewing for centuries. Ranbir, hardened by years in the desert, feared nothing. Fighting to the death was his preference, and his pain made him dangerous.

Our new allies were the wild card. They seemed to love the man they knew as Kade like a brother, and if they fought with the same fire, they could match Maddox's fury.

But Malik—he was the enigma. He didn't strike me as a fighter, nor was he physically imposing. What did he have on the line that could compare to the rest of us? Maya was safe, he wasn't hooked on regenerator, and I wasn't willing to believe he was fighting for his biological son. Maybe he was the hero Maya claimed him to be, or maybe he had something to prove. I didn't know. But if he wanted my respect—and to be called a part of my family—he'd have to earn it.

As for me . . . I was as dangerous as any of them. A mother's love can move mountains, and mine had burned forever. I wasn't sure Marcus knew how much I loved him or how my heart had splintered by what we had done to each other. But I'd walk over hot coals—would gladly give my life—to save him and hear him say "I love you" to me just once.

If it came to that, I'd burn the Citadel to the ground for him.

It's often said that those who have nothing left to lose are the most dangerous. Maybe that's true. But our enemies were about to learn that those with everything on the line are far worse. My group was fueled by the pain of unrequited love, a thirst for revenge, and the madness that only surfaces when your friends' lives hang in the balance.

And Maddox? He was about to find out just how dangerous that could be.

Chapter 18

Blinding Hubris

Dr. Amaar: 2337

T he news of Maddox's victory spread like wildfire through the Citadel. I was one of the first to ride the mechanical lift up to the planet's surface, eager to see the spoils of his conquest. As the lift ascended, the sheer mass of the recovered craft came into view, its size dwarfing those we had set out in. Shielding my eyes from the rising sun, I marveled at the sight—a miracle and a second chance.

The people of Earth must have forgotten us after so many years. Aside from those wealthy enough to preserve themselves in cryosleep chambers, our investors were long dead. Mission Vocury II was probably an afterthought. A deep space exploratory tragedy that warned future generations not to chase after the fountain of youth.

Little did they know that not only had I found it, but that I was the architect of its creation and the master of its healing waters.

The history books will be rewritten, but not nearly soon enough. Without a gravity drive on the Wolf Moon, six hundred years will have passed before my triumphant return to Earth. By then, humanity will have achieved technological wonders that will astonish those of us who had lived on Vocury. But none of their achievements will rival mine.

I will return as a man out of time—forgotten by many yet envied by all. The greatest scientists of the twenty-seventh century will look upon my discoveries in awe. They'll seek out Vocury to experiment for themselves, walking the path I have carved out for them. If their names are remembered at all, they'll be recalled as followers, mere disciples of my genius.

Corporations, politicians, and world leaders will fight to get their hands on what I will bring home. With access to untainted human embryos, I will perfect the regenerator and serve it to the masses. Diseases once thought incurable will vanish. A new era will dawn—time itself will be measured as before Dr. Amaar and after. The human race will be grateful to live in an age where death is no longer feared. I will be a god among them. They will no longer fearfully pray to deities, for I will deliver them from their judgment day.

When I finally reached the surface, Maddox and his team had already disembarked, pleased with their victory. I walked over to my hulking enforcer and extended a hand in congratulations, but he brushed it aside.

"Your whiny brat of a son is still on board. The simple fool led us right to them. You're welcome," Maddox said dismissively. "Now get us home."

I had brought a group of workers, and with the soldiers—minus Maddox—we had more than enough manpower to get started.

"Strip her down," I ordered. "Remove every last piece of unnecessary equipment. And I do mean all of it. Wake the sleepers and put them to work. I want everything on this ship except the embryo freezers cleared out in ten hours. You"—I pointed to one of Maddox's higher-ranking men—"you're in charge of loading. Move the bulk containers, lab equipment, and Vice to the surface. Leave the Praxi children until we're ready to go. I don't want them running off. We launch in forty-eight hours."

"Yes, sir."

Once the work had begun, I boarded the ship and found Taj sitting in the cargo hold looking particularly defeated.

"You're going to get stepped on if you sit there and pout," I said. "Get on your feet and out of the way."

"What have you done?" Taj asked, shaking his head.

"I've saved mankind and given our people a second chance, that's what I've done. You've been given more than any of them and you're the only one who doesn't seem to appreciate it."

Taj stood, using the sound of my voice to seek me out. "What did you give them, Father?"

"I've cured their diseases and given them eternal life." I scoffed. "I'd like to see you do better."

"And what did you give me?"

"I gave you life, boy. In the most impossible of situations, I brought you into this world. I sacrificed more than you'll ever know. And for my troubles, you've given me nothing but contempt and ungratefulness."

"Then tell me," he demanded. "No more lies. What did you sacrifice?"

"You wouldn't understand," I said dismissively, turning away. But Taj followed, grabbing my arm.

"I may be blind, but I see more than you think," he said, his voice rising. "What did you do to my mother?"

"She died in childbirth," I repeated, as I had countless times before.

"Liar!" Taj's grip tightened. "That's nowhere near the full story and you know it! She died because you made her an experiment, didn't she? What lies did you spin to get her on your operating table?"

"I'm not entertaining this conversation," I replied, attempting to yank my arm from his grip, but his grip held firm.

"How long had it been since anyone conceived? A hundred years? More? You must have been so desperate. Achieving all this brilliant work to extend life, just to destroy everyone's ability to create it in the process."

"You know nothing." I grit my teeth.

"I know everything," Taj spat. "I'm blind because of you. I don't have a mother or anything resembling a family because of you. Regenerator is your greatest achievement, and it's so toxic that you can't let me touch it. You've murdered, enslaved, and mutilated an alien race, and you've destroyed the lives of everyone here. And now you want to take that to Alexis' home?"

"That girl has twisted your weak mind. Neither she nor you understand the costs of greatness. You mourn your mother as if you knew her, as if you could feel her loss. She was my wife!" I shouted. "You curse my name for turning her from barren to fertile, but she knew the risks of carrying you."

"Don't do this, Father." Taj pleaded. "You can stop. Tess says it's not too late to reverse the damage, but you have to stop."

"You'd trust the word of a traitor over your flesh and blood?"

Taj paused, his grip on my arm loosening as his hands moved to my shoulders. His face inches from mine, he asked softly, "Have you ever looked me in the eyes when lying to me?"

I couldn't answer. Claiming I had would be another lie.

"Go to your quarters and rest," I commanded. "The desert heat has made you delirious."

"Very well," he conceded, releasing me. "But this isn't over. My new friends are coming, and they won't stop until your head rolls."

I tried to take Taj's forearm to guide him out of the ship, but he wasn't interested in my assistance. He felt his way along on his own and my gut knotted in regret.

I should have told the boy the truth from the start. In failing to do so, I had cultivated his hate. Deep down, I knew blaming him for his mother's death was a coping mechanism, but I wasn't strong enough to shoulder the load myself.

The only path to repairing our relationship was forward. Taj needed to see Earth and the welcome we would receive. Only upon witnessing how desperately those people needed me would he understand my value and ethics. In time, he would come to appreciate my work. And once I perfected it, perhaps he could enjoy the fruits of it himself. There were untainted human embryos aboard the Wolf Moon. Soon, my greatest work would be complete.

In two days, we would be among the stars once more. We would leave this rock behind, and I would continue my legacy as it was meant to be.

Chapter 19
Going Underground
Gia: 2337

Humans are a complicated species. My kind had studied them for thousands of years, but nothing can prepare you for living among them. Every action they take is bound to an emotion, and in comparison to Praxi, humans often act in extremes. Their love yearns harder. Their hate burns hotter. Their need for acceptance, revenge, and justice is incomparable. They make snap decisions in the moment based entirely on emotion, but also possess incredibly long memories for those who have helped or hurt them.

These are not the traits of Praxi. When I was young, I was taught that our kind have control of their emotions. That we express and exchange our feelings freely, and in doing so, we make decisions rationally and pragmatically. As a child, I thought we existed on a higher plane than humans. My people had long since given up on wars, religious conflicts, and the trivial politics that plagued mankind. We thought our DNA was superior. But after living among them—and coming to love them—I know that's not true.

Our differences were in culture. Most Praxi learned to walk a higher path because they were taught well by their elders. We weren't inherently better than humans; we simply had more time to learn.

I didn't have the luxury of completing that education. The only parent I had known was the one from stories that seemed to act more human than Praxi at times. Gio hadn't even spent much time around Ranbir and his friends, but those experiences had changed him. He took unnecessary and irrational risks to help them, and though his loss to me was great, it was not without a lesson.

I follow in my father's legacy as a Praxi who inexplicably fell in love with humans. We both had reasons to distrust and even hate them, yet somehow, we ended up in the company of individuals who showed us a different side to them.

If it weren't for Tess, I would have been as good as dead. If it weren't for Maya and Ranbir, I would have lost my way. Every day I spent among them, I became more human. A Praxi child raised on the culture of man. Taught to act with emotions and even speak their dialect. The day Dr. Amaar cut out my sensory capabilities was the end of one life, and the day Ranbir taught me to speak was the beginning of another.

I wasn't fully Praxi and I wasn't fully human.

There was a strange emptiness inside of me where the bioelectric connections to something greater had been severed, yet I could still sense an ability to reach out, though I did not know what for. Grasping for that invisible connection caused a discharge of electrical current, which, while effective as a weapon, wasn't its true purpose. At the time, it felt like a strange curse. Little did I know that my unique connection to something beyond me would serve a purpose one day.

It was nearing dusk, and our ragtag assembly of humans and Praxi acting entirely on emotion had made our way to the nearest train pad. At this hour, workers would typically be returning to their crumbling homes, numbing themselves to the reality of their lives.

On this day, however, there was no one riding the gravity pads through the desert. There was only so much room on a single freighter, and there wasn't a soul left on Vocury who wanted to be left behind. Our ride came to a stop, and we hopped on to head toward danger. But before I could engage the drive, a voice called out from behind.

"Wait! Wait for us!"

Dani approached, struggling to support two sickly figures draped over her shoulders, with more bedraggled souls trailing behind her.

"Oh," she said as she took notice of who she had been flagging down. "Where the hell do you guys think you're going?"

"The train only makes one stop," I replied.

Dani helped those she carried onto the platform and stood aside so the others could climb aboard.

"They'll never let you leave," she callously informed us.

"No shit," Ranbir snapped.

"You idiots." Dani shook her head. "You're going to get yourselves killed, and everyone else in the process." She paused.

"Where is Kade?" When no one answered, she pressed harder. "Tess, where the hell is Kade?"

"I don't have anything to say to you."

"Maddox took him." Double-A answered. "He wants Maya, but he'll settle for the next best thing if he has to."

"But he's alive?"

"We think so," Ranbir said.

Dani was incredulous.

"And what—you're going to go in fists blazing and punch your way to victory?"

"The ship is too big to take underground," I said. "It's just sitting out there in the sand. All we have to do is get on board."

"That's some plan," Dani said sarcastically. "You eight against what, like, sixty soldiers and one pissed off giant? They'll see you coming from a mile away."

"This is very helpful," Malik complained.

"You have a better idea?" I challenged her.

Tess glared. "Who cares what she thinks."

Dani scanned our faces and sighed. She stepped off the platform and waved her arm for us to join her. "Dammit, come on, before I change my mind."

One by one, we stepped off until only Tess remained. The gravity thrusters hummed a warning that the train was about to embark, and rather than argue with her, I jumped back on, slung Tess over my shoulder, and carried her off. The train zoomed away toward the Citadel, carrying the last of the addicts, leaving us behind with Dani, our fate in the hands of a wild card.

"This better be good," Tess muttered as we followed Dani back toward the village we had come from.

"I can sneak you into the lower levels and maybe even help you find Kade, but after that, it's up to you. If you maniacs somehow pull this off, I expect to be on board when you leave. And if you fail, those of you who survive better remember that I helped."

"Always an angle," Tess condescended.

"You played your hand. I played mine. If you had treated me like an equal instead of deceiving me, maybe we wouldn't be in this mess."

"Right, it's my fault that you ratted me out to Amaar. I forgot," Tess snapped sarcastically.

"Shut up!" Rix barked at both of them, but we all felt his annoyance.

"Seriously," Dixie echoed.

We followed Dani back into town and through the doors of one of her trademark pharmacies.

"Stay here," she told us as she ran up the swooping exterior staircase and disappeared. Moments later, there was a clang, and she reappeared behind the bars in the wall. After a few bolts and locks were unfastened, she swung the cage door open but raised a hand before we could enter.

Dani peeled back the rug covering the floor, then pried a hook under one of the wooden boards to jar it loose. Once free, the surrounding flooring was able to be raised, exposing the hatchway beneath.

Lowering herself down a wooden ladder, she looked back up at the rest of us and grinned. "Hope nobody is claustrophobic."

Ranbir went next, followed by Taz, Malik, and the others. It was slow going as they lowered into the pit one by one, and only Rix and I remained.

"It's a trap," Rix said.

"It's not a trap, you big coward. You're just afraid of tight spaces."

"I am not."

"Then what is it? Afraid of the dark?" I laughed as I dropped two legs down the hole and used my third to grip the ladder.

"Would you come on?" my voice echoed into the chamber.

As my feet hit the floor, I discovered that we were in a hidden underground passage carved deep into the ground beneath Vocury. Rix just behind me, I crawled through the dark tunnel, the air thick as the chorus of everyone's whining voices mixed and echoed throughout the corridor.

By the time we reached what appeared to be a home dug out of the earth, and were able to stand a bit, we must have been fifty feet underground. A small bed, multiple lanterns, a rectangular table with two chairs, and some clothing and personal effects filled the space, and a labyrinth of tunnels branched off from it.

"Kade's condo," Dani announced, pointing first to the tunnels on the left and right. "Village, village," she indicated before gesturing straight ahead. "Storage, and then Citadel."

"That sneaky bastard." Double-A laughed.

"I guess we have our answer to where that boy always slips off to," Taz said, and Dixie grunted in agreement. "It must have taken years to move all this mud."

"There was never any shortage of time—until now, I guess. Come," Dani said, leading us into the tunnel to the Citadel.

Again we went in, one by one, with Rix and I taking up the rear.

"See? No trap," I teased him.

"That mouth of yours is worse than the humans," he bantered back.

The next passage wasn't nearly as long, opening up to a much larger underground chamber. Inside was a trove of supplies that Marcus had collected for himself—tools, storage bins filled with multicolored pills, and an array of salvaged equipment he'd stolen from the Omaha. Dani immediately began sorting through the stash, shifting boxes and bins from one spot to another.

"Keep it moving," Tess demanded.

"If you're in a hurry, be my guest. There's something in here that I think you're going to want, though."

"Look at everything he's been hoarding down here," Dixie said as she rifled through piles of clothing. "There's going to be some changes in our organization when this thing is over."

"He's been slowly parsing out our score to the freaking villagers over the years," Double-A complained.

"Got it!" Dani shouted as she raised a flat silver device the size of her head. "Here's the real reason why the Citadel guard never made a move on Kade."

"Easy with that!" Ranbir panicked as he recognized the seismic gravity charge.

"Kade's insurance plan," Dani said as she caressed the cylinder's smooth surface before passing it to Ranbir.

Tess seethed. "Stop calling him that."

"Why?" Dani smirked. "I knew him a hell of a lot better than you ever did. That's the name he picked, and unless he tells me any different, Kade is what I'll call him."

Tess stepped into Dani's personal space. "That's who he became, not who he is."

"You're still so egotistical." Dani shook her head. "Believe it or not, we're not all shaped by your actions or inactions. Some of us actually make our own decisions independent of you. You're not that important, and Kade was better off without you."

Tess raised an open palm to strike Dani, but before the blow could land, Rix surprisingly caught Tess' wrist. His quick action was a perfect example of a Praxi's understanding of emotion that I was as unable to observe as my human counterparts.

Rix and I owed our lives to Tess, and where I would take her side in every matter, Rix was capable of reacting with full perception of the emotional landscape.

"Take a look around you, Tess," Dani's voice lowered to an approachable calm. "You think your son squirreled this all away for himself? Who do you think has kept these people alive in the desert all these years? Who put shirts on their backs, shoes on their feet, and gave them a safe place to sleep? Who negotiated peace and maintained the trade that gave the slaves a sliver of freedom and hope?"

She huffed out a breath. "It wasn't you, and it wasn't you, either, Ranbir"—Dani's gaze swept for Ranbir without success—"You want to save Kade and call him Marcus while you do it? That's fine by me. But don't pretend like he's some monster of your making. You don't need to save him from himself."

"That's quite enough," Rix interjected, almost certainly taking stock of the rising tensions between the two women.

"So, he set this great example for you, and what did you do with it?" Tess interrogated Dani. "You fed these poor people the very elixir that would keep them enslaved. Did you ever try to help them? Or did you just facilitate their trading their sustenance and hydration for opiates and speed? Did you even bother to warn them?"

"I did what I had to do to survive! I didn't create this mess, but I had to live through it just like everyone else."

"Enough!" I shouted. "If the two of you survive this, you can kill each other when it's over. We have one chance to get this right, and there are too few of us to find success while divided."

"So what do we do with the bomb?" Taz asked. "Use it as a diversion? Try to plant it on the ship? Blow up the Citadel?"

"Nobody is blowing up anything until my people are safe," Rix declared as I nodded along.

I appreciated my human friends' commitment to their centuries-long mission, but the tortured Praxi had to come first. We couldn't allow them to be taken to Earth.

"The Citadel mines are only fifteen minutes up the tunnel." Dani pointed to the carved-out path. "Once inside, I can get you access to the laboratories and the Praxi med tubes. There might be some resistance, but you should be able to get the drop on them. If we free the children, we could plant the explosive there, rendezvous back here, and trigger it remotely."

"It might bring the entire Citadel down," Double-A mused. "It's a good diversion, and will create an atmosphere of panic, but we're screwed if that ship gets off the surface without us. They have water, power, and production in the Citadel. That's not a horrible consolation prize should we fail."

"Not to mention the fact that it would kill hundreds of innocent people, and potentially my son," Tess added.

"Right, and all that," Double-A conceded.

"We go for the Wolf," Malik said. "Use the tunnels to sneak into the Citadel and keep things quiet. Free the Praxi, search for Marcus, and get as close as we can to the surface without being detected. If we get caught or cornered, we use the explosive as a threat."

"Or most of us could fight and one of us could plant it on the ship," Taz suggested.

"If one of us can get on the ship, they might as well get to the bridge and take off," Malik pointed out.

"And I suppose in this scenario, you think that's you?" Dixie asked, though her framing was more of an accusation.

"Any of the rest of you know how to pilot that thing? It's got to be me or Ranbir," Malik responded, turning his head to look for the only other capable pilot. "Ranbir?" There was no answer. "Chop?" he called out, voice rising in urgency.

"Where'd he go?" I blurted, panic setting in.

Double-A punched the wall. "That damned fool has run off with the explosive!"

"To do what, though?" Dixie asked.

"Oh shit," Tess said. "He's going for the ship, and I doubt he has any intentions of trying to steal it."

"Well, come on!" Rix challenged us.

He leaned forward and went barreling down the tunnel at a speed only I was able to replicate. I wasted no time following, the humans left in our wake even though we couldn't see where we were going. I dragged one hand across the rocky tunnel wall and focused my energy as though I were trying to communicate with Rix.

As I did, my body emitted an electrical current and the sparks created flashes of light when my touch met the conductive minerals in the rocks. It was as though there were small flashes of lightning guiding our way forward and showing the path to those behind us.

By the time we reached the end, we found ourselves standing in a dimly lit cavern. The space was vast and empty, and I imagine my voice would have echoed with terrifying thunder had I called out for Ranbir. The air had a heavy dampness to it, as though it was more poisoned by the proximity to Vice than on the surface. The ground and walls were jagged calcified rock that had been chipped away daily by human hands.

When I was a child, the lower mines were small and pristine. My people knew how to find the Vice within the stones, but the humans didn't have our knowledge. They smashed their way in every direction, hollowing out the space with tunnels and passageways in every direction in search of their lifeblood. Their recklessness had turned a once organized mine into a disaster zone that was unfamiliar to me.

I looked back down the tunnel to where there was approaching lantern light and soft voices arguing with each other. There was no time to wait for them or get caught up in their human concerns. The Praxi were our priority, and if we didn't get to them before Ranbir foolishly announced our presence, we might not get a second chance.

Rix and I hurried to the elevator shaft, forced it open, and climbed up toward the industrial level. To our surprise, the only human in sight was a hunched over, unconscious male, his leather armor and gear removed.

"Still pretty resourceful for an old man," Rix joked at Ranbir's path having carved its way out ahead of us.

There was an audible ruckus off in the distance, but there was too much space and equipment between us to see what kind of predicament Ranbir was getting into. I could feel Rix's desire to help our friend, but we couldn't veer off course. I had the passion of a human, and my sights were set on freeing the kin we had left behind.

"He's distracting them. We must take advantage."

"He's in distress," Rix pleaded with me.

"Stay on task. Bring the lift to our level and hold it here," I whispered.

I snuck ahead into the manufacturing center with disgust as I looked upon the way the humans had perverted our equipment. They had turned our birthing center into an industrial nightmare. Where once was new life now only death remained.

I was twenty paces in before I had to duck behind ratty equipment to hide from some passing humans rushing toward the other end of the factory. Ranbir could get himself into a pinch and trigger the device at any moment, so there was no time to waste.

I kept to the shadows, creeping along the perimeter before coming to the main center structure where I was born. I hadn't taken two steps inside before my eyes met those of three individuals in lab coats and all of us shared a moment of panic. The trio stopped removing tubes and packing equipment to stare me down and look at one another as if trying to figure out what they should do.

"Going somewhere with them?" I asked, my gaze shifting to the tubes filled with frail Praxi children behind the glass.

If only I still possessed the ability to emote—maybe then I could make those humans feel my pain, make them understand and finally do the right thing for a change. But all I had was my voice, and the most powerful note it could strike was rage.

"I'm going to give you three a chance to live," I bargained with them. "I'm in something of a hurry, and instead of popping all your heads off and rearranging them on the wrong bodies, I'll let you help me and then you can be on your way."

"Wh-whatever y-y-you w-want," one of them stammered.

"Open the tubes, unplug the children, and help them out," I ordered, fighting to keep control. I stepped toward the door to check the hallway.

"How many?" I asked as the first of the children was released from bondage.

"Thirteen."

I knelt beside the first child, who clung to my leg for support. Tracing a finger over the scar on his head, I looked up at the doctors, eyes narrowing in suspicion. "All of them?"

"What do you mean?" the frightened doctor responded nervously.

"You know exactly what I mean."

"We're not surgeons—we didn't do it!" they pleaded, their voices trembling in fear of the retribution they deserved.

"Just get them out," I growled through clenched teeth. "What about upstairs? How many in the labs?"

"They've already been moved. The teenagers are on the ship."

"Fuck," I groaned. "Come on, little ones. Climb on." I scooped up two children in my arms and leaned over so a third could climb onto my back.

"Let's move!" I snapped at the humans.

Once all thirteen were freed, I forced the scientists to carry the ones who couldn't walk. I peered through the door, waiting for the right moment, and as soon as a few men ran past, we bolted toward freedom. There was no longer any yelling from the other end of the bay, and I wasn't sure what that meant for Ranbir.

By the time I returned with the children, our human compatriots were already stepping off the lift. Tess gasped at the sight of the children, inspecting their wounds.

"So many," she whispered.

"You can fix them, right?" I asked, hope tinging my voice.

"I don't know. Maybe."

"Get them on the lift." Rix urged, his voice calm and reassuring. "Come, my young friends. Feel the gentle emotional embrace of an elder. Your suffering is over."

I hadn't felt warmth like that from Rix for as long as I knew him. It was exponentially more powerful than any rage he had ever shared, and just as I was remembering what that felt like, he turned to look upon the three humans who had held our little children in captivity. His hate burned through them, and I was shocked he didn't kill them right then and there.

Cradling the children in my arms, I stepped onto the lift with the others.

"Gia? Where are you going?" Tess asked.

"I'm going to get them to safety. Through the tunnels and at least as far as Marcus' cave."

"We need you," Malik begged me.

"They need me more."

I switched off the stop button and the lift began to lower down the shaft. My eyes met Rix's as we parted, and I feared it would be the last time I saw him.

"Rix—the older children are on the ship. You must save them."

I couldn't see him by the time he responded, but I sensed the steely resolve in his words.

"I'll bring them home."

If the Citadel guard had any sense, they wouldn't stand in his way. Rix may have allowed a stay of execution for the three scientists, but I doubt he'd control himself once the young ones weren't around to witness his rage.

Chapter 20

Blood For Blood

Malik Emmanuel: 2337

There wasn't time to ponder in the moment, but if there had been, I would have felt quite selfish. The gravity of our situation was dire for a dozen reasons, yet all I could think about was preventing Ranbir from doing anything foolish. He wasn't the same man I had known on Earth, and I didn't doubt for a second that he'd detonate that charge to prevent Amaar's escape.

I didn't press forward because I wanted to save Earth, rescue the Praxi children, or even spare Alexis from having to face a difficult decision. I went headfirst into battle because, above all, I needed to know what Ranbir would find in the dream tube. I had to know if I had experienced something real in the beyond, and Ranbir was the only person who could answer that question.

"What are we waiting for?" I asked. "Come on!"

Rix was the first to spring into action, sprinting ahead on his three legs through the mechanical maze of equipment. The rest of us followed without hesitation, no longer bothering to hide. We zigzagged through the Praxi machinery, catching up to Rix only when he stopped to deal with a group of Citadelians and guards.

Towering on two legs, Rix swung his third like a weapon, sending one of them flying to the left and another to the right. In a stand-up fight, there were none among them who could go toe to toe with him save Maddox. Our situation was sure to come to blows, and if that chemically-enhanced freak was in the middle of it, we stood no chance without Rix.

It took us five minutes to make our way across the production floor, and it would have been double if not for Rix either trampling over or swatting those who stood in our way. By the time we made it to the other end of the bay, the enormous mechanical lift had secured itself at the surface, cutting off the sunlight from pouring through the opening.

There were no less than a hundred Citadelians from all walks of life and levels of dependency congregated together. They parted for Rix, allowing us to reach the control panel where three soldiers frantically pressed buttons, trying to bring the lift back down. They didn't seem interested in a fight—outnumbered for once, or maybe just desperate to escape the planet.

"No one is going home if that maniac has his way," one of the men said about Ranbir.

"You'd be wise to maybe keep your mouth shut right now," Tess warned him.

"Why? You going to—" the soldier began before Rix leaned back on two legs and gave him a firm kick to the chest, sending him flying a good ten feet.

"Eh." Tess threw up her hands in disappointment. "That's why. What about you bozos? Have anything snappy to add, or do you want to maybe just bring that lift down here for the rest of us?"

"You remind me of someone," I complimented her with a small smile.

"Back in the day, Maya threw her own punches," Double-A teased.

"You want a fresh one too, smart guy?" Tess quipped, glancing up as sunlight flooded the area again. The giant steel lift groaned as it descended toward us. "Come on, come on, come on."

We started boarding before the platform even touched down. Violence and the threat of explosion waited above, but the Citadelians rushed to climb aboard with us. There was no time to waste letting every one of them join us, and if the fools knew what was good for them, they'd find a place to hide and pray we succeeded.

The lift ascended with about twenty Citadelians aboard, some of the more desperate clinging to the edge, either pulling themselves up or letting go before the drop became too high.

"Can't this thing go any faster?" I muttered, kicking the control box in frustration.

As we neared the surface, the sounds of conflict grew louder—shouts, orders, and chaos. Chop wasn't immediately visible, but we could see a cluster of soldiers slowly converging toward the ship. Equipment lay scattered around, some ripped from the ship, some still waiting to be loaded. Most of the sleep chambers had been ripped out, with only a few opened.

I ran to the nearest tube and pressed my hand against the glass to find it warm under the Vocury sun. Inside was a slumbering member of my crew, and without life support, they could already be dead.

Panic gripped me as I fumbled with the latches, finally prying the lid open. His skin was warm, but that didn't mean anything in this heat. I placed my hand on his chest—barely, just barely, I felt the rise and fall of his breath. Relief flooded through me.

"Help me! We have to open them all!" I shouted, but my friends had already become distracted by Ranbir's standoff.

Luckily, a few dozen Citadelians and even members of my original crew who had been woken were looking on and I quickly put them to work. "Everyone! Hey! These people are going to die if we don't get these chambers opened. Come here. Watch."

I quickly demonstrated how to unlatch the lids and remove the breathing apparatuses and IVs. Normally, I'd be more thorough, but I was far too distracted with worry for Ranbir.

"Open them all and help them out if they wake, but don't rush them." I pointed to a woman who was watching but unmoving. "You there—get in those crates and find hydrator. These people will need it. Go!"

Once the work had begun, I raced to join the others who had slowly made their way to the rear hatch of the ship. Ranbir stood elevated as he backed up the ramp, soldiers and my friends following closely behind.

"Don't make me do it!" Ranbir warned them.

"He's bluffing," one of the soldiers taunted.

"No, he's not," Tess answered him before turning to Ranbir. "Come on, buddy. Let's think this through."

"Get! Back!" The tension in Ranbir's voice was palpable as he glanced between us and the soldiers. "If all of you don't move away right now, I'll take every last one of you with me." He paused, his eyes lingering on Tess. "I've got this under control."

The Citadel forces slowly backed away down the ramp. When they didn't move fast enough for Ranbir's liking, he raised the gravity charge above his head as a threat. He might have been out of his mind, but for the moment, he bent our enemies to his will.

If he truly didn't value his life any longer, he could have ended it right then and there. Maddox's men were spooked enough to give him space, and those of us who cared for him complied because he seemed to have a plan. All he needed to do was push a single button and the mission he had set out on centuries ago would be complete. It might not have been a total victory, but an hour prior we didn't think we had much chance at all.

"Where is Marcus?" Ranbir shouted at the soldiers. When they didn't recognize the name, he asked again, annoyed. "Kade! Kade! Where's Kade? What did you do with him?"

"Easy now," one of the soldiers replied. "He's sedated on board. Trigger that device, and you'll kill him."

It was a clear manipulation, but it didn't mean he was wrong. Judging by Tess' lack of reaction, she must have had some faith that Ranbir hadn't gone completely mad.

"He's in the infirmary," a voice calmly stated from behind Ranbir before Dr. Amaar walked into view. He could have exited the craft and taken himself out of harm's way, but he didn't seem to have any intention of leaving the Wolf Moon after he had waited so long for it.

"No need to fetch him. He's resting. You're all welcome to join him. Tess, why don't you come check on him yourself?" Amaar tempted her.

"Nobody move," Ranbir ordered, his eyes narrowing at the doctor. "You—go get the boy and the rest of your crew."

"This is unnecessary," Amaar replied, keeping his voice even. "Governor Chopra, think politically. There's room for all of us on board. We can forget this place, return home, and you'll be hailed a hero for bringing healing to Earth. They'll probably even make you Prime Minister. Think of the good you could do. We could save so many lives together."

Ranbir wasn't buying it.

"Let me make this crystal clear. You are never ever getting back to Earth. My friends and I are either taking this ship and undoing the hell you've unleashed here, or I'm blowing it to pieces. You can die with me in the blast if you'd like. It makes no difference. If you really want to save lives, clear your crew out. Wait patiently, play nice, and we'll give you and everyone else a fresh start on Prius."

Amaar shook his head, his gaze unwavering. "And have all my work be lost in the ether? What a waste. I might as well be dead. No. I won't be aging out. Nor will anyone else, not on my watch. I'm offering you a truce, and I don't believe you're in any position to turn it down."

Ranbir's eyes burned with defiance.

"Try me."

"Come everyone," Amaar addressed the masses. "Let's find out if the governor is truly willing to sacrifice us all for his cause."

Ranbir had painted himself—and all of us—into a corner. Amaar wasn't going to budge, and we'd only give him more leverage if we stepped closer to the blast radius. None of us had much choice, though.

Marcus was on board, as were the adolescent Praxi and the embryos needed for Tess' elixir. Ranbir was the only one of us with the nerve to do what must be done, and if he triggered that device, I might never know the truth behind my dream world. He had to live, even if it meant we were left marooned on Vocury forever.

I was the first to approach the ramp, and that was all the signal Rix and Tess needed to join me.

"You guys, don't," Ranbir warned, genuine fear creeping into his voice. "We can't let them leave."

Tess stepped forward, hands raised in a calming gesture.

"I have to save my son. You understand?" she asked him softly.

"And my kin." Rix joined her.

"You can come with us," Dr. Amaar echoed his sentiment. "You might as well . . . because you can't have the Praxi children, and I have no intention of releasing Kade. It's all or nothing."

"They don't belong to you!" Rix's fury surged through the air, hitting Amaar like a tidal wave. "How long has it been since you've felt the psychological weight of the terrors you unleashed on my people? Did you cut the ability to express themselves from every one of them?"

Dr. Amaar staggered, gripping his head as he collapsed.

"Get out! Get out!" he screamed.

"Maybe I should take your tongue. Strip you of everything that makes you human," Rix threatened him, driving the doctor to further depths of madness.

"Enough!" A booming voice cut through the tension as Maddox approached from the forward decks, Marcus slung over his shoulder. He dropped Marcus at the doctor's feet and turned to face Ranbir.

"A deal's a deal. Where is she?"

"She's dead," Chop lied. "And if you don't control yourself, we'll all be joining her soon."

"Prove it or blow us all up. I don't care."

"We're leaving, Maddox," Tess interjected. "It's not too late for you. I can fix everything. You can go home."

"Shut your mouth!" Maddox hollered, pointing his gravity stick at her. "You know my terms. This isn't a negotiation."

"The hell it isn't," Ranbir challenged him. "Get off the ship."

Maddox ran a bandaged hand across his mouth as he studied Ranbir. He slowly but confidently began to walk toward him, maintaining eye contact.

"Stop!" Ranbir demanded as Maddox stepped nearly close enough to swipe at him with his weapon. "I'm not playing with you."

"Good. I like a man with conviction. Go on, Governor. I've been ready to die for some time now."

Chop's hand trembled around the detonator, his thumb hovering over the trigger. If I stood closer, I imagine I could've seen the sweat beads forming on his forehead and his chest heaving with his rapid breaths. His eyes flicked to us, seemingly examining the distance and calculating if we were outside the blast radius. Maddox kept moving, step by step, forcing Ranbir to retreat further into the ship to create more of a gap between us. He wasn't bluffing after all.

"Hey! Chop!" I called out, my voice steady but urgent. "Don't do it, man. There has to be another way."

"There isn't, and that's okay. I've been ready for a while. I'm going to Em."

"Chop, no!"

"Do it." Maddox kept up the pressure. "Go on, do it."

With less than five feet between them, Maddox could have struck Ranbir if he was willing to risk the press of that button. In the sickest parts of his soul, I think Maddox wanted it to happen.

"It's Emilia!" I shouted. "She's waiting for you, but not like this. I've seen her, Chop. I can't explain it, but it's true. You have to see for yourself."

Ranbir's glossy eyes met mine before he turned away. By the time he looked back at Maddox, the beast had his hand wrapped around Ranbir's, though he didn't struggle for control over the device. Maddox could have wrestled it away, but he left the decision in Chop's hands.

"Last chance," Maddox warned him as his grip tightened.

Chop looked up at him and called out to us one final time. "I'm sorry, my friends. This is the end."

His eyes closed and his thumb mashed the trigger. When the bomb didn't immediately send gravity waves in every direction, he frantically pressed it again and again.

"Oh shit," he groaned.

Maddox wrenched the malfunctioning device out of Chop's hands, tossed it to the side, and proceeded to discard Ranbir from the cargo hold with a single swing of his stick. Next up was Marcus, and Rix immediately began charging into the ship toward them. Before Rix could reach his target, however, Maddox had clubbed Marcus and sent him barreling into Rix, knocking both off the side of the ramp.

"Kill them," Maddox callously ordered his men, then stomped to the edge of the ship, shouting at the masses of Citadelians gathered below. "If you want off this shithole, you have five minutes. Move your asses!"

The chaos that erupted was our saving grace. Hundreds of Citadelians surged toward the Wolf, shoving, trampling, and fighting for a chance to escape. The panic was spreading, and though the initial wave would clear soon, hundreds more were still flooding up from the depths of the Citadel to join the fray.

Double-A came to Ranbir's aid, and once he was back on his feet, I turned my attention to completing the mission. The others were locked in small, frenzied fights amid the flood of people, so I slipped quietly into the crowd. Keeping my head low, I moved swiftly, knowing that my friends would need my help.

I hurried along, taking short, stuttering steps as I blended into the tight mass of bodies on the ramp. As the Citadelians boarded, they spread out in the ship with looks of relief, making way for those still pouring in behind them. Guards were yelling and pointing, directing traffic, but I kept my head down, sneaking past toward the forward decks.

I reached the freezers without incident and quickly opened the casing to fish out a handful of frozen embryos. I filled my pocket with five little ice spheres that would serve as the precursor to Tess' antidote and then pressed my luck further by searching for Taj. I don't know exactly what he meant to Alexis, but we promised not to come back without him, and that was a good enough reason for me.

I stalked through the living quarters, but the hectic situation had spread deeper into the ship. People were crammed into every available space, shoving and shouting as they scrambled for a place to settle for the journey home. The noise was deafening, but I yelled out anyway.

"Taj!" I called repeatedly, sticking my head into doorways, hoping to spot the young man.

"Come on, kid, where you at?" I mumbled to myself. "Taj!" I called again.

"Security!" Dr. Amaar's voice rang out through the corridor. "Intruder!"

"Oh, shit. That's not good," I muttered under my breath. "Taj! It's now or never!"

"In here," came a soft reply, echoing faintly down the hall.

I hadn't pushed past more than a couple of people before the guards had me by my shoulders and yanked me away. They dragged me back the way I came, and the doc smiled villainously at me as I tried to kick and jerk my way free.

"You're too late," Amaar sneered, turning toward the bridge. "Get us in the air," he barked to no one in particular.

My captors hauled me through the cargo hold, and just as I yanked one arm free, the ship rose off the ground and pointed skyward. A few dozen of us lost our balance and went sliding down the rear ramp, the majority falling to the surface below. I held on tight—fantasies of pulling myself up, stowing away, and commandeering the vessel filled me—but my grip failed, and I dropped twenty feet onto the bodies below.

Maddox threw Rix off his back and howled with rage at the ascending craft.

"AMAAR!"

We stood there, a few dozen Citadelians, various members of the Wolf Moon's crew, twenty brutes, and the rest of us—all left behind, watching as the rear ramp closed and the ship burned the tiniest bit of triaxum to break free from the planet's gravity.

Marcus was still lying prone in the dirt as the ship's shadow passed over him. Taz shrugged off the soldier he was wrestling with and limped backward. Ranbir had blood leaking from his nose down over his mouth and chin. And Tess, Dixie, and Double-A all had various areas of swelling on their faces and bloodstains on their clothes.

For the moment, the fight was over as our adversaries realized they'd been abandoned by their friends, and the rest of us realized that we had failed.

"Nooooo!" Maddox yelled.

"It's over, Maddox." Tess tried to calm him, but the beast had gone feral.

He stomped toward Marcus, picked up his gravity stick, and raised it above his head to hammer his wounded enemy. Before the blow could land, Rix slammed into his side and the two rolled around momentarily. Tess and Taz raced to take advantage of Maddox being grounded, and the rest of us were pulled back into hand-to-hand combat with the remaining men.

"Stop!" I shouted but was met with a fist to the back of my head that toppled me over and nearly knocked me unconscious.

From my perspective, there wasn't anything left to fight over. Everyone left behind had lost, and there was no point in killing each other. I couldn't understand how intensely hot the fires of rage burned after centuries of hate, though.

The last of Maddox's men had nothing left to fight for except their leader, and there was no way we were talking him down. He had lost everything and had nothing left to live for. We were either going to have to kill Maddox or die by his hand.

There were no more challenges to throw down or cards to play. Honor, tradition, and ceremony had deserted us. Only blood, hate, and sweat remained.

Tess tried to throw body shots at Maddox as he grappled with Taz, but she caught a wicked backhand that sent blood spraying from her mouth and her body spinning toward the ground. Rix again took Maddox's back but was quickly shaken off. Maddox drove a powerful forward kick into Taz's chest, impressively pushing him back some eight feet, and if Taz had known what was good for him, he would hit the dirt.

Meanwhile, Ranbir was trading punches with two soldiers and not doing so well. Still dizzy, I picked myself up and zeroed in on one of the men to tackle. But before I could act, we all froze, horror-stricken by what we saw.

Maddox had wound back his stick and swung it with full force into the side of Taz's head. The blow nearly decapitated him, and the gravity wave from the weapon hurled his limp body across the ground, spraying blood for thirty feet before Taz's corpse slammed into the dirt.

"No!" Double-A screamed but refrained from charging at Maddox and meeting the same fate.

"He killed Seamus!" Dixie cried out, as if there was any doubt.

Ranbir blocked the next punch thrown at him and stepped back. "Enough! We surrender."

I understood where he was coming from but was shocked that Ranbir would be the one to give up. He had a death wish, but apparently didn't desire the same for the rest of us.

"I'm not taking prisoners," Maddox growled. "You know what I want."

His men circled behind him, giving the rest of us the chance to gather ourselves together. There was no time to make a plan, and no options left. Maddox dragged his club through the dirt as his men stepped aside, clearing a path toward Marcus.

A tense silence fell over our group as we exchanged grim looks. Then, with a collective surge of desperation, we charged.

"Come on, you bastard!" Rix raged as he steamed ahead of us.

Maddox turned, bracing for a low tackle, but Rix exploded from the ground and leaped clear over him, striking Maddox in the head as he passed over top. Rix landed near Marcus, matching Maddox's violent rage as he sent soldiers flying this way and that. Maddox swung around to strike him, but his men were already swarming and getting absolutely trounced by Rix as he went wild.

I plowed into Maddox's side but barely moved the mountain of a man. Luckily, Ranbir and Dixie were right behind me, and together, we managed to knock him off balance. Ranbir pounced, pinning Maddox to the ground and hammering both fists into his face.

Dixie and I thrashed and kicked at Maddox, but it seemed to do no good. With a single punch, he threw Ranbir off and rolled to his feet in one swift motion, shrugging off our attacks as if they were nothing. With a single swing into Dixie's shoulder, he sent her barreling away, her pained yells indicating the amount of damage done. He then turned to swing his stick down on Ranbir but instead drove it into the sand as Ranbir quickly rolled away. As I helped him to his feet, we shared a look and a head nod before charging into Maddox before he could refocus himself.

We didn't get within six feet before having to dodge attacks. Maddox continued advancing on us and became frustrated when his swings came up empty.

He cocked back, grunted, and finally just threw the weapon at us. Ranbir tried to step in front of me and take the brunt of the blow, but plenty of it caught me as well, and I got my first taste of what weaponized gravity feels like. It caught me in the right shoulder, and it was as though every muscle and cell were collapsing in on itself with the invisible force of gravity rearranging my insides.

"Ugh," I groaned as I gripped my shoulder and massaged my chest. I turned to Ranbir who was face down in the dirt and was relieved when he turned on his side.

"You okay?" I asked him.

"Not really," he groaned. "I don't see a way out of this."

"We either get our hands on that weapon or we're headed to see our ladies the old-fashioned way."

By the time either of us could recover and scurry to grab Maddox's stick, he had already retrieved it from the dirt. I hurried away on my knees and forced myself to my feet as he stalked in our direction, but Ranbir couldn't pick himself up before Maddox stood over him, a leg on either side.

"You wanted to die. I'm happy to oblige."

Tess, Dixie, and Double-A were defeated. Rix continued raging on, but the soldiers swarmed him and held onto his powerful legs to neutralize his attacks. I was the only one within range to do anything about Maddox's impending kill shot, and I had already seen how ineffective I was when charging at him.

Maybe it was time for me to return to Lydia and discover if I had truly experienced the afterlife. I could think of worse ways to go than trying to save a friend.

Before I could begin my final charge, a voice rang out across the battle-field.

"What kind of pussy uses a weapon against a fallen enemy half their size?!"

I shielded my eyes against the sunset to find Maya, Alexis, Gia, and even Stacks walking into view with the last of the daylight burning behind them like a desert mirage.

"You're in some shit now, pal!" Dixie yelled.

Maddox disregarded Ranbir and turned his attention to Maya. His eyes narrowed and his grip tightened around his stick.

"So. After all this time, you're still alive."

"Not for lack of trying."

She was my same old Maya. Three hundred years couldn't cure her of that smart-mouth and swagger.

"Killing her won't change anything," Tess reasoned. "We'll still be stuck here, and you won't feel any better. You can't bring your boy back, but you can honor him."

"If the roles were reversed and your little boy was dead, it would be Maya standing where I am and you know it," Maddox seethed through gritted bloodstained teeth. His hateful eyes stared at Maya across the battlefield as he stated definitively, "Blood for blood."

"That's fine by me," Gia jumped in. "Give no quarter. Receive none."

Maya pulled a handful of accelerator from her pocket and ground them up into Alexis' open palm until there was a small pile of powder. She lowered her face, pressed her nose to the stimulant, and snorted enough to kill a bear.

"Oof," she yelped as she plugged one nostril and the next to take it all in. "Hit it," she directed Stacks to finish off the drug, to which he obliged.

Maya bounced on her feet as she taunted Maddox. "Let's go, you big dumb animal. You want vengeance? Come and take it!"

"And you"—Maddox pointed his stick at Alexis—"you owe me a finger," he declared as he exposed his wounded hand.

"Yeah?" Alexis didn't miss a beat. "You're in luck. I've got two for ya," she responded confidently, flipping him the bird with both of her middle fingers.

Gia lovingly slapped Alexis on the back. "You've got spirit, human. Maybe stay behind me, though."

Maddox charged at them, and Gia moved to meet him head-on, with Maya close behind. Stacks went barreling into the soldiers roughing up Double-A and Dixie, and Alexis wisely held back. I rushed to help Ranbir, and while he was in no condition to continue to fight, he got on his feet anyway.

Gia slid to avoid a swipe from Maddox, then delivered a powerful kick to his side. As he was thrown off balance, Maya hustled in, kicked him in the knee, and threw a few quick punches to his gut. Rather than going for a strategic retreat, she clamped onto his arm holding the weapon and held on for dear life.

"Somebody get it!" she screamed at us.

I had to leave Ranbir behind to seize this opportunity, and he collapsed to his knees. By the time I reached the scrum, Maddox had smashed his fist into Maya's face and dropped her like she was nothing more than a nuisance.

He must have sensed me coming because he turned in my direction—but before he could act, Gia was striking again. She pushed two hands into his back and let out a primal electrical scream that shocked the brute. His grip loosened, the device falling and hovering over the ground, and I quickly swooped in to grab it and get clear.

Gia kept up the pressure, shooting a current through Maddox every time she hit him. Every punch came with something extra, and Maddox was incapable of striking back without being electrocuted.

He would land a punch, and every collision sent his hand snapping back. Without his weapon, Gia had him neutralized. Maddox was in a constant state of retreat, and with Maya joining Gia, they had him stumbling backward as he absorbed blow after blow.

I turned my attention to helping the others, specifically Rix. If he were to break free, this fight would be all but over. Six men were accosting him, essentially holding him in place so he couldn't do further damage. I hit the first man in the back, and the downward motion of my swing drove him into the dirt.

"Oh, wow! I'm so, so sorry."

I felt bad for them, but if they weren't going to surrender, they were going to get hit with the club. I swung at the next man and he went careening across the ground as the others released Rix and turned their attention to me.

"Fellas, I don't want to hurt you," I warned them.

I took a few steps back while they continued slowly advancing on me. Stacks headbutted the final soldier holding onto Rix and then bellowed "Sammy Sosa their asses!" at me.

I swung on the nearest man and made contact with his left arm, sending him flying to the dirt with a loud thud.

"This isn't even fair," I said with a guilty laugh.

"Batter up." Stacks motioned for me to pass off the duty, so I tossed the stick near his feet. He picked it up and took the stance of a right-handed batter.

"This is how McGwire did it," he announced and then blasted a soldier like he was driving one over the left field wall. "Down the left field line. Is it enough?" Stacks narrated, like Joe Buck doing a play-by-play. "There it is! Sixty-two. You are the new single-season home run king."

Once Rix was freed, Stacks offered him a hand to bring him up on his three knees.

"Whaddaya say, tripod?" he playfully prompted Rix. "Fight together instead of against each other for a change?"

"Just this once." Rix grinned.

With Stacks now in charge, his friends rallied behind him and sent Maddox's men scattering. Rix and I rushed toward the others, and even though they didn't seem to need our aid, Rix went headfirst into combat regardless. He jumped, landing a fist to Maddox's head and rolled to a stop near Gia.

The two of them pressed forward, swinging limbs at their enemy until Maddox was on his back and they were mounted over him. Gia screamed once more and kept two palms against his chest like a defibrillator meant to stop his heart rather than start it.

"That's plenty," Maya dissuaded Gia from finishing him off.

"His fate is not yours to decide," Gia responded.

"He has to pay," Rix added.

"He's beaten," I joined Maya in her sentiment. "This isn't the Praxi way."

"I'm not Praxi! Not anymore. Not after what he did to me and my people," Gia said.

Tess limped to us, and she and Maya leaned against one another to stabilize themselves.

"He didn't do that to you. I did. I thought I could fix things, but I made them so much worse."

"Don't listen to them," Maddox snarled, blood dribbling down his chin. "Finish it. There's nothing left for me here."

I knelt next to Gia and placed a hand on her arm. I received some of the shock, but she stopped when she realized I was absorbing it. Then, Maya placed a hand on her, Tess following suit.

"You are Praxi," I reinforced. "No matter how many human characteristics you adopt, no one can take that from you."

Gia hung her head and sobbed, her hands still pressed against Maddox's chest. Her tears rolled off her cheeks and fell in single drops onto his face as if they were his own. Even Rix placed a hand on her, and I don't think he did it because he necessarily agreed. We were authentic in our mercy, and it was enough to soften even the hardest Praxi heart.

"Gia. It's over. Let him be."

"It's over," I echoed as I removed my hand.

We all stood, and Maya pulled me in for a hug.

"I've missed you," her voice cracked as we all started to calm down.

"I've missed you, too. I never should have left in the first place."

"You did good, Malik." Tess nodded her head. "Real good." She hugged Maya and her grip tightened on the back of Maya's shirt. "Can we start over?" she whispered to her.

"Did you ever stop?" Maya had lost hundreds of years to shameful, isolated addiction, and throughout it all, Tess had never given up on her.

I couldn't imagine what they had been through, or how torturous the divide between them must have been, but even amid great loss, there was hope that love could be rekindled. Not just for Tess and Maya, but for all of us.

Alexis, Ranbir, and the others joined us in our sweet moment, well-earned after such a sour defeat.

"Where's Taj?" Alexis asked. "Is he okay?"

"He was on the ship," I answered. "I think he's fine, but I couldn't free him . . . I'm sorry."

"So they're gone?" Alexis looked stunned. "Just like that? They got away?"

"I couldn't stop them," Ranbir told her, sorrow in his eyes.

"Oh my God, I'll never see him again," Alexis said softly. "That's it. He's gone forever, and we're all going to die here."

"It's not all bad news," I interjected. "I got some embryos."

Both Tess and Alexis perked up and I'm not sure which was more excited by my revelation.

"Malik, I underestimated you," Tess admitted with a smile. "You've saved us!"

"That's my dawg." Maya grinned.

"I could kiss you!" Alexis rejoiced. "I don't know what I would have done. Can't even think about it."

"Well, now you don't have to." Tess beamed. "Let me get a look at them."

I reached into my pocket and my savior's smirk evaporated from my face. The ice casing had cracked during the melee and melted away in the heat.

The embryos, once safely preserved, were now a lukewarm, soupy mess. I gripped what I could, liquid seeping between my fingers, and revealed the disaster that they had become.

Tess' eyes widened in alarm. "Put it back!" she gasped, frantically cupping her hands beneath mine. "Don't lose any of it. We have to get to the labs. Now!"

Chapter 21

Depression in the Face of Joy
Alexis X: 2337

We retreated inside, and while the Citadel offered us hope, the mood was somber. Tess and Dani put aside their differences and joined each other in the lab, Maddox was locked in his quarters, and the rest of us patched ourselves up. Ranbir, Marcus, and a few of the soldiers were in worse shape, but an extra dose of regenerator and some rest would have them back on their feet in no time.

No one would look at me, and when they did, it was as though they saw a ghost. During a day filled with bad news, everyone but me expected more of the same. I held onto hope that Tess could salvage something from those embryos, get everyone clean, and allow me to keep my unborn child.

Being trapped on Vocury without Taj would be hard, but I was surrounded by the people who meant the most to me. I was convinced that I was going to have a daughter and, regardless of our situation, we would make the best of it.

Tess would find a way. She had to.

Once the wounded were tended to, the others hauled in the stock left behind, including the discarded sleep chambers. A team of twenty, led by Maya, sought out the Omaha to move what remained of their supplies to the Citadel. A separate team of twenty went with Rix into the tunnels to retrieve Marcus' cache of hidden treasures and the children hidden below. Two of the Citadelians brought the water reclaimers back online, and everyone else foraged through the lower levels for anything of value.

Double-A, Dixie, and Stacks buried Taz but refrained from giving him a proper funeral until the rest of the Dawgs resurfaced. Despite their differences, I imagined Ranbir and Maya would want to attend when the time came as well. They were all friends once, and if we were going to start over and survive, they would have to be friends again.

Things settled down after a day, and a mini town hall was called for everyone to give an accounting of events and discuss our options. Rix and Gia had returned with the children they had liberated, and they joined Maya, Malik, and the Dawgs in the heart of the Citadel's pharma mall to hash it out.

Under normal circumstances, I would have had my nose right in the middle of everything, but my presence complicated things. Everyone else was in survival mode, and rather than stand among them and have their opinions censored by my presence, I hid behind the counter of one of the kiosks and eavesdropped on the conversation.

"Alright, here's the situation," Gia explained. "There's ninety-four of us and with the water back online, there should be plenty for everyone. We recovered enough triaxum from the Omaha to keep the power on indefinitely and there's plenty of space indoors to live comfortably."

"If that's the only good news, I'd rather you just lead with the bad," Stacks complained.

"Shut up, Stacks." Malik took the position of the enforcer now that Maya was crashing hard on the comedown from the accelerator.

"Amaar left a lot behind," Gia continued. "Between Marcus' stash, what we found in Dani's warehouse, and the leftovers from the Omaha, we have one hundred and eighty-four cases of sustainer. If we ration it, that's about six years of life."

"Screw that," Double-A scoffed. "How many of them soldiers are there?"

"Twenty-two, counting Maddox," Rix piped up.

"Well, there you go," Double-A said. "Cut them off. That's an extra few years for the rest of us."

"Out of the question," Malik said firmly.

"Just yesterday they were trying to kill us," Dixie grumbled.

"We're not starving anybody. I don't want to hear it," Malik said. "Gia, continue."

"As I was saying, that's six years, but there's only enough regenerator for fifteen weeks. If Tess can't use the cells from the recovered embryos or her antidote doesn't work, every human will age out long before the sustainer runs dry."

"Nah. No way. That girl is pregnant," Stacks referred to me, further drawing my attention. "She needs to step up and do the right thing."

"Keep your voice down," Malik ordered. "Nobody, and I do mean nobody, is to say a single word to Alexis about this. Don't pressure her, don't ask her about it, nothing. God willing, it won't come to that, but if it does, that's her call."

"Easy for you to say," Dixie jumped in. "You don't need regenerator. The two of you, your sleepy crew, and all the tripods can live happily ever after while the rest of us age out. You've got no skin in this game."

"Well, I do," Maya said weakly, her former hungover state back in full effect. "We've lived long enough, and if any of you crosses her on the matter, I'll take another head full of accelerator and give you a quicker death than aging out."

"I second that motion," Ranbir announced as he limped up behind Maya and gave her a fist bump. "I say if nothing works, the rest of us should check out early with some dignity intact. Gia, how long would the sustainer last Malik, Alexis, her child, the other travelers, and the Praxi?"

Gia closed her eyes and calculated the adjustment. "Forty-six Earth years, give or take."

"Good," Ranbir said. "I don't know about the rest of you, but I'm ready."

My eyes began to well with tears as I listened in on my friends so valiantly defending me. To me, it had only been a few months since we had all been together. To Maya and Ranbir, I must have been only a fragment of their centuries-distant past.

All that time had passed, and both were still ready to die for my right to choose. Maya was tough as nails and Ranbir had lost a part of himself, but no one had more heart than either of them.

"Wouldn't one abortion be easier than putting a couple of those Praxi kids back in the tanks and making more regenerator?" Double-A asked, quickly changing his tone when he felt the rage coming from Rix. "I'm not like, saying that we should, but one fetus seems like a smaller bill than another lifetime of enslavement and dissection and the sort."

"That's off the table," Gia said. "Under no circumstances. You humans have pillaged my people for long enough. You've extended your lives far beyond your typical spans. If this is the end for you, I will bid you a fond farewell and miss my friends without wavering."

"Then Tess better figure this shit out, 'cause I'm not feeling real peachy about our lack of options," Dixie said. "If it comes down to that girl choosing between the rest of us and her own flesh and blood—well, that's a coin I don't want to flip."

The elevator dinged, alerting everyone that news was arriving from the labs, and Tess and Dani stepped off, draped in their lab coats, to deliver it. I peeked up over the ledge to watch them, but they were too far across the borough for me to read their facial expressions. Everyone shifted their attention to them, and no one spoke as Tess nervously ran her hand through her hair.

"Well?" Stacks finally asked. "How bad is it?"

Tess sighed. "Where is Alexis?"

"Oh shit," Double-A moaned.

"She's around here somewhere," Malik said. "Did I ruin the embryos?"

"I'm afraid so," Tess answered. "I can't do anything with them."

"That's it. We're screwed." Double-A cursed.

"Then so be it." Maya declared as she struggled to stand. "Some of us wasted it but we had our time." Her gaze flicked to Tess, filled with regret.

My stomach churned painfully, like a wet rag having the water twisted out of it. These were my friends, their lives torn apart, yet here they were, standing by me even as they faced their end. I had the power to give them six more years, and a second chance at happiness, but it would cost me more than I could bear.

How could I possibly decide?

I wished Taj were here—I knew what he'd say—but he wasn't. And the decision weighed on me like an anchor tied to my ankle, threatening to pull me under forever. Either I would be the reason my friends died, or I'd be the mother who ended her child's life before it even began.

I couldn't listen to them argue over my fate any longer. Tears streamed down my face before I even stood up. My voice trembled as I choked out, "It's okay. I'm here."

Everyone turned toward me as I approached, their lives hanging on my next words. I was a jury of one, and what I was about to say could be their death sentence. I swallowed hard, every part of me screaming not to do it, like the life growing within me was wailing for its right to survive.

I sucked in a sharp, deep breath, my heart breaking, and managed to utter, "I'll . . ." before the weight of it all overwhelmed me. I couldn't say the words or commit to my fate.

Malik was the first to wrap me in a hug, followed by Tess and Maya, who rubbed my back gently.

"You don't have to," Maya whispered. "We'll understand."

I was crying so hard that I couldn't even respond. They would give their lives for me, and the universe was calling upon me to sacrifice for them. No matter what I chose, I might never forgive myself.

I could feel each of them judging my reaction and gauging which way I might be leaning. The more vocal members in favor of living on didn't speak openly once I stood before them, probably because they thought they were in the clear. Double-A, Dixie, and Stacks had no idea what my pregnancy meant to me, and they were unwise to assume their salvation.

"Do you think we could talk in private?" I asked Tess.

"Me?" She blinked in surprise, drawing everyone's attention.

"Come on." I beckoned to her as I hastily made my exit toward the elevators. I couldn't do this in front of everyone.

"Alexis," Ranbir's voice rose just as I was about to step inside. "Don't do it."

Stacks tried to cut him off, but Ranbir pressed on.

"Each of us has shoveled loads of sand into our hourglass of time. Six years is nothing more than another spoonful. Our graves are dug either way, but you don't have to join us. Neither does Malik, our Praxi friends, or your child. You came here to make peace and establish a colony even though I stood in your way. Well, I'm telling you now, you were right. Finish what you started. Live your lives better than we lived ours."

I wish everyone shared his sentiment. Ranbir and I wanted the same thing, but I think we were alone in our desire. No matter how gracious and supportive my friends were, I couldn't believe that the instinct to survive had abandoned them. Even if it had, I'd still need to live on knowing that I had chosen myself and my child over them.

This looming decision seemed an even worse fate than whatever Dr. Amaar had been planning for my pregnancy. At least if he had gotten his way, I'd have someone else to blame.

Tess and I boarded the elevator and the moment the doors closed, I broke the silence.

"Tess. Tell me. What do I do?"

"I can't counsel you, and it's not because I stand to lose too much. You don't have a morally sound option and I'm truly sorry that you have to be the one to choose."

"Help me. Please," I begged her. "Give me any reason to keep my child. Anything. What would you do?"

The elevator doors opened to the laboratory level, and it felt like being at the footsteps of Hell. We could have gone anywhere to speak privately, but somewhere deep inside of me, I knew what I had to do, and I was subconsciously leading myself to it. Every step toward the operating room felt like it was sealing my fate.

"If I were you, I'd listen to Ranbir. He's right, but maybe for the wrong reasons. You deserve to be a mother because you're already loving like one. We'd do anything for our children. My only son hates me, and I'd still crawl over broken glass for him. The only words Marcus ever shared with me have been spoken in hate, and still, I can't give up on him. I'd do unspeakable things for the chance to start over. To hold him as a baby and hear his first words again. To shape him into an honorable young man. If I were you, I'd give up everything for the life of my child."

Tess' advice should have cemented my decision to carry my child to term, but it had the opposite effect. Marcus would be healed soon, and with only weeks to live, their relationship might never heal.

Things had happened so fast since I discovered my friends were still alive, and I hadn't been able to process everything they sacrificed and the sorrows that drowned them in the ocean of time.

Had they not committed themselves to centuries of loss while waiting for our arrival, I may very well have been dead. I stood on the edge of an impossible decision, ready to jump, but my feet wouldn't budge. I needed one last push to force me into doing the unthinkable.

I looked at Tess.

"What about Maya? What will become of the two of you?"

"I don't know. Some fractures are too great. Maya has been to the depths, and I don't know if she can claw her way back."

"Do you still love her?" I asked pointedly.

Tess blinked rapidly, trying to stop her tears before they could flow, and her mouth clamped up tightly. Her lips collapsed and twisted as she bottled her breakdown. It was as though she couldn't bring herself to speak her love out loud for fear that it would break the dam that had restrained her emotions for years. She simply nodded her head yes, swallowed hard, and looked away.

I didn't give my decision another second of thought. There were no more mental pros and cons to be weighed. As horrible as it was, this had to be done. My friends were there when I needed them, and it had cost them everything. I couldn't turn my back on them now.

"I'll do it," I said softly. The words didn't taste like my own. Before Tess could try to talk me out of it or offer condolences that would shake my nerve, I pressed on.

"I want it done quickly, I want to be put under, and I don't want any visitors when I wake. Can you do that for me?"

"Yeah, I can do that," Tess replied, resigned to my decision.

We entered the operating room and Tess busied herself with sterilizing her tools as I disrobed and shimmied onto the table. As she covered me with a lab coat, I pushed my earbuds in to take my mind off the nightmare. I was down to one percent battery power, and even with the device set to random, karma seemed to haunt me with the song choice.

The opening guitar strums of Lightning Crashes by Live filled my ears and I wished there was another way. If only things were as they were in the song. The circle of life takes the mother while the child survives.

I ran my hand over my belly and fully owned what I was about to do. I wasn't a careless young woman anymore; I felt the weight of my awful responsibility. There was the beating heart of a little girl within me—and she would never take her first breath so that many others could take their next.

It's said that "the needs of the many outweigh the needs of the few, or the one," but I know now that sentiment is only shared by the many. Until you look the needs of the one dead in the eyes, you can't truly understand what it is to sacrifice. Morality and pragmatism don't mix.

I removed one earbud and pressed it to my belly to share a small taste of the life I could not give to my little one. "Lightning crashes, an old mother cries," I sang softly along with the opening verse, wondering if my daughter could hear it. This awful pain was my punishment for disregarding life when I was younger. A lesson the universe tried to teach me many years ago, and karma was now finishing the job.

"I'm so sorry," I sobbed. "So fucking sorry."

Tess stroked my hair gently. "I'm going to give you a sedative now," she said softly. I nodded, unable to speak. "The terrible things I've done at this operating table . . ." she said to herself, her voice trailing off.

I closed my eyes to trap the tears threatening to escape and my breathing fluttered with gasps as I cried. "The angel closes her eyes," I sang amid my sobbing, "The confusion that was hers belongs now to the baby down the hall." My body became light as I began to slip into unconsciousness, and just as I was about to fall under, the battery on my phone finally died. The last few lyrics lingered on my lips, a soft, painful lullaby meant for the child who would never hear them again . . . and then, I slipped away.

***

When I woke, I experienced that brief, disorienting moment after a deep nap when your mind struggles to catch up with reality. For a moment, I thought I was back on Earth and that everything—the horror, the sacrifice—had been a bad dream. I've never enjoyed that foggy feeling, but just this once, I wished it had lasted a minute longer.

As my vision cleared, I found myself sitting upright and dressed. Tess was gone, but I had not been left alone to ponder the terrible weight on my soul.

"Easy now," Dani said. "You're going to be a little wobbly. Let's go slow."

"Is it done?" I asked.

"Listen, uh, we don't really know each other. The first time I met you, I thought I had struck it rich."

"Please. I don't want to—" I tried to stop her, but she continued.

"Just listen to what I have to say. We had been waiting for you for so long. So, so long. Most of us didn't think The Travelers were a real thing, and then there you were. You looked so formal in your uniform, and I just thought, ya know, maybe you did actually come to save us. I immediately tried to cash in on the bounty, and I hoped that Dr. Amaar would weasel his way onto your ship and take us home. To me, that was being saved. But nothing happened for a long time, and then things went down the way they did, and I wasn't saved at all."

She laughed humorously before continuing. "I mean, here I still am, marooned on this damn rock. Yesterday, I would have gladly taken the ride to Earth and stayed hooked forever. What I'm trying to say is, you did save me. You saved everyone. It wasn't Ranbir. It wasn't Maya or Malik. Not the Praxi kids. You. You saved me. I just wanted to say thank you. I don't know if I can ever repay you for your loss, but I'm going to try. I'm going to be better."

I pursed my lips and my eyes instantly welled up again. I couldn't answer Dani without breaking down, so I simply nodded my head. I knew I was going to hear statements of gratitude from many others, and every one of them would be a painful reminder. I'm sure my friends were waiting to comfort me, but I didn't want to see anyone. My shame and pain were too fresh.

I avoided checking in on Tess in her lab and rode the elevator to the main level. It was only a short walk to the stairwell, but everyone was still loitering around waiting for their miracle.

I kept my head down, briskly rounded the corner, and made it up two flights of stairs before realizing that I had never climbed the entire way to the sixth floor on my own. With one arm in a sling and the other gripping the railing, I pulled myself to the top feeling that the Vocury gravity was equal to the weight of my sadness. Without Taj, I was left to bear this burden alone.

For three days, I laid in bed, ignoring every knock on my door. I wasn't even sure if Tess had been successful, and in my depressive state, I naturally feared that I had aborted my child for nothing. I'd never been so low in all my life.

Even when I was on the run from the authorities and Emilia turned on me, at least my anger and sadness were aimed outward. The self-imposed isolation was suffocating, but I couldn't face the world, knowing I was the architect of my own misery.

I couldn't eat and I barely slept. Eventually, I had enough of my self-loathing, and I just wanted to dull the pain for a while. There's no way Amaar made off with all of his goodies amid the melee, so I figured I would wait until after dark and then go foraging around the lower levels for something that could make me forget and help me sleep.

The sun had been down for hours when I snuck out of my room and down the stairs. There was no one on the main level, so I seized the moment to fill my pockets with a few sustainers in case my appetite returned.

I rode the elevator down to the manufacturing level and was surprised to find the lights on and the space filled with someone's soft humming. I traced the sound to its source and found Maya lying on top of a steel crate.

"What are you doing?" I asked her.

"Jesus! Why you creeping up on me?"

She swung her feet over the ledge and sat upright.

"I'm looking for something and I didn't want to speak to anyone to get it."

"Sounds familiar."

"Well, what is there for someone who doesn't want to feel anymore?"

Maya looked down at the crate. "I'm not sure. This here is the only container not marked as regenerator that didn't make it to the surface. I haven't opened it yet."

"Hop off there and let's have a look."

Maya drummed her heels against the side of the steel box and examined me closely. She opened her mouth, took a breath, and acted as though she was about to speak multiple times, though she didn't say anything as she continued to search for the right words.

"Are you going to move or what?"

"I'm not sure."

"Maya, move. I just want to catch a buzz and go back to bed. Can we not make this a whole thing?"

"I came down here two nights ago and walked laps around this box. I must have almost opened it a hundred times. Came back last night too. I'm gonna get high. I'm not gonna get high. And back and forth. This is the longest I've been clean since we arrived. Three whole days. Some accomplishment, right?"

"Have to start somewhere."

"True. I can make it four days tomorrow, but this fucker is still going to be sitting here like a ticking time bomb waiting to explode. If Tess' cure doesn't work, she's going to be the first one to age out, and I'll no longer have any reason not to pry this lid open."

"Yeah, well, I'm already at that breaking point, so if you want to avoid temptation, maybe you should go upstairs while I take a peek inside."

Maya completely ignored my desire to get high.

"Did Ranbir tell you everything that happened?"

"I doubt it was everything, but he told us a lot."

"Hmm. Did he tell you what a terrible mother I was?"

"Of course not."

"He's a good shit. He wouldn't say it directly. You picked it up from context though, yeah?" Maya asked rhetorically, continuing before I could answer. "I screwed my kid up real good. I'd get sad, I'd drink more, hate myself, drink more, neglect my kid, drink more. Numbing the pain was the only answer I knew. I know you're going through it right now, too."

Maya stared at me, and when I avoided eye contact, she jumped down to stand face-to-face with me.

"Look at me," she said with a softer tone than she usually used. "I know you're hurting, but this isn't the answer. Pain is quicksand. If you fight it, that shit will take you under, ya feel me? You can't medicate it away. You just got to sit in that shit, real still-like, and let the people around you pull you out."

I bit my upper lip, and my hands began to tremble as all my emotions bubbled to the surface.

"Maybe I want to be pulled under," I responded, my voice trembling.

"Maybe," Maya conceded, "but I won't let you. You start popping these pills and you might blow your chance. You can still be a mother one day, and I'd be willing to bet you'd be a damn good one."

I don't know if Maya was trying to break through to me, but she crushed my defenses perfectly. I didn't want to stand in front of her and cry, which made her tight hug appreciated. I didn't have the strength to speak it out loud, but my dream of being a mother was dead. I could create life, but my irresponsibility stood in the way of carrying it to term.

Who knows what kind of damage I was capable of if I ever actually got the chance to raise a child? They would end up ruined, and my depression would only sink further.

I stood quietly in front of Maya pondering the shadow I had cast over my own motherhood. This solemn state could have gone on for hours had Maya not broken the ice. "You have to do something for me," she said quietly, almost as if she was unsure about the favor she was about to ask of me.

I wasn't alone in facing my demons.

"Name it," I replied.

"There's a torch over there on that workstation. I need you to do what I cannot."

Maya cracked the seal on the container and threw the lid back, revealing neatly stacked packages of pills, a graveyard of her past addictions. She clenched a fist as she stared down at the evil that had left her in a centuries-long spiral. Her voice barely audible, she whispered, "Burn it."

So I did.

The plastic casings quickly melted away as I set the flame to the top row, the fire crackling and spreading to devour the pills. I traced the torch across the entire surface until black smoke rolled off of the growing embers and I was forced to step back.

"Got any marshmallows?" I asked sarcastically.

"I wish. I'd do unspeakable things for solid food."

We opened the industrial hatch that led to the surface to release the smoke and found a comfortable place to sit as the fire consumed the contents of the crate.

Neither one of us spoke while we watched the drugs go up in smoke. Maya was dealing with her pain, and I was processing mine. For a brief moment, my depression escaped me, but it was still right there waiting for me when I was scared awake with my head on Maya's shoulder. Oddly though, I was at ease and had slept better than I had in days. That tiny bonfire with a friend was exactly what both of us needed.

The next week wasn't easy, and it was going to take me a long time to heal, but at least I had my friends. Ten days had passed since Tess injected herself with the first dose of her concoction and she hadn't experienced any withdrawals from the regenerator. Thankfully, my sacrifice wasn't an empty one, though everyone's smiling faces as they found new life reminded me of what it had cost.

Within each of them was a small part of my daughter who would never taste life. She would have to live on through them, and we were going to have to make the best of our second chance to properly honor her brief existence. There wasn't much hope of ever escaping Vocury, and we only had six years of life remaining, but I wouldn't count us out just yet.

Everyone but Ranbir took their dose of Tess' elixir. Even Maddox, though locked away, still wanted to live on. Chop had seen enough though, and neither Maya nor Malik, or even his precious Praxi friends, could talk some sense into him.

He had made up his mind, and there's only one person I've ever known with the brute stubbornness and callous directness necessary to get through to him: Emilia.

Chapter 22

Across Space and Time
Ranbir Chopra: 2337

C hop! Let's go," Malik's voice echoed from behind my door as he pounded on it.

I stood in front of the mirror examining my facial hair that was either falling out or turning white. My legs were weak and my head was dizzy as the last of the regenerator flushed out of my system. I had maybe two painful days of life left in me and one final promise to fulfill.

I had failed. I couldn't keep Maya clean. I didn't do enough to raise Marcus right. Even after three hundred years of preparation, I had allowed Dr. Amaar to escape. In a few centuries, mankind would be introduced to pharmaceutical poisons that would make hydrocodone look like Flintstones vitamins.

There was no glorious death left for me. I would take this one last ride with Malik, and after that, I was done with this life. I'd only be remembered for a few years by the survivors.

Explorers who traveled to Vocury many centuries in the future would disregard my skeletal remains as just another common failure of a man. The dream of a Prius retirement plan was so far in my past that I could no longer remember it.

Malik's knocking persisted so I sluggishly dragged myself to the door and opened it. I knew I looked like death, but my appearance didn't seem to dampen his spirits.

"Everything is ready, and Tess is waiting for us."

"I'm sorry, my friend. I really don't want to do this. Please, just let me go," I begged him.

"It will feel like an hour of your time. I swear. Just go in, have a look around, and debrief me afterward. If you still want to die after that, then so be it."

"You really think I'm going to dream of Emilia and that it's going to change my mind?"

"I don't know. I've already said too much. I need your subconscious as clear as possible."

"Why me?" I asked as I had a dozen times before. "Send anyone else in. I'm done, man."

"It has to be you, and I can't tell you why." Malik put his hands on my shoulders and locked eyes with me. "Please. You promised me."

"Alright, alright," I conceded as I joined Malik in the hallway. "Lead the way."

We took the short elevator ride to the labs and Tess greeted us in a room set up for their little science experiment. The space was clear, save for one of the recovered dream tubes, which was hooked up to a power source. A single-drawer chamber was open, like a coffin, just waiting for me to climb in.

"Whoa, not so fast." Tess grabbed my arm. "There's going to be a little pinch," she advised before inserting an IV into my arm. "Now, I will have to give you a little bit of regenerator to keep you pumping in this condition, but once you're comatose, it won't take much."

"When this is over, I'm done," I repeated my desire for euthanasia.

"No one will stand in your way," Malik said confidently.

It was as though he didn't believe in my desire for death, or like he thought a single dream could change hundreds of years of depressive resolve.

"We've lowered the compound so that you'll get just enough to take you under but not enough to keep you there. You'll be sleeping for about two days before the sedative reaches its pinnacle."

"If my calculations are correct," Tess added, "you should be in the dream state for maybe thirty minutes. You may sleep for another day or two after the sedative wears off, but you shouldn't feel a minute of it."

"Fine. Let's get this show on the road," I said.

"I'll never be far away, and I can track your vitals and change your levels if needed." Tess held me up as I lifted one leg after another into the sleep tank and settled in.

"Alright. One last adventure."

"Thanks, Chop. This means a lot to me. Hopefully you'll know why by the next time we speak," Malik said.

"See you on the other side," I replied as they pushed the drawer into the contraption, and I closed my eyes.

***

Bacon. Do I smell bacon?

I opened my eyes, unaware that I had already fallen asleep. Fully dressed, I lay on a bed, sunlight peeking through the curtains of a small basement window. I sat up, found my shoes neatly placed beside the bed, and turned toward the dresser mirror. My beard had been freshly trimmed and restored to its black state.

"Huh," I said to myself as I ran my hands through my thick head of hair.

I exited the bedroom and walked into a living room with children's toys stored in boxes along the wall. I began to climb the stairs to the main floor of the home, the crackling of a frying pan softly echoing in the distance. Reaching the top of the stairs, I closed my eyes and basked in the delicious aroma of breakfast meats; I could practically taste them.

"Mom?" I instinctively asked, half expecting to relive a childhood memory. Instead, I found a fit white woman in a sundress tending to the stovetop, and she didn't seem the least bit startled by my presence.

"Hungry, Captain?" she asked.

"You have no idea," I replied, licking my lips. The thought of solid food after all these years was enough to placate my inquisitive mind.

"Been expecting you, sugar. Why don't you have a seat at the table? I'm sure you have many questions, but I think you'll agree that mine are more important. Firstly, how do you take your eggs?"

"Scrambled, ma'am," I answered. "With cheese, if you have it."

"Good man. Secondly, coffee or orange juice?"

"I'd love an orange juice."

"Kids! Come meet Captain Chopra!" she shouted. "They're so excited."

"I'm sorry, who are you?" I asked her.

"Oh, come on, sweetie. You know."

Two mixed-race children ran into the kitchen and the adolescent boy and young girl approached to examine me.

"I'm Marcus," the boy said, and rather than offer a handshake, he poked his finger into my shoulder and it passed through me. "He's all liquid, just like Dad," Marcus said to the woman.

"I know, baby. Would you please pour Captain Chopra an orange juice?"

"It's just Chop. Or Ranbir," I corrected her softly.

"Well, we knew you as Captain Chopra, you see. We were there the day you rocketed off with that little alien to test the Jump Point. That was a long time ago, but I still remember it like it was yesterday."

"And who is this little darling?" I asked, even though I was already piecing things together.

"I'm Maisie," the little girl announced proudly. She stood up straight and offered me the most adorable salute.

"My God . . ." I said softly.

"I know what you're thinking," the woman said. "'Is this real, or did my mind just picture Malik's wife this beautiful and his children this lovely?'"

She laughed and looked over at her family. "We're a good-looking bunch, aren't we?"

"You're Lydia," I said as a matter of fact.

"In the flesh. Well, sort of." She smirked.

"I-I don't even know what to say," I stammered.

"Don't say anything. Eat."

Lydia placed a plate of community bacon on the table, and I wasn't shy about digging in.

"Oh, my! Bacon, where you been all my life?" I exclaimed as the perfect crispy piece soaked into my taste buds.

"I presume your current adventure has led you back to that rascal husband of mine. Did he send you in here to check up on us?"

"He was pretty cagey about the whole thing, but I think you might be right."

"And how is my darling? Behaving himself?"

"He's healthy, but things haven't exactly gone according to plan."

"Is Daddy coming home soon?" Maisie asked me.

"If this place is what I think it is, he's not going to be away for too much longer," I answered her. "None of us will, me least of all."

"Sounds like the two of you still have some work to do," Lydia said. "When you see him again, you tell him that Mama doesn't want him coming home until the world is done with him."

"In our current situation, I don't think there's much more he can offer the world, but I'll deliver the message."

"God's not done with him yet, or else he'd be here. The same goes for you."

Lydia placed a plate of eggs in front of me then went to work on preparing breakfast for the kids.

"You're taking this a lot better than Malik did. Lordy, that man had a million questions. Always so skeptical."

Maisie snuck her fork into my pile of eggs and held a single silencing finger up to her smile. I slid the plate between us, and we shared in Lydia's goodness as she continued.

"The least you could do is ask 'Why here?' You could have woken anywhere. Why do you suppose you're in our breakfast nook? We've heard so much about you, but we've never even met."

"As much as I've heard about you? I don't know . . ." I laughed. "I'm not sure why I'm here, but I think I understand my friend a little better now."

"You're certainly better-mannered than our other house guest." Lydia chuckled. "I've had to threaten to rinse her mouth out with soap on occasion, but I see why you're so fond of her. I reckoned you might come looking for her at some point."

A genuine smile lit my face, something I hadn't felt in years.

"Emilia? She's really here?"

"Well, of course. You were bound to show up wherever she was, and our home was as good of a reprieve from the storm as one could hope for. She's out back. Come look."

Lydia led me to the window and pulled the curtains aside.

There . . . God, there was Emilia, sitting on a bench swing with a book in her hands, a small umbrella shielding her from the rain falling all around her.

I rushed to the back door and found myself at the edge of a storm. I stood in the sun, but only steps ahead was a perimeter of rain that seemed to encircle Emilia twenty feet in every direction.

As I stepped into the rain, my presence cut through it. Every step closer to her made the clouds above grow smaller. By the time I walked right up behind her, the entire storm had evaporated.

"I knew you'd come," Emilia said without turning to me.

She sat up from the swing, walked around it, and stood before me. My eyes devoured every inch of her, my jaw hanging agape, and my tears began to flow. Her face was covered in her old scars, but as the storm washed away, so did her physical blemishes.

"What is this?" I asked, questioning the reality of the dream for the first time.

"Sit," she ordered, and I complied. "Are you here or are you really here?" she asked me.

Emilia reached out slowly, her hand only inches from my face, and she paused as though she was afraid of the answer. I moved my head toward her touch and her hand passed through my cheek. A creeping smile crossed her face as she looked down at me.

"You're still alive! How is that possible?"

"It's a long story."

"No shit. I have waited and waited and waited for you."

Emilia looked to the sky and closed her eyes as the sun shone on her face. "I haven't felt the sun in eons," she said as she basked in it.

She looked so gorgeous, I couldn't help myself. I sprung out of my seat, desperate to feel her—but my hand passed through her neck and my lips couldn't feel her kiss.

"Annoying, isn't it?" she asked. "I appreciate you trying, though," she added with a smirk.

"This is torture. I need to be able to touch you."

"And you could, hypothetically, if you were dead."

"I'm so close. You have no idea. Everything has gone bad and I'm ready to come to you. Not through this dream state, but for real this time."

"That's cute and all, but then we'd both be dead and where's the fun in that?"

"I'll show you how fun it'll be," I smirked.

"Oh, I bet you would," she flirted back as though we were on a first date. "I've had a lot of time to think, though. Malik was in here a while back and then he left. Now you're in here and I imagine you won't be staying long, either."

"I can stay forever. I'm ready!"

"Shhh, dum-dum. I'm sure your heart is involved, but you're thinking with your dick again. If you guys can come and go as you please, then what the hell is keeping me here?"

"You're dead, sweetie."

"You a master of the afterlife now or something? It should go without saying, but these aren't our bodies. Whatever you've done to bring your consciousness here, there has to be a way for me to do the reverse."

"I wouldn't even know where to begin."

"Whatever you used to get in here. That's where you begin."

"Even if it were possible, we'd still be stuck on Vocury with only a handful of years to live."

"I don't care if we're stuck in West Virginia with only minutes to live. One problem at a time."

"I don't know, Em. This is beyond me. I could just die, and we could be together."

"You really gonna make me do a callback?" she asked with a raised eyebrow.

I gave her a confused look, and she put both hands on the sides of my face without allowing them to pass through my translucent skin. Her eyes locked with mine as she said, "You. Do. Not. Have. My. Permission. To. Die."

I couldn't help but smile. She was still my same old Emilia. There was nothing I wouldn't do for her, and even faced with an impossible chore, I was unable to deny her. She was convinced there was a way for us to be together again in life, and just like that, I found a new resolve to live on in her service.

"Close your eyes," she ordered. "Where are you right now?"

"I'm in a dream tank developed from Praxi tech. I'm heavily sedated."

"Who is there with you?"

"Maya, Malik, and Alexis."

"Got the whole gang together again, huh? Who else?"

"Tess is here."

"Who's Tess?" Emilia's voice cut through with a hint of jealousy. I opened one eye to see her scowling and she shut me down. "Ah! Focus."

"She's Maya's wife."

"Tell me about her."

"She's a doctor, a scientist, and a researcher. She's very sweet. A determined woman. You'd like her."

"And smart? What kind of scientist?"

"Yes, she's extremely intelligent, but she's been through a lot. She's a medical professional, and she knows a great deal about biology."

"That's good. That's real good. She'll be useful. Who else is there?"

"There's some soldiers, some everyday citizens, some pirates, and some colonists. Also Gia and Rix, along with some Praxi youth."

"There's Praxi where you're at? Open your eyes!"

"Oh, right. Yes! Emilia, it's Gio's daughter! We found her—and she's not like the others."

I had so much to tell, but Emilia wasn't interested in a three-hundred-year history lesson.

"Eh, eh, eh, eh, eh." Emilia pointed at me. "Slow down. If anybody is going to understand what's going on here, it's the Praxi. Them and Tess. That's your team. You can fill me in on all the other details when you get me out here."

"If," I corrected her.

"No, not 'if.' When," she replied sharply. "Think about it. Malik's consciousness went straight to his family and yours came straight to me. We're bonded forever across space and time and whatever the hell this place is. Every door you walk through leads to me."

"I love it when you're accidentally romantic." I grinned.

Emilia ignored my reignited puppy love and plowed ahead.

"Find the right door and pull me through it. Exhaust every last option. If there's no other way, then and only then, will I be waiting here for you."

A slow smile crept across my face as I realized that one way or another, the love I had for Emilia had not only survived for three hundred years but would continue to live on.

"What are you grinning about?" she asked playfully as she mirrored my happiness.

"You're the first person to try to escape the afterlife. It's very on-brand."

"I'm a stubborn bitch," she quipped.

"You certainly are."

"But you love me, don't you?"

"I certainly do."

"Then say it."

"I love you. Across time and space."

"Good." Emilia leaned forward until we were almost nose-to-nose, even though we couldn't make contact. "Prove it," she whispered seductively. "You want to touch me again? Make the impossible possible."

With the power of foresight, I would have gotten off the regenerator, given up long ago, and gone to Emilia. Our mission to Vocury had only delayed the inevitable. Every moment waiting for Malik and Alexis to arrive was wasted. I spent all those years longing for Emilia while she was right here waiting for me.

Perhaps I wasn't meant to know about what awaited me in the great beyond. Maybe among all my failures, I still served a purpose. My friends had survived, and Malik had presented the opportunity for my soul to seek out Emilia's.

It was as though she had willed me from the grave to this moment out of sheer tenaciousness. No woman had ever been able to replace her, and I wasn't able to die because Emilia held on just as tight as I did. It was as though she had kept me alive until I was in a position to potentially repay the favor.

When Malik sent me in, he was looking for answers. He needed someone to confirm that what he had experienced wasn't a figment of his imagination, and I feared what he might do when he learned the truth. With only a few years of sustainable life afforded on Vocury, what was there to keep him among the land of the living?

I know what I would do if I were in his shoes. I'd ignore Lydia's call to continue to make the world a better place, check out early, and go to my family. It was going to be my job to offer him a better alternative—hope.

What a coward I had been for giving up on life.

I had spent so much time wanting to die that I had forgotten what it meant to live. Sure, we had lost, but my friends had survived. Knowing that they would need me should have been enough to shake my depression, but I could not see.

If I didn't surrender, then maybe neither would they. Emilia didn't believe the afterlife could contain her, and if she was right, then perhaps we'd all collectively believe in the unbelievable. Maybe Vocury wouldn't be our end after all if we continued to fight.

I sat on the swing in Lydia's backyard, Emilia by my side. She had given me new purpose and a reason to live, albeit a silly one. I needed to take my newfound positivity and spread it among my friends like a virus. If it caught on, there might be hope that we could survive and escape our prison.

Now was not the time to give up.

I became lightheaded as we talked, and my breathing became shallow.

"This is it," I announced. "I'm being called back to the land of the living."

"Sit still," Emilia ordered. She slid over until our bodies became one. I placed my hands on my knees and Emilia mirrored my posture perfectly.

"You think it's going to be that easy, huh?" I asked.

"Can't hurt to try. Explore every option, remember?"

"If there's a way, I'll find it," I promised.

My body began to phase in and out. My heart raced, my vision faded, and my breathing intensified. Just as I was about to slip away, I could feel Emilia within me. I recognized her touch and scent. It was a millisecond of a lucid memory brought to life, and before I could express the joy in that connection, I was gone.

My eyes opened to the sting of fluorescent lights. I reached out in the sleep chamber, half expecting to find Emilia lying next to me, but I was alone as always. She might not have physically traveled back with me, but a part of her resided within my soul.

"Don't try to get out," Tess cautioned. "I'm going to get Malik."

I laid there crying tears of joy for a few minutes. As far as I was concerned, Emilia was still alive. No matter what came next, I'd be able to go on with the knowledge that one way or another, we'd be together forever.

I imagined that comfort could have saved the lives of millions before me who had fallen into depression. There was no amount of therapy or prescriptions that could deliver anything close to the relief I was experiencing. I had lived in my pain and made it my home; now, it was only a part of my past.

Malik excitedly burst into the room, Tess following shortly behind him. He stood at my bedside and offered me his hand so I could sit up.

"Did you dream?" he asked.

"No, I lived. More in thirty minutes than I have in three centuries."

"What did you find?"

"A southern belle, her two children, and the love of my life."

Malik placed a shaking hand on my shoulder and his teary eyes found my own. "It was . . . you saw them?" His voice shook. "My Lydia? Marcus and Maisie?"

I nodded.

"It's real!" Malik exclaimed.

"I have a message for you," I said, pausing for dramatic effect. "She said that 'Mama doesn't want you coming home until the world is done with you.'"

"What more could the world possibly need from me?"

I pondered the lesson I had learned about my new purpose and shared it with Malik. "I need you. Maya needs you. Alexis needs you. What about you, Tess? You need Malik?"

Tess and Malik made eye contact and there was a brief moment of uncomfortableness.

"You know what?" Tess answered, "I think I might."

That's exactly what Malik needed to hear, and it's coincidently the same mindset that had set me free. Like it or not, we needed each other. The love we shared bound us together, and neither death, loss, depression, nor addiction could break those chains.

Malik's love for his family and my love for Emilia had kept us connected across dimensions. If we were going to live on and find each other in the next life, we'd all have to love the same.

Hope must remain.

"What about Emilia?" Malik asked. "Did you see her?"

I got goosebumps at the mere mention of her name, almost as though she were residing just under my skin.

"She's enjoying some of Lydia's southern hospitality . . . at least for now."

Malik raised an eyebrow, and before he could launch an inquisition, I piqued his interest further with a little mystery.

"We've got work to do. You're not going to believe this."

Afterword

Thank you so much for reading this series! I can't possibly convey to you what your support means to me. I've put everything I've got into writing these books, and yet, they would be nothing without you, the reader.

If you love this series, please share it with anyone you can! Getting ratings and reviews on Amazon and Goodreads, along with positive word of mouth is more a powerful marketing tool than any ad I could run. I'm small-time over here, and your support could make all the difference. Thank you!

Lastly, thank you to everyone who made this dream possible. My name might be on the cover, but this book doesn't get made without my support team. Anna, my absolute dynamo of an editor, and my closest friends, family, and fans. You all know who you are, and I love you!

Coming Soon: The Contact Series: Book 3

Vengeful Contact

Made in the USA
Monee, IL
04 December 2024

72038376R00174